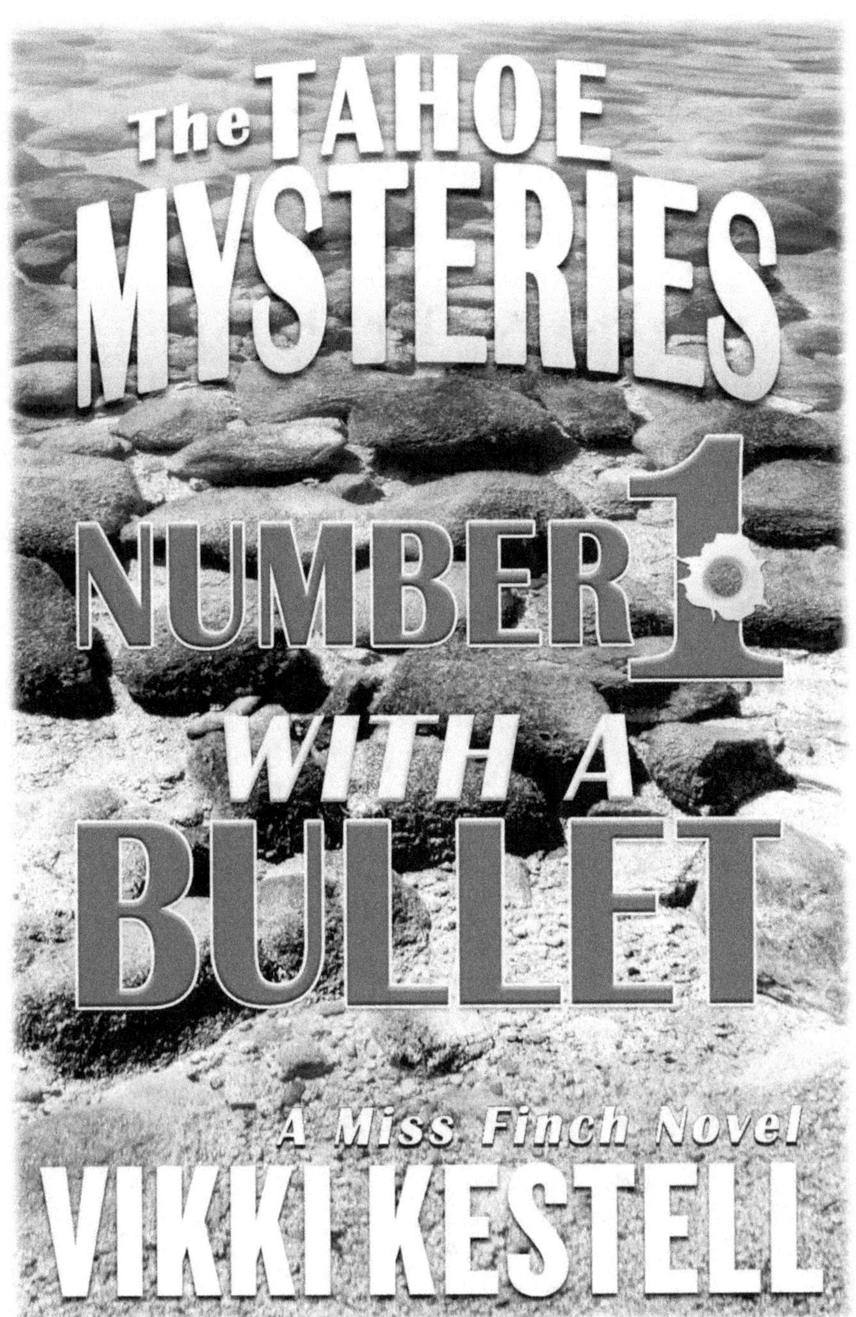

Faith-Filled Fiction™

www.faith-filledfiction.com | www.vikkikestell.com

NUMBER 1
WITH A BULLET

THE TAHOE MYSTERIES | BOOK 1
Vikki Kestell
Also Available in eBook Format

BOOKS BY VIKKI KESTELL

THE TAHOE MYSTERIES

Book 1: *Number 1 with a Bullet*
Book 2: *Be Quick or be Dead*, 2025
Book 3: *Death on the Big Blue*, 2026
Murder by Accident, A Miss Finch Prequel, 2025

A PRAIRIE HERITAGE

Book 1: *A Rose Blooms Twice*
Book 2: *Wild Heart on the Prairie*
Book 3: Joy on This Mountain
Book 4: *The Captive Within*
Book 5: *Stolen*
Book 6: *Lost Are Found*
Book 7: *All God's Promises*
Book 8: *The Heart of Joy—A Short Story*
Book 9: *Rose of RiverBend*

GIRLS FROM THE MOUNTAIN

Book 1: *Tabitha*
Book 2: *Tory*
Book 3: *Sarah Redeemed*

LAYNIE PORTLAND

Book 1: *Laynie Portland, Spy Rising*
Book 2: *Laynie Portland, Retired Spy*
Book 3: *Laynie Portland, Renegade Spy*
Book 4: *Laynie Portland, Spy Resurrected*
Book 5: *Vyper, A Laynie Portland Sequel*

NANOSTEALTH

Book 1: *Stealthy Steps*
Book 2: *Stealth Power*
Book 3: *Stealth Retribution*
Book 4: *Deep State Stealth*
Book 5: *Stealth Insurgence*
Book 6: *Stealth Triumph*
Book 7: *Stealth Genesis,*
   A Nanostealth Prequel

NUMBER 1
WITH A BULLET

THE TAHOE MYSTERIES | BOOK 1
Vikki Kestell
Also Available in eBook Format

EVERY SHERLOCK NEEDS HIS WATSON, every Hercule Poirot his Captain Hastings. Who else could tell their stories that we might share in their adventures?

Meet Simon Fletcher, a recently (and reluctantly) retired Marine, at present the facilities and security manager for Lake Tahoe's exclusive Bright Star Summer RV Residence. Enter Miss BD Finch, who shortly embroils Simon Fletcher in mystery, mayhem, and . . . murder.

Life at Bright Star takes several left-hand turns when the diminutive and enigmatic Miss Finch, driving a restored classic panel wagon and towing a seventeen-foot travel trailer, attempts to check in. Indeed, it seems that Miss Finch herself, in addition to her *non*exclusive and somewhat unusual "rig," is never what people expect. Those around her generally find themselves knocked off-kilter, including and especially those she's scrutinizing—because although our delightfully unpredictable Miss Finch has many talents, she is also an investigator. *The private kind.*

And when Miss Finch arrives on the south shore of Lake Tahoe for a summer of rest and recuperation? To put it bluntly, her R&R does *not* go as planned. Rather, "things" go oddly awry. Dangerously awry.

Prepare yourself for . . . **The Tahoe Mysteries**.

Book 1: *Number 1 with a Bullet*
Book 2: *Be Quick or Be Dead,* 2025
Book 3: *Death on the Big Blue,* 2026
Murder by Accident, A Miss Finch Prequel, 2025

DEDICATION

"This is dedicated to the One I love."

ACKNOWLEDGEMENTS

All my thanks, appreciation, and love
to my esteemed teammates,
Cheryl Adkins and **Greg McCann**
continually demonstrating that they are
—BEST IN CLASS—

SCRIPTURE QUOTATIONS

The HOLY BIBLE,
NEW INTERNATIONAL VERSION®, NIV®
Copyright ©1973, 1978, 1984, 2011 by Biblica, Inc.®
Used by permission. All rights reserved worldwide.

COVER DESIGN

Vikki Kestell

CHAPTER 1

BRIGHT STAR SUMMER RV RESIDENCE, SOUTH END OF LAKE TAHOE

WEDNESDAY PRIOR TO MEMORIAL DAY, MAY 21

SIMON FLETCHER TURNED right off the paved road and drove his pickup around to the back side of the refurbished log cabin that served as his employer's office. He parked, then strode to the front side of the cabin, stepped out onto the road and faced the park's entrance, just beyond the office. He pressed the button on the remote in his pocket and watched Bright Star's bronze gates slide apart.

With chin tucked and arms folded across his chest, Bright Star's Facilities and Security Manager glared through the open entrance with the intensity of a Marine drill instructor inspecting a ragged row of raw recruits at oh four thirty in the dark a.m.—which was exactly how Simon viewed his Bright Star responsibilities: His purpose was to shape, shine, mold, cajole, or pummel the pieces and parts of Bright Star residing under his purview until each one exceeded his expectations.

Barely topping five feet nine but wide and muscled across the chest, Simon was a rock of a man, a machine unacquainted with the word "quit." From his strong physical presence to a "get it done" work ethic, Simon's every action oozed purpose. No detail escaped him, nor did he tolerate much in the way of nonsense.

Simon's fellow Marine MPs had laughingly referred to him as the Corps' human armored fighting vehicle. They'd nod sagely, and in the same way they might say, "We need an M1 Abrams to bust through that concrete barrier," they would shout, "This drunken brawl requires our resident tank: Call in the Fletcher!"

They weren't far off the mark. Simon Fletcher was, more often than not, inclined to roll over or through any impediment foolish enough to plant itself between him and his objective.

Feeling a familiar anger rising, he sniffed and reminded himself, *The Corps is in your rearview mirror, Fletcher. All twenty years of it. Nothing for you there, so stop looking back.*

A snide voice replied, *Once a Marine, always a Marine, Fletch. Semper fi.*

"Yeah, yeah."

Whatever.

Simon had prided himself on his accomplishments in the Corps, but now two years out from his discharge, he no longer thought of himself as anything special. Near the end of his second year of civilian life, he considered himself an average guy with sandy hair, light brown eyes, and bland features capped by a nose that had been broken twice, set once.

At forty-eight years of age, he had nothing to show for his years in the Corps—no career, wife, kids, or living relations. As far as Simon was concerned, the family he'd chosen and poured his life's blood into had turned its back on him.

His years in the Marines aside, in this last year he had become a valued worker and a steady, faithful partner to Joe and Holly Mitchell, Bright Star's owners. He was helpful and friendly with people, too—with the exception of the aforementioned "foolish impediment" type. And rarely did friend or acquaintance of any length call him by his given name, Simon. Sooner or later, everyone fell into using his last name, Fletcher, or its shortened version, "Fletch."

Backlit by the early morning sun, Simon stood before Bright Star's open gate and mentally gauged the park's readiness to receive its first residents. Residents who would begin arriving midday tomorrow.

He tried to put himself in their shoes: *If I were an incoming guest, what would catch my eye as I arrived?*

The gate itself was as beautiful as it was imposing, a splendid work of hardened steel and metal sculpture. Custom-designed and built for the park, the gate featured Bright Star's bronzed logo. Holly Mitchell generally kept the gate open during the day while she staffed the office but closed and locked outside of office hours. The automated gate retracted when residents entered their personal code on the gate's keypad. A Bright Star employee could also open or close the gate by pressing a button inside the office or on a remote such as the one Simon held.

Of course, Holly had requested certain features to protect the privacy of Bright Star's residents. To satisfy her, Simon had posted prominent signage several yards before the gate. In flowing gold letters, the sign declared,

BRIGHT STAR SUMMER RV RESIDENCE
PRIVATE PROPERTY
Visitors Must Check In at Office

Simon thought Holly had exhibited a bit of paranoia when she insisted Bright Star's gate be "extra strong so our residents feel safe," but she wrote the checks. After Simon finished his work with the fabricators, the installed gate could withstand the impact of a half-ton pickup truck—as could the tall steel fence set in concrete extending twenty-five feet from the gate on both sides, the fence's two ends vanishing into forest shrubbery.

Holly had actually lobbied for fencing the entire park, but her husband, Joe, had put his foot down.

"We're trying to give our guests a piece of the great outdoors, Hol," Joe had protested, "not a prison cell. Besides, we can't afford such an expense."

Joe's reaction didn't keep Holly from assigning Simon the task of installing a four-camera video surveillance system to capture video of the road leading up to Bright Star's gate. Over Bright Star's private road, from where it joined the main road, stood an arched sign displaying Bright Star's bronzed logo and smaller words declaring, "Office Ahead." Simon had mounted the first camera there, capturing images of all vehicles that turned in. He located the second and third cameras along the half-mile stretch of road leading to the office, and a final camera at the gate. A monitor on the office counter displayed the video feed, cycling through the four camera views every few seconds.

The gate and cameras couldn't guarantee the residents' security, but they went a long way toward projecting the perception of privacy.

Speaking of privacy . . .

Simon walked through the open entrance. A broad swath of freshly laid and striped asphalt scribed a graceful, elongated circuit from the gate, through the park's forest and past all the RV sites, and returning to the gate. Simon knew every twist and turn of that wide, one-way loop like the back of his own hand, just like he knew every inch of Bright Star's thirty acres. He'd spent the last nine months hard at work alongside Joe and Holly, helping them bring their dream of a unique summer RV park to birth.

"One ritzy, glorified campground," he muttered under his breath.

The park was much more, although Simon wouldn't admit it to just anyone. Fact was, he was proud of Bright Star and its unique flavor.

Twenty-four pristine RV sites poked their long double driveways into the park's perimeter loop like so many spokes on a very out-of-round wheel. Each RV site, in addition to being set far back from the road, was shaded by a canopy of tall pines and endowed with a full RV hookup (including cable and internet), a sizeable patch of perfectly edged grass, and a tidy paved patio area complete with firepit, picnic table, and chilled drinking water dispenser. Every site's driveway also provided a level pad for its resident's RV and ample parking for the resident's vehicles. The kicker? Forty feet or more of natural mountain verdure separated the sites one from another, effectively achieving the impression of peaceful mountain solitude for the occupants of each site.

Simon shifted his internal gaze. Yes, the RV sites were impressive, and pictures of the various sites on Bright Star's website had done them justice. Still, it was the architectural renderings of the large "island" built up in the center of the park that clinched the deal for most prospective residents.

The island's tapered promontory jutted toward the park entrance, commanding the attention of all comers—as it was designed to do. Four ascending tiers climbed the promontory and were crowned with banks of concealed water jets. From those jets, sprays of water leapt, twirled, and pirouetted in mesmerizing cadence to soft music, while hidden lights infused the spurts and feathery showers with intense color.

Or at least they did in the fountain designer's colorful animation.

Simon smiled to himself. *Can't wait to see them in action again.*

The promontory with its terraces of gamboling water dancers was the taste that tantalized, the crooked finger that beckoned visitors into the park and onward toward the island's further attractions . . . and said further attractions did not disappoint.

Next, the island showcased a splendid though modest-sized swimming complex. The complex's main pool, closest to the dancing water feature, had a large three-to-five-foot-deep section dedicated to family fun. The deck on one side sported two water slides. On the far end of the family pool was a twelve-foot "deep end" reserved for a single spring board and two diving platforms of varying heights.

Residents could also enjoy an adult-only lap pool with three warmed swim lanes, each forty feet in length. A six-foot wall separated the family pool from the swim lanes, reducing the noise coming from the family pools for those wanting to enjoy a more sedate swim time.

Within the swimming complex's main enclosure, residents and their guests would also find two hot tubs, three lounging areas, a half dozen shaded patio tables, and two exquisitely appointed restrooms for showering and changing into or out of swim wear.

Lastly, the complex boasted a zero-to-ten-inch-deep wading and spray pool for toddlers, complete with tiny water slide, close parental seating, and its own restrooms. The kiddie section sat within a separate enclosure, unattached to the rest of the swimming complex, for safety reasons.

Aside from the dancing water feature, the swimming complex was Bright Star's definitive jewel and leading attraction.

"But wait! There's more," Simon snickered.

Down the island from those appealing amenities, atop a picture-perfect lawn, awaited a barbecue zone, furnished with gas grills and shaded picnic tables for the residents' pleasure. Farther across the grass was an inviting group firepit encircled by log seating. On the grass beyond the firepit stood a volleyball *slash* badminton net, and beyond the net, a fenced pickleball court.

A large cabin at the farthest end of the island served as an indoor rec facility. One side of the rec facility was dedicated to group events and included a community kitchen and dining room. The other half of the building was split between a small gym equipped with weights, cardio machines, mats for stretching, and a game room stocked with board games, puzzles, and video game consoles. A low structure off to the side of the rec facility bore the sign, "Bright Star Resident Laundry Facility."

The amenities on the island were interconnected by broad paths of local stone and mortar. Simon and his boss, Joe, had painstakingly laid every foot of those paths. Given that the majority of their clientele were likely to be retirees, Simon and Joe had made certain the path surfaces were flat and smooth with nary a single trip hazard, while solar lighting along the paths ensured easy navigation after dark.

Simon nodded to himself. The park's features and facilities had that "brand-new" sparkle to them because they were, in fact, brand-new. Furthermore, every aspect of the park shouted "select," "private," and "discriminating"—which was the whole point.

Bright Star was the only Tahoe RV park to bill itself as a summer *residence*. One did not stay overnight at Bright Star or check in one week and check out the next. No, in this RV park, guests paid handsomely (and in advance) to call Bright Star their home away from home for the entire season, Memorial Day weekend through Labor Day.

Twenty-three candidates had flocked to Bright Star's website and each shelled out thirty-six grand, the equivalent of twelve thousand dollars a month, to spend the summer at Bright Star. The last berth to be booked at Bright Star—a worry that had plagued Holly—had finally been filled just two weeks ago.

"And we're almost ready for them," Simon murmured, "although it's a mighty big 'almost.'"

Half of Simon's job as Bright Star's facilities and security manager was to maintain the island and its amenities in its "brand-new" state. With the exception of one essential element, all features were up and operational, inspected, approved, and certified where required. But the "one essential element," the single impediment facing Simon before Bright Star's grand opening?

"The swimming complex's blasted water pump," he growled.

Simon needed the pump that fed and cycled water to the dancing water feature and the several pools, and he needed it *today*. The original pump, a large and complex piece of hardware, electronics, and accompanying software, ordered six months in advance, had functioned perfectly.

Until it didn't.

The fountains had danced and twirled to Holly, Joe, and Simon's shared delight. But an hour into the pump's trial performance, it failed and died.

Simon's call to Bright Star's Vegas supplier—after he had recited the pump's serial number to the supplier and he had checked the manufacturer's website—revealed that Bright Star's pump was subject to a national recall. The problem was a fabricating defect resulting in faulty chips on the pump's motherboard. Worse, the recall had depleted the manufacturer's warehouse of that model, meaning Bright Star's pump was now out of stock.

As it turned out, *thanks be to God*, their supplier had an extra pump of the desired model on their shelves. Joe had reeled Holly down from the office ceiling, and the freight company had delivered Bright Star's replacement pump two weeks ago.

Except . . .

Except the crated pump had arrived looking like it had fallen off the truck somewhere between Vegas and Tahoe, bounced down the highway, endured a glancing encounter with a semi, and cartwheeled onto the shoulder . . . where it was scraped off the road, returned to the truck, and delivered to Bright Star with a smarmy smile and an affable but disingenuous "sign here, please."

As Simon recalled the delivery guy's false warmth, a scowl traversed his weathered face, a scowl that could have melted the bronzed Bright Star logo right off the entrance gate. Simon clenched his teeth. He wasn't a cursing kind of guy, but after twenty years in the Corps, he'd become acquainted with every swear word known to the English language, along with a smattering of Spanish ones. He may not have uttered those curse words aloud; nonetheless, his personal convictions didn't keep those words from popping into his head during trying situations where they'd pound on the door of his mind, hoping to wear him down, trying to make their way into the open air.

"Nope. Get lost," he growled aloud, waggling his tense shoulders. "I don't use the mouth with which I praise God to also utter obscenities. Beat it!"

Simon had refused to sign for the pump and told the driver to wait while he photographed the moose-sized crate (crushed on two sides, caved in on another) to document the exterior damage. While the driver protested the delay, Simon tried to swivel the crate into the light to get a better shot. The driver shut his mouth and found something else to do when loose bits of the shattered pump fell from a crack in the crate onto the truck's floor.

"Good grief," Simon had muttered. He took pictures of the broken bits and sent all the photos via email to the supplier in Las Vegas, then followed up with a phone call to the supplier's office.

"I've declined delivery of the pump," Simon told him. "Check your inbox for the details."

After reviewing Simon's photos, the man on the other end of the call was suitably apologetic. "I don't blame you. Look, I'm sorry this happened, and I'll lambast the freight company. Unfortunately and like I told you earlier, that particular pump is in high demand across the casino industry to run their water features, and thus is on back order. You can thank your lucky stars, though, because I have one of those pumps coming in later this month. I can have it to you . . . one sec."

I don't thank stars, lucky or otherwise, Simon had declared silently. *God, are you listening? I really need you right now. Please help.*

He heard the clicking of a mouse as the man searched his inventory.

"Earliest I can get it to you is late Tuesday."

"Really? *This* Tuesday?"

"Nope, sorry. I meant the Tuesday before Memorial Day, about two weeks from now."

"Outstanding," Simon had muttered under his breath. Then, admitting they would at least have a working pump before Bright Star's opening day, he added a heartfelt, *Thank you, Lord!*

Unless something else had gone wrong, the supplier should have delivered the pump as promised late yesterday afternoon. Simon would have personally checked the delivery when it arrived, but he'd had to leave work early for an urgent root canal. With the pump's arrival, Simon's sole priority as he clocked into work this morning, the Wednesday prior to Memorial Day weekend, was to install said pump, connect the various elements of the fountain and swimming complex's plumbing to the pump, update the pump's automation software on the swimming complex's laptop, and put the system back to work.

With the pump system up and operational, Simon would be able to fill the several pools, cycle the water and chemicals through the entire system and, *finally*, test the water to meet the Health Department's commercial pool requirements.

It irked Simon that today was supposed to have been his first day off in three weeks. He needed the brief respite after months of concentrated effort. It was supposed to have been a peaceful pause before Lake Tahoe's summer insanity officially kicked off.

"But nooo," he groused. "Instead of a well-deserved day off, Bright Star's swimming complex is giving *me* a complex—not to mention, now that the numbing for my root canal is wearing off, my jaw feels like it was kicked by a mule."

At present, the fountains, pools, and hot tubs were dry as dust. And until the pumping system was online, Bright Star's "jewel" would remain sadly lusterless.

Simon muttered a line he knew by heart: "Filling those pools could take up to eighteen hours. Nevertheless, God willing, I *will* get it done and the complex *will* open on time. *Oorah.*"

Simon turned and walked back toward the front of Bright Star's office. About the same time, Holly Mitchell burst from the cabin's doorway, the screen door slapping closed behind her. They met on the grass between the office and the road.

Holly was in her early fifties, a redhead trending toward gray. She was pleasant enough to work for—unless she was disturbed or anxious—and one look told Simon that Holly was totally rocking her disturbed and anxious alter ego. Her fading red curls trembled, and she clenched and unclenched her hands as she spoke.

"Fletcher, you have no idea how glad I am to see you! We have a bit of an emergency here, and I need your help."

Simon wasn't all that surprised. Working with Joe was great—he took problems in stride. But working for Holly followed a pattern: New day? New crisis.

"Nothing's on fire. Don't see any residents queuing up ahead of their move-in date. What's the big emergency?"

Besides our problem child of a swimming complex? Please don't go there, Holly. My stress meter is pegged out without you standing on it too.

Holly went there.

"Well, *the pools*, of course! The replacement pump arrived last evening, but can you believe this? The supplier sent *the wrong one!* Of course, the delivery guy just shrugged. As soon as Joe realized it was the wrong model, he called the supplier, after which he jumped in his truck and headed for Vegas to get the right one. The supplier promised to have it ready to load into Joe's truck first thing today.

"Joe drove through the night until he got to Vegas, then slept in his truck in the supplier's parking lot until the sun came up. He called a few minutes ago to say he's catching some breakfast and will be waiting at the supplier's door when they open this morning. He'll head back as soon as they load the *right* pump onto the bed of his truck."

She licked her lips. "Fletch, if the pool isn't filled by tomorrow, midday, the five residents scheduled to check in every hour from noon forward will not be merely disappointed. Oh, *no*, not simply 'put out.' They will be disgruntled, Simon, *disgruntled!* And you know how disgruntled people love to post negative reviews online! One couple, the Gormans, are bringing their granddaughters to Tahoe for the holiday weekend, and our swimming complex, in particular, figures high in their plans. *High*, Fletch!"

Simon stifled a yawn as Holly droned on. *Need. More. Coffee.*

"We don't dare launch our inaugural season on a sour note, Fletch, not after the way we've promoted Bright Star's grand opening. The residents' leases state that if they find substantive fault with Bright Star's advertised accommodations or amenities, they have five days to request a full refund. Fletch, we *can't afford* to refund any of our reservations. We need that money to pay you and operate the park through the summer season and-and-and to support Joe and me during the offseason."

The thirty acres Bright Star sat on, approximately halfway between Mount Tallac Trail and Fallen Leaf Lake, had originally belonged to Joe's grandparents and had been used in decades past as a summer camp, complete with horses and stables. Under a local zoning "grandfather" clause, long-term use of the land as a summer camp had afforded the Mitchells significant leeway in how they could renovate and utilize the property going forward.

Consequently, when Joe Mitchell inherited his grandfather's Tahoe property, he and Holly had retired early from their San Diego real estate business and moved to the modest cabin Joe's grandparents had lived in. Over the sixteen months since then, they had sunk their life savings and the profits from the sale of their company—plus a hefty mortgage—into turning a dated summer camp into a luxury RV paradise. It was no big secret to Simon that Joe and Holly's financial future depended on Bright Star being a success.

The nearer opening day loomed, the more anxious Holly became. And when Holly tensed up? She tended to micromanage.

Simon unfolded his arms. "Yeah, yeah. No pump, no pool, no *bueno*. I get it, Hol. Don't sweat it; when Joe gets here, I'll jump on the installation and get the pools filled on time. When do you expect him back?"

"He should be here late this afternoon, but with Joe out on the road, that leaves us shorthanded. I need you to take on Joe's tasks today, Fletch. Of course, the minute he gets here, you can switch to the pump install."

"Roger. Do all of Joe's chores, then install the pump when he gets here with it. Any specific issues I should know about?"

Holly hedged. "Well, there's Skipper."

Skipper Mitchell, Joe and Holly's fourteen-year-old nephew, had been with them an entire week, but it hadn't required the full seven days to convince the three of them that the kid was a right royal pain.

"What's he done this time?"

"Nothing, but that's just it. He won't do anything. I can't get him to unlock his bedroom door, let alone get him started on his chores, and I'm depending on him today. Especially today."

She shook her head. "I don't know if I can abide that boy through the entire summer, Fletch. I simply cannot tolerate the level of . . . disorder that follows him around."

Simon snorted. Skipper was under a form of house arrest as the condition of his probation. To complicate matters, Kathy, the boy's mother and the Mitchells' sister-in-law—*former* sister-in-law—could not miss work while Skipper was on probation without risking her job. So, at her request and with Joe and Holly's agreement, the judge overseeing Skipper's case had sentenced the boy to a summer of labor under his uncle and aunt's supervision. The alternative would have left Skipper alone at home through the summer, wearing an ankle monitor, but without structure or supervision, while his mother worked.

A recipe for further trouble if I've ever seen one, Simon thought. *The odds of that kid making it through the summer without breaking the conditions of his probation? Pretty much nonexistent.*

A year ago, to the Mitchells' dismay, Skipper's dad, Pete—Joe's much younger brother—had bailed on his family. He'd disappeared and his whereabouts remained unknown, which left his wife to support and raise their son on her own.

Now Skipper is a ticking time bomb, pushing the envelope hard, finding new ways to express his anger daily. Not unlike a few pimple-faced Marine recruits I've encountered over the years who were given the choice: join up or go to jail.

And what a ball of fun they were when out on their first leave as a Marine. Full of themselves and looking for trouble.

"I was hoping you would talk to him, Fletch. After all, he'll be working for you once we open."

Simon rubbed the back of his neck. "Talking isn't likely to put things right in that boy. The kid needs routine, physically demanding labor, and a firm hand. Someone to help him learn personal accountability."

"You fit the bill perfectly, Fletch, which is why I'm asking for your help. For example, he was supposed to help Joe hang the residents' site banners today."

A wrought iron pole with a perpendicular side arm stood at the head of each resident's double driveway. The pole's side arm was designed to display a vertical flag easily seen from the road. Holly had made the twenty-four colorful banners herself, adding to each one a site number and the residents' last name in applique. She was justifiably proud of the welcoming touch the banners would provide.

Simon shook his head. "Look, I'm a military cop by training, not a nursemaid, Holly. My style would be to bust open the kid's door, flip over his bed, and dump him onto the floor. But I'm not an MP any longer and he's not a Marine recruit. I'm not going to roust that spoiled kid from bed if he's too lazy to get up."

Holly's eyes glistened. "Please, Fletch?"

Well, crud.

Simon blew out a long breath. "Can't promise it will improve his sorry attitude, but I'll at least get him moving today. Now, is that everything?"

Holly fidgeted. "Just one more . . . item." She glanced through Bright Star's entrance and down the road to the right where Site 1 was tucked into the trees, its driveway not even visible from the gate. "Our first resident arrives today."

Simon's jaw about hit the floor. "Are you kidding me, Holly? Today is Wednesday. Residents aren't supposed to start checking in until tomorrow, noon. Those are *your* rules—no one checks in before the Thursday preceding Memorial Day weekend. No. One."

Fixing her eyes on the grass, Holly toed the broad leaves of a budding dandelion. "This isn't on me, Fletch. Joe made some kind of special exception for this woman, and he didn't even consult me! Of course I knew she was registered, but then yesterday Joe announced that, for some reason, she needs to check in a day early. Because he owes her some sort of a big favor, he made the exception."

Simon's brows drew together. "What kind of favor?"

"I have no idea, and believe me, I've asked. But whenever I've tried to put the question to Joe, he clams up like it's a big, dark secret or something. Anyway, this woman asked specifically for Site 1 because it backs up to the creek. Joe told me she studied the park's layout online and apparently likes the sound of a babbling brook nearby."

Simon made a disgusted noise. "And she's checking in today? Good grief! Like we don't have enough going on. Fine. We'll figure it out. What time is she due?"

"Joe said about 11:00." Then she looked up and skewered Simon with her gaze. "I need you to park her RV, Fletch."

Crud and double crud.

Bright Star rules dictated that only designated Bright Star employees were allowed to position and park resident RVs. Joe was an absolute savant at backing up the type and size of luxury RV Bright Star's residents were expected to bring. Simon was no slouch at the task, but he didn't have the artistry or flair Joe did. And the bigger the RV, the less confident Simon felt.

"What's this woman driving or hauling?"

Holly's mouth tightened. "And that's another thing, Fletcher. Bright Star is an *exclusive* summer residence. Do you know how stringent our requirements must be for us to actualize and model that exclusive status?"

Simon did know, and he quickly nodded his head hoping she'd skip over the lecture. Nope. Nothing could deter Holly from reiterating those stringent requirements aloud as though he'd never heard them.

She ticked them off on her fingers. "Resident RVs must be a minimum of thirty feet in length.

"Resident RVs must be no older than seven years.

"Resident RVs must be clean and well maintained with no noticeable neglect, damage, missing parts, or discoloration to the frame or paint.

"Resident RVs must be leveled and skirted within 24 hours of arrival.

"Resident RV systems must be compatible with and connected to Bright Star's electrical, water, and septic systems within 24 hours of arrival and during the entirety of the residency period.

"Residents must maintain their RV and assigned site in a manner that reflects and honors the spirit of Bright Star Summer RV Residence—with the exception of their site's lawn, of course. The sprinklers will water it, and Joe will mow the grass weekly."

"So what's the problem? If she signed the lease, she agreed to the terms."

Holly fidgeted and dug her shoe into the doomed dandelion. "Joe said . . ."

"Joe said what?"

With a huff, Holly muttered, "Joe said he'd made two concessions for this-this-this *woman*, this *Miss Finch*."

"Miss Finch, huh? And, pray tell, what two concessions did Joe make on this mysterious woman's behalf?"

"Don't tease me, Simon Fletcher! This is not a subject to make light of."

"Sure, Holly. What allowances did Joe extend to the woman?"

"Well, the first was allowing her to check in a day early. He would not elaborate on the second, but he said . . . he *promised* me that it would not lower Bright Star's standards."

Simon looked aside. "Interesting."

"*Not* interesting. Annoying. Maddening. And-and-and *wrong!*"

Simon slid a hand across his mouth to smother the laugh threatening to jump out. Holly was nothing if not melodramatic concerning her precious standards.

An inappropriate display of humor successfully averted, Simon suggested, "Why don't we wait until this Miss Finch arrives before we worry about how her rig might impact Bright Star? In the meantime, I'll attempt to get Skipper moving so he and I can get the site banners hung."

Holly nodded her agreement. "Thank you, Fletcher."

<hr>

SIMON LEFT THE OFFICE, glancing at the sign in the door's window that read, "Bright Star Office Hours, Monday-Saturday, 9:00 a.m. to 5:00 p.m.; Sundays, 1:00 to 5:00 p.m." He grabbed the keys to one of the park's two service vehicles—small, fuel-efficient pickups emblazoned with Bright

Star's copper-tinted logo. He and Joe used the pickups to haul maintenance and groundskeeping tools, cleaning supplies, firewood, and anything else that needed hauling.

Simon pointed the truck down the road that led away from the office and turned left at the side road just two-hundred yards from Bright Star's gate. A minute later he parked at the Mitchells' cabin. His own cabin, once the bunkhouse of the stable hands who'd worked for Joe's grandparents' summer camp, was off the next turn down the road.

Holly had left the front door unlocked, so Simon didn't knock. He went inside, stood in the small living room, and listened. All was quiet. He turned his head, still listening. There it was: the breathy in-and-out sounds of deep sleep coming from the second bedroom.

Simon tried the bedroom door, but as Holly had told him, it was locked. *Just a push-button knob lock. No need to break anything.*

Simon pulled his Allen wrench multi-tool from its pouch on his belt, selected its thinnest wrench, and inserted it into the hole in the knob to pop the lock. He stood in the open doorway and surveyed the room, starting with Skipper. The kid lay on his belly under a wild tangle of covers, his head on a fluffy pillow, face turned to the side, one arm dangling over the side of the bed.

Ah, youth! Sleeping on my stomach with my head angled like that would give me an all-day crick in the neck—sort of like the pain in the neck this kid is.

He turned his attention on the room. Discarded clothes, crumbs, crumpled candy wrappers, empty soda cans, and an open bag of chips littered the floor.

Simon spoke aloud with blatant disregard for Skipper's state of repose. "This place reeks like a pigsty. No wonder Holly doesn't think she can tolerate this kid's *disorder*."

Skipper twitched. His tousled head jerked up from the pillow. He flipped over and stared around in confusion. When he spotted Simon, he sat up. The kid was startled, but he managed to cover his fluster with a challenge.

"Fletcher! What the *blank* are you doing in my room?"

"Technically? Not your room, Skippy. Belongs to your aunt and uncle. Oh. And I'd advise you not to curse at me. I don't appreciate it."

"Yeah, well, my door was locked! You had no right to unlock it and barge in here—and my name's not Skippy; it's *Skipper*."

"Again, *not your room*, SkipBo. Belongs to your aunt and uncle. And since you didn't show up for work on time, your aunt gave me permission to roust you from your bed."

"I'm not working for them, and you can't make me. They aren't even paying me, and that's illegal. Now get out!"

Skipper grabbed at the covers, pulled them over his shoulders, flopped over, and buried his head in the pillow.

Simon took hold of the covers, and in one smooth move, yanked them off the bed onto the floor.

Skipper came up shouting, "I'm calling the cops on you, Fletch!"

Simon tossed the boy his cellphone. "Here. Use mine. You don't have one—and if you did? I doubt you could find it in this mess. By the way, while you're on the line with the police, don't forget to tell them the conditions of your probation."

That did the trick. Blinking in sudden uncertainty, Skipper sank in on himself.

Simon didn't let him stay there. "Get out of bed, nugget. We're burning daylight."

"My name is *Skipper!*" Under the outrage lurked tears.

Simon stepped to the side of the bed. "I'll use your proper name when you start holding up your end of the bargain. You agreed to the judge's terms, to his allowing you to come here instead of spending the summer at home under house arrest."

"Like I had a stinking choice."

"You had a choice, kid—in fact, you had several choices. Despite your mother's instructions, you chose to hang out with two up-and-coming criminals. Despite their bad reputations and the amount of trouble they'd already been in, you chose to pal around with them and follow in their footsteps. And despite knowing the difference between right and wrong, you chose to watch them start a fire in your school's cafeteria. *Those were the choices you made.*"

Simon picked up the half-empty bag of chips and squeezed the bag, crushing its contents to chip dust. Then he opened the bag and emptied it into the room's trash can.

"Today, you have another choice, *Skippy*. Get your butt out of bed and get to work or no food. Nothing. Not a bite."

"That's child abuse!"

"Good. We do agree on one thing: You, Skipperoo, are a child."

Skipper jumped to his feet, trembling with rage. "I am not!"

"As long as you behave like a child, you *are* a child, Skipperdoodle. And the judge's order dictated the conditions of your probation, not your aunt or uncle. You're to be paid for the work you do with room and board. Period. We're standing in the room your uncle has graciously allowed you to sleep in—*if* you work. Board means daily food. No work? No food and no expectation of privacy."

Skipper opened his mouth to retort, but Simon wasn't having anymore of the kid's lip.

He edged as close to Skipper as he could without actually touching him, standard military police intimidation tactic. He leaned in nose to nose, eye to eye, his countenance as fixed and unyielding as a rock, and roared.

"*Get. Your. Clothes. On. Nugget!* Now! Now! Now!"

Skipper withered under Simon's bellows. The instant Simon stepped back, Skipper grabbed a pair of dirty jeans from the floor and yanked them up and over his boxers. He scrambled for shirt, socks, and shoes, and pulled them on too. Uncertain what to do next, he slid a nervous glance toward Simon.

"Are you a human being or a dumb animal?" Simon barked. "Make that bed! When you're done, police this room, take out the trash, and get in the truck!"

Skipper hurried to comply.

Minutes later, with Simon nipping at his heels, Skipper ran from the Mitchells' cabin and jumped into the truck's passenger seat.

———— ◆ ————

AFTER THREE HOURS of labor, Simon and Skipper reported back to the park office. They had hung all twenty-four site banners, cleaned the bathrooms in the swimming complex (not that they had been used or needed cleaning), wiped down the kitchen and other parts of the rec cabin—the bathrooms, game room, and gym, and swept all the floors. Outside, they had tightened the sagging volleyball/badminton net.

It hadn't been fun for either of them.

Simon had kept pressure on the boy the same way his unit's staff sergeant used to establish his personal and unit expectations and to ensure that the Marines in his charge performed to his exacting standards—until they did so without supervision. Regardless of the task at hand, Simon kept Skipper jumping and running, never giving him a moment's peace or rest.

When Holly came out of the back room that served as her personal office, she leaned her elbows on the counter between her and them and waited for Simon to report their progress.

He rehearsed their finished tasks, then asked, "What else do you have for us this morning?"

Holly looked from Skipper's downcast eyes to Simon and back. "I'd like a supply of firewood stacked under the rec cabin's eaves for use in the group firepit."

Bright Star had six cords of firewood stacked to one side of the office, along with a huge pile of kindling. Residents could pick up what they needed for their site's firepit at any time or request that a park employee deliver a fresh supply to their site.

"Can do. What else?"

Holly pointed to a rolling laundry bin filled with neatly folded towels. "Just finished folding those towels. Stock them in the swimming complex's changing rooms, please."

"Consider it done. Happy to help. Right, Skipper?"

Simon lifted his chin toward Skipper and waited.

"Um, right, Fletch."

Simon then tipped his head toward the laundry bin, and Skipper quick-stepped to the bin and dragged it toward the door.

"Well!" Holly breathed. "The age of miracles has not passed away after all."

"We're coming along," was all Simon replied.

"Good. Now get out of here," she tossed over her shoulder on her way back through her office door. "I have paperwork to do."

He followed Skipper and the laundry bin to the door and grabbed the bin's back edge, giving it the assist needed to propel the bin's wheels over the threshold and onto the cabin's low porch.

That was the moment a vintage two-door panel wagon eased to a stop in front of the office and Skipper and Simon's forward motion came to an abrupt halt. The passenger's side of the panel wagon faced the office, so Simon could not see the driver. Besides, he was too busy gawking at the car to notice much else.

"*Wow*," Simon exclaimed under his breath. He stepped off the porch to ogle the car up close.

The classic car had been meticulously restored, its body a deep smoky blue, the paint job exquisite. Every inch of the wood paneling that covered the passenger side of the car gleamed, including the trim that ran down the side to the car's rounded rear corner. Simon resisted the urge to stroke the blue front fender—that was a classic car "no-no"—even as he took in the car's shiny new tires and their wide, blindingly white sidewalls.

Skipper joined Simon in his examination of the car's hood. "What kinda car *is* this?" he demanded.

Reverence in his voice, Simon answered, "This, my boy, is a 1950 Ford Custom Country Squire—a panel wagon commonly known as a 'woody.'"

Skipper echoed Simon's sentiments. "Er, *wow*."

The TAHOE MYSTERIES

CHAPTER 2

SIMON WAS SO ENGROSSED in the details of the vintage vehicle that he had paid no attention to the driver, and did not readily notice when she got out and hobbled her way to the front of the car. Not until a quiet voice said,

"1951, actually."

Simon dragged his eyes off the car. Did a reluctant about-face, then swiveled his head left and right.

"Down here," the woman murmured.

He looked down.

The woman before him was short. Not merely short, but really short. Possibly inches below the five-foot mark—not that he, Simon, was any measure of "tallness." He compensated for his lack of height in muscle mass.

When the woman shifted a little of her weight onto a cane, Simon glanced lower. She wore a child-size "boot" strapped around her left calf, ankle, and foot, one of those stiff orthopedic walking contraptions prescribed post-surgery or after an injury to protect a foot or leg while it was healing.

His perusal moved back up and took inventory. An out-and-out riot of curling black hair sprinkled lightly with silver framed the woman's face, a face surprisingly unlined for her age.

Which I'd put in her mid-to-late fifties?

She'd somehow managed to juggle a can of Zero Sugar Cherry Dr. Pepper along with the cane, because about then she took a swig.

Gah! How can she drink that stuff?

"Happens to be my favorite. Probably drink three or four cans a day."

Simon mentally smacked himself on the forehead. "I apologize for staring, ma'am. Impolite of me."

He redirected his attention to her face, and found that *she* was studying *him*. Yet, when he looked closer, his brows lifted: Two dark brown orbs—not unlike two glossy Junior Mints—stared steadily at him from under eyelids fringed by thick, stubby black lashes. But it was the hooded, almond shape of her eyes that surprised him most.

"One-half Korean, father's side, legal immigrant, 1960."

Simon frowned. *I'm getting real tired of you reading my mind, lady.*

To change the subject, he turned his scrutiny back onto her car. "So, not 1950 but 1951, you said?"

"Yes. You were correct on the rest, though. It is a Ford Custom Country Squire."

"Well, it's in amazing condition. Did you—"

"Restore it myself? Yes, but with the advice and help of professional restoration gurus."

"And those whitewalls—"

"Custom refabrications of the originals."

"Custom refabrications must be—"

"Pricey? Yes."

"The wood—"

"Paneling? Mahogany trimmed in maple."

"The original 239 cubic-inch flathead V8—"

"With Offenhauser heads? Certainly. Precisely rebuilt, of course."

"Well, it's absolutely gorgeous—"

She tapped her cane on the road's asphalt. "Pardon me for cutting short our fascinating tête-à-tête, but is this where I check in?"

"Check in? Oh! You're our early resident? Miss Finch?"

She inclined her head. "One and the same."

Simon extended his hand. The cool fingers the woman placed in his palm were as diminutive as the rest of her.

"Simon Fletcher, Bright Star Facilities and Security Manager. I'll be parking your RV for you—"

Simon's tunnel vision and rapturous perusal of the vintage panel wagon had blinded him to what the woody towed behind it. He lifted his gaze to her rig and nearly choked.

It wasn't a motor home. Wasn't a fifth wheel or a luxury trailer. It certainly wasn't, per Bright Star's stiff standards, a qualifying RV of any type or model.

Attached to the bumper of Miss Finch's vintage vehicle was a travel trailer. The trailer's paint design was a unique and exquisite combination of cream, gray, and the same smoky blue as the body of the woody.

Unfortunately, the pleasing paint job could not disguise the unmistakable and commonplace outline of a seventeen-foot Casita.

Simon slowly ticked off Bright Star's RV requirements one by one.

Resident RVs must be a minimum of thirty feet in length.

Well, that's a fail.

Resident RVs must be no older than seven years.

I suppose it could *be seven years old or newer—but highly unlikely.*

Resident RVs must be clean and well maintained with no noticeable neglect, damage, missing parts, or discoloration to the frame or paint.

Okay, it passes that standard. Certainly has an impressive paint job.

But even if the trailer were new enough to qualify for a Bright Star berth, it was nowhere close to the required minimum length of thirty feet, and Holly would kick hard at that violation. Worse yet, common travel trailers in general defied the gravest of Holly's rules—unstated but implicit though that rule might be: *Bright Star was for luxury RVs only.* The park's rules and high-dollar season fees were all about ensuring that nothing of an inferior class take up residence within Bright Star's hallowed grounds.

Simon kept his expression carefully neutral. Nevertheless, as a Marine, he was well acquainted with that old, anglicized, and diluted military adage: *No plan survives first contact with the enemy.* In other words, whatever "special exceptions" Joe may have promised Miss Finch? In Joe's absence, they were unlikely to survive first encounter with Holly. She'd die on that hill before she'd allow Miss Finch's common little travel trailer to take up residence at Bright Star and besmirch its reputation.

As a further aside? Simon would take neither fame nor fortune to stand in Joe's shoes when he returned from Vegas with the pool pump.

Joe, you are a braver man than I am.

"Skipper?"

The boy gave an annoyed huff. "What now?"

"Run inside and let Holly know our season's first resident has arrived."

"Yeah, whatever." With an impatient sigh, he dragged his feet up the porch to deliver the message.

A minute later, he dragged them back. "She'll be right here."

"Right here" gave Simon the moment he needed to put his arm around Skipper's shoulders, pull him aside, and issue a whispered caution.

"Before Holly gets here, make yourself scarce, kid. The fur's about to fly."

"Oh, yeah?" Wide-eyed, Skipper retreated to the side of the office where he could duck out of sight behind cords of firewood should tangible fur actually fly in his direction.

Simon glanced back to Miss Finch. She seemed calm and unfazed, but she did push a wispy curl away from her eyes. She then reached into the handbag slung crosswise across her body and retrieved an envelope.

Simon slid his hands into his pockets and shunted a crooked smile in her direction. "Mrs. Mitchell will be here directly."

She returned his smile with a soft one of her own. "So I gathered," she murmured.

Simon saw something glimmer in those dark-chocolaty eyes of hers, and an irrational impression nudged its way into his mind. *Why, Junior, ah do believe thar's steel a-lurkin' behind them thar chocolate drops.*

He squinted. Shook off the cowardly impulse to join Skipper around the corner of the cabin to avoid the coming unpleasantness.

You're a Marine, Fletcher. You've waded into drunken brawls, put down raging riots, and faced enemy fire. Stand your ground!

He was instantly irritated when he found Miss Finch still studying him. "What?"

"How long have you been out?"

"Out of what?"

"Military. Marine Corps. Lifer. Separated less than a year ago, I wager."

"And who told you that?"

"You did."

Simon hoisted his hands to his hips. "Says *you*."

Carefully, she lifted her walking stick and pointed it at his head. "You're not yet comfortable with a fuller civilian hairstyle, but I imagine Mrs. Mitchell deemed the Corps' 'regulation cut' to be a bit off-putting to her upscale clientele, so she asked you to grow out your hair."

She pursed her lips, then added, "I take back the word *asked*. She made it a condition of employment."

Marines are the definition of stoic. They do not allow the unexpected to rattle them. Do not easily show emotion. Simon had spent twenty years plowing that particular groove in his brain's gray matter. Had it down cold.

"And you could tell all of that from my hair?"

"Not from your hair but from your actions. You drew my attention to your discomfort."

Simon felt weirdly defensive and off-balance. He was beginning to wonder if the lady was telepathic. He hardened his frown. "And when did I do that?"

"The three times your hand rubbed your neck and hairline since I arrived. You dislike and remain unaccepting of your hair's longer length."

Holly appeared on the office porch. She scanned the panel wagon and its towed burden. Her brows shot up. Her head moved slowly side to side.

"Oh, no. No, no, no. *No*. This will *not* do."

As Holly stepped off the porch, Miss Finch hobbled forward, smiled, and held out her hand.

"Good morning. Miss Finch. I have a reservation and am checking in."

Holly ignored the outstretched hand before her and drew herself up—not at all necessary as she had at least six inches on the smaller woman.

"Miss Finch, I am Mrs. Mitchell, Bright Star's office manager. I'm afraid there's been a misunderstanding. Since you claim to have a reservation, I must assume that you downloaded and printed a copy of the lease from our website, then signed it and brought it with you?"

Miss Finch's set smile did not waver. "Actually, Joe sent me a revised lease, one that made an exception for the length of my RV and that granted me an early check-in for today. He signed and dated the lease before sending it. I have a photocopy . . . if you're interested?"

Holly froze momentarily. Regained her chilly but superior demeanor. "Where is the lease with Joe's original signature?"

"Ah. The original, with Joe's handwritten revisions and dated signature, is in the safe within my RV. This certified copy of the revised lease with both of our signatures, thus a completely legal substitute for the original, is for your files." Miss Finch extended the envelope toward Holly.

Holly slowly took the envelope. "My husband mentioned that he owed you a favor, but in the thirty-one years we've been married, he has, not once, alluded to such a thing. I had never even heard him speak your name before he logged your reservation." She lifted her chin. "Just how do you know him?"

Miss Finch placed both hands on the head of her cane. "My acquaintance with Joe, although brief, goes back a number of years. We knew each other less than a month, and it was at the end of his military service during the Gulf War. You may ask him to share the particulars with you, if you like. It will make no difference at this late date."

Holly studied Miss Finch. "Joe was wounded in that war. He spent his last weeks of service in a military hospital in Germany."

The diminutive woman inclined her head once but added nothing.

Holly squared her shoulders and lifted her chin, her body language telegraphing her decision. "I apologize for the inconvenience, Miss Finch, but just as one cannot make a silk purse from a sow's ear, I cannot allow you with your, er, *travel trailer* to take up residence at Bright Star in blatant contravention of our exacting standards—standards all of our residents agree to and expect from fellow residents. I will discuss this situation with my husband when he returns from Vegas and am certain he will agree with me."

Miss Finch again inclined her head. "I understand your position, although I must reiterate that I hold a binding lease signed by the property owner." Her cordial manner remained fixed, even when she murmured, "Joe is, I believe, the property owner?"

Simon cringed. Talk about ruffling feathers! Miss Finch couldn't have said anything more contentious and certain to raise Holly's ire. He had heard the Mitchells argue over the issue of Bright Star ownership three times. Ownership of the *land* on which Bright Star stood had been Joe's tool of last resort when he was dead set against one of Holly's campaigns and was determined not to let her have her way. Sadly, that argument never seemed as effective as he would have wished.

Yes, Joe's grandfather had left the thirty acres to Joe as sole and separate property. On the other hand, the Mitchells had funneled their joint savings and other joint assets into turning the old summer camp into a luxury RV park. Nonetheless, whenever Holly pushed Joe for a decision he balked at, the issue of land ownership always came up. In those heated moments, Simon felt for Joe: It was the only card he had left to play.

The office phone rang, giving Holly a valid reason to break off the "discussion" where it stood in stalemate. She addressed Simon, saying, "Do not park Miss Finch's *trailer*, Fletch," as she swept across the porch and through the office doorway.

Simon cut a guilty glance at Miss Finch's back. He opened his mouth to—

"You need not apologize, Mr. Fletcher." She looked aside and sighed. "This is between me and Mrs. Mitchell. And possibly Mr. Mitchell."

Simon sputtered and snapped his jaws together. *She's not looking at me, not even facing my direction, yet she knows what I'm thinking?*

The woman turned toward him, the faintest of smiles tugging at her mouth. "My, my. Are you aware that you are rubbing your hairline again, Mr. Fletcher?"

Simon jerked his hand off his head and shoved it in the back pocket of his jeans.

At that moment, a shriek erupted from the office followed by Holly screaming, "Fletch! Fletcher! Help!"

Simon raced for the office door, catching a glimpse of Miss Finch's startled expression as he blew by her.

———— • ————

HOLLY SAT IN A CRUMPLED heap on the stool behind the office counter when Simon found her. She was still on the phone, weeping silently, listening to the voice on the other end, and scribbling frantic notes.

When she gulped and demanded, "Where? Which hospital?" Simon reached across the counter, put a hand on her shoulder, and squeezed gently. She glanced at him, grateful for his comforting presence.

Finally, Holly hung up the phone and tried to pull herself together. "Fletcher."

"I'm here, Holly. Tell me what's going on."

She sobbed once. "It's Joe. A semi ran him off the road just north of Vegas, and his truck rolled over. He's got a fractured leg, possible internal injuries, and God knows what else! They're taking him by ambulance to a Vegas hospital. His truck is totaled . . . I have no idea about the pump."

She lifted her wet gaze to Simon. "Fletch, what am I going to do?"

"Which hospital, Holly?"

"It's . . . I wrote it down. Here it is. UMC Trauma Center."

"Okay, this is what you're going to do. You're going to get in my pickup and let me drive you down to Vegas." He exhaled slowly. "I'll track down Joe's truck and the pool pump. If the pump wasn't totaled along with Joe's truck, I will haul it back here ASAP."

"But Fletch, we can't leave! We have guests arriving tomorrow!" She stared at the binder on the desk holding the check-in schedule. "But I also cannot leave Joe, as serious as his condition is, alone in the hospital. I cannot! I refuse to! And if you drive me down there, I won't have a car to get around. Oh, dear. No, I think you should stay here, and-and-and I should drive myself—"

She ended on a choking sob, put her elbows on the counter, and dropped her face onto her hands.

"Holly, with the shock you've been handed, you're in no fit shape to drive. I will take you. I'll handle the details, too, get you a hotel room and arrange for a rental car so you can drive back and forth to the hospital. After we see how Joe is doing, I'll leave you with him and do my best to find the pump and arrive back here before noon tomorrow when the first resident checks in. I'll drive all night if need be. Don't worry; I'll take care of things."

The screen door slapped closed behind Skipper. He trotted up beside Simon. "Is Uncle Joe all right?"

"He will be," Simon murmured, determined to be positive.

As though Skipper weren't standing right in front of her, Holly groaned and whispered, "But what do I do with *him*, Fletcher? We can't leave him here by himself—the judge ruled he had to be under continuous supervision. Even if we *did* leave him here alone, there's no telling what kind of mischief he'd get into! I suppose we need to take him with us."

"Perhaps I can be of assistance."

Holly scowled; Simon turned around, surprised to find Miss Finch, both hands resting on the head of her cane, standing inside the office door.

"*You*," Holly ground out, "are not a resident and cannot stay here."

Miss Finch gently inclined her head. "Perhaps. However, I *can* supervise this young man while you are gone, Mrs. Mitchell."

"No! I will not allow—"

"Thank you," Simon interjected, cutting Holly off. "We accept your gracious offer."

Skipper protested. "What the hay? You don't even know this old biddy. I can stay here on my own."

Holly opened her mouth, but Simon held up his hand in the universal sign for "stop." Holly subsided before she could wind herself into a full fit.

Beside Simon, Skipper seethed. "I don't need a babysitter."

Simon answered the young man. "We talked about this back in your room, *Skippy*. Act like an adult and you'll be treated like an adult. Act like a child, and you'll be treated like a child."

Red-faced, Skipper protested, "Well, I'm not a child—I'm fourteen years old! The law says I'm old enough to be left alone."

"Yeah, you *should* be responsible enough to be left alone, which is why, when you aided and abetted your buddies in starting that fire, you lost both your credibility and your freedom. And just to point out the obvious? When your aunt and uncle agreed to have you spend the summer here, they obligated themselves to follow the judge's supervision order *to the letter*.

"Miss Finch has, out of the kindness of her heart, agreed to step in and keep an eye on you. You either stay here *and mind her*, or you ride to Vegas and back with me. Fourteen or more hours with me in my pickup, my choice of music nonstop, or remain at Bright Star under Miss Finch's supervision. Which will it be?"

Skipper growled low in his throat. "Stay."

"I need you to say that you will follow Miss Finch's instructions while I am gone."

Skipper cut angry eyes toward Miss Finch. "Whatever."

"Say it, *Skipperoo*."

Between gritted teeth, the boy fumed, "My name is *Skipper!*"

"Your name is *mud* if I don't hear you say *aloud* that you'll follow Miss Finch's instructions."

Skipper glared at Simon. "I will."

"You will what?"

His glare less pronounced, Skipper sniffed and muttered, "I will follow her instructions."

"Thank you."

"But I'll sleep in my own room in Uncle Joe's cabin."

"No. Nope. *Nuh-uh*."

Miss Finch spoke. "I have a table that makes into a single bed. Skipper is welcome to sleep there. All he needs is a sleeping bag and a pillow."

Holly found her voice. "But you cannot park that-that *trailer* at Bright Star!"

"Yes, I believe you made yourself clear on that point," Miss Finch replied, "but for me to keep an eye on both Bright Star and Skipper, it will be necessary for me to park my trailer somewhere . . . close by."

Holly huffed. "You may park behind the office. *Out of sight*. Plug into the outlet on the back side of the cabin. And Skipper may sleep in your . . . trailer."

"We appreciate your kindness and thank you, Miss Finch," Simon replied. "Will those arrangements work for you?"

Skipper edged in close to Simon and whispered for all to hear, "No way! Not sleepin' in some creepy lady's moldy old trailer!"

Simon pushed his face into Skipper's. "You'll do what I say you'll do or you and I will have another meeting of the minds, Skipperoni. *Do you get me?* When I return from Vegas, you can bunk at my place—top bunk only. No negotiation on that point. Until then, you stay with Miss Finch."

"*Fine*." Skipper subsided, but shot a dirty look in Miss Finch's direction.

Miss Finch.

Simon had saved his toughest words for her.

"Here's how it's going to go, Miss Finch. After I locate that miserable pool pump, I will break every speed limit between here and Vegas to get back before our first resident arrives tomorrow at noon. That said . . ."

He startled Holly and Skipper by stalking across the room to where the little woman stood near the door. He "gifted" her his most suspect-intimidating glare. "While we do appreciate your assistance, should anything shady happen while I'm gone, you'll have me to deal with."

It was said for Holly's reassurance more than any distrust of Miss Finch, yet Simon blinked in surprise. The cold, menacing face of stone he'd perfected as a military cop, combined with the sudden and blatant intrusion into the individual's personal space, had never failed to intimidate perps, young Marines, or most anyone else. So what was that twinkle swimming around behind that woman's two shiny brown orbs?

Wait. Where did it go? Simon backed up a step. *It was right there . . . and now it's gone?*

Unfazed and unintimidated, Miss Finch cleared her throat. "Right you are, Mr. Fletcher. I am accountable to you."

She then addressed herself to Holly. "Mrs. Mitchell, I believe we got off on the wrong foot. You must be terribly concerned about Joe. In your absence, please allow me to watch over Skipper for you while you see to Joe's care. And do not be concerned for your lovely RV park. With Skipper's help, I'll safeguard it today, and Simon has promised to be back tomorrow before your residents begin arriving. Please go, with peace of mind, and be with your dear husband."

Holly appealed to Simon, who saw the crusty shell around Holly crack. He nodded his approval.

Holly licked her lips. "I-I . . . well, all right. Thank you for your offer, Miss Finch."

"Not at all. Happy to be of service."

She pulled a business card from the handbag slung crosswise across her body and slid it across the counter to Simon. "I apologize for the crossed-out number. I have a new phone and haven't updated my cards. I've printed my current number at the bottom. Call any time. And your number is?"

Simon rattled it off. She typed his number carefully into her phone.

Then Simon gestured to Holly. "Grab whatever you need from your office. We'll stop at your place so you can pack a bag, but we leave pronto."

CHAPTER 3

SIMON WALKED HOLLY ACROSS the parking lot and into the hospital, noting the time on a prominent wall clock—after 7 p.m. They had stopped only once to gas up, grab coffee, and use the restrooms. He hadn't eaten since breakfast, and his stomach was staging a revolt.

He and Holly were directed to the ICU nurses' station. There, the doctor on shift told them that Joe was listed in guarded but stable condition, then shared the results of the tests they'd run on Joe.

"He's in better shape than he was when they brought him in, so we're cautiously optimistic. However, in addition to sustaining a compound fracture of his left leg, Joe has a small internal bleed. We're keeping a close eye on that bleed, which is why he's in the ICU. We've scheduled him for two surgeries tomorrow, the first to locate and close the bleed, the second to set and pin his leg."

A tearful Holly asked, "Is he awake?"

"Not at the moment. We sedated him to ease his pain and keep him still. When he wakes up, the nurses will let him know you're here. Feel free to make yourself at home in the ICU lobby while you wait."

The harried doctor departed, and a nurse showed Simon and Holly to the ICU's lobby.

Simon spoke. "Holly, I need to locate that pump. When you were on the phone with the police, did they give you an accident report number?"

"Yes. I wrote it down . . . somewhere."

"Maybe you left your notes on the office counter?"

"Oh, bother! I think I did."

"I'll call and ask Miss Finch if she can find them. And shall I get you a room for the night?"

"Don't trouble yourself, Fletcher. I won't leave Joe while he's in danger. I can get a room tomorrow."

"Okay, then I'll get out of here and—"

"Fletcher?"

"Yeah?"

"Fletch, you know how to pray, don't you?"

He hesitated before replying, "Yeah, I do. Would you like me to pray with you right now?"

"Please. I-I don't remember how, Fletch. I try, but I cannot find the words."

They were alone in the waiting area, so Simon steered Holly to some chairs. They sat down and he took her hand in his. He sucked in a deep breath. Let it out.

Lord, it's been a while for me too. Please help me.

He began, "Lord God, I stand before you in the mighty name of Jesus. I ask you to come, by the power of your Holy Spirit, to minister to Holly's needs. Lord, you know her heart; in fact, you know her inside and out. You know what she needs, even before she does. Please speak peace to her heart and mind and draw her close to Jesus, your only begotten Son and the Savior of the world.

"And at this time, Lord, Holly and I also ask for healing for Joe's body. Lord, we thank you for preserving his life and thank you for the excellent care he is receiving. Please be with the doctors and nurses as they continue to attend Joe. We thank you for hearing our prayers. Amen."

"Amen," Holly sniffled and gripped his fingers. "Thank you, Fletch. I don't know what we'd do without you."

Simon bobbed his head. "I'm glad I can help. You have my cell number. Call if you need anything. Anything at all. I'll be out looking for Joe's truck and the pump. When I find the pump, I'll head straight back to Bright Star."

On his way out of the hospital, Simon's phone vibrated. He plucked it from his pocket. A text waited for him. He didn't recognize the number, but he opened and read the message.

Police Accident Report
Number 27.33652B
LVMPD phone 702.828.3111
BD Finch

"Ah. Our new acquaintance. And it's *BD* Finch, is it? Wonder what the B and D stand for."

With grudging respect for the woman's thoughtfulness, Simon touched the Las Vegas Metropolitan Police Department phone number to dial it. He read off the accident report number to the officer who answered his call.

"Give me a minute," the officer said.

Simon waited.

"Yup. Found it."

"What I need to know is where the truck was towed," he told her. When she replied, he said, "Great. Do you happen to have their number? Yeah? Let me jot that down. Thanks for your help."

But to his dismay, he soon discovered that knowing where to find Joe's truck and the elusive pump was merely the first step in retrieving said pump. When Simon called the tow yard, instead of a person, he got a recording.

"You have reached Assurance Towing. Our regular business hours are 8:00 a.m. to 6:00 p.m., Monday through Saturday, closed on Sundays. If you have reached us after hours and require a tow, press 2 to connect to our dispatch service. Please note that our dispatch service cannot provide information on already towed vehicles in our storage lot. For that information, leave your name and number, and we will return your call during our next scheduled business day."

"Closed and won't open until 8:00 a.m. tomorrow morning? And after that I have a seven-hour drive back to Tahoe?"

Simon scrubbed at the back of his neck in frustration. He was a man of action, who, at the moment, had no avenue of action open to him.

That is, until an ill-advised (not to mention illegal) idea popped into his head.

"Are you nuts, Fletcher? No way! I'm not breaking into a tow yard probably guarded by a pack of junkyard rottweilers just to rescue a blasted pool pump. And even if I were to wait until after dark and *somehow* gain access into that place, wander around and *somehow* find Joe's truck in the dark, and then *somehow* wrestle the pump's crate onto my truck? All that 'somehow' is more likely to get me arrested than put me back at Bright Star by noon tomorrow."

He stared at his phone. "And getting arrested won't help Joe and Holly a bit. I'm sorry my old nature even suggested such a thing, Lord."

Talking to the Lord twice in one day, Fletch? Something of a recent record.

"Shut up," he growled.

He made his way across the parking lot and climbed into his truck. With a disgusted shake of his head, he dialed the newest number in its contact list.

She picked up the call on its second ring. "BD Finch here."

She pronounced those two initials as a single word, "BeeDee."

He caught himself again wondering what her initials stood for, then yanked himself back to the situation at hand.

"Miss Finch, it's Simon Fletcher."

Simon heard Skipper's voice in the background demand, "Hey! Ask him how my Uncle Joe's doing!"

A brief moment of silence passed before he heard a muttered, "Sorry, Miss Finch."

Wow. Not a word spoken by Miss Finch, but she managed to pry an apology from the kid? That's a trick I'd like to add to my repertoire.

Miss Finch came back on the line. "Mr. Fletcher, is there word on Mr. Mitchell's condition?"

"Guarded but cautiously optimistic. He'll be having surgery tomorrow. They will look for internal bleeding then set his leg."

"Thanks be to God! Now, what can I do for you, Mr. Fletcher?"

"First, I appreciate the text you sent. I called the police with the accident number, got the name of the tow yard, then called them. Unfortunately, they're closed for the night and won't open until morning. Don't know what I'll find, either. I mean, if Joe's truck was totaled, I have to think the pump would have also sustained significant damage."

He spewed some pent-up worry. "Long story short, that pool pump pretty much determines whether Bright Star's first week of the season is a success or a complete blowout. If, because the pool is closed, some of the residents back out of their leases, they are eligible for full refunds . . ." He let the sentence fizzle out.

She murmured, "Ah. I believe I understand your concern."

The silence on the line lingered, but it wasn't an uncomfortable silence. Simon had the sense that Miss Finch was thinking. When she did speak, she surprised him.

"Mr. Fletcher, do you by chance have the model number of that pump handy?"

"Uh, well, yeah. I do." *Know it by heart at this point.*

"Be so kind as to read it off to me."

Simon was tired, discouraged, and ravenous, spiraling fast toward downright cantankerous, but it was easier to give her what she asked for than to push back on her request. He recited the pump's model number to humor the woman.

No matter how you slice it, lady, even should I get back to Bright Star late tomorrow with a working pump, it's still going to take twelve to eighteen hours to fill those pools, cycle the chemicals, then heat and test the water. No doubt about it, those first residents will arrive tomorrow to a closed swimming complex. Big ouch.

Which reminded him.

"Uh, Miss Finch?"

"Yes, Mr. Fletcher?"

"Because I can't get access to the tow yard until they open tomorrow, I can't possibly make it back to Bright Star by noon. Best guess puts me back between three and four o'clock. Possibly later."

"Not to worry. I have perused the schedule in the book Mrs. Mitchell left on the counter. Five residents are scheduled to arrive, in hourly sequence, beginning at noon. I will see them settled in satisfactory style, and Skipper will assist me."

Recollection of another sticky issue hit Simon, and he had the sudden urge to rip his hair out. "Uh, Miss Finch?"

"Yes?"

"In your lease, do you recall reading Bright Star's rule on the parking of resident RVs?"

"Mmm, yes. I do recall that rule. Again, please do not concern yourself; we'll muddle through. Anything else?"

Simon flinched. *She's going to ask the residents to park their own rigs?* He again found himself calling on heaven. *Dear Lord, please help us!*

He stared out the front window of his truck, turning over the few options left to him.

I suppose what Holly doesn't know, Holly can't have a cow about. And if the residents park their own rigs, hopefully I can repair whatever damage they've wreaked before Holly gets back.

He'd forgotten he was still on the phone until Miss Finch's voice startled him.

"Mr. Fletcher? Do you have anything else?"

"No. Nope. That's it. Thanks again, Miss Finch. You . . . frankly, you're a godsend."

A puff of feigned indignation floated to him over the miles.

"I've been called worse, Mr. Fletcher. You don't scare me."

A laugh burst from his chest. "Thanks. I needed that. And please call me Fletcher, Miss Finch, or just Fletch, if you prefer."

"Very well. Have a restful evening, Fletcher."

"You too."

Simon clicked off his phone. Visions of flattened electrical boxes and crushed septic lines danced in his head alongside notions of runaway luxury RVs jouncing over the fixed parking curbs at the end of each site's asphalt drive, then disappearing into thick forest. Those mental images made him shudder, *but* . . . but for some reason, he wasn't actually all that concerned.

"Lord, I don't need to know how you intend to get us through this situation. Just . . . please don't allow too much damage, particularly to our residents' RVs? And Lord? Thank you for sending Miss Finch at exactly the right time. I ask you to bless her."

Sheesh. Four prayers in a day, Fletch? Why, it's like having a camp meeting.

"Can it, would ya? Gimme a break."

About then, the roar from his stomach intruded. "Yeah, yeah. Hold your horses. Guess I'd better get a room for the night before they're all taken."

He saw a motel with a vacancy sign ahead. He got out of his truck under the motel's portico and secured a room. He added Holly's name to the room, then texted her the information. He would use the room tonight then turn it over to her for the remainder of her stay in Vegas.

"Oh, yeah. And arrange for a rental car to be delivered to her at the hospital."

His stomach bellowed again.

"I hear you! Next stop? Food. And lots of it."

------●------

THURSDAY PRIOR TO MEMORIAL DAY

SIMON PARKED AT ASSURANCE Towing at 7:45 the following morning. Soon after, three cars parked near him. Their occupants headed for the employee entrance. One driver noticed him and strode to Simon's window.

"Morning. I'm the manager here. Can I help you?"

"Yes, thanks. My employers' truck was in an accident yesterday and was towed here. I need to pick up the crate that was in the truck's bed. Got a letter here from the truck's co-owner giving me permission to take the crate."

"Red late-model Ford F-150?"

"That's the one."

The guy shook his head. "Totaled, I'm afraid."

"I figured as much. I'm after the crate it was carrying."

The manager's next words chilled him.

"Yeah, you're welcome to take what's left of it. Follow me."

The manager walked ahead of Simon to his office. He grabbed two hard hats, handed Simon one, then led the way through a maze of wrecked vehicles.

Simon heard the *clank* and *scree* of the crusher starting up and identified the whine of a forklift across the yard, but he scarcely recognized Joe's truck when they came to it. The semi's sideswipe had sent Joe's truck into a roll, and the crate, still tied down in the truck's bed, had taken the brunt of the rollover. It was crushed from the top down.

"I hope you didn't pack your granny's good china in there," the guy joked.

Simon didn't laugh. "Borrow a crowbar from you?"

Simon tore into the wood and packing material until he'd exposed what he'd dreaded: shards of metal, plastic, and glass from broken valves and gauges.

"Tough luck, man," the manager muttered.

Simon put his phone in his pickup's dash-mounted phone holder and dialed Bright Star's supplier before he left the parking lot. "Joe was bringing the replacement pump home when a semi ran him off the road. Yeah, he's bad off at the moment. We think he's going to be okay, but the pump is trashed. We need another, pronto."

The supplier's exasperation came across to Simon. "Dude, like I told you, that was the only pump of its kind we had coming in—and that model is backordered. Too bad Joe was hit *after* he picked up the pump."

"He wouldn't have been hit at all if you'd delivered the right model in the first place."

The man sighed. "I hear you. You won't need to pay for its replacement. Still, I estimate six weeks *minimum* before we can get our hands on another pump of that model."

"Then I'd appreciate it if you'd get it ordered today—although if our swimming pools are dry for the next six weeks, I have to wonder if, by the time the next pump arrives, our RV park won't be as empty as its pools are."

Who knew we'd need that stinking pump just to stay in business?

"Rotten luck, man, but like I said, the Trident 7000 is the most utilized pump model in Vegas because it runs many of the large water features the casinos brag about."

"You've told me that, but—" A lightbulb switched on in Simon's head. "Say, do you think any of your casino customers keep a spare pump on hand?"

The supplier perked up. "That's a great question. Wait one."

Simon listened to mouse clicks and mutters as the man worked his way through his inventory records.

"Looks like Blue Lagoon bought two pumps back in January, one to replace their broken unit, the other to keep in reserve. I suspect they won't want to part with the spare, though. Competition being what it is, those casinos cannot afford for their water features to be offline even a day."

"I hear you. Nonetheless, I should at least call and make an attempt to buy their spare."

"Yeah? Well, good luck with that."

———●———

HE HAD FASTENED HIS seatbelt when he heard the *ding* of an arriving text. He glanced at the lock screen's preview. He didn't recognize this number either, but he swiped to the text anyway.

Hey fletch its skipper
Miss Finch give me this cheap
phone so she could getahold
of me when im out working
said i should text you the number
in case you wanted to call me or
something its a really dumb phone
but anyway this is me

Not a single punctuation mark. Rife with misspellings and poor grammar. Yeah, Simon could believe the text came from Skipper. He added the number to his contacts, then replied,

Thanks for the text, Skip.
I have your number now.

Yup. I have your number, kid.
Another text came through almost immediately.

My name is Skipper
NOT SKIP

———◆———

THE FACILITIES MANAGER AT Blue Lagoon, a guy named Mobius, sounded sympathetic. "Sorry, man, but the reason we keep a spare pump in storage is because our working pump crashed on this past New Year's Day. What a fiasco! Took a week to procure a replacement and get it installed, my boss nipping at my backside the whole time, so I ordered a spare. Glad I did; I hear they're even harder to come by these days."

Mobius must have put his hand over the phone, because Simon heard a muffled aside, "Hey, Jack! Get that ladder over to the crew in the parking garage pronto. Thanks."

Then he was back. "Sorry about the interruption. It's always a three-ring circus over here—and we're not even close to being the biggest attraction on the strip, you know, and competition for customers is stinking fierce. Last New Year's when our pump went out and our water features were down for a week, we lost a chunk of revenue.

"My boss told me if we ever again got caught without a replacement pump, I'd be out of a job. Now you know why I need to keep that spare on hand. I swear, though, if I were at liberty to sell our spare to you, I would."

"Sure. I appreciate your circumstances."

Simon clicked off the call, pulled over to the curb, and parked. "Lord? I've pounded on every door I know to pound on, to no avail. Please help us; we're really in a bind here. And I ask you to help Joe and Holly over at the hospital." He sighed. "I suppose I need to pray for myself too. With Joe out of commission, a lot of his work will fall to me. Please help me, Lord God."

Sheesh. Getting to be a habit, Fletch—you know, prayer? Or should I say it's getting to be a habit again?

"Yeah? What of it? And is talking to myself in any way normal?"

With no additional options before him, Simon pointed his truck north on US-95. He was an hour into his drive home when Holly's question at the hospital began to nag at him.

Fletch, you know how to pray, don't you?

Simon had hesitated before replying to her. Why?

Maybe because the sore spot in his heart was still mighty tender, more so on some days than on others.

I was supposed to serve in the Corps until I hit the mandatory retirement age, not quit early. I never planned for this civilian life! I don't belong here. Don't even know what I'm doing if I'm no longer a Marine.

That voice rang in his head again. *Once a Marine; always a Marine.*

Simon felt that same old anger rising in his chest. "Even when they treat you like dirt and kick you to the curb?"

Under the increasingly politicized culture of the military and the pressure coming down from on high for the enlisted to conform to that culture, *knowing how to pray* had gone from being an asset to being akin to a bucket of dried cement attached to Simon's career. Ignoring the veiled (and not-so-veiled) threats of his commanding officers by continuing to lead his fellow MPs in prayer and Bible study? He'd effectively painted a bullseye on his back. Simon's last two years in his beloved Corps had been taxing, to say the least.

Annual fitness reports were the primary means of evaluating a Marine's performance. FITREP evaluations determined promotion, career designation, retention, resident school, command, and duty assignments. Basically, those reports influenced every aspect of a Marine's future in the Corps . . . and Simon had received downgraded FITREPs two years running.

After eighteen years of fitness reports where the comparative assessment section read THE EMINENTLY QUALIFIED MARINE, I was downgraded to A QUALIFIED MARINE.

Basically, "barely a Marine."

Only one tier above UNSATISFACTORY.

Why? Because I refused to kowtow to their ungodly agenda.

Simon sighed. *You know I'm no quitter, Lord, but look where serving you got me.*

They forced me out.

CHAPTER 4

SIMON PARKED HIS PICKUP in his usual slot behind Bright Star's office. It was a quarter after four in the afternoon. He was stiff, hungry, and bone tired, even with the power nap he'd grabbed at the Luning rest area. Didn't matter. Before he went home for the day, he needed to see for himself, had to assess whatever damage would be waiting for him to repair the following morning.

I will not call Holly with an update until I have the facts in hand and a plan in place to soothe the residents and save the tattered remnants of Bright Star's reputation.

The office was closed and locked with the "Be Back Soon!" sign on display, right next to the sign with Bright Star's office hours. Simon let himself in and studied the check-in roster.

"Miss Finch must be with the Kinzers, Site 5. Check in at 4:00 p.m. Better get over there quick as I can."

He slid into one of the maintenance trucks, buzzed through the open gates, passed Bright Star's dancing fountains on his left, rounded the first curve, and pulled up sharply before he passed Site 1 on his right.

"What in the world have we here?"

The site was occupied.

Miss Finch's glorified seventeen-foot Casita rested at the rear of the site, radiating every indication of having resided *in situ* for a month or more. Whoever had backed the trailer into the site had used the driveway's double width to pivot the trailer at an oblique angle across the asphalt, slanting the trailer's door toward both the site and the road in a pleasant, open manner.

An awning, printed in the same classy blues, cream, and gray colors as the trailer's paint job, shaded the trailer's length. Beneath the awning, Simon spied a smoky blue patio rug trimmed in gray. Two color-coordinated lawn chairs, one youth-sized, one adult-sized, waited for their occupants just outside the trailer's door, a round side table stationed between the chairs. And a pot holding a trailing geranium hung from the near corner of the awning, spilling soft pink buds and blossoms from its dangling green branches.

The overall effect was sweet.

Homey.

Peaceful.

"Huh. For a sow's ear, that trailer turned out pretty nice. Actually? I kinda like it."

But would Holly appreciate it?

I'm not taking that bet, no matter how enticing the odds. But I do need a closer look.

Simon climbed out of the truck and walked farther into the site.

"She's already got her siding up? And . . . holy cow. What is *that?*"

He studied the contrivance under the far end of the awning. It appeared to be a very narrow screened room that took up about a third of the awning's width. The strange "room" butted up to and attached to the trailer.

Mystified, Simon walked closer, peered into the room, and noted its uncommon furnishings: three carpeted posts of varying heights. The posts each had one or two holes punched straight through them with a series of transparent tubes connecting the posts. A two-foot wide carpet runner attached near the room's ceiling hung down one wall, and a strange roost resembling a miniature hammock cut one of the room's high corners—

A pair of glittering blue eyes stared out of the hammock.

Straight through Simon.

Then a shadow on the floor of the screened room crept toward him and snarled low in its throat.

Simon jumped back. "What in the world?"

The room was not, Simon realized in a rush, intended to protect campers from mosquitos.

He backed away. Retreated to his ride. Cranked the engine and hurried up the road toward Site 5, blitzing by the new residents in Site 2.

Get back to them later, he told himself.

Just before Site 5, Simon's mini maintenance truck came to an abrupt stop, nose to nose with the new residents' gigantic king-cab pickup. The big truck and its towed load blocked the road entirely, which was exactly why resident check-ins were staggered. The truck was in the process of backing a Luxe Elite fifth wheel—all five hundred thousand dollars *plus* of it—down the site's driveway.

Visible to him through the truck's windshield, but focused on her task, sat Miss Finch. Simon couldn't figure out what she was sitting on that lifted her high enough to, barely, peer out the pickup's windshield. And maybe it didn't matter, because regardless of what it was? She still looked every bit the elementary school kiddo pretending to drive her daddy's big rig.

No way could she reach that truck's pedals.

"Oh, no, no, no, no, no," Simon moaned. He scrambled down from the maintenance truck, shouting and waving his hands. Trying his best to get her attention.

A grinning Skipper skidded to a stop next to him. "Hey, Fletch! Glad you're back."

"Don't just stand there! Help me get her attention before she crashes the Kinzers' RV!"

Skipper touched his arm. "Uh, I wouldn't interrupt her if I were you, Fletch. She doesn't like it."

Miss Finch revved the truck's engine, and with sure, measured speed, backed the forty-four-foot fifth wheel down the drive into its slot.

Simon was convinced that the next sound he heard would be the harsh *scree* of half a million dollars plowing into the electrical service box and its post. Instead a cheer rose up from down the driveway.

He ran to the head of the site. Peered down the double driveway. Spied two orange traffic cones, one centered on the far end of the drive, the closer cone halfway up the drive but lined up on the far one. He blinked with astonishment when he realized the passenger-side rear corner of the fifth wheel was now perfectly aligned with the far cone, while the near corner of the rig stood a whisper from the near cone.

A balding gent sporting a loud Hawaiian shirt strode up the drive. He looked Simon up and down. "Hey there. I'm Ray Kinzer. You are?"

"Simon Fletcher, Bright Star Facilities and Security Manager." Simon extended his hand, and they shook.

"Great to meet you." He pointed into his site. "That's my wife Irene. Man, your Miss Finch is a real crackerjack! Backed my rig up in one smooth go. Picture perfect! Couldn't have done it nearly as well myself. Extraordinary. You can bet I'll be telling my friends about her."

"Uh, right. We're . . . lucky to have her."

A Marine never wastes a golden opportunity.

"Have to agree with you. Excuse me, though. I need to help Miss Finch down from my cab, unhook my rig, and get 'er leveled."

Simon moved with Ray around to the driver's side of his truck, curiosity eating him up.

How in the world could she reach the pedals? And what about that orthopedic boot on her left foot?

The truck engine shut off, its cab door flew open, and Miss Finch poked her head out. "Skipper! My tools, if you please."

Skipper ran like one possessed to deliver the asked-for tools. "I can do it for you, Miss Finch. Please let me?"

"Very well. Thank you."

In the meantime, Ray Kinzer had stepped up to his truck. "May I help you down, Miss Finch?"

"Thank you, no, but please take my cushion." She tossed something to him—a firm cushion at least eight inches thick. Then, holding to the truck's grab bar, she swung herself out of the truck cab, hopped on her right foot to the first step, second step, and onto the ground.

The instant she landed, Skipper offered Miss Finch's cane to her. As she steadied herself, he pulled himself onto the first step and, leaning inside the cab, went to work on whatever it was that needed tools.

Miss Finch, intent on what she was saying to Ray, nearly missed Simon as she hobbled by him.

"Oh! Hello, Fletcher. Didn't see you there. Glad you made it back."

"And I'm glad . . . to see things are in good shape. Er, anything to report?"

"Only that the previous four residents checked in when expected. Other than that, no, nothing of note."

"And did you also . . . park the other residents' RVs?"

"Why, yes. We managed to muddle through."

A mischievous spark flared within the chocolate-drops lurking behind half-staff eyelids and was gone just as quickly as it had appeared.

Skipper hustled up to her just then with his hands full. "Disconnected and removed your pedal extenders, Miss Finch. Shall I take them and your tools and cushion back to your site?"

"I would appreciate it, Skipper."

"Consider it done!" He raced off, tossing, "Happy to help!" over his shoulder.

Simon gaped. "Who is that kid and what did you do with the Mitchells' budding delinquent?"

"Oh, him? Yes, I had to yank a knot in his neck two or three times before he straightened up. Perhaps we'll see the spoiled child in him diminish somewhat over the summer, but I predict that the brat inside is not only alive and well, but will likely prove difficult to tame. Takes time and a steady hand, you know."

She side-eyed him. "I did notice that a few hours in *your* company markedly improved what came out of his mouth. If you listened closely just now, you heard him parrot your language."

Consider it done? Happy to help? Simon scratched his chin and scanned overhead. *Nope. No pigs cruising the atmo.*

Miss Finch huffed. "If that is all, Fletcher, I need to remind the Kinzers to have their siding up by this time tomorrow." She began to limp down the driveway toward Ray and Irene.

"Wait. Just a second?"

She turned toward him.

"You've been busy."

"An understatement."

"But you had time to move into Site 1."

"When you left me in charge, did you really expect me to camp behind the office? If you recall, I have a signed lease for Site 1, a binding contract, for which I paid the full price, in advance, as required."

Simon's hands twitched and started to move of their own accord. He sent them to his hips and ordered them to stay there.

I will not rub the back of my neck for this woman to comment upon.

"Fine. Holly will not like it, but since Joe signed off on your exceptions, I'm okay with them. Actually, I like your setup."

Simon tendered a blasé expression that made her brows twitch upward.

Ha! Wasn't the answer you were expecting, was it? Surprise! And as much as I'd like to demand an explanation of whatever exotic creatures you keep in your little pen, that's a can of worms I prefer to open at a later date.

Miss Finch recovered herself quickly. "Thank you, Fletcher. Anything else?"

"Well, I suppose I thought, in my absence, that the residents would be parking their rigs themselves. I'm surprised—amazed, actually—that a, um, what's the correct term? A vertically challenged individual such as yourself could back a large RV so, er, efficiently."

His wording and tone came out mangled.

Awkward and condescending.

Not at all what he'd intended.

Yikes.

What he got in return was a shot of acid rain across the bow.

"Shall we set the record straight, *Mr.* Fletcher? First, I am short, not 'vertically challenged.' Second, height, either the abundance of or the lack thereof, has no impact on intelligence or God-given ability. Third? As far as maneuvering a big rig goes, I became quite adept *when I drove a two-trailer road train cross country for an entire year*, back in the day. And by the by? I never go anywhere without my seat cushion and pedal extenders. I need them to drive my panel wagon and back my own trailer as well as any large RV that might present itself."

She closed her mouth and pivoted on her good foot.

If she hadn't been gimping away from him with help from that cane, she would have been stomping off in high dudgeon—whatever the expression "in high dudgeon" meant.

He hazarded a last look at Miss Finch—just as she teetered and went down.

Simon sprinted to her. "Are you all right?"

"Yes, I'm fine."

"What happened?"

"My ankle has a wicked penchant for duplicity. One moment it supports me; the next it does not. Give me a hand up, if you please."

He got her up and hung on until she was steady on her feet.

"Thank you."

Without another word, she hobbled away.

Simon grimaced. "Way to go, Marine. Think you've done enough damage here?"

Why, yes. Thank you for asking.

"Well, you can shut it."

He got into the maintenance truck and moved down the road, stopping at the occupied sites to introduce himself and visit with the new residents, Holly's cautions ringing in his ears.

Whatever you say, Fletch, do not mention the swimming complex.

He met the Bigalows, Chet and Justine, in Site 10. They were a newly retired couple from Florida who had met one fateful summer long ago in Tahoe City on the west side of the lake. They would spend the summer at Bright Star in their Newmar King Aire and rekindling the romance they'd found while exploring Lake Tahoe forty-five years ago.

In Site 11, just beyond the Bigalows, Simon chatted up the Bhattacharya family. The couple had recently sold their business and home in West Virginia, bought a Coachmen Encore with the optional bunkbeds, and taken their family of four on the road, towing a compact car behind them.

"We homeschool," Mrs. Bhattacharya explained, "so we thought we'd base ourselves at Tahoe for the summer and take several field trips on the side."

"We're going to see the redwoods and sequoias," their eleven-year-old son chipped in.

"And the Pacific Ocean," his nine-year-old sister added.

"I hope you have a blast," Simon said with a smile.

Lastly, Simon met the Gormans in Site 21. The Gormans were the couple who'd leased a site at Bright Star specifically to have a pool available for their granddaughters over Memorial Day weekend.

Simon was anxious to prevent the conversation from veering toward that dry gulch presently billing itself as Bright Star's swimming complex. The Gorman's 40-foot Class C Tiffin Phaeton was parked with the same precision as the Kinzers' fifth wheel, so he ventured to ask how they had liked Miss Finch's services.

"That Miss Finch? What a gal," Mr. Gorman bragged. "Parked our Phaeton on a dime." He looked around. "And this site is great. Roomy and private, like having our own mountain property within spittin' distance of the lake. We'll be here all season, with our grown kids and granddarlings cycling through every couple of weeks."

He grinned. "Two of our granddaughters are with us this weekend, although you'll have to meet them another time. Right now, they're down the road at the pool."

"What?" The word leapt from Simon's mouth before he knew it was lurking there.

"The pool. Swimming complex."

"Right. Good talk. See you later. Bye."

Simon jumped in his ride and, disregarding the park's speed limit, floored it. He pushed the little truck hard around the last curve before the swimming complex. At the same instant a *very* recent memory punched him in the solar plexus, sucking the breath out of his lungs.

Hold up just a blessed moment. That can't be right, can it?. I must be misremembering things. Right. I must. No other explanation possible!

He stomped on the brakes and stopped in the middle of the road, leaving tread marks on the new asphalt. He needed to study the scene stuck in his head.

I'd just returned from Vegas. I got in this truck and drove through the open gate. Passed Bright Star's dancing fountains on my left, drove around the curve, and came upon Site 1 only to discover that Miss Finch had taken over the site. I paused to check out her setup.

Wait. What?

I passed Bright Star's dancing fountains?

Those fountains could *not* dance without a pool pump and its accompanying computer program that synchronized the fountain's jets, music, and light functions.

But I saw the fountains. I know I did—and the jets were on!

Simon again punched the accelerator on the mini truck. When he came abreast of the swimming complex, he slid the truck into one of the complex's parking slots. The moment he got out, the sounds of girlie giggles and splattering water slapped him upside his face. He quick-walked up the steps to the pool enclosure. Stepped through the gate.

Two early teen girls frolicked in the shallow end of the family pool, splashing each other, laughing with glee. While the shallow end was *not* bone dry as it had been before he left for Vegas, it was, unmistakably, a bare foot and a half deep. He studied the depth and decided it *might* be slowly filling, but it was nowhere in the vicinity of three feet deep.

And the water has to be pretty cold.

Sending a matter-of-fact nod to the girls, Simon strode toward the pool's deep end. Its level was past eight of the requisite twelve feet. Unlike the family side of the pool, the deep end was roped off. A sign hung from the diving board declared "Deep End Closed Until Friday."

"The pools are filling . . ." Simon muttered. "But how in the world?"

Pulling his set of facilities keys from his rear pocket, he walked to the entrance of the pump house behind the changing rooms, unlocked the door, and went down a flight of steps to the pump room. The room itself was as far underground as the pool's deep end.

There, in what had been the gaping hole where the pump belonged, was a functioning doppelganger. He stared at it. Listened to the whooshing sounds of pressurized flowing water.

An itch started in the back of his head, made its way down to his shoulders, crawled along his arms, and settled in his fingers. The longer he stared, the more the creeping sensation expanded. Simon shoved his itching hands into his front pockets, pulled them out and rubbed them up and down the denim legs of his jeans.

"Get a grip, Fletcher. Has to be a logical explanation."

Ya think, Fletch?

He checked the pump's model number. *Trident 7000.* As it should be. He tapped one or two gauges. Nothing out of the norm. Went to the pump house's desk and opened the laptop that controlled the pump's many functions. He toggled through the various windows of the software.

It wasn't *only* that a new pump had miraculously appeared.

"Pro job. Whoever installed this pump knew what they were doing. They even set the water features in motion."

But who, other than himself, would have had access to the keys of Bright Star's facilities? Who else could have unlocked the pump house and granted entrance to the mysterious pump installer?

Well, *her*, of course.

Simon squared his shoulders and went in search of Miss Finch.

CHAPTER 5

SIMON DIDN'T HAVE TO look far to find the woman. She was cooking up burgers and corn on the cob on Site 1's grill. No trace of a guilty or conniving conscience touched her countenance.

"Ah, Mr. Fletcher. You're early. Dinner won't be ready for another ten or fifteen minutes."

Simon's stomach wanted to reach out and hug the woman.

The MP side of his brain wanted to slap her.

Hold up there, Marine. Get a grip.

"Uh . . . did you imply that you're fixing dinner for me?"

She shrugged. "For you, for Skipper, for me. Goodness, but we worked hard today. I'm certain we could all use a hot, filling meal—and tomorrow will be even busier than today. I suggest we plan tomorrow's meals tonight."

She'd moved her lawn chairs nearby and pointed her burger flipper at the larger of the two. "Have a seat if you like."

"I sat in my truck for fourteen of the past thirty-six hours, thanks. If you don't mind, I'll keep stretching my legs."

She glanced up. "Well, you won't likely be sitting much tomorrow. According to the schedule, we have eight residents checking in, one every hour on the hour, beginning at 8:00 a.m., with a short reprieve at noon. One of us should staff the office while the other parks the rigs. We can switch off when the other needs a break."

The reason Simon had tracked her down flew out the window.

Wait just a cotton pickin' minute! How did this woman, overnight, go from total stranger to "we" and "one of us"?

Before he could speak, her features fell into thoughtful lines, and she added, "We will be so busy, I figure we should order in for lunch and eat on the fly. By the way, Skipper—that budding delinquent we spoke of earlier—ended the day as a terrific helper. Once I'd taught him how to mount and remove the pedal extenders, he was eager to own the task. I believe the boy has an aptitude for mechanical things, and I would appreciate it if you would loan him to me again tomorrow—unless, that is, you would like to take over parking the rigs?"

"Me, park those wheeled monstrosities? Not on your life. You, on the other hand, seem to have that duty down pat."

He thought he heard her snicker, but she'd turned her head away so he wasn't certain.

He cleared his throat. "Speaking of Skipper, where is the young man?"

"I sent him to the Mitchells' cabin to fetch buns, condiments, and anything else edible he could rustle up. I have not had time to lay in groceries. Been a bit occupied otherwise."

When she looked his way, she was laughing softly to herself. "This was not how I envisioned my first days of retirement, if you must know."

"You're retired?"

"Call it a trial run."

"Guess I didn't think you were old enough to retire."

Another snicker. "Well, I am sixty-two. Right on the cusp, according to some sources."

"You're how old? Sixty-two? No way!"

"I assure you I am. To complicate matters, this *thing*," she pointed the burger flipper at her orthopedic boot, "forced me to take off several weeks last semester. I managed to get my students safely to the end of the term—in spite of the incompetent substitutes the dean brought in, I might say—but since I have a ways to go before my ankle is again fully functioning, I thought I would spend my summer of rehab in a pleasant environment while simultaneously testing the waters of retirement."

"Several weeks last semester? Your students? Substitutes the dean brought in? What kind of work do you do?"

She began to flip the burgers on her grill. "Oh, I consider myself widely diversified, actually. Among other things, I teach a class at UCLA."

Simon's jaw dropped so precipitously he thought it had unhinged itself and was in danger of landing on the paved patio. "You're a professor?"

"Heavens, no. Nothing so exalted as all that." She quirked one eyebrow in his direction. "I authored a little tome, *Forensics of a Traffic Accident*. The book is nothing to shout about, but it somehow caught on in its associated disciplines."

"You wrote a book."

"Ah. Two books to date, actually. The second, *Forensics of a Suicide*, is due to come out in January. Both are, more or less, exhaustive how-to investigative guides, inclusive of a variety of case studies. The first book is married to a little online program I designed."

"You wrote a computer program."

She drives semis. Teaches at a university. Writes books and computer programs. Is there anything this woman can't do?

"Me, a computer programmer? Not on your life. I am nowhere nearly tech savvy enough to undertake such an endeavor."

Simon was unreasonably placated by Miss Finch's confession.

Until she spoke again.

"Of course, I designed the schema for the program and its associated parameters, then worked with a small team of programmers and animators to bring the product to market. Users of the program input scene photographs, measurements, and other data collected during their investigation; the program then employs AI to generate an animated 3D recreation of the event. Students taking my class use the program free of charge during their enrollment period."

She turned to the grill and nudged the steaming foil-wrapped ears of corn. "The program has garnered a respectable following. Of course, medical examiners and law enforcement departments pay a monthly subscription fee to use the program."

"But *of course* they do, while you teach your book's college course at a world-class university."

Rather apologetically, she added, "Mmm. My classes are cross-listed, which generally results in an enrollment mix of criminology, criminal law, and medical students—three disciplines with very different objectives in mind. My, but we do have lively discussions."

The preconceptions Simon had attached to Miss Finch less than twenty-four hours ago were busy crashing to the ground. Through the debris field whipping around in his head, he fumbled to recall why he'd raced over to her site.

Oh, yeah. Right. I need to ask her about the—

His intention flew away when a breathless Skipper arrived hauling two grocery bags.

"Hey, Fletch! Hey, Miss Finch. I've got buns, condominiums, coupla tomatoes, a sweet onion, and a bag of barbecue chips."

"Condominiums?" Simon was baffled.

"He means condiments."

"Yeah. Condiments. Ketchup, mayo, mustard, relish."

"Well done, Skipper, and good timing at that; the food is almost ready. Mr. Fletcher, while Skipper fetches my little folding table and another chair, if you would poke your head into my abode, you'll see the place settings within easy reach."

Actually, Simon was dying to "poke" his head into Miss Finch's little trailer. But, as he approached the door, movement within the screened room startled him. As he tried to locate the movement, it was followed by a hissing growl.

He shivered. *Man, I forgot about her menagerie.*

He stepped through the trailer's narrow door and spied the plates and flatware on the little counter to his left. He grabbed them up, taking the momentary opportunity to look around. He didn't know whether to be impressed or distressed.

"If this is a refurbished Casita, it has to be the most fascinating makeover in the brand's history." At the same time, it was obvious to Simon that the interior was designed to accommodate an individual much smaller than himself.

"Whatever floats your boat," he muttered, "but confined to this rig, I would suffer an attack of claustrophobic panic."

The table was up and waiting when he returned to the firepit, so he set out the place settings. Miss Finch slid the burgers and corn onto a platter, and they sat down—Simon and Skipper scarcely able to get their knees under the shortened table, which, on the other hand, fit Miss Finch to a T.

While Miss Finch sliced onion and tomato, Simon and Skipper prepped their hamburger buns. And Simon, again, recalled his question.

For heaven's sake, ask that woman about the pool pump, Simon Fletcher!

But before he could form the words, Miss Finch asked, "Would you kindly bless the food, Mr. Fletcher?"

"It's just Fletcher," Simon reminded her.

"Or Fletch," Skipper supplied.

"But that was before I insulted you earlier, at the Kinzers' site, Miss Finch," Simon added softly, "for which I apologize."

"Apology accepted . . . Fletcher. Please pray before the food cools."

Sheesh. And don't forget to ask about the pump while you're eating!

Simon grabbed Skipper's hand and reached out his other hand for Miss Finch. The mitt she slipped into his was so much smaller than Skipper's, he was almost convinced that he was holding hands with a kid.

"Lord, we thank you for this food and for this first day of Bright Star's season. Thank you for pulling a success out of the mess of obstacles and problems we faced today. We thank you for your many blessings, Lord. In Jesus' name, amen."

"Amen," Miss Finch echoed him.

Skipper just rolled his eyes. "Now that you're back, Fletch, can I sleep at your place?"

Simon lifted his burger and his stomach lurched. "Sure, kid. Top bunk."

"Cool."

They dug in. Simon downed his ear of corn and two burgers so fast that he couldn't recall pausing to chew. He stared at Miss Finch's plate. She had cut her lone burger in half and was slowly working her way through the first half.

She caught him coveting the contents of her plate. "I never eat more than half a burger or sandwich, Fletcher. If you're still hungry, you may have my other—"

Simon whipped the half burger off her plate and onto his so fast the slipstream almost pulled her across the table. Then he poured half the bag of chips onto his plate. "Guess I'm hungry."

"Do tell," was Miss Finch's dry response.

"Hey! Save some chips for me!" Skipper protested.

"I did."

"Nuh-uh! The bag's almost empty!"

Miss Finch sighed. "Cannot take you children anywhere."

"That's not fair!" Skipper groused.

Simon ignored her dig by changing the subject.

"Say, Miss Finch," he said, "since we're less formal with each other now, are you inclined to tell me what the BD in BD Finch stands for?"

She sighed a well-practiced, longsuffering sigh. "Only since you *insist*. However, it is enough that you know my parents gave my grandfather the honor of naming his only grandchild, me."

"What about your grandmother? Didn't she get a say?"

"I never met her, actually. She and my grandfather married when he was but seventeen and she, fifteen. Young marriages were quite common back then, you know."

Miss Finch sighed. "My grandmother passed away not long after my father's birth, leaving my grandfather to raise him from infancy to adulthood. My grandfather never remarried. He had but one picture of my grandmother, their wedding photograph, which I treasure to this day."

"So your father allowed your grandfather to name you?"

"Yes, and he named me after my grandmother. In Korean, our names have a common but precious meaning. The transliteration in English, on the other hand—due to my beloved grandfather's understanding of English being less than fluent when I was born—is not a suitable name for an adult. Thus, when I grew older, I elected not to use the English transliteration he was determined to bestow upon me."

"Okaaaay . . . Not sure I got all that."

"'All that' as you call it, amounts to either BD Finch or Miss Finch. Period."

"Pronounced BeeDee, you say?"

"Pronounced *Miss Finch*, Mr. Fletcher."

"Er, got it . . . Miss Finch."

His hunger partially satiated, Simon picked up the last chip on his plate and recalled his thrice-derailed question. "Uh, Miss Finch, how is it that the swimming complex has a functioning pool pump?"

She pointed the briefest of glances at him before turning her attention to the last bites of her half burger.

"We have a functioning pool pump? How . . . fortuitous."

"Don't make me laugh. I know it was you."

"Why, what makes you think *I* had anything to do with it?"

"*Pfft!* Who else even knew about it? Besides, I spent twenty years in the military police—and not all of it was breaking up bar brawls. I joined the Criminal Investigation Division and trained in investigative procedures and interrogation techniques. Participated in many criminal investigations. Led a few case investigations myself."

Her chin twitched, and she fixed a curious gaze on him. "Did you now? Tell me more."

"Nah, but nice try. When we spoke on the phone while I was in Vegas, you asked for the pump's model number, and somehow or other you acquired a pump of that model? Do you also pull rabbits out of a top hat? Seeing that you were the only person at Bright Star who had access to the keys that unlock the pump room, answer the question, please."

She did not look up as she popped the last bite of her half burger in her mouth. "Took you long enough to ask that question, Mr. Fletcher."

"Yeah, well, I've been a little on the busy side—*and it's just Fletcher*, Miss Finch. But, since I know that the particular model we needed is back-ordered nationwide and couldn't be had for love nor money, out with it: How'd you do it?"

She lifted one shoulder. "Let us just say I made a few calls and located a Vegas casino's facilities manager who had a spare pump of that model in his inventory."

"A spare? What—are you talking about Blue Lagoon?"

"One and the same."

"But Mobius *swore* he couldn't sell me his spare!"

"Ah, you spoke to him, did you? What a coincidence. I can only surmise that Mobius, having promised the pump to me late last evening—and also perhaps for personal reasons—chose not to confide our business arrangement to you. Either way, his decision was justifiable, I should think. Did he mention that his continued employment at Blue Lagoon is contingent upon the uninterrupted function of that casino's water features? Mobius would be foolish not to keep our transaction under wraps so that, as far as his boss is aware, the spare hasn't budged from Blue Lagoon's inventory."

"But how do you even know this Mobius dude? How did you convince him to sell the pump to you?"

And did that woman just waggle her eyebrows at me?

"Oh, once upon a time, in a land far, far away, during my rebellious years, I might add, I dealt Black Jack at the Nugget."

"The Nugget?"

"The Golden Nugget."

"Don't know that casino—not," he temporized, "that I'm familiar with any of the Vegas casinos. I don't gamble, and I only moved to Tahoe a little more than a year ago."

"After you separated from the Marines?"

"Changing the subject will get you nowhere."

She uttered a little *heh-heh* under her breath. "Had to try. Let's see, where was I? Oh, yes. The Golden Nugget is no more. It was sold to MGM Grand in 2000 and renamed the MGM Mirage. In any event, during my time at the Nugget, Mobius was the casino's pit boss." She shrugged her shoulders. "My stint at the Nugget lasted a scant six months, but during that time I did Mobius a favor."

"Had to have been a mighty big favor, and . . ." He broke off, frowning.

Didn't you say Joe owed you a favor too?

Yes, she did!

Wasn't asking you.

"And?"

"And that doesn't explain how you got the pump delivered and installed before I returned from Vegas."

She continued to study him, her hooded eyes probing, prying . . .

Probing and prying for what?

She tilted her head a little to one side. "Very well. As it happens, I asked Mobius to arrange air transport to the landing strip nearest us and to send along two suitable members of his crew to drive the pump from the airport to Bright Star and install it for us. They arrived quite early this morning. Finished and left just after ten o'clock."

Incredulous and shaking his head, Simon muttered, "I saw that the pools are still filling up but that the Gorman's granddaughters were using the family side of the pool. Happily, I might add."

She shrugged. "I overheard Mrs. Mitchell's concerns regarding the Gormans and their grandchildren. I reasoned that the Gormans might not mind if the pool was only half full as long as the girls weren't disappointed. I did, of course, personally inform them that the pool was in the process of filling. I also had Skipper post signage warning all comers that the deep end was closed until tomorrow when the pools would be full and several degrees warmer. Takes time to heat that much pool water."

Simon was still struggling to digest her revelations. "You took liberties while we left you in charge. Expensive liberties, I might add, like giving Skipper a phone."

"No expense involved there. I had a spare phone hanging around. Just a basic, prepaid model. I did not relish chasing the boy around the park to keep tabs on him, you see."

"Huh. Just happened to have a spare handy?"

"Yes. I picked it up at a convenience store in Sacramento . . . after I mislaid my own cellphone. Since then, I've acquired my usual model phone."

Simon felt the small twinge of a doubt. *Bought a disposable phone after you mislaid your cell? I don't think it's your style to ever 'mislay' anything, lady.*

"Consider it a loan to the boy," she added.

"I guess you lending him the phone is acceptable—and yes, it will help me keep him corralled—but the other stuff? The really expensive stuff?"

"I admit that my actions were not entirely by the book and will cost Bright Star a pretty penny. On the other hand, bad press is the costliest of all business expenses. It is the gift that keeps on giving—on and on and on, *ad nauseam*. Mobius will send the Mitchells a bill for those expenses."

"Holly will be thrilled. Overcome, I might add."

Note to self: Be far away when the bill arrives.

"And what about the pool chemicals and required testing?"

"I left those tasks for you. If you add the chemicals after the pool closes this evening, they will cycle through overnight. You should be able to test the water first thing in the morning. If the test results are within acceptable limits, will that permit you to open the entirety of the swimming complex at its regular posted time?"

Simon was trying his best to poke holes in her reasoning. "Yeah, well—"

"Well then, you do see that I engaged in what amounts to a small calculated risk? My intention was to avoid the two occurrences Mrs. Mitchell fears most, one, the Gormans and others demanding a refund, and two, those irate former Bright Star residents posting negative reviews on Yelp and elsewhere on their way out. As I said before, bad online reviews are eternal."

"Uh . . . okay. I get it."

"Of course, if Joe is unwilling to pay the cost of flying the pump and two of Mobius's men to Tahoe and back, I suppose I must admit to overreach and spring for the expense myself."

Simon scrubbed his tired face. "Maybe. And maybe, once he's thought through the alternatives you've outlined, he'll come to the right conclusion, and yet—"

"*And yet*," Miss Finch filled in, "I heartily recommend, in the strongest possible terms, that we refrain from informing Mrs. Mitchell of my rather inventive liberties and allow Joe that privilege."

Simon had no issue admitting to the wisdom of her suggestion. "You bet your ever-lovin' life we 'refrain' from telling her!"

Even Skipper yukked it up. "Yeah, man! Pick another day to die!"

Miss Finch smiled, her hooded eyes dropping to slits, their corners crinkling in a pleasant manner. "Then we are agreed. Still, do not forget, Fletcher, that you owe Mobius a pump, along with your profuse thanks. When the pump you ordered from the supplier finally comes in, please have it delivered to Blue Lagoon posthaste."

He grinned back, the load of stress under which he'd been toiling easing up. "Roger that, Miss Finch. Now I have just one more question."

"Really? I find that I have exhausted my supply of answers, Fletcher."

Simon snorted. "I doubt that's even a remote possibility. What I want to know is, what in the world are you keeping in that-that-that cage thing attached to your trailer?"

"Do you refer to my 'catio'?"

"Catio? As in rhymes with patio?"

"The same."

"Sooo, you keep a cat in the catio?"

"One generally does. My precious kitty loves the great outdoors, but her favorite thing is schmoozing it up with new people. Sadly, she cannot be trusted not to live up to her name."

"Which is . . ."

Skipper opened his mouth to interject the answer, when Miss Finch's raised index finger subdued him.

Hey . . . how'd she do that?

"We shall get to your question in due time, Fletcher. In any event, except when we are taking a walk or sitting out of doors together, I prefer to confine my feline darling to the catio and, by doing so, keep peace with my neighbors —or, for that matter, any hapless stranger passing by. I don't leave her in the catio alone, of course. Hugo spends most of his time with her. Hugo and my cat are quite attached to each other, you see."

"Not yet, I don't. What's a Hugo?"

"Ah. I suppose introductions are now in order."

Miss Finch got up, went to the catio, and opened the door to the screened room. "Hello, my darlings. Come out and meet our visitors."

Simon watched a small Airedale exit first.

No. Cute, but too small for an Airedale. Could pass for a stuffed animal. Similar to an Airedale in conformation and markings, though. Welsh terrier?

The dog, his tan "whiskery" muzzle barely reaching Miss Finch's knees, circled her three times before he sat and leaned in to be petted. She patted and scratched and whispered to him. As she walked over to the table, the dog walked to heel on her right.

"Fletcher, this is Hugo; Hugo, this is Fletcher. Fletcher? Hugo is a well-behaved gentleman. And Hugo? I believe Fletcher is a good man."

She said aside to Simon, "I have already introduced Skipper to Hugo."

"Hugo and I are buds," Skipper declared. "He slept on the floor next to my bed in Miss Finch's trailer last night."

Hugo looked to Miss Finch. She nodded. He trotted over to Simon, sniffed his hand and the legs of his worn jeans, then sat. Waiting.

Simon knew when to and when not to touch a strange dog. Since Hugo had approached him and sat, Simon took it for permission to pet him. He rested his hand lightly on Hugo's head, then he gently massaged Hugo between his ears, working up to a light scratch.

Hugo's eyes closed in bliss.

When he'd milked Simon for several minute's worth of affection, Hugo trotted to the catio door, barked once, then turned his tail to the door.

A blur of flying fury landed, crouching, atop Hugo's back.

It hissed. Hugo moved forward.

"And the other penny drops," Miss Finch whispered.

"*That* is your cat?"

Simon noticed Skipper had backed away, so he stood, wary.

"Careful, man. I mean it!" Skipper warned. "Don't let Hugo near you if Pouncer is driving."

"If Pouncer is *driving?* And that's your cat's name? Pouncer?"

"One of several monikers I attempted to assign her when I found her as a kitten. As time progressed, however, Pouncer seemed most apropos . . . *quite* apropos, I should say."

"Look out!" Skipper shouted.

About then, Hugo trotted up to Simon and fired a fusillade of ferocious fur from his back.

Simon instinctively threw up his hands to repel boarders.

The attempt did not save him.

The cat slipped through Simon's defenses and landed on his chest, claws extended like grappling hooks, said hooks finding purchase in Simon's work shirt and skin.

"*Ow!* Get it off me!"

Skipper hollered, "Hold still! Don't fight it, Fletch!"

But Simon was desperate. He grabbed at the cat, only to have his hands scored and bloodied six ways from Sunday while the cat made her way up to his left shoulder and around the back of his neck.

Miss Finch reached for Simon's hands and pulled them down. "Stand still, Fletcher! Do stop struggling!"

"Yeah, man!" Skipper shouted. "Resistance is futile—you've been Borged by the Borg Queen, so stop jumpin' around!"

Simon froze in place, convinced that Miss Finch's cat was about to sink her fangs into his jugular. Instead, she draped herself across the back of his neck, attaching her front claws to the shirt over his right shoulder, her rear claws digging in on his left shoulder.

"There. Now just be still," Miss Finch whispered.

Simon opened his mouth; she flattened her hand over it.

"Not. A. Peep."

Still as stone, Simon waited. A low rumble, similar to the ignition of a muscle car's engine, ignited behind his right ear. The rumble leveled out and resolved into a deep, satisfied purr.

Simon's gaze sought out Miss Finch. She was again smiling, her eyes nearly closed, those pleasant crinkles showing themselves.

"You could have warned me."

"Yes, I could have. But when I said her favorite thing is schmoozing it up with new people, I wasn't exaggerating. Pouncer loves new people, and 'pouncing' is her preferred method of introduction."

She shook her head. "Sadly, her advances are often misinterpreted. When she was a kitten, I called her Percher because, as you have witnessed, she gravitates to the tallest human around her that she might perch, quite happily, across their shoulders. You do note that she is purring, yes?"

"I can't hear you," Simon half-shouted. "Someone's running a chainsaw next to my head."

"Very funny." Miss Finch patted her chest. "Come here, my darling. This man doesn't appreciate your finer qualities."

Pouncer scrabbled her back legs from Simon's left shoulder to his right and leapt into Miss Finch's arms. When she turned toward him, Simon was at last able to take stock of her.

Pouncer was a small Siamese, lean and most definitely lithe, with a gorgeous contrasting coat. Her brilliant blue eyes stared with arch disdain into his hazel ones. She flicked one dark-tipped ear, then hopped from Miss Finch's arms onto Hugo's back. Hugo immediately trotted back to the catio where Pouncer dethroned herself and walked, tail in the air, through the open door.

And that wasn't all. As soon as Pouncer entered the catio, Hugo nosed the door shut, and Simon heard the latch click.

"Well, I'll be a monkey's uncle."

"Hugo and Pouncer have a lovely symbiotic relationship."

"You don't say."

He rubbed one perforated shoulder. "Guess I'll be going now. Need to stanch the bleeding and disinfect my wounds. Thanks again for dinner."

He turned toward Skipper. "Grab your stuff and put it in my truck. You can hang out in the rec hall until I'm ready to go home. I . . . I suppose I'll call you when it's time."

Simon kept himself busy that evening until the pool officially closed. He then added the required chemicals, set the pump to recirculate them, and locked up for the evening. As he drove Skipper to his cabin, he revisited the events of the last thirty-six hours, beginning with the arrival of Bright Star's first and, without question, most unusual summer resident to date.

In Simon's estimation, one thing was certain: This Miss Finch was a great deal more interesting than he'd initially reckoned.

CHAPTER 6

SIMON GOT AN EARLY start to his workday the next morning. Skipping his usual morning run, he checked first on the swimming complex, found the various water levels as they should be, drew samples from the pools, tested the samples, and recorded the results in his log book.

Satisfied that the complex could open in full, he removed the tape and signage from the deep end, then returned to the office and closed himself into Holly's private office.

He called Holly with the update he'd promised her and caught her as she was leaving her hotel.

"Simon! I'm glad to hear from you, but Joe's doctor is meeting with us in forty minutes to discuss Joe's treatment plan going forward. The doctor mentioned yesterday that Joe would need to stay in the hospital several more days and in Vegas a bit after that, so just give me the bottom line: Did everyone scheduled to check in arrive? Were there any mishaps parking their rigs? What have you been telling them about the swimming complex? Did the Gormans demand a refund? And did you get rid of that Miss Finch and her awful little travel trailer?"

Simon hissed under his breath. *Did I get rid of Miss Finch and her awful little travel trailer? Lady, I do* not *know how to break the news to you.*

But maybe he could gloss over the details? Slough off her questions for a few days? Set the "Miss Finch Problem" on the back burner?

"Actually, things at Bright Star are great, Holly."

"What? They are?"

"Yup. All scheduled residents are settling in. No mishaps, the Gormans are fine, and Miss Finch hasn't been a problem. Listen, we've got a full day ahead of us with eight more residents checking in, starting in half an hour, so I don't have time to tell you more. Give Joe my best, mkay? Yup. Talk later."

Simon slammed the phone onto its cradle and exhaled.

"What Holly doesn't know won't hurt me."

Miss Finch stood on the other side of the screen door leaning on her cane. "Did you mean 'what Holly doesn't know won't hurt her'?"

"That's a big nope."

She laughed under her breath. "You did not tell her I occupied my site, did you?"

"Noper than nope."

"Coward."

"Oorah."

"Fine. What Holly does not know and all that. However, our first residents of the day just pulled up. They are twenty minutes ahead of schedule, but I don't mind getting them settled, if you don't mind checking them in early."

"Not a problem. I'll give Skipper a call to come help you."

"Yes, thank you. I could use him."

"And I'm glad he's actually helping. I'll order lunch around 11:30 and holler at you when it arrives."

———●———

THE THREE OF THEM shared a large pizza and a side salad at noon. Simon had posted a conspicuous sign on the office's front door saying they were closed from noon to 12:45, which should have granted them a breather before their 1:00 p.m. resident arrived.

Should have granted them a breather, but service industries are rife with the notorious "those people."

"I feel I ought to give you a heads up regarding my near neighbor in Site 2," Miss Finch said picking her way through a slice of supreme—one olive, pineapple tidbit, and sliver of pepperoni at a time.

Simon was too busy chowing down to care. "Oh?"

"A Mrs. Rickert, checked in yesterday? Recently widowed. Persistently critical. Remarked concerning my rig, 'Blatant disregard for the rules. Blot on Bright Star's reputation.' Those and a number of other equally disparaging remarks."

"Got distracted and forgot to introduce myself to her. I'll pay her a visit after lunch."

"I doubt you will need to."

"Yeah, bet she comes lookin' for ya, Fletch," Skipper offered. "She isn't a very nice lady."

"Or a patient one," Miss Finch added.

Someone pounded on the office door.

"Daresay, that would be her," Miss Finch said quietly.

Disgusted, Simon dropped his half-eaten slice on his plate. When he opened the office door, the woman facing him was nothing like he'd envisioned. Mrs. Rickert, widowed and persistently critical, was not a stout matron of fifty or sixty years, helmet hair permanently shellacked into place with spray-on lacquer as thick as decoupage.

No, the new resident was perhaps thirty-five, a striking blue-eyed blond with an even more striking figure. It was all Simon could do not to gape. As it was, he had to retract his eyeballs, both of which had popped out of his head on springs that bounced up one side of Mrs. Rickert's striking figure and down the other.

Every bit of Mrs. Rickert was "easy" on Simon's eyes . . . until his perusal reached the woman's face. Obviously aware of with how her figure affected men, her thin mouth was twisted up in a smirk while her jaws slowly worked a piece of gum.

"Are you the manager?"

"I'm filling in for the manager, yes. You are?"

"Mrs. Terri Rickert, Site 2. I have a complaint regarding the resident in Site 1. Two complaints, in fact."

"Mrs. Rickert, did you by chance read the sign on the door before you knocked?"

"Of course, but I could hear that you were inside."

"Yes, ma'am. Our staff members are inside . . . eating their lunch." Simon opened the door wider and gestured toward Skipper and Miss Finch.

When Mrs. Rickert spied Miss Finch, she frowned. "That woman's trailer falls far below the standards of this summer residence—and her cat is a menace!"

"Mrs. Rickert, we have five more residents arriving this afternoon. When I have time, I will come by and take note of your complaints."

"I'm already here. Please take note of them now."

Simon felt his temper rising. "Nope. We're on our lunch break. I'll drop by your site shortly after one o'clock." He shut the door in her face with a little more emphasis than necessary and returned to his lunch.

"Boy, if Aunt Holly saw you slam the door on a resident, she'd have a cow."

Simon could see the whites of Skipper's eyes. All the way around. He picked up his half-eaten slice of pizza.

"No one asked you, Skipper, but if you're that concerned, I could have you take a notebook to Mrs. Rickert's site and have you register her complaints. Like right now."

"Hey! I'm still eating!"

"My point exactly."

BY THE END OF THAT very long day, Simon had met and checked in eight registered residents, Miss Finch had parked their rigs, and Simon had found fifteen minutes to deal with Terri Rickert. He drove a maintenance truck to Site 2 and knocked on her door. She was gratified to see him, but after she'd rehearsed both of her complaints three times in full detail, he called a halt to the woman's umbrage.

"Mrs. Rickert, the owner of Bright Star, Joe Mitchell, was in a serious vehicle accident three days ago or he would be responding to your complaints himself. I can, however, tell you that Miss Finch is an old and valued friend of Mr. Mitchell's and that he personally approved the exceptions to Miss Finch's RV. I would add that, Miss Finch's rig, although deviating from Bright Star's required norms, has not nor will it in any manner negatively impact Bright Star's ambiance or reputation. Its exterior is quite tasteful, in point of fact."

She opened her mouth, but Simon held up his hand. "I haven't finished, ma'am. Furthermore, because Joe was taken to the ER in Vegas yesterday, I had to drive Mrs. Mitchell down to be with him. If Miss Finch hadn't been available and disposed to manage your check-in, you would have had to wait until I returned from Vegas to back it in for you—and trust me, you want Miss Finch handling your rig, not me."

"Well, what about—"

"Her cat? Yes, let's talk about Miss Finch's cat. If I understand correctly, you went into Miss Finch's site, without invitation, to complain about the length of her trailer. Do I have that part right?"

Mrs. Rickert, sensing the tide pulling against her, hesitated. "Yes, I did approach Miss Finch . . . in her site, but I did not venture off the driveway before that menace *jumped on me!*"

"I understand. However, I hardly see how your keeping to her driveway, and I emphasize that it is *her* driveway, changes the facts of the matter. In essence, you trespassed on Miss Finch's site. I believe that when you approached her, she was holding her cat, was she not?"

"Y-yes, she was holding it—but then it jumped on me!"

"Mrs. Rickert, did Miss Finch, in any way, warn you to keep back?"

"Um . . . she may have said something to that effect, but that does not alter the point that her *trailer* is in gross violation of the residency requirements!"

"I find her trailer to have the finest exterior paint job in the park."

"But her trailer is not seven years old or newer!"

"Actually, its total refurbishment, from stem to stern, is less than a year old—besides which, as I said earlier, the owner, Mr. Mitchell, approved the exceptions himself."

Mrs. Rickert's mouth hardened, but Simon's stint as a Marine MP had made him a master at dealing with difficult people and challenging situations.

"Taking all circumstances into consideration, your lease with Bright Star grants you recourse, Mrs. Rickert. You have five days from check-in to withdraw from your lease and receive a full refund."

"Withdraw from my . . . you mean leave after I've just arrived?"

"Yes, ma'am."

"Well, I never! You're kicking *me* out instead of her?"

"No, ma'am, we are not kicking you out nor do we wish you to leave. I'm saying your lease gives you the option to withdraw if you so choose. Should you choose to withdraw within five days of yesterday's date, you will receive a full refund."

But Holly will have my head on a pike if she has to reimburse your fee.

Mrs. Rickert took a step back. "I see." Those two words were as icy as a Russian gulag in February.

"Additionally, I would be remiss if I did not add that one of Bright Star's unique attributes is the quality of our residents' sites—how large the sites are, how far back from the road they sit, not to mention the distance between sites, all to ensure our residents' sense of privacy.

"To speak plainly, Mrs. Rickert, every resident has an expectation of that privacy within their site as well as mutual civility from and among the other Bright Star residents elsewhere on Bright Star's grounds. Should you choose to trespass on Miss Finch's site a second time or should you accost her on our grounds to berate her for the exceptions the owner has granted her, we may be obliged to take strong measures."

Mrs. Rickert frowned. "What do you mean? What strong measures?"

"I really see only one resolution should the problem continue. At that point, yes, we would be forced to evict you."

Simon was operating *way* beyond his authority, but he was experienced with bullies, their sense of entitlement, and their tactics. And most bullies, faced with public censure or expulsion, would back down.

Mrs. Rickert did not disappoint.

"No, er, I'm sure—that is, I would not want to, er, leave Bright Star after just settling in."

"Nor would we wish to lose you, ma'am. If you can commit to me that you will stay out of Miss Finch's site and if you can keep your comments concerning Miss Finch's rig to yourself, we can call this issue closed. As for her cat? Rule of thumb: If you don't approach Pouncer, she won't bother you."

"Pouncer? That cat's name is *Pouncer?*"

"Yes. And I can say from personal experience that Pouncer is a lover, not a fighter. When she pounces, it is only to make your acquaintance and to, er, snuggle up to you while lying across your shoulders."

"Well, I never!"

"Again, if you do not trespass on Miss Finch's site, that situation will not recur." Simon had a thought. "Oh. And when I said, 'If you can keep your comments concerning Miss Finch's rig to yourself,' I did mean *to yourself.*"

He leaned in a little. "I had better not hear gossip or complaints about Miss Finch traveling through the park via our other residents."

Mrs. Rickert spun on her heel, marched to the front door of the Class A motor home that was easily worth three-quarters of a million dollars, and slammed the door behind her.

As Simon climbed into the maintenance truck, he muttered, "Sheesh. If I'd been married to you, lady, I think I would have jumped out the nearest window."

CHAPTER 7

SATURDAY PASSED FOR SIMON, Skipper, and Miss Finch in much the same vein as Friday had until, by that evening, a total of nineteen of Bright Star's twenty-four summer residents were settled in their sites.

In Site 13, Simon met three sisters, Dina, Gracia, and Margola Benowitz, who looked remarkably alike and close in age.

"We have all retired in the past three years," Dina Benowitz told him, with pride shining from her eyes. "Margola, being youngest, is the most recent to retire, so now the three of us—we're best friends, you know—are available to vacation any time we choose. We pooled our money to buy this RV so we might travel around and see the US together."

"I hope you enjoy your summer at Bright Star," Simon replied.

The three smiled and nodded in exactly the same manner, and Simon grinned at their mutual delight.

After leaving the sisters, Simon introduced himself to soft-spoken Marie Santini, a mousy, middle-aged single with stringy hair and an elderly boxer named Napoleon. Her spanking new thirty-two-foot Class A Forest River, parked in Site 19, was the smallest RV residing at Bright Star, barring Miss Finch's trailer. Still, Simon knew Santini's Forest River was no slouch in the luxury department.

When she caught him studying her rig, she offered softly, "My dad bought this RV for me when I told him I wanted to get away, perhaps spend the summer here."

Simon whistled. "Must be nice."

The woman was shy, but she smiled a little while she unwrapped a stick of gum. "You know how dads are. My dad would do anything for me . . . well, almost anything."

By the time the workday ended, Simon, Skipper, and Miss Finch were exhausted . . . with Miss Finch demonstrating a new hitch in her giddy up.

A markedly more pronounced limp.

"What happened?" Simon demanded, hands on his hips.

Miss Finch scowled at him.

Skipper's eyes jinked from Simon to Miss Finch and back. He slowly eased himself out from between Simon and Miss Finch.

Simon sniggered to himself, *Kid doesn't know which of us to be more afraid of.*

He added, aloud, "Look, Miss Finch, if you hurt yourself while on the job, I have to log the incident and take you to get checked out. Workers' Comp and all that."

"Unnecessary."

"I'll decide what's necessary. What happened?"

Through clenched teeth she muttered, "You have seen me hop down from one of those big rigs. Not an issue. And nothing more happened today than I landed a mite too hard on my left foot. All I need do is elevate my foot and ice the ankle."

"That's it? Still seems like I should get you checked out—just to be on the safe side."

"I have already spoken to my physical therapist. As he's told me a hundred times, the pain in my ankle is residual soft tissue damage with little to be done for it other than easy walking, the passage of time, and avoiding precipitous impact. If the pain continues or worsens, he'll ask my surgeon to call a nearby Tahoe clinic and request that they give me an injection."

Simon studied the set of Miss Finch's mouth. "I've made an executive decision. Rather than go to the bother of cooking a meal, I've decided to order pizza for us."

Miss Finch sighed. "Pizza again?"

"You have my vote," Skipper declared. "Pepperoni with pineapple!"

"You don't have a vote, Skip.

Simon ordered two large pizzas, after which they gathered around Miss Finch's firepit. The woman's foot was packed in ice and resting on a cushion atop a short stool.

Simon and Skipper feasted on the pizza while Miss Finch worked on her one and only slice.

"Before we retire for the night, let's talk about tomorrow," Simon said. "Since the next two residents won't be checking in until the afternoon, two and three o'clock respectively, and since our final three residents have elected to check in Tuesday, after the madness of the holiday weekend is over and done, and seeing as how the office is usually closed until one o'clock on Sundays, that leaves tomorrow morning wide open for some personal time."

He looked at Miss Finch. "If your foot cannot bear weight by tomorrow afternoon, I'll park the guests' rigs. Somehow or other."

"Yay personal time!" Skipper enthused. "Man, I am gonna sleep in till noon! You guys have about wore me out."

"I would not mind a bit of a breather myself tomorrow, Fletcher," Miss Finch said. "What are your plans for the morning?"

"Church. I'm planning to attend Sunday worship service." It was a recent plan. The idea had just now popped into his head.

I know, Lord. It's been too long.

"Ha! You can count me out for that," Skipper declared around a mouthful of pizza.

"I suppose that depends, Skippy."

"Yeah? Depends on what?" he sneered, "'Cuz, I ain't going and you can't make me."

Simon laid his hands on the table and concentrated on keeping his splayed fingers there instead of wrapping themselves around Skipper's throat of their own will. He waited until Skipper, sensing the tension radiating from Simon, noticed.

He looked from Simon to Miss Finch and back. His mouth still stuffed with food, he muttered, "What? Did I miss something?"

"Only the obvious, kid: According to the judge, *you*, Skipperoni—with pineapple—are not to go anywhere or be *left* anywhere without adult supervision. Thus, unless Miss Finch were to agree to babysit you while I go to church, you *will* be accompanying me."

With a derisive sniff, Skipper shifted his attention to Miss Finch. She was making the usual inroads through her single slice of pizza, examining each small bite before she put it into her mouth as though she'd never before in her life encountered hand-tossed pan crust and a combination of cheese, sausage, olives, and mushrooms.

Skipper swallowed his current mouthful. "Is that okay with you, Miss Finch?"

"Hmm?"

"Is it okay if I stay with you while Fletch goes to church tomorrow?"

"It's perfectly fine by me," she replied.

Skipper beamed. "Cool. Thanks!"

She lifted one shoulder. "Of course, I'll be going to church, too, so you are welcome to ride along with me. Or ride with Fletcher. I believe either way will satisfy the judge's supervision requirement."

Skipper's lips flattened. "That's just great. You guys are forcing me to go to your dumb old church."

Miss Finch tipped her head to the side. "Have you ever been to church, Skipper?"

"Huh? Well . . . not 'zactly."

"It's a yes or no question, young man."

He flushed red. "I been to a funeral once. At a church."

"Not at all the same as participating in a worship service—although I've attended a few memorial gatherings that were more uplifting than many a Sunday morning in my experience. Nothing quite like an avid believer's homegoing to set God's people to worshipping!"

"I've seen the same," Simon affirmed. "Which church do you plan to attend tomorrow?"

"As I'm unacquainted with the Bible-teaching churches in and around South Lake Tahoe, I thought I would tag along with you. Is that all right?"

"Want to ride with us?"

"Why, yes, thank you."

Skipper slouched down in his chair. "Super. Get half a day off and where do I have to go? Church! Good thing Monday is a holiday, 'cuz I'm sick to death of work, work, and more work."

"Uh, hate to break the news to you, Skippy, but what is a holiday to most people will actually be one of our busiest work days. The office needs to be open all of Memorial Day while you and I take care of our guests' needs."

Skipper swore under his breath.

Simon leaned toward him. "What did you say?"

Skipper's head jerked up. "Uh, nothing much. Nothing at all. Just, um, God bless America."

"Outstanding."

———— ● ————

MISS FINCH LEANED HEAVILY on her cane as they left church the following morning, and Skipper was uncharacteristically subdued. Simon glanced over his head at Miss Finch and winked. She winked in return.

"Say," she said. "Since it's coming up on noon, shall we stop at a restaurant for brunch? My treat."

Skipper brightened. "Cool! And can we have pancakes?"

"I know a waffle place right off Lake Tahoe Boulevard," Simon replied. "They have pancakes too, but I'll be paying. No, don't argue with me, lady. Consider it a well-deserved bonus."

Apparently the waffle house was popular because the three of them had to wait half an hour for a table. The service, on the other hand, once they'd been seated, was lightning quick.

As Skipper tucked into a tall stack of pancakes, Simon asked, "Say, Miss Finch. When you texted me in Vegas, before I had your contact info, you signed your text BD Finch. What does BD stand for?"

"Why?"

"Why what?"

"Why do you wish to know?"

Simon shrugged. "Just curious."

"Very well. Tell your curiosity that BD is Latin for two words loosely translated to English as my-ob."

Skipper snarked, "My-ob? What kinda word is that?"

"Yeah, what Skipper asked," Simon muttered.

"Ah! My-ob is a word closely related to Nunya."

Skipper screwed up his face. "What's nunya?"

Simon sighed. "It's nunya business, Skip."

The boy reddened. "You wanted to know what that dumb word, my-ob, means. If it's none of my business, it's none of yours either!"

"Yup, and that's her answer to my question. Apparently BD stands for none of my business, just as my-ob, or MYOB, happens to be the abbreviation for 'mind your own business.'"

"You guys are nuts." Thoroughly disgusted, Skipper returned his attention to his plate.

"Suppose we choose another topic of conversation?" Simon asked.

"Lovely idea. How about the pastor's sermon?"

The morning's lesson had been on Romans 5, verses 3 and 4, beginning partway through the verse.

> *. . . We also celebrate in our tribulations,*
> *knowing that tribulation*
> *brings about perseverance;*
> *and perseverance, proven character;*
> *and proven character, hope . . .*

With his head tipped to one side thoughtfully, Simon said, "I really appreciated Pastor Neilson bringing out the meaning of the Greek word *hypomone*, translated as perseverance or patience in that passage. I especially liked the part where, according to Vine's Expository Dictionary, one aspect of perseverance is 'to remain under' difficult circumstances or commitments. That definition resonated with me. I mean, today most of us refuse to endure even simple discomfort; we immediately run away from hard situations, declaring how unfair our lot is. As a result, we don't grow.

"But during New Testament times? The majority of people had few choices open to them. They couldn't just shuck off a job they didn't like. It wasn't that easy to change jobs or find another one. They couldn't declare bankruptcy in order to escape the pressure of debt; they couldn't opt out of servitude or slavery. Today, though, we enjoy many freedoms. We can move anywhere we like. We can change jobs with a fair amount of ease. We can divorce our spouse to leave a difficult marriage. Fact is? Most of us can—and do—bail at the first hint of anything uncomfortable, painful, or difficult to see to completion."

Miss Finch nodded. "I agree. As the pastor said, it's easy for us Americans to er, *squirt out from under* distasteful, challenging, arduous, or onerous responsibilities—except when running away is impossible, like with this blasted ankle of mine. I cannot leave it behind, yet living with it is hard and often painful."

Simon felt for her. "I'm sorry you're in pain, Miss Finch."

"Thank you. At least those same verses also tell us that remaining and working through hard times is what produces 'proven character,' something sadly missing in today's culture. I wish more people understood that the sum of their regular and habitual actions determines their personal character, that if you always run away from your responsibilities, you will never grow, never mature."

Skipper stared at Miss Finch, for a change, his heart an open book. "Is that . . . do you think . . . I mean, my dad leaving and all?"

She gently laid one of her small hands on Skipper's. "Divorce is certainly a common example of choosing to flee a lifetime commitment. However, I hope that you, rather than dwelling on your father's character flaws, will choose instead to work on your own character by completing the tasks you've committed yourself to and by remaining under the pressure of a situation you cannot change, such as the judge's conditions for your probation."

Simon saw that Skipper was thinking hard on Miss Finch's words, so he said nothing, leaving the boy to process her advice.

Ten minutes later, after devouring a second plate of pancakes, Skipper sat back, burped, and sighed. "That was epic."

"You're welcome," Simon said.

"Yeah."

"Is that how your mother taught you to show appreciation?"

"Uh, right. Thanks . . . for the pancakes. I liked them a lot."

"Better. Say, did I see you talking with a couple of other teens after church?"

Skipper lifted his shoulders. "Yeah, I met a couple of guys. I guess the church has what they called 'youth group' meetings on Thursday evenings. The guys I talked to told me that they do some cool stuff, like archery, games, and movies. They invited me to come . . . but I told them I couldn't."

Miss Finch cleared her throat. "What if . . . what if Simon or if I were to take you to youth group and wait in the church lobby or parking lot until the meeting was over? Technically, someone would still be watching over you."

Skipper blinked. "You'd do that?"

"I would . . . if Fletcher thinks the arrangement will satisfy the court's requirements."

Simon nodded. "We could make it work. That is, if you want to go."

Skipper looked down at his plate. "Yeah. I think I'd like to go. It's . . . it's kinda lonely at Bright Star without other kids around."

Simon smiled. "I'll call the church office and tell the youth pastor to expect you Thursday evening."

———◆———

AFTER LUNCH, SIMON MANNED the office, while Skipper assisted Miss Finch as she situated the two RVs checking into Bright Star that day. Following those check-ins, Simon had Miss Finch staff the office, where she answered an endless flow of questions and requests.

As for Simon and Skipper, they roamed the park through the remainder of the day. If the two of them weren't delivering firewood, they were policing the grounds, cleaning and restocking bathrooms, and tidying the game room.

Preparing for the onslaught at dawn tomorrow.

Memorial Day.

CHAPTER 8

MEMORIAL DAY

THE PARK WAS ALIVE with the shouts, shrieks, and laughter of families at play. All elements of the swimming complex were utilized to capacity. Barbecue grills operated nonstop, filling the park with the tantalizing scents of sizzling burgers, steaks, and ribs. The volleyball and pickleball courts and the rec hall were in ongoing demand.

But Simon, Skipper, and Miss Finch? They labored on without a smidgen of holiday respite.

When 5:00 p.m. Monday rolled around signaling the formal end of Memorial Day weekend, Simon and Miss Finch decided to again eat out. Simon's truck idled near the office porch while he and Skipper waited for Miss Finch to join them. They watched as she flipped the sign in the office window from Open to Closed and locked the door on her way out and limped to the truck.

"Retirement is looking better by the moment," she huffed as she reached the truck's open door.

"Hurry up, lady—I'm starving!" Skipper groused in Miss Finch's direction.

"Skipperdoodle, if I catch you speaking rudely to Miss Finch again, I'll jerk a knot in your neck so tight you won't be able to swallow whatever you put in your mouth," Simon growled.

Miss Finch climbed with slow weariness into the truck's cab. "Not if I get to him first."

Skipper, sandwiched between the two of them, scowled undaunted. "Work, work, work! We work so much, I haven't had a decent meal in days."

"Really? You didn't stuff yourself at that waffle house yesterday?"

"Simon's right. We ate out just yesterday afternoon. So, how about we stop by Joe and Holly's cabin and let you forage for yourself," Miss Finch murmured. "Hopefully you can scavenge something edible there. I mean, we wouldn't want you to starve on our way to the restaurant. We'll allow you to sit in Simon's truck and eat what you've found at Joe and Holly's cabin while we go inside to a nice dinner."

Simon nodded. "Sounds like a plan, and feeding two mouths rather than three will save me some bucks."

Skipper's jaws snapped shut, and he folded his arms across his chest.

Simon held in the snarky guffaw that rose in his throat. Here he was, saddled with a fourteen-year-old boy whose mother was doing the best she could without a husband and father to help raise their son—no easy feat, as Simon was finding out for himself.

Maybe, Simon thought, *maybe handling this kid is less like herding cats and more like dealing with a neglected puppy. One second he's sweet and docile, but the next moment he might snarl and snap at the hand that feeds him.*

He shook his head. *From day to day or hour to hour, I never know which Skipper is going to show up or which personality will manifest itself. I've seen him be polite and compliant, but he's also regularly rude, lazy, and ungrateful. Oh, and he's always pushing his boundaries. I suppose it doesn't help that boys his age are bags of raging hormones.*

He sighed. *Lord, I'm in no way qualified to handle a teen but . . . just like the pastor was teaching yesterday, I have committed myself to watching over Skipper while Joe and Holly are away. I cannot bail or 'squirt out' from under that responsibility no matter how difficult or distasteful the task.*

So, Lord? Would you please help me help this kid?

———◦———

THE THREE OF THEM, replete and in much better spirits after eating, were headed back to Bright Star when Simon's cellphone rang.

"That's Holly's ringtone."

Simon didn't need Holly to know Miss Finch would be on the call with her. He side-eyed Miss Finch and put a finger across his lips. She nodded.

Then Simon handed his phone to Skipper. "Put the call on speaker for me, please, and, uh, don't mention that Miss Finch is riding with us, okay?"

"Sure, Fletch."

There it is: the cheerful, compliant Skipper. For the moment.

"Hello, Fletch? Are you there?"

"Hey, Holly. I'm driving so you're on speaker. Skipper is also with me."

"Joe's with me and we have you on speaker too."

"Hey, Joe! How's it going?"

They heard Joe heave a great sigh. "Progress is slow but I'm not complaining. I'm downright glad just to be alive, to tell you the truth."

"We're glad, too, Joe, but don't rush your recovery—we need you all healed up when you come home. Say, when do you get out of the hospital?"

Holly spoke up. "He was discharged late this afternoon, although because of the holiday, we wasted most of the day waiting around. Waiting for Joe's doctor to discharge him to the rehab center, waiting for the rehab's transport van to arrive, waiting at the rehab office to get him checked in, waiting for them to take him to his room and get him settled there."

Simon steered the conversation back on track. "And are you settled in now, Joe?"

"Good to go, Fletcher. PT starts first thing tomorrow. Have to take it slow and easy until my bones and internal injuries knit a bit more, but at least my muscles won't be atrophying further while I'm healing. The staff people here know what they're doing."

"How long will they keep you, do you think?"

"Doc says that if I make sufficient progress over the next two weeks, I'll graduate to a walking boot and can come home. Sorry to say, though, that even then, I'll have to continue to rely on you for a lot of the work, Fletch. I'll only be allowed to, for example, drive the mower and perform similar tasks that won't stress my leg or my insides as they heal. No lifting, no standing or walking too long. That sort of thing."

"Don't worry, Joe. Skipper and I will keep handling the heavy lifting once you're home. And you, Holly? What are your plans now that Joe's in rehab?"

She hesitated. "Well, I suppose that depends upon you and Skipper. I mean, we're thrilled with how you've managed the move-ins and that the residents seem to be enjoying themselves. Your texts and updates are quite reassuring in that regard . . ."

Her voice trailed off.

"And now you want to know if we can continue to hold the fort. Specifically, you want to know how long we can manage without you?"

"Well, I *would* like to stay on here, at least until I see how Joe tolerates his therapy. Do you think you and Skipper can manage say, another three days?"

"Nope. No can do."

Simon was so firm and quick in his response that Skipper and Miss Finch's heads jerked in his direction like they'd been yanked by the same string.

Holly must have been equally stunned. "What? You can't?"

Simon's smile was tight. "Since I have both of you on this call, Holly, I should apprise you of a few facts. Fact one, Bright Star owes the successful start of its first season to the unstinting assistance of Miss Finch."

Holly sputtered and tried to cut him off.

Simon wasn't having it. "Don't you horn in on me, Holly Mitchell. I have things to say—and you need to listen up."

Joe must have shushed Holly at that point, because he said, "Go ahead, Fletch. We're all ears."

"Thanks, Joe. The truth is, without Miss Finch's assistance from the day she arrived until now, Skipper and I could *not* have managed everything. Miss Finch has worked right alongside us, hour by hour and day by day, straight through this hectic weekend. So, I took the liberty of putting her on the payroll and logging her hours. Double time on Memorial Day, of course."

The invisible string that had jerked Skipper and Miss Finch's heads in unison now tugged open their jaws in tandem. Then Simon grimaced in embarrassment as Holly's indignation echoed through the truck's cab—and abruptly cut off when a party on the other end of the call, presumably Joe, pressed the mute button. Simon glanced at Miss Finch and offered a silent apology.

She shook her head and mouthed, "Not necessary."

A moment later, Joe unmuted his end and answered Simon. "Good call putting Miss Finch on the payroll, Fletch. It was both the right and the legal thing to do. What else did you wish to tell us?"

"Thanks, Joe. Just to be clear, until Holly returns and picks up the slack around Bright Star, I'll continue logging the hours Miss Finch works so she is appropriately compensated. The only other matter of note is that I authorized Miss Finch to take up residence in Site 1. She did have a signed contract, after all, paid in full."

Simon, Skipper, and Miss Finch heard the first words of a protest in the background, cut short when Joe again muted the call.

"Guess they're sorting things out," Simon commented under his breath, drawing a snort from Skipper.

When Joe unmuted the call, he replied. "That, too, was the right decision, Fletch. Do you have anything else to tell us?"

"Yes, I do—and this is the kicker. You and Holly owe Miss Finch a huge debt of gratitude, because without her? Bright Star would be spending the season without a functioning swimming complex."

Across the miles, they heard a startled Joe say, "What?"

For a change, Holly was silent.

Must have stunned her, Simon thought with a smile, *and it takes a lot to stun that woman.*

"You heard me. Without Miss Finch, our swimming complex would still be closed and would remain so most of the season."

Holly started to say something, but Joe interrupted. "I think you'd better explain, Fletch."

"Sure, Joe; it's pretty cut and dry, really. When your truck was hit, it rolled."

"Rolled a couple of times, if memory serves," Joe muttered. "I don't recall the precise moment the semi hit me or most of what happened afterward, but whenever I close my eyes, I experience a vivid recollection, a déjà vu sort of sensation, of me, inside my truck, rolling over and over and over. I relive the jarring impact of the truck landing on its side, then the roof, then its other side, and so on, the seatbelt cutting into me again and again."

He shuddered. "It's a nightmare I'm having trouble getting rid of, and I've got deep bruises from my seatbelt's shoulder strap to prove it happened.

Other than that creepy, recurring memory, though, until I woke up in the hospital? Nothing."

"I'm truly sorry about all this, Joe."

"Thanks, Fletch. Doctor says it takes a while to get past this kind of trauma."

Simon hesitated. *Yeah, I know, Lord. I've wallowed in the juices of my own trauma long enough. It's high time I put it behind me. Get back to living my faith out loud.*

He rolled the words he was reluctant to say around in his mouth before finally he blurted, "I've been praying for you, Joe, and I'll keep right on praying until you're back home with us."

Simon couldn't tell if Joe was shocked, touched, annoyed, or all three. The man said nothing for a moment, then muttered, "I appreciate that, Fletch. You want to finish telling us about the swimming complex? I mean, from what I recall of Miss Finch—and that was decades ago—she was a force to be reckoned with, but conjuring a pool pump out of thin air? This I need to hear about."

"You're not wrong about her, Joe. Well, as you can probably imagine, the pump you had tied down in the back of your truck took a beating when the truck rolled. Like your truck, the pump's crate was crushed. When I tore open the crate, the pump was a total loss. I called our supplier and ordered yet another pump, but he said it would be six weeks to get it in. Maybe longer. And without the swimming complex, who knows how many of Bright Star's residents might have demanded refunds?"

"But you said—"

"Getting to it, Joe. Unbeknownst to me, Miss Finch, after I'd left to drive Holly down to Vegas, started making phone calls on her own. She discovered that one of the casinos was holding our exact model pump in stock as a spare. As it turns out, Miss Finch actually knew the facilities manager from a long time ago, and—"

A great belly laugh erupted from Joe, followed by groans of pain. "*Ow, ow, ow!* Man, Fletch! Don't make me laugh like that. I'm black and blue and sore everywhere. Please don't hurt me!"

Simon winced. "Don't make you laugh? How in the world did I do that?"

Joe chuckled and again groaned. "Sorry. Just . . . *ow!* You got to the part where you said, 'Turns out Miss Finch actually knew the facilities manager,' and I knew right off what you were going to say next."

Simon slid a suspicious glance in Miss Finch's direction. Her mouth was slightly pursed, her eyes two flat slits fixed studiously on the road ahead. For all she gave away, Joe and Simon could have been discussing the weather. Except . . . except Simon thought her shoulders jiggled. Just a little.

Is that woman, that annoying *woman, laughing?*

Having lost the direction of the conversation, an impatient Skipper looked from Simon to Miss Finch and back. "You ever gonna finish, Fletch?"

"Your manners ever going to improve, Skipper-dee-doo-dah?" Simon growled. "Sorry, Joe. Back to Miss Finch and the casino's facilities manager. When I said she knew the guy, you knew what was coming next, did you?"

"Yup. I'd lay money on it."

"Care to share?"

Another laugh turned into a moan before Joe answered, "Yeah, okay, so the casino's facilities manager? She said he owed her a favor—am I right?"

Simon's eyes jinked across the truck's cab to Miss Finch. He no longer had to guess if she were laughing. Her shoulders visibly shook. Unable to stop—or unwilling to; Simon didn't know which—she turned her face to her door's window and wrapped her arms around her middle—precious good that did!

"Brat!" Simon hissed.

Skipper again looked from him to Miss Finch and back. He may not have known what was going on, but he grinned anyway.

"Fletch? Fletcher?"

"Sorry, Joe. So you knew she'd say the guy owed her a favor, did you?"

"Sure did. That woman collects favors like I collect fishing lures."

"Huh. That so."

"Yup. She got ahold of that guy's arm, twisted gently, and *presto chango!* He was wondrously convinced to sell his pump to us. Tell me I'm wrong."

"Twisted his arm, yes, but rather than pay him for his pump, we'll be replacing his spare with our back-ordered one when it comes in."

Simon didn't bother rehearsing the rest of the details, the cost of flying the pump and installers from Vegas to Tahoe. That was an expense to address on another day. Like when the bill arrived.

"In any event, by the time I got back to Bright Star, the pools were filling up and our guests were happy."

"That woman is worth her weight in gold, Fletch. You tell her that for me, will you? In fact, we're grateful to the three of you for your unstinting efforts on our behalf and Bright Star's."

"Thanks, Joe. I'll . . . let her know. Talk later."

When the call ended, Simon and his passengers were quiet. For less than half a minute. Then Skipper declared, "Well, I don't think it's fair. If Miss Finch is getting paid, I should get paid too."

Aaand the rude, quarrelsome teen was back.

Simon shook his head. "We've already gone over this, Skipper. You're eating well, aren't you? Have a decent place to sleep? Learning valuable life skills? You should count yourself lucky to be spending your summer here and not stuck in your mom's apartment with an ankle monitor strapped to your leg. Besides, now that Memorial Day weekend is over, things at Bright Star will calm down. You'll have less to do each day and can use the swimming complex or game room during your afternoon off time. Not a bad deal, if you ask me.

"So, if you ever again feel inclined to embrace a couple of budding young criminals as your models of maturity, remind yourself of the *awful* restraints you're under right now, because next time could be worse. Much worse."

Skipper folded his arms across his chest and lapsed into a sullen silence.

Simon smiled serenely over Skipper's head. Miss Finch returned his smile with a placid smile of her own, her eyes doing that crinkling at the corners thing Simon was starting to like.

———•———

THEY WELCOMED THE LAST of Bright Star's summer occupants Tuesday afternoon, and that evening, Simon called a "meet and greet" with the residents. In preparation, he and Skipper built a fire in the group firepit. Miss Finch, having suggested that snacks and a beverage would be in keeping with Bright Star's high standards, zipped off to town where she used Simon's Bright Star credit card to purchase lemonade and a variety of treats and finger foods.

A good showing of residents turned out. Simon, Miss Finch, and even Skipper (under dire threat) smiled and shook hands all around.

Simon met Wes and Polly Trujillo, a charming couple in Site 15, early eighties, out to see America.

"Spent last summer in Montana and last winter in St. Augustine," Wes said. "Lots of sights and fun in between. We plan to head for Yuma this fall."

Tom Peterman, Site 24, introduced himself too. "I'm retired and a wanderer by nature. Live in my RV year round."

It was a pleasant evening, and the snacks Miss Finch had laid out quickly disappeared.

"Like a hoard of locusts," she muttered out of the side of her mouth to Simon.

"Be nice."

"Hmph."

Simon stepped up onto one of the seating logs and clapped his hands to get the residents' attention. "Folks, thank you for coming to Bright Star's very first meet and greet. We're off to a great start for this summer's fun and relaxation."

He heard murmurs of agreement in response.

"Before I dismiss us, I'd just like to run through one or two housekeeping items. The most important thing I could share is how we can enjoy this beautiful park safely." He ticked off the most common items—pool safety rules, the 15-miles-per-hour speed limit within the park, and the gate protocols.

"Bright Star staff will keep the gate open most days to coincide with office hours. However, be sure you have your gate code memorized so you can get in and out of the park when the gate is closed.

"And last, but definitely not least, fire safety. We live in the shadow of Mount Tallac and are privileged to enjoy this park's lush greenery and many tall trees. I think we also love a campfire on a cool evening, don't we? So I ask you, please be careful how you manage your firepits, barbecues, tiki torches, and so on—particularly when the winds pick up. Only a spark could turn our paradise into a pile of ashes, so *please*, if the wind comes up, be extra careful."

From the frowns Simon observed, he saw that no one cared for the idea of a forest fire tearing through Bright Star's gorgeous landscape.

"One last point of order. In the unhappy event of a fire in or near the park, we will activate Bright Star's emergency protocols. What happens if we do? We've mounted speakers in strategic locations throughout the park, speakers such as that one." Simon gestured to Skipper, who stood across the lawn and beneath a speaker fixed under the eaves of the rec cabin. Skipper grinned and pointed up to the speaker.

Simon continued. "In case of fire or other emergency, the speakers will broadcast a siren—and trust me, folks, you *will* hear it."

A titter rippled through the gathering.

"So, day or night, if you hear the siren, you are to leave the park *immediately* using the means of transportation most available to you. Take nothing with you as you go other than your pets and purse or wallet with ID. The emergency system will also automatically unlock and open the gate to the park and keep it open for easy egress. Any questions?"

No one spoke, and several residents shook their heads.

"All right then! Have a wonderful time here at Bright Star."

Simon's last remark raised an enthusiastic round of applause and a chorus of "Thank yous."

⁕

THE CRUSH OF MEMORIAL DAY weekend behind them and the chaos of moving in residents now complete, Simon and his staff of two settled into a nicely mellow routine. Miss Finch kept daily office hours, 9:00 a.m. to 5:00 p.m., while Simon and Skipper handled the grounds and facilities.

As Simon had assured Skipper, the boy earned free time each afternoon by completing his chores to Simon's expectations. The kid was eager to get to his work in the morning and earn additional time off in the afternoon. Most of that time off was spent in the game room on one of the video game consoles.

Of course, Holly should have returned to Bright Star by midweek to relieve Miss Finch. So where was she? She'd texted Simon Wednesday morning that she'd changed her mind and would be staying on in Vegas until Joe was released to come home.

"Way to go, Holly," Simon grumbled. "Leave it to you to find a way to 'punish' me for circumventing you and permitting Miss Finch to stay in the park—not to mention punishing Miss Finch for, out of the goodness of her heart, saving your bacon! Sheesh. That old saying, 'no good deed goes unpunished' isn't far off the mark after all."

THURSDAY EVENING, Simon drove Skipper to the church's youth group meeting and introduced him to Pastor Kent, the group's leader.

Simon pulled the young man aside for a word. "I appreciate you making Skipper feel welcome. We just have a few court-ordered requirements."

To his credit, the youth pastor didn't blink or flinch. "Whatever we can do."

"Thanks. I need to remain close by. Say, the lobby or even the parking lot."

"Feel free to wait here in the lobby. We gather here for snacks, then meet in the fellowship hall, just over there. Trust me, you'll be able to hear us."

"Super. And, well, can you let me know ASAP, should Skipper disappear?"

"Yup. I'll keep a close eye on him for you."

"Thanks again, Pastor."

Simon drove Skipper back to Bright Star afterward. "How was the meeting?"

"It was okay."

"Talk to anyone in particular?"

Skipper shrugged. "Just Zane and Kevin."

Simon considered those four words progress indeed.

BRIGHT STAR'S MORE RELAXED routine lasted until Friday afternoon when the residents' various guests began arriving for the weekend. For Simon, Miss Finch, and Skipper, it meant that their "more relaxed" workload picked up and continued at a frenetic pace through the weekend.

Saturday morning as Simon and Skipper started their work, Skipper discovered that the Gorman's granddaughters, Becka and Melissa, had returned to spend the weekend and the following week with their grandparents. He arranged to meet the girls that afternoon in the family pool.

Simon was taking weekly water samples when Skipper and the girls entered the family pool. They hadn't been there long before another visiting teen joined their little cadre.

"Hey," Skipper said. "Want to swim with us?"

The newcomer wasn't shy. "Sure. Actually, I'm really glad to find some other kids around. My folks plan to send me to stay here with my uncle and aunt most weekends this summer. I thought sure it would be a dead bore."

"No chance of that. We're having a blast. What's your name?" Becka asked.

"Bryce Muller."

"Bryce, I'm Becka. This is my sister, Melissa. And this is Skipper."

"What site are you in?" Melissa asked.

"We're in Site 7. My parents and I recently moved to Portland where they took new jobs. They are ER physicians. Sadly, until they get some seniority, they have to work most every weekend. They flew me down here so I'm not home by myself too much."

"You flew here?"

Simon could hear the amazement in Skipper's question.

"Sure. My dad is a pilot and owns his own plane. We fly lots of places, especially to ski."

Simon flinched when Skipper said, "I've never been on a plane."

"What?" Melissa was astounded. "Never?"

Simon saw Becka nudge her sister. "Mind your manners, Mel."

"Oh. Er, sorry, Skipper. That was rude of me."

Skipper shrugged. "No worries. Want to practice diving?"

Simon finished collecting his samples and exited the pool enclosure. As he walked away, he decided that he was okay with what he saw in Skipper, especially that he was making friends.

And they sound like decent kids, kids who will be a good influence on him.

Like Miss Finch said.

———◆———

SIMON, MISS FINCH, AND Skipper again attended church in town Sunday morning. Afterward, Skipper mingled with some of the boys his age, and on the drive home, he had a request.

"Fletch, can Zane and Kevin come swim here sometime this week in the afternoon?"

"Huh. Let me think on that, okay?"

Skipper's attitude jumped lanes in an instant. He crossed his arms and muttered, "Figured you'd say no."

"Did you hear me say no? You did not. I said let me think on it—and don't bug me about it while I'm thinking."

Simon sighed internally. *Lord, I am not cut out for this. I need a vacation. And a raise.*

CHAPTER 9

SOMETIME DURING SUNDAY NIGHT, uncharacteristically hot, sticky weather descended on the lake and its surrounds and settled in to stay. Early the first Tuesday in June, after restless sleep and with temperatures already rising, Simon dragged himself out of bed.

"Ugh."

Move it, Marine.

"Oorah."

Skipper hung over the edge of the top bunk, lost in his dreams. As he usually did and because it was still early, Simon let the kid sleep while he got himself up and moving. He set a pot of coffee brewing, made his bunk, and policed the cabin. The cabin's open floorplan was easy to keep tidy: the bunkbeds to one side, kitchenette across the back wall, workout area in the middle, small bathroom through a door past the bunks.

Fifteen minutes later, wearing shorts, t-shirt, and running shoes, steaming coffee in hand, Simon pointed his truck down Bright Star's private road. He turned left at the main road, then right where the road intersected Emerald Bay Road, and drove until he reached the western outskirts of South Lake Tahoe's residential area. He parked, then jogged across Emerald Bay Road, heading north until, a few blocks later, he hit the Pope-Baldwin Bike Path.

Even at six in the morning, residents and tourists alike were already out in force, some on bicycles, most, like Simon, on foot. Essentially mirroring Emerald Bay Road, the wide, paved trail ran from South Lake Tahoe to Spring Creek Road, just shy of four miles. Simon would run the length and back, reveling in the breathtaking views of Mount Tallac on one side and, on the other side, the occasional glimpses of Lake Tahoe's shimmering blue water with the peaks of the Sierra Nevada mountain range as backdrop.

About three miles into his return route, he usually diverged onto a dirt path loop that left the trail then reconnected about half a mile from his starting point. Simon's smart watch told him that adding in the loop got him to an even nine miles total, a route that usually took him just under an hour and a half to run. He should have eaten up the distance in an hour, but that was back when he was younger and stronger.

At this moment? This morning, Simon's knees were stiff and his calves tight. He set a modest pace that would allow his legs to gradually warm up. He needed to stretch them out before he demanded a faster pace from them.

Kowtowing to your age, are you?

Maybe he was starting to show every one of his forty-eight years, but he would go down swinging before he let advancing age dictate to him.

You're as slow as a slug. Pick up your pace, Marine!

"Shut your pie hole. I'm warming up."

He was approaching Camp Richardson Campground, about a mile and half into his run when he ran past a hobbling figure with dark, frowsy hair. Could have been a stranger, but the homely dog walking beside her was a solid giveaway.

Or was the giveaway that *cat*, riding with regal loftiness atop the dog?

Lazy beast.

He glanced behind him. It was Miss Finch all right. She was wearing shorts, walking shoes, a t-shirt, and features set in unhappy but determined lines. From what he'd seen as he passed her by, she also had a death grip on her cane.

Huh. Not a good look for you, lady. Not at all.

Unlike you too.

An hour later, on his way back, Simon had stuck to the trail, ignoring the dirt loop he usually tacked on.. For some reason, he felt compelled to seek out Miss Finch. When he found her, she was perched on a fallen log just off the trail, Hugo sprawled across her feet, Pouncer nestled in her arms. A dribble of blood ran from her knee to her ankle, and her ever-present cane was nowhere to be seen.

Miss Finch's glower, on the other hand, was publicly evident.

Simon's approach was cautious. "Morning."

She didn't seem surprised to see him. "Yes, it is morning."

Hugo peered up at Simon. His rheumy eyes flicked toward his mistress, then back to Simon. Like he was trying to convey a message.

Is that dog . . . pleading with me?

"Did you take a fall?"

"Congratulations, Mr. Fletcher. You have acquired the much sought-after ability to state the obvious."

"And you have developed a new skill: a proclivity for accidents. Isn't this your *third* fall since you arrived here?"

"And they say you can't teach an old dog new tricks."

He put his hands on his hips. "Uh, I don't see your cane. Did you lose it?"

Miss Finch did not respond, but Hugo blinked twice.

Once for yes; twice for no?

"Do you know where it is?"

Hugo blinked once.

Huh. I may be on to something.

"How long have you been sitting here, Miss Finch?"

The woman sighed, and Hugo's tail thumped the ground in sympathy.

Simon squatted and scratched behind Hugo's ears. Tongue lolling, eyes closed, Hugo leaned into Simon's hand. Meanwhile, Simon used the opportunity to squint at Miss Finch's knee. It was skinned up pretty good, but the bleeding had crusted over.

Needs cleaning and an antibiotic ointment.

Next, he scanned the area on both sides of the trail. When he didn't immediately spot Miss Finch's cane, he got up and walked a wide circle around the log, searching. He found the cane about a dozen feet from where she sat. Not near the trail itself but in the bushes a yard or two distant.

Where she had to have pitched it.

He retrieved the cane and, without a word, leaned it against the fallen log near her. Hugo thumped his tail in thanks.

Apparently, there was nothing wrong with Miss Finch's hearing. She perked up abruptly, and peered down the trail. Simon heard something too. The tinkling of some kind of bell. He swiveled around and spotted two cyclists coming toward them.

He glanced at Miss Finch and saw that she was focused on the riders. They slowed out of respect for pedestrians as they rode by, an older, white-haired couple, grinning with happy abandon. Simon's inspection got snagged by the bikes themselves.

Interesting.

The woman, in her mid-seventies Simon decided, *ring-a-dinged* her little bike bell and giggled as she passed by. Giggled like a little kid.

Simon snickered under his breath, but Miss Finch sort of folded in on herself.

A moist nose nudged Simon's hand. He looked down. Hugo's eyes were in full-on pleading mode.

Yeah, yeah. And just what do you expect me to do, huh?

With a huff, he said, "Well, I need to get going. Finish my run. I'm parked that way, near the beginning of the trail. See you later. Back at Bright Star."

Miss Finch nodded. Said nothing.

Hugo whimpered.

———•———

FIFTEEN MINUTES LATER, Simon reached his truck. He was sweating a bucket and needed to shower before heading to work. But he couldn't seem to get Miss Finch's look of defeat out of his head.

Lord, what would you have me do? I have a boatload of work ahead of me today, tasks that shouldn't be put off.

Still, he couldn't shake the sense that Miss Finch needed him. And truthfully? He needed her to staff the office.

But what can I do, Lord? That's one stubborn lady.

The urgent feeling only increased.

With a resigned sigh, he pointed his truck down Emerald Bay Road, watching the bike trail on his right, scanning through the trees and bushes standing between the shoulder and the trail. When he caught sight of Miss Finch, still sitting on the log where he'd left her, he pulled onto the shoulder, set his emergency flashers, and got out. Jogged around a couple bushes and trees, and came up to her.

Hugo stood and barked a greeting. Pouncer hissed her joy at his return. Miss Finch blinked in surprise.

"What are you doing back here? I thought you had to work."

"You also have work, don't you? Or have you quit on me?"

"I'm no quitter!"

"Could have fooled me. Get up. I'm taking you to your car."

It was testament to her sunken spirits that she didn't protest when Simon put his arm under hers, hauled her to her feet, and handed over her cane.

She grimaced.

"Hurts that bad?"

"It certainly does not hurt *good*."

"I've got a first aid kit in my truck. When we get to your car, I'll swab that lovely scrape you acquired this morning and slap a bandage on it."

"It is not my knee that hurts, Fletcher; it is my blasted *foot*."

"Huh. I can't do anything about that, but I can clean up that scrape on your knee. Let's go."

He led the way, and she hobbled slowly behind him. Hugo took up the rear, Princess Pouncer yawning her boredom while riding Hugo in regal style.

Simon boosted Miss Finch into the passenger seat and fastened her seatbelt. As soon as he moved away, Pouncer hopped into her lap. Hugo jumped up and sprawled on the floor below Miss Finch's dangling feet.

"Where are you parked?" Simon asked from the driver's seat.

"Down at the beach."

"Right." Simon knew she meant Baldwin Beach, about two miles from where she'd sat down on that log and also the only beach on the trail with public parking.

She brightened up a bit as he drove. "Thank you, Simon. I was rubbernecking at the lovely scenery, not paying enough attention to how far I had come until my ankle really started hurting. Then, because I was not adequately watching the trail, I tripped and skinned my knee."

"Likely bruised your knee a bit too. Might stiffen up some."

She sighed. "Already has. I was not looking forward to the walk back to my car."

"I get you. I've rehabbed a few injuries in my day. Say, care to tell me what's wrong with your foot or whatever it is that's not working right?"

"That is personal business, *Mr.* Fletcher."

"Hey! What's with that "Mr." business again? I asked about your *foot*. I didn't ask you for your life's story or demand that you confess your deepest, darkest secrets."

Although I wouldn't mind knowing more about you since I find you rather intriguing.

She folded her arms. "*Hmph.*"

Simon jerked the wheel toward the shoulder and stopped. "Excuse me for being a caring human being! You want to get out now? Here?"

Pouncer's eyes dilated. She stiffened, showed her fangs, and growled at him.

"You knock that off!" Simon growled back. "*My truck*, not yours, you brat."

Pouncer, caught mid-hiss, recoiled, scrabbled her way out of Miss Finch's lap onto the floor, and cringed behind Hugo's back.

"Why you little coward!"

He looked up in time to catch Miss Finch's hand dart to her mouth.

Simon was still fuming. "Are you laughing at me?"

Her shoulders quivered; her head moved side to side, but her fingers stayed over her mouth.

"Your hands aren't big enough to hide that smarmy smile, lady."

She gave in and chuckled aloud. "I'm not laughing at you. I'm laughing because you called Pouncer's bluff. Good for you! She is far too accustomed to ruling by intimidation."

Simon glanced at the truck's floorboards. Pouncer had turned her back to him and tucked her head down low. On the other hand, Hugo's tongue hung out to one side and his mouth was turned up in a happy grin.

"Rules by intimidation, does she? You don't say."

He drove back onto the road, turned right onto Baldwin Beach Road, and made his way to the parking lot at the road's far end. Her panel wagon was easy to spot, and he came to a stop behind it, then retrieved the first aid kit from under his seat.

"Stay put but swivel toward the door, if you please. That will make it easier for me to treat your knee."

He opened her door, and she obediently swung her legs toward him. Her knee was already a scabby mess where the blood had dried. He tore open a fast-food handwashing packet and laid the moist sheet across the wound to soften the crusted blood, then opened another sheet to scrub the trickles of dried blood down her leg. When he'd finished, he went to work on her knee, gently sponging the scrape.

"Yeah, you've picked up some tiny gravel bits. Those will have to wait until we get back to Bright Star and apply some hydrogen peroxide to boil them out. In the meantime, I'll dab everything with antibiotic ointment and bandage you up."

When he'd finished, he asked, "Need some help getting down?"

She stared straight ahead and didn't move.

He waited.

Finally, she exhaled and said, "This past February I was in a car crash all too like the one Joe was in, poor man, except I was T-boned on the driver's side. I sustained a minor concussion and a broken ankle. I had surgery to set my ankle and was in the hospital for several days after. I suppose . . . I suppose that is one reason I volunteered to help in Joe and Holly's absence. I understand the long recovery Joe is facing."

Simon frowned. "That was, what, three months ago?"

"Fourteen weeks, to be precise."

"What about the truck that hit you? Did the owner have insurance? How's the other driver faring?"

"How the driver is faring is highly dependent upon the advance reservations he made for his eternal destination."

Simon blanched. "He *died?*"

She slid her eyes toward him. "His demise would make a great public service announcement on the virtues of using your seatbelt. He expired on the hood of my car."

To herself rather than Simon she muttered, "I still see him . . . sprawled across the hood of my vehicle, his blood splattered on the windshield and everywhere else."

Simon scrambled to get the conversation away from the depressing details and back on track. "Sounds terrible . . . but after fourteen weeks, your foot still pains you to walk on it?"

"At times unbearably."

"And your doctor—"

"Yes, you have hit upon the 'bone' of contention between me and my surgeon, Fletcher—pun intended. He claims I am not rotating, stretching, walking, and otherwise using my foot enough; I insist that I experience a stabbing pain in my ankle when I walk and that the pain increases rather than decreases the more I use my foot."

"You've followed your physical therapy orders?"

Her eyes narrowed. "Is the Grinch green, Mr. Fletcher?"

"Sorry. Just asking."

"I have, with difficulty, completed every regimen foisted upon me, but the pain when I put weight on my foot is frequently sharp and worsens when I walk. My physical therapist is baffled, my surgeon is as dense as a box of rocks, and I am . . . beyond frustrated."

"Did—"

Now that she'd opened the tap, more came pouring out. Much more.

"I have always been an active individual, Fletcher. Until *this*, I have traveled extensively, snow skied, water skied, run half-marathons, rock climbed, and parasailed. Now, I am saddled with an ankle that refuses to heal and a doctor *who will not listen* and who treats me like a doddering old fool! This-this-this forced inactivity is not at all who I am!"

On that exasperated declaration, she stood in the truck's doorway on her good foot and reached for the truck's grab bar to hop down out of the truck.

Simon held up a hand, the glimmer of an idea unfolding in his head.

"Hold up a sec."

"What?"

He shook his head, still thinking. Finally, he said, "Let's take a little drive, shall we?"

"A drive? You will make us both late to work this morning, Fletcher."

He shrugged. "So the office opens an hour late. Sue me."

"But . . . where are we going and why?"

"Not far. You'll see."

"I do not have time for this nonsense—"

"You don't have time? Really? Ten minutes ago you were stranded alongside the trail. I'm your boss, and I say you have plenty of time. Get back in that seat and buckle up."

Meekly, she sat and swiveled forward.

Hugo's tail thumped in approval.

CHAPTER 10

SIMON RETRACED HIS ROUTE Into South Lake Tahoe and drove deeper into town. The sign in the lot where he parked read **Tallac Trail Bikes**. He went around his truck and opened Miss Finch's door.

She had read the sign and refused to get out. "No. Take me back to my car, *Mr.* Fletcher."

"I think you should see what I have in mind first."

"And I disagree. I already know that I cannot ride a bike in my present condition."

"Again, I think you should see what I have in mind."

"After which you will return me to my car?"

"Yup."

"This is coercion."

"Yes it is. Let's go."

Glowering disapproval, she allowed him to help her down where she stood on her good leg until she had her cane and her balance in hand.

"Hugo? Pouncer? Come." The animals did as she asked. Hugo stood off to her side, and with a lithe leap, Pouncer jumped onto his back.

Adding a sniff, Miss Finch said, "I refuse to leave my darlings in a vehicle during hot weather."

"Understood."

He walked ahead of her and opened the shop door. While he waited for her to catch up, he hollered inside, "Yo, Jasper! You there?"

A head appeared in the doorway leading to the shop's side room. "Is that Simon Fletcher?"

"In the flesh, man."

They did that "man hug" thing where they bumped chests and pounded each other's back.

"What can I do for you, Fletch?"

"I have a customer for you. Special, so be nice."

"I'm always nice."

"Oh? Then why do I have to ask you to be nice?"

Jasper snorted and walked toward Miss Finch.

"Ma'am, my name is Jasper Gifford. My friends call me Jasper."

She reluctantly took his extended hand. "BD Finch. You may call me Miss Finch."

He nodded slowly. "Well, Miss Finch, this is my shop. I take it you're interested in trying one of my electric bikes?"

"Not in the slightest. I was bamboozled into coming here, although . . ." A curious and wistful expression flitted across her face. The same expression Simon had seen when the older couple had ridden by them on the trail.

She cleared her throat. "When you say electric bikes, do you mean the kind with little motors on them?"

"Yes, ma'am. Small electric motors." Jasper took in her height and asked, "Shall we take a look at my inventory?" He nodded toward her cane. "No riding required, I assure you. Just a look-see, although I will say that when new riders feel ready for a test ride, we simply open the garage door back there. They give a little twist to the throttle and ride around the empty lot behind my shop."

She hobbled behind him to the bike display, all the while muttering, "But I do not see the *point* of an electric bike, I really do not. How is that actual exercise?"

Jasper wheeled out the smallest bike in his inventory. Put the kickstand down, inserted a key into the bike's battery, turned and withdrew it, then pushed a button on the controller. Rested his hand on the seat. "Sixteen-inch wheels. Step-through frame. Adjustable seat and handlebars. This bike is the ideal size for you."

Her upper lip curled in disdain. "Wonderful. The necessary accoutrements to complete the look are a red fez, a ringmaster, and a complement of circus clowns."

Jasper guffawed and grinned at Simon. "I like her."

Simon grunted. "Can you get her on the bike? That's all I ask."

"Sure. Okay, so Miss Finch, the bike may be small, but I promise it is the right size for you. Let's at least give it a try."

"Let's? Will you be riding on the bike with me, Mr. Gifford?"

Jasper snort-laughed. "That, Miss Finch, truly would be a circus. Let me rephrase: I would like you to try this bike. I believe you will like it."

Miss Finch, her greedy eyes roving over the bike, still protested, "But this battery-driven snake oil you are hawking? What is the *point?*"

"Two points actually. The first is that you are in control. At all times, you pick the level of pedal assist you want or need."

She tapped her cane on the shop floor. "Explain 'pedal assist,' please."

He pointed to the bike's controller. "See this number? The electric motor has five levels of pedal assist, numbers one through five. Need help on that hill coming up? Move the pedal assist up. Prefer to pedal more? Move the pedal assist down. Your call; you are in control—but to answer your question, the point is that, at all times, you are pedaling, and pedaling is exercise."

"Unlikely. And your second point?"

"Ah! That one's easy. The second point is that you'll feel like a kid again. You know: Faster than a speeding bullet. More powerful than a locomotive. Able to leap tall buildings in a single bound? Like that. Painful knees or feet? In most cases, much less of a problem or no problem at all. Again, you are in control of how much assistance you need or want."

She pursed her mouth and moved closer to the bike and studied its features. "You don't say."

Jasper stood to the left of the bike and put both of his hands on the handlebars. "Let me demonstrate how to safely mount the bike. Nudge the kickstand up. Squeeze and hold the brakes. Slip one leg through the frame like this." He demonstrated—although his large frame now straddling the bike looked patently ludicrous.

"Once you're standing astride the bike, scoot backward onto the seat. Toe the right pedal until it is in an 'up' position."

He saw that she was watching closely.

"Put your right foot on that pedal, use the throttle to gently start your forward motion, then begin to pedal. Use the brakes to slow and stop as you would any bike."

He clambered off. "Let's get the handlebars and seat set for you, shall we?" His expert eye darted between her and the aforementioned bike parts, as he lowered both the handlebars and the seat to best fit her.

"That should do it."

She hobbled up to the bike. Handed off her cane to Simon without a backward glance. Gripping the handlebars and brakes, she shifted her weight to her left leg. She grimaced but maneuvered her right leg through the bike anyway. As soon as her right foot touched the floor on the other side of the "step through," she shifted her weight onto it, then slid her backside onto the seat. Exhaled.

"How's that feel?" Jasper asked.

"Not . . . terrible."

"Can you touch both feet to the ground while seated?"

Miss Finch inched her left leg to the floor until the bike was balanced between both feet and she was still comfortably seated.

"Now use the toe of your right foot to nudge the pedal up and place the ball of your foot on the pedal."

She did so. As soon as her foot was firmly on the pedal, she leaned more of her weight on it and sighed with relief.

Jasper, quick to perceive where her pain came from, asked, "Not too much discomfort on your left, er, foot?"

"No; I'm able to keep most of my weight off it in this position."

Her hand twitched next to the throttle, above the right handlebar grip.

"Yes, that's the throttle. A gentle turn toward yourself activates it. How about I open the garage door?"

"But . . ."

"It's a bike. Your body knows how to ride a bike even if it's been years."

"More like decades," she muttered. "So, I just pedal?"

"Yep. Think you can manage to pedal with your injured foot?"

She sighed. "That is the question, and I do not yet know the answer."

He put a helmet on her head, adjusted and fastened the straps under her chin.

"Shall we find out? Give the bike a bit of throttle just to get you going, then release the throttle and pedal around the test lot. The lot connects to a bike trail should you decide to ride farther."

She sniffed. "Trifling chance of that."

Jasper hit a button on the wall and the garage door rose. "Ride on out."

Miss Finch stared out the opening to the modest asphalt lot beyond. She swallowed. Then her hand gently turned the throttle. She gasped as, without a sound, the bike moved forward. She wobbled, then began to pedal, and the bike rolled out the door. Around the lot she went, her brows knitted in concentration as she learned the bike's controls.

Simon called to her, "How does your ankle feel?"

She flashed him a thumbs up. On her fourth go-round in the test lot, her head came up. A smile crept across her mouth.

And widened.

Simon saw the exact moment it happened. She grinned and pointed the bike toward the lot's outlet, shouting over her shoulder, "I shall return!"

The last words he heard were, "Take care of Hugo and Pouncer!" followed by the *ring-a-ding* of the bike's little bell.

Simon grinned. "Thanks, bro. You've made my day and hers, too, I think."

Jasper laughed. "Your Miss Finch is quite the character."

"Ya think?"

"I'd say she's already hooked, too. Good thing I've got that size bike in stock." He glanced at Simon. "She's really cute, Fletch. How old do you think she is?"

"Sixty-two, if she's to be believed."

"You're joking!"

"Nope."

"Well, shoot. I was thinking of asking her to dinner, but . . . naw. Too old for me." He looked around. "Where's that dog of hers? And was that a cat riding on his back?"

"Yup." Simon lifted his voice. "Hugo! Come, boy."

Hugo trotted to him, eyes bright and curious. Pouncer, seeing Simon reach his hand toward Hugo's head, leapt off. Tail in the air, she stalked to a safe distance, sat down, and with tail twitching side to side, stared steely blue daggers at him.

"This is Hugo. The stuck-up queen in the corner is Pouncer."

"Hello, Hugo."

Hugo leaned into Jasper's hand, closed his eyes, let his tongue loll out the side of his happy maw.

Jasper chuckled. "Y'know, sometimes Airedales and this related breed of terrier don't seem quite real to me. Like, when they sit really still like this? They remind me of—"

"Remind you of a stuffed animal?"

"That's it! A life-size stuffed animal. And what's with the cat riding on his back?"

"Princess Pouncer: Ruler of the Realm and Empress of Ego. Hugo is her subservient lackey. Fair warning? Don't get too close to the princess. She didn't come by her name on accident."

While they waited for Miss Finch's return, Jasper poured Simon a cup of coffee. Found a dog treat for Hugo. Stayed clear of Pouncer.

Thirty minutes later, Miss Finch still hadn't returned.

"I gotta call my young Jedi apprentice, Jasper. Be right back."

Simon went outside and stood by his truck to call Skipper. The boy didn't answer, so Simon left voice mail. "Yeah, Skipper, just letting you know I'm running a few errands in town and they are taking longer than expected. Be back as soon as possible, but in my absence, I need you to walk yourself down to the office, unlock the door, and staff it until I return."

When he came back inside, he found Jasper standing as still as Lot's salt-pillar wife. Pouncer, on the other hand, lounged with languid nonchalance across Jasper's shoulders, her claws securing her station.

Jasper pleaded softly, "Help me, Fletch!"

"I told you to steer clear of that cat."

"But she-she-she ambushed me! Hugo came up to my side for more scratches, as nice as pie, but *she* was riding atop him, and I wasn't paying attention! As I bent to pet Hugo, *she* launched herself onto me! Now every pincushion in the world has my condolences."

Pouncer yawned and dug her front claws into Jasper's collarbone.

"*Yow!*"

Simon moved closer—but not too close. "Pouncer, get down."

She sneered at him, yawned, then capitulated, making Jasper flinch multiple times as she readied herself to dismount. Simon had, wisely, moved back a couple of yards to avoid becoming a waypoint on Pouncer's route to the floor.

About then, Miss Finch rode through Jasper's open garage door into the shop. Her cheeks were rosy. She couldn't stop smiling. Jasper held the bike steady for her to dismount, but with the exception of a grimace as she put her left foot on the ground, she managed herself well.

"Mr. Gifford, I have questions."

"And I have answers, Miss Finch. Fire away."

"If I were to purchase a bike from you, how would . . . how would I load it into my car? A piece of the road from my RV park down to the bike trail is pretty much all gravel."

He nodded. "Yeah, you should avoid riding on loose gravel while your, er, foot is healing and until you're more confident on your bike. As for loading it into your car? This little gem weighs in at just thirty-six pounds. Easy to manage. Take the battery off and it weighs eight pounds less. It also folds in half. What do you drive?"

"A 1951 Ford Custom Country Squire."

"An actual woody? For real? Are you serious?"

"Serious as a heart attack."

Jasper looked to Simon. "Man, I'm in love."

Jasper's laughing declaration irked Simon. "You said she was too old, remember?"

Jasper turned back to Miss Finch and ran into a wall of ice.

"I'm too old for what?"

Jasper flinched. "Uh, pay no mind to that doofus, Miss Finch. And to answer your question about transporting this bike? Open the tailgate of your woody, attach a small pet ramp to the rear of the car, and roll the bike up and in, then lay it down. Small wheels and, like I said, thirty-six pounds or less if you take the battery off first. Easy peasy."

Miss Finch thought a moment. "Excuse me while I make a quick call."

When she returned, she said, "My physical therapist says anything that will get me moving without pain is all right in his book."

She patted the seat of the bike she'd ridden. "Do you have a bike like this in stock?"

"Sure do. Will you be wanting a helmet and mirrors also?"

"Yes, please."

Simon smirked. "I'd testify in court that I just now saw dollar signs flipping over in place of your eyeballs, Jasper."

"Ha-ha. Very funny."

"And I'll expect my usual cut."

Miss Finch and Jasper answered simultaneously: "What?"

———●———

HALF AN HOUR LATER, Simon pulled out of Jasper's lot, a boxed eBike in the bed of his truck along with a rack and an attachable pet basket for the front wheel, plus two sacks containing a new helmet, dry chain lubricant, handlebar mirrors, tools, and other bicycle paraphernalia. A smiling Miss Finch rode in his passenger seat, Pouncer and Hugo on the floor.

Simon definitely preferred a contented Miss Finch to a defeated one.

"Don't know if you are aware, Miss Finch, but Bright Star sits on thirty acres, and much of the property is crisscrossed through the forest with what used to be horse riding trails but are now beautiful walking trails—or, in your case, cycling trails. Most resident sites on the south side of the park have feeder paths that lead to the main trails. Your side of the park, being backed by the creek, doesn't have direct access to the trail system, but you can use the trailhead just across the road from the swimming complex."

"My wild days of riding motocross are far behind me, Fletch. I believe I will stick to smooth pavement from here on in."

"Holy cow! You rode *motocross?*"

"I enjoyed the thrill of it quite early in my youth. I even competed for a few years, first locally and regionally, then in the Women's Motocross Nationals where I earned my riding name, *Sprite.*"

"*Sprite?* That name is all kinda perfect for you. Gotta say, I like it. A lot."

She dropped her chin. "Thank you. I was good, but I was never quite crazy enough to advance to any significant level in the national standings."

"You, never quite crazy *enough?* So you do admit that you *were* crazy to ride motocross, albeit the ordinary, run-of-the-mill crazy?"

"Don't be snide, Fletcher. It does not become you."

"Then tell me you aren't afraid of the few tame dirt trails Bright Star offers?"

"Not afraid, *Mr.* Fletcher. Rather, I choose to exercise the measure of prudence the good Lord gave me and that my age dictates."

She gazed into the distance as she delved further into her memories. "Let me see . . . in 1996—as a largely symbolic gesture since I quit competitive motocross when I hit my thirties—I became a founding member of the Women's Motocross League. It was lovely that women finally had their own league and could make their own rules."

"You astound me, all the things you've done. Nearly every conversation includes 'I once did this' or 'I once did that.' I half expect you to say that you volunteer as a brain surgeon and advise the President on foreign policy in your spare time, or go on about how you were once a test pilot."

"I earned my pilot's license back in 1986, but—"

"Stop already! Next you'll be letting slip that you were admitted to NASA's astronaut program."

"Well, I did train for and applied to—"

"Shut it, lady; I don't want to hear it," Simon growled. "And what was *that?* Are you laughing at me?"

"Why, Fletcher! Would I laugh at your expense?"

He jerked his eyes toward his passenger; Miss Finch, prim and relaxed, had her full attention fixed on the road ahead. But Pouncer, who wouldn't miss an opportunity to hiss at him for all the catnip in Saskatoon, poked her head up from behind Hugo, bared her fangs, and warbled low in her throat.

"You, Little Miss Pouncer, are a charlatan," Simon replied. He bared his teeth and hissed back at her for good measure. Her eyes flashed wide before she ducked her head back into Hugo's protective shadow.

They returned to Miss Finch's car. He helped her down and waited until she drove away to follow her back to Bright Star. He drove directly to Site 1, unloaded the boxes and sacks, and stacked them against her trailer.

"Need help assembling your bike?" he asked.

"I don't believe so. According to Jasper, it's mostly assembled already. What remains is to mount the front wheel, rotate, straighten, and tighten the handlebars, add the bike seat and front rack, and charge the battery. I appreciate your offer, though."

"Well, should you need a hand, give me a call." He remembered something. "Oh. And don't forget to clean the dirt out of your skinned knee before you get too distracted."

She sighed. "Ah, yes. Thank you for the reminder, Fletcher. And please tell Skipper I'll be there to relieve him as soon as I tend to my knee."

"Nope. I'm giving you the day off. Skipper can run the office today."

"I appreciate your kindness, Fletcher."

"Just be sure to get your knee cleaned up before you get too engrossed with your bike."

"Yes. I will." She hesitated. "And thank you for an unexpectedly good morning, the best I've had in a while. To show my appreciation, I'd like to make you dinner."

Simon perked up. "Free food? When and where?"

"Right here. Six o'clock. Don't be late, or I cannot vouch for the condition of your 'free food.'"

The TAHOE
MYSTERIES

CHAPTER 11

SIMON APPEARED AT THE door of Miss Finch's trailer at six o'clock straight up, arriving with the onset of a fine, misting shower. Miss Finch's new bike, assembled and ready to go, leaned against the trailer under the awning where it was sheltered from the rain.

Simon knocked. He bore flowers for his hostess, their blooms carefully folded into several sheets of tissue paper. When she opened the door, he extended the flowers to her with a smile. "If I understand correctly, a lady can never have enough flowers. Am I right?"

With mock acidity, she demanded, "Pray tell, which of the meanings that I might attach to your greeting should I understand to be the correct one? That ladies, in general, can never have enough flowers or that *I* am a lady who can never have enough flowers? And does my agreement with you affect the possibility of your being correct?"

"Swell. If I'd known you'd be serving up a grammar lesson with dinner, I would have gifted you a side of Strunk and White instead of flowers."

She *heh-heh-hehed* under her breath and tucked a wild curl of hair behind her ear. "Well said, Fletcher, and thank you. I do enjoy a fresh-cut bouquet, but only on occasion. Pouncer tends to get a little overly excited at the prospect of shredding flower petals and their leaves."

"Why am I not surprised."

She stepped back, using the narrow countertop to keep from putting her full weight on her left leg. "You had best come inside. I don't believe we can dine comfortably in the rain, although I'm grateful that this shower is likely to bring down the unseasonably high temperatures."

"I, too, am all for a more moderate temperature, but is there actually room for both of us in there?"

"Very witty, Fletcher. I recommend that you take this seat." She pointed to the nearer of two cushioned seats flanking her small table already set with dinnerware for two. "And I caution you not to move about. You are likely to trip me up should you sneeze, cough, or breathe heavily."

He chuckled, stepped inside, and obediently sat, observing the woman's accustomed can of Zero Sugar Cherry Dr. Pepper at her place setting. "So how's your knee doing? Leg stiffen up at all?"

"You were right about bits of finer gravel in my scrape, but I believe the H_2O_2 boiled all of it out. Icing my knee several times this afternoon worked wonders on the swelling too. Not terribly stiff at the moment."

She turned to what was sizzling in a pan atop the stove, the stove being a little two-burner affair.

"Smells good."

"Ordinary pan-fried chicken, I'm afraid, a tad overdone on the outside, but not yet cooked through."

"I love fried chicken."

"As you have not yet tasted mine, you should, perhaps, reserve your accolades."

"And here I expected you to whip out your *Le Cordon Bleu* diploma."

"Sadly, I failed their master course. They said I . . . came up short."

Simon choked on a laugh. "You angling for a Golden Globe in self-deprecation?"

"Why bother? I am already the acknowledged Mistress of Modesty. Now be quiet while I try to salvage our dinner."

Simon snickered but was glad of the opportunity to look around without being too obvious. He'd been wanting to better understand her living arrangements. It helped that he had looked up this Casita model's floorplan. For example, he knew that the rear third of the trailer was supposed to be taken up by a dinette table with bench seats on both sides. The tabletop was designed to drop onto the front edges of both benches. Lay the bench cushions across the tabletop and *presto chango!* Instant double bed.

Neither a table with two bench seats nor a double bed, however, was what he'd glimpsed the evening he'd poked his head into the trailer to retrieve Miss Finch's place settings for three. At present, while seated inside at Miss Finch's invitation, he had time to study what he'd only partially seen.

Instead of the schematic's full-sized dinette, he saw a tabletop cut to half its intended width. He looked more closely and saw that the half-width surface, supported by its two original posts, was closer to the bench on the left than it had been built to be, leaving the half-width table hanging slightly over the bench seat on the left. To what purpose? Apparently, to accommodate the single bed where the bench seat on the right had been widened.

Huh. The table looks to be several inches shorter than factory-built too. And I'm thinking it must be mounted on rails so that she can push the table to a working distance from herself while she's seated on the left-hand bench. Alternatively, she can slide the table all the way to the left as it is at present, giving her plenty of room to get in and out of the bed on the right.

He noted a laptop or tablet tucked into a pocket attached to the back left wall and a small printer on the table. That's when something else caught his eye.

What's that?

The window above the bench on the left was different than the other windows. The glass on one side had been removed and replaced by a dark panel in which was set a smallish door that swung from hinges at the door's top.

Huh. Gotta be a pet door that leads to a pet ramp in her "catio."

A framed photo on the wall near the laptop caught his eye. The black and white image was of a curly-haired child and a noticeably small older man. The girl was turned sideways to the camera, and she stared into the man's face with frank adoration.

"Is that you with your grandfather in that photo?"

"It is."

"You told me earlier that he named you. Would you mind if I bring up the topic of your initials one last time? Merely for the sake of clarity, of course."

"Are you wholly unversed in the concept of boundaries, *Mr.* Fletcher?"

Simon affected a pious air. "Sadly, I'm not as well versed as I should be. After you respond to my invasive questions, would you be so kind as to school me on the subject?"

"I would delight in such a schooling."

Simon half grimaced, half chuckled. "Yikes."

She shook her head. "You are not unlike Hugo with a bone, Simon Fletcher. Since you simply will not leave it be, please get on with it."

"I will, thank you. So, should I pronounce your initials BeeDee?"

"The appropriate pronunciation is *Miss Finch.*"

"Huh. Reminds me of this riddle I know. How about this? If you can solve my riddle, I'll never ask about your name again."

"And if I do not solve it?"

"You tell me your full name."

"Hmph. Might be worth the risk. I warn you, though: I am quite good at riddles."

"I'm willing if you are."

"Very well."

He looked toward her desk. "I require a piece of paper and a pen."

She supplied them and watched through slitted eyes while Simon wrote on the paper,

M R ✶✶ s M R

M No ✶✶ s!

O S A R!

C D E D B D iis?

"What are those?" Miss Finch pointed to the ✶✶s.

"For you to solve."

She picked up the paper and studied it. Minutes passed, and she still studied it . . . although the set of her mouth tightened.

"Give up?"

"No."

"If you can't solve the riddle, you'll have to tell me what your initials stand for."

"I comprehend the nature and scope of our wager, *Mr.* Fletcher."

After another ten minutes, Simon muttered, "I should have set a time limit on your attempt to solve the puzzle."

"Indeed, you should have. As I said, I comprehend the *scope* of our wager . . . so I will, as they say, 'put a pin in this and get back to you.'"

"And when will that be?"

"When I have the solution."

"Cheater!"

"Details are important, and presumption is ever the enemy of truth, Fletcher. We did not agree to a timeline."

Simon grumbled, "Fine! Have it your way."

This should teach me not to take you at face value, lady. You are far more devious than you let on.

He returned to the previous subject. "You said your grandfather was an immigrant. Did he take well to American ways?"

"He did not, at least not initially, and it did not help that my father, contrariwise, chose to fully integrate. It stunned my grandfather when my father fell in love with and married my mother, a white woman of full Irish parentage. His upset did not last long, however. I was told he and my mother learned to love each other. And if any disappointment remained? Grandfather got over it when I was born."

She lifted a brow. "It is, you may comprehend, uncommon for an Asian to have curly hair, so I must credit my wildly wayward locks to my mother, who had a full head of glorious black curls."

"I like them," Simon said, with a grin. "Or maybe I just like how they pester you."

"Why am I not surprised? But back to my family. It wounded my grandfather's heart deeply when my father elected to legally change our Korean family name to an English approximation. My parents were both high school teachers, you see, and they felt strongly that they needed to 'fit in' at their respective schools.

"As a result of the name change, Grandfather tended to overemphasize my Korean heritage, hoping to pass on to me what he could of it. He often looked after me while my parents worked, and I was his willing and doting audience. Thus, as a child at his knee, I gained keen insight into the Korea of his youth."

She hesitated. "We were really quite close."

"I imagine he has passed away by now?"

"Yes. He lived to the vigorous age of ninety-three, although he never seemed to grow old. My parents perished in a car crash when I was but thirteen, and he cared for me until I was of age. He passed away . . . unexpectedly eleven years ago. My last surviving relative."

"I'm sorry for your loss, Miss Finch, and I get it. I have no remaining family ties either. In general conversation, people tend to share their family's doings and notable events. Leaves me with nothing to contribute."

Lord, you know the Corps was my family. It will always be my family! So I'm still wondering why you took my life in a whole other direction. Where's my purpose now, Lord? A little guidance here, even a hint or two, would be appreciated.

Simon's perusal returned to the bed on the right. *Man, that is one very short mattress. Has to be custom made.*

"I don't require the length of a regular twin bed," she said from the stove, "Fifty-four inches may be a snug fit even for me, but it is comfortable enough. Oh. And a friend who manufactures memory foam mattresses made the mattress to my specifications."

"How did you know what I was thinking?" *And what favor did this guy owe you?*

"Your eyes were fixed on my custom office area and my, shall we say, *distinctive* sleeping arrangements."

"Ha! But those are not your trailer's only unique customizations, are they? How, if I may ask, did you come by this curious renovation?"

She put the lid on the frying pan she'd been watching, reduced the heat, and turned toward him. "An old friend owned this relatively new trailer. He had parked it in his back yard and, to his regret, allowed his grandson to live in it."

She made a *tsking* sound. "My friend was ignorant of his grandson's source of income. The young man was cooking meth—right where I am standing, mind you—until the trailer caught fire. They were quite fortunate in that regard, both the young man and my friend. The lab could have easily exploded, killing the grandson, and taking out part of my friend's house.

"Instead, thanks be to God, rather than being explosive, the fire was relatively ordinary in nature, and the young man escaped unscathed. As it was, though, by the time the fire department arrived and put out the fire, much of the trailer's interior was either charred or infused with toxic smoke fumes."

"You took the wreckage off your friend's hands?"

"I thought it quite the deal, actually. He wished the wreckage gone immediately, so I paid him a dollar for the title and had it towed to a small warehouse where I could work on it."

"You did the renovations yourself?"

"The majority. I stripped the trailer down to its bones and refurbished it from stem to stern with assistance and advice from friends who are professionals in the field. New wiring, plumbing, insulation, and inside paneling. New fixtures and appliances."

She opened the microwave and took down a covered dish, "I wanted a trailer light enough to tow with my panel wagon, you see, and I desired certain creature comforts, amenities, and customizations, such as a permanent sleeping nook for myself with ready office space close by. And since I am fond of learning new skills, I enjoyed the remodel process."

"You got everything you wanted?"

She set the covered dish on the table. "I believe so. I wished to retain the dinette as a work station, you see, but I did not care for the idea of folding up the bedding each morning and setting the dinette to rights, then repeating the process in reverse each evening. I mean, what if I wished to take a nap during the day? Making up the bed each time I needed to lie down was a continual bother I did not care to put up with. My customizations did away with that inconvenience."

Simon nodded. "I take your point. Your other customizations interest me too. Tell me about them?"

"Very well. As another essential upgrade, I installed a tankless water heater that provides instant hot water to the kitchen sink and my tiny shower."

"Nice improvement."

"Thank you; I agree. I also did not care for the Casita's unimaginative and blasé white exterior. I prefer to surround myself with a color palette that both delights and soothes."

"I see you matched up the trailer to your woody. Both paint jobs are stunning."

"Thank you again. While planning the design, I chose a color scheme that would harmonize with another customization: solar power. I mounted a number of flexible, 200 watt monocrystalline solar panels atop my trailer's roof. The sultry blues and grays of my custom paint job complement the panels while simultaneously drawing the eye away from the panels and along the sinuous design flowing along the trailer's sides. The panels charge two large batteries—you are sitting on them—and the batteries will run my lights and light appliances should I choose to camp off-grid."

Simon nodded. "Great enhancement."

"I required the addition of a small security system as well. It feeds off its own solar panel when armed."

"Nice."

"Unfortunately, the system only covers my doors and windows. I will look into a perimeter system at some point."

"Good thinking. What about wastewater and sewage?"

"Both upgraded with new pipes and fittings but within the constraints of available space, of course. For example, the whole of my little bathroom's enclosure, including toilet and sink, was designed to serve as the shower stall—with no way to expand it. No matter! While it might present a tight fit for others, it serves me well enough."

Just then, a form pushed through the swinging door over the left-side bench. It landed softly on Miss Finch's desk, then onto the bench seat. The form sat, twitched her tail, and stared hard at Simon, her blue, slightly crossed eyes flashing.

Miss Finch said, "Hello, Pouncer. Yes, we have a guest, so be civil."

"Civil? Is she aware of the term?"

"The preponderance of evidence would not support such a conjecture. However, she does know it is her dinner time."

Hugo poked his nose through the swinging door and uttered his rough bark.

Miss Finch bent over and, perusing her half-height refrigerator, removed two packages. "Yes, it is dinner time, Hugo. You may come in."

Hugo bounced through the swinging door and sat on the bench before Miss Finch's desk alongside Pouncer. He grinned at Simon. Simon grinned back.

Miss Finch set two small plates on the desk before her pets. They waited while she prayed, "Lord, we thank you for this bounty. Amen."

While her pets bent to their dinner, she removed a salad from the fridge and placed it on the table in front of Simon. Then she picked up the frying pan and forked three sorry-looking pieces of chicken onto Simon's plate and one piece onto hers.

"Er, *yum?*" Simon said as he stared at two charred thighs and a singed drumstick.

"This is your fault, you know. You and *your riddle*. In any event, you had better pray a blessing over your chicken, Fletcher, and a potent blessing at that."

"Actually, I'm thinking of calling for the elders of the church and a large carafe of anointing oil."

CHAPTER 12

WEDNESDAY STARTED OUT ON par with the previous day, albeit ten degrees cooler, thanks to the rain they'd received overnight. Simon left Skipper sleeping while he went for his morning run. As he ran, he drank in the fresh air and reveled in the crystal-clear color of the lake nicknamed "Big Blue." The high point of his run, however, was when he heard the repeated tinkling of a bike bell not far behind him, gaining on him quickly.

He waved as a bicycle, Hugo and Pouncer hanging out of its front basket, blew past him, its rider laughing in high hilarity.

"Good for you, Miss Finch!" he said to himself.

He finished his run in decent time and returned to his cabin to shower.

Skipper was still dead to the world as he usually was. He slept on, oblivious, while Simon finished his shower and started breakfast.

The boy had not been pleased to man the office for eight hours straight yesterday, even after hearing that Miss Finch had taken a fall. Assigned to the office until 5:00 p.m., he missed his afternoon hours off and grumbled about it all evening. Simon counted himself fortunate not to have been around to witness Skipper's version of customer service during the day.

Hope none of the residents file a complaint.

"Hey, Skipper, time to get up. We leave for work in ten minutes."

Skipper mumbled a few unintelligible words.

Simon took a deep, calming breath. *Lord, I'm weary of tussling with this kid every morning just to get him moving. Tired of having to cajole him out of bed, of having him ignore me.*

"Skipper, get up."

No response.

"Skipper! Get up. Breakfast is almost ready."

"Don't want to."

"And I don't care. Get up."

"You can't make me."

Simon's tolerance died right there.

He strode to the bunkbeds, grabbed Skipper's arm, and dragged him off the bunk, letting him crash the last couple of feet to the floor. Skipper came up fighting mad, swearing a blue streak. He threw himself at Simon, cursing, punching, kicking.

He never once made contact.

Simon dodged Skipper's flying fists and feet, then shoved the boy backward. Off balance, the kid fell to the floor on his buttocks. He bounced up, determined to pound on Simon.

Simon shoved him again. Hard. This time, Skipper landed on his backside and skidded two feet. Slower this time, Skipper picked himself up.

Simon, hands on his hips, asked, "Are you done?"

"No!"

Skipper threw himself at Simon a third time. Simon feinted left, then the crack of his palm on Skipper's jaw rang through the cabin. Skipper reeled backward, hands on his face, staring in disbelief.

"You can't do that! I-I I'll call the cops on you!"

"Be my guest. It's called self-defense for a reason, kid."

"But why . . . why do you have to be so-so-so mean?"

"Me? Mean? What about you? We have jobs, and you're too lazy to even get yourself out of bed, Skippy. What does that make you?"

"Don't call me Skippy, you-you-you—" Skipper found a gratifying curse word and inserted it.

Simon growled back, "You know what, you spoiled brat? Life with you is like a bowl of cherries—it's *the pits*—and I'm sick of it. Joe and Holly aren't paying me enough to deal with your attitude and lip."

"But you treat me like a kid! You rag on me all day and-and-and call me names!"

"I treat you like a kid? Don't you mean like a baby? That's right. *A baby.* Do I need to change your diaper too?"

Simon studied Skipper and saw something he'd been waiting for.

Hoping for.

The fight in him died. Instead of belligerence, the kid was close to tears.

Maybe he's ready to listen.

Simon yanked one of his two chairs away from the table. "Sit. We need to talk."

"I don't want to."

"*Sit your butt down!*" Simon roared.

Skipper sat. Simon sat. Neither of them spoke.

The eggs on the stove burned.

Simon blew out a breath. Got up. Turned off the burner. Put the smoking skillet in the sink.

The stink of scorched eggs was strong. He opened the cabin door. Smoke and stench wafted away.

He sat again. "Look, Skipper, I have tried many times to treat you like an adult, but it hasn't worked, and frankly? You don't deserve it. I can't treat you like an adult because you're *not* an adult. You're still a child. Do you want to know how I can tell you're still a child?"

"Why bother asking?" Skipper spat at him. "You'll tell me anyway!"

"I'm asking because until you decide to listen, you won't care about what I tell you. I'll ask you once more—do you *want* to know how I can tell that you're a child?"

Skipper kicked his foot against the table's leg. "Whatever."

"Fine. *Whatever*. We'll keep going along like we have been until you decide that you want things to change."

Simon got up, grabbed a couple of granola bars, and tossed one to the boy. "Let's go. We're already late."

Skipper stared at the tabletop. "Wait. I . . . I'll listen."

Simon slowly sat. "Okay. But if you backtalk me again, that's it."

"I *said* I'd listen."

"And there's the lip." He got up. "Come on. We have bathrooms to clean."

"No. Stop. I'm . . . sorry."

Simon sighed. Sat. Drummed his fingers on the table. After a minute he said quietly, "The way I can tell that you're immature is how you react when I remind you of why you're here, why you're under house arrest."

"I do everything you tell me to do, and I do what the stupid judge said I had to do! What more do you expect?"

"Again, it's how you react when I remind you of why you're here."

"I know I blew it. I know why I have to work all summer. I know it already!"

"What you just said? '*I* know I blew it. *I* know why I have to work all summer. *I* know it already.' I, I, I. Everything you said is about *you*, Skipper. See, you only think of yourself. What about the damage you've done to other people? Do you care about that?"

"What damage? What other people?"

Skipper's response was pure victim: all belligerence and blame.

Simon's blood began to heat.

"What other people? You've just made my point, Skipperdoodle."

Skipper jumped to his feet, kicking over his chair. He kicked it again for good measure. "Don't call me that!"

"Why not?"

"Because . . . because it's disrespectful and-and just plain mean!"

Simon got up and slowly moved into Skipper's personal space. "And why should I care how you feel?"

Skipper backed up. Simon stayed with him. Three more steps, and Skipper's back was against the bunkbeds.

Simon loomed over the boy. He repeated, "Why should I care how you feel, Skipper?"

When Skipper didn't answer, Simon added, "Why should I care about your feelings when you don't care about the feelings of anyone else?"

Skipper's mouth trembled. "But . . . I mean, what are you talking about? Whose feelings?"

The pressure inside Simon released.

Finally. Thank you, Lord!

"Your actions matter, Skippy, and your bad behavior affects other people—principally those who love you. Let's start with your mom, shall we?"

Simon saw the barest glimmer of understanding cross the boy's face, so he pressed ahead. "Do you care about *her* feelings, Skipper? Have you any idea how hard her life is without you screwing her over too?"

The boy's lips parted. Nothing came out.

"Your dad didn't just leave *you*, Skipper. He left her too. Can you imagine how that made her feel? How worthless it makes her feel every stinking day? On top of that, your dad left her to raise you on her own. No help, no child support, not even a forwarding address. Well, did she throw in the towel? Does she refuse to get up each morning? Does she call in sick and stay home to eat bon-bons and watch movies? No, she does not.

"Instead, she does her best and works hard, long hours every day to feed you, clothe you, make the car payment, and keep the mortgage paid—and how do you thank her? How do you treat her? How do you repay her for the love and selfless devotion she lavishes on you?"

Simon softened his voice to answer his own questions. "Your thankless attitude and poor choices have deeply wounded your mom, Skipper. Talk about kicking someone in the gut while they're already down! And the worst part of it? You're so self-centered and self-indulged, you're such *a child*, that you don't even see it."

Skipper blinked back tears. "I-I never thought . . . I didn't realize . . ."

"That's right—you don't think! You don't realize! Just like yesterday, you couldn't have cared less that Miss Finch, who is under *zero* obligation to help us, needed a day off. She tripped and fell, skinned her knee really good, *but you don't care.* You never gave her needs a thought just like you never cut your mom any slack, because in your head, *everything is about you.*

"And while we're on the topic of 'all about you,' have you considered how your uncle and aunt feel? Joe and Holly love your mom, and they love you—or they wouldn't have taken responsibility for you this summer. So, how do you repay them? How do you show your appreciation? With a cruddy, selfish attitude, that's how.

"And what about me? Why am *I* strapped with a lazy, rebellious, self-centered child? What did I do to deserve having to put up with you? Have you considered that? So why should any of us care how *you* feel?"

Skipper stared straight ahead, his lower lip caught between his teeth. He shivered once, then began to tremble. The kid's body shook until he folded and slowly sank to the cabin floor, his arms on knees, his head on his arms.

Simon couldn't help but hear the boy's muffled sobs. He placed a gentle hand on Skipper's quivering shoulder, sighed, and closed his eyes.

It's a start, Lord God. I pray this is a new beginning, and I thank you.

THE RIDE INTO WORK was quiet, but to Simon's relief, it wasn't a 'storm's a-brewin'' kind of quiet.

Simon could tell Skipper was thinking. And sorrowing, he hoped.

Lord, please help Skipper today. And please help me? I admit that I'm not doing a bang-up job with this kid. I mean, what do I know about raising kids? Whenever he pushes my buttons, I immediately lose my temper! Just, please . . . help us?

Miss Finch had the office open and a load of towels in the washer when they got to Bright Star. He said good morning, then quietly issued Skipper instructions.

"And when you finish those tasks, come find me. We need to knock down weeds around the buildings and edge the walkways today before we mow the grass tomorrow. I'll show you how to use the string trimmer. You can work alongside me while I run the edger."

Skipper nodded and headed off to do what Simon had asked of him.

Simon found himself praying again. *Lord, please help us.*

MISS FINCH COLLARED Simon after lunch. "Fletcher, I can't help but notice how subdued Skipper is today. Is he all right?"

"He will be. We had a rather blunt heart-to-heart this morning. Perhaps he's reflecting on what we talked about. I'm praying that the Lord will open his eyes. Show him what a pain in the backside he's been. Work a change in him."

"Ah." She thought a long moment. "I wonder. May I ask two favors of you, Fletcher?"

"You're asking me for favors? And here I thought you were in the habit of collecting favors."

"Please. This is serious."

"Sorry. Of course, I'll help. What do you need?"

"First, let me close the office an hour early. Second, after I close the office, please drive me down to Jasper's bike shop."

"Are you having a problem with your bike?"

"Not at all. Just . . . out of the kindness of your heart, do me these favors."

He slowly nodded.

"Thank you."

SIMON AND MISS FINCH returned to Bright Star close to five o'clock with a gleaming emerald green mountain bike in the bed of Simon's truck. The bike was compact and boasted fat, knobby tires suited for riding dirt trails. As they passed the dancing fountains, Miss Finch called the phone she'd loaned to Skipper and put it on speaker.

"Skipper, would you please come to my site?"

"Can it wait, Miss Finch? I'm in the middle of a game with Becka."

"I apologize for interrupting, but I have something for you."

Simon heard Skipper talking aside to the two Gorman teens. "Gotta go do something for Miss Finch."

When he came back on the line, he said, "Be there in a sec, Miss Finch."

"Good man. See you soon."

Simon backed into Miss Finch's site, put the truck in park, and got out. Miss Finch joined him on her driveway.

Simon asked, "What in the world possessed you to buy a bike for Skipper?"

"Mr. and Mrs. Gorman's granddaughters won't be visiting their grandparents every day through the summer, Fletcher. Skipper already spends too much time alone, and he'll be by himself many more days before summer ends. Being alone that much isn't healthy for a growing, developing boy."

"Huh. I hadn't thought about it that way."

"I suppose it's been a minute since you were a boy?"

"Very funny. How does a bike help Skipper?"

"Ah. Well, when you told me about the lovely trails around the park, all of them on Bright Star property, I realized Skipper could hike them without technically breaking his parole. But then I wondered if he might not enjoy riding them even more."

Simon shrugged. "You could be right."

"He might also enjoy riding the Pope-Baldwin Bike Path with me once or twice."

"You think you could pry him out of his bunk to ride with you early in the morning? Ha! I wish you luck with that one."

"But as long as he's with me, it would be permissible for him to ride the trail, am I right?"

"Yes. As long as he remains with you and follows your instructions."

"Also . . . and I hesitate to bring it up, but on the way home from church Sunday, Skipper asked if his new friends from the youth group could come swim here some afternoon."

"I said I'd think about it."

"And have you thought about it?"

Simon had totally spaced Skipper's request. At Miss Finch's gentle reminder, he experienced a guilty little squeeze around his heart.

"I suppose having two friends swim here with him couldn't hurt."

"Skipper spending time with other young men his age? Young men who, according to the women I've spoken to at church, are good, well-behaved boys who have already committed their lives to Christ? Not only will spending time with young friends of such quality not hurt Skipper, I think they may very well help him. And isn't that what his summer probation is really about? You, Joe, and Holly helping Skipper to acknowledge his mistakes while pointing him in a better direction? We mustn't only point out his failings, Fletcher."

Simon ran a hand over his face and rubbed it hard. "All right. All right! You've convinced me. As far as his friends swimming here at Bright Star goes? I can permit it for the present, but Holly will likely nix the whole idea the moment she gets back."

"If the boys do well and cause no problems, perhaps I'll speak to Joe about Skipper and his friends before Joe and Holly return."

"Doing an end run around Holly won't put you in her good graces."

"Holly has good graces? And do I stand any chance of finding myself in them?"

"Ha-ha."

Simon and Miss Finch heard Skipper trotting down the road. The kid turned in at Miss Finch's site and skidded to a stop in front of them.

"Here I am. What did you need, Miss Finch?"

"I believe I said I had something *for* you, Skipper." She eyed Simon, then shifted her gaze momentarily to his truck. He nodded in return.

Skipper squinted at the westward-slanting sun. "I thought you meant you had something for me to do."

"Not at this moment. Rather, I felt that your work for Bright Star deserved a little 'well done,' a small token of appreciation. So . . ."

Simon lifted the bike out of his truck and placed it on the driveway.

Skipper stared at the bike's flashy green finish and blinked stupidly.

"I bought this bike for you, Skipper. Fletcher tells me Bright Star is surrounded by thirty acres of paths and trails through the forest."

"You bought this bike . . . for me?"

"Indeed. Go on. You can touch it. Try it on for size."

"I can show you how to raise and lower the seat," Simon suggested, "if it's not the right height for you."

Skipper still stared. He began to tremble, and his eyes blinked rapidly.

"Now, Skipper, it's all right," Miss Finch murmured. "Your work here has been improving."

But Skipper's head dropped, and his shoulders shook.

Miss Finch's eyes widened. She telegraphed her alarm to Simon, and tipped her head in Skipper's direction.

Simon sighed, moved close to Skipper and, a bit awkwardly, put his arm around the boy's shoulders.

Then the kid lost it.

Sobbing, he blubbered, "I don't deserve anything nice. I-I've been mean and rude and a brat. I'm . . . I'm s-s-s-sorry!"

Simon squeezed Skipper's shoulders a little. "Yeah, you're right, Skipper, and I'm glad to hear you admit your faults. I think . . . I think that admitting that you've been mean, rude, and a brat is a good first step in the right direction."

About then, they heard other footfalls on the road, two individuals jogging toward Miss Finch's site. Moments later, Becka and Melissa Gorman halted at the top of Miss Finch's driveway.

They took in the scene, including Skipper's red, blubbering face, in a glance.

Melissa backed up a step and whispered, "Sorry," but Becka fidgeted, obviously wanting to comfort her friend but feeling awkward about intruding.

"It's all right, girls," Miss Finch said, smiling. "Skipper just got a new bike, and he's so happy that he's a bit . . . overcome."

The girls moved closer and ogled the bike.

"Super cool bike!" Becka said. "But where can Skipper ride it around here other than the road through the park?"

"He can ride all over Bright Star's property," Miss Finch replied. "Thirty acres of forest trails."

"Whoa!" Becka breathed.

Melissa agreed. "Totally!"

The girls looked at each other.

"Do you think Grandpa might buy us bikes?" Melissa asked her sister.

"You might point him to Jasper at Tallac Trail Bikes," Miss Finch murmured. "I believe he rents bikes in addition to selling them."

Skipper was getting himself under control, so Simon, again awkwardly, dropped the arm he'd wrapped around the boy's shoulder.

"Hey, Skipper," Becka said, grinning. "I like your new ride! It's really *bad*."

Miss Finch's lips parted. "It's bad?"

Skipper wiped his face with the tail of his t-shirt. "Bad means cool, Miss Finch." He turned to Becka. "You think so?"

The girls answered simultaneously, "Oh, yeah! Totally wicked!"

A perplexed Miss Finch moved her head slowly side to side; Simon just grinned at her bemusement.

Melissa addressed Skipper. "Maybe we can get our grandpa to rent bikes for us this week and we can ride through the forest together?"

A little smile worked its way onto Skipper's face. "Miss Finch says the woods have acres and acres of trails."

The girls again looked to each other and simultaneously turned on their heels. "We'll be back! Gonna go ask Grandma and Grandpa!"

When they raced off, Skipper put one hesitant hand on his bike. His fingers caressed the glossy, sparkling paint of the bike's top rail.

"Why don't you give that bike a try," Simon suggested.

Skipper glanced up at him. "Can I?"

"Yup. Just as soon as you thank Miss Finch."

Skipper's hand jumped off the bike like it had been scalded. He took two steps toward Miss Finch. "I'm sorry. I didn't mean to be a jerk and not say thank you. Truly."

Miss Finch, a self-satisfied smirk now tugging at her mouth, said, "You are most welcome, Skipper. Do you like it? Does the color suit you?"

"Do I like it?" He again wiped his eyes, then studied the bike from stem to stern. He slowly shook his head. "Nope. I don't like it. *I love it.*"

———————•———————

SKIPPER SPENT THE REST of the evening cruising up and down the road, racing around the circuit, generally having a blast, only surrendering the bike and allowing Simon to lock it up inside the office when Simon threatened not to order enough pizza for the two of them.

During dinner Skipper told Simon that he'd shown off his bike to Mr. and Mrs. Gorman. They had agreed to call Tallac Trail Bikes in the morning to see about renting bikes for Becka and Melissa.

With stars in his eyes and a mouth stuffed with cheesy pizza, he raved, "Miss Finch is the best, isn't she, Fletch? I can't wait until tomorrow afternoon to go explore the trails."

Simon, grinning on the inside, answered, "Yup. Our Miss Finch surely is something else. Just don't shirk your chores tomorrow. If you do them well, I'll cut you some slack and make sure you have several hours to ride the trails afterward."

"Okay, Fletch."

Okay, Fletch?

Did a snowball just land in the hot place and snuff out a couple flames?

CHAPTER 13

THURSDAY, MIDMORNING, FOUND Simon using a long-handled net to fish out whatever had made it into the pools overnight, while Skipper pulled the garbage bags from the pools' various trash bins. The tinkling of dueling bike bells caught their attention. Skipper ran to the wrought iron fence surrounding the swimming complex. Soon his ecstatic hoots—and the fact that he was bouncing up and down—caused Simon to stop what he was doing and go check out what was of such great consequence.

Becka and Melissa, on new bikes, were scribing circle eights on the road bordering the swimming facility. Except for color, their bikes were identical to Skipper's bike. Becka's bike was red; Melissa's was blue.

"You got 'em, you got 'em!" Skipper hollered through the fence rails, hardly able to contain himself.

"Yes, and we can't wait to ride the trails," Becka shouted back, while pointing at the trailhead not far up the road near the office.

Melissa stopped her bike abreast of Skipper. "Come on, let's go, Skipper!"

Simon watched Skipper's joy collapse in on itself. He half expected to see the kid melt down or throw a tantrum, but Skipper surprised him and did neither. The boy swallowed and sucked up his disappointment. Holding his regret inside, he shook his head. "Sorry, Melissa, I can't. Not until this afternoon. Gotta finish my work first."

"Oh." Melissa looked aside. "Okay. Well . . . guess we'll see you then."

She and Becka pedaled away, and Skipper returned his attention to the trash bag he was tying up. Simon watched him closely. The kid didn't cry. Didn't pout, murmur, or complain. Simon heard no grumbled protests.

Yet even with all that in Skipper's favor, a bigger picture of dejection Simon had never seen . . . except maybe when wiry Gunnery Sergeant Barker, age 59, had whipped an arrogant raw recruit during an epic arm wrestling contest. The event took place after the recruit, one Private Jenkins, raised on a farm and already a hulking brute of a man at age nineteen, had bragged nonstop to his fellow recruits about being his community's arm wrestling champion. According to Jenkins, he'd bested every comer in his Tennessee county.

Jenkins declared, furthermore, that he could beat any man on the base.

Gunny Barker, a head shorter than Jenkins, but a bred-in-the-bone Marine who'd cooed "Oorah" as the doc pulled him from his mother's womb, took exception to the boy's bluster and braggadocio. Chest-to-chest with Jenkins, he'd growled, "Challenge accepted."

Nearly the entire base, including the commandant, turned out to witness the competition, with many of the spectators making surreptitious side bets, the odds favoring Private Jenkins. But as the competition began, it soon became clear that, regardless of the size difference between the two men, they were not so unevenly matched. For twenty protracted minutes the two men hung in a stalemate of superior mass vs. unyielding resolve. Unfortunately for Private Jenkins, Gunny Barker had earned his stripes in what that young man lacked: pure, unadulterated tenacity.

Eventually, Jenkins' determination faltered, and Gunny Barker—a colder, more calculating Marine Simon had never met—made his move.

Bottom line? Although Gunny Barker wore his right arm in a sling for a week following the competition, Private Jenkins suffered the taunts of his fellow Marines for months.

Simon frowned. What had brought that memory to the surface? Was it to remind him that Skipper wasn't another lazy, undisciplined, snot-nosed Marine recruit in basic training but rather a young teen in his formative years? And hadn't the boy turned a corner?

What was it Miss Finch had said about Skipper needing good friends?

"Not only will spending time with young friends of such quality not hurt Skipper, I think they may very well help him."

Simon sighed to himself. "If you say so, Miss Finch. What do I know?"

He called out across the family pool, "Hey, Skipper?"

The kid turned, his eyes downcast, lips pressed tightly together. "Almost done with the trash, Fletch. Then I'll get after wiping down the tables and chairs."

Well done, kid, Simon thought.

The next word out of Simon's mouth was, "No."

No? Where did that come from? What are you talking about, Simon Fletcher?

Skipper was clearly confused. "No, Fletch? Did you want me to do something else instead?"

"Uh, no, I'd . . . I'd, uh, like you to take the rest of the day off."

"What?"

"Go ride your bike with Becka and Melissa, but make sure to stay on Bright Star property, you hear me? We need to follow the judge's order to the letter. That means you don't cross any fence lines, got it?"

Skipper slowly nodded, his lower lip quivering. "Y-yes. Got it. Th-thank you, Fletch."

"You're welcome, kid. Take your phone with you so I can reach you if I need to. Understood? Oh. And you can have friends from church over to swim at Bright Star. Just not on the weekends when we have a lot of visitors—and only after you've finished your work that day, of course."

Skipper, vibrating with pent-up excitement, responded, "Yes, *sir!*"

He dropped the trash bag where he stood, yanked open the fence's gate, and galloped down the slope toward the road, shouting after the girls, "Hey Becka! Hey, Melissa! Wait up! I can go with you! Wait for me—gotta grab my bike from the office!"

⁎

THAT EVENING, SIMON and Skipper shared a bucket of fried chicken and a heaping bowl of mashed potatoes with Miss Finch. She provided a side salad and a plate of sliced watermelon.

Skipper ate with gusto, and all he could talk about was how cool riding the dirt trails through the woods had been. As for Miss Finch and Simon? They exchanged small, knowing smiles across her short little table. Neither of them had ever seen Skipper this exuberant.

"Hey, Miss Finch? Becka and Melissa are driving up to Incline Village with their grandparents tomorrow morning, but they said they should be back in the afternoon. Do you want to ride with us around four o'clock after they get back?"

Miss Finch's half-staff eyelids opened wide. "Who, me?"

"Well, you have that cool new bike."

"At my age, I should probably stick to paved trails, Skipper."

"But the dirt trails are nice, you'll see! A couple of little hills and bumps that are fun to jump over, but hardly any rocks or tree roots at all. I mean, yes, a couple of the trails are rough and washed out, and some of the trails have fun little jumps and all, but you can avoid them easily enough. Besides, we mostly ride the easy trails."

He took a bite and kept talking. "Why, there's even a cool little bridge over the creek way west of the RV loop. When we cross the bridge, we can ride on the north side of Bright Star's property too. Got some awesome jumps there—but like I said, you don't have to ride those trails. Anyway, you should at least check it out. I think you'd have a blast with us."

Miss Finch considered his offer. "Is that so? Hmm. Well, perhaps I'll, uh, *check it out*, as you suggest. Who knows? If I don't at least take a look, I may be passing up a rare opportunity to 'have a blast'—and we can't have that, can we?"

"Awesome!"

Simon grinned. "Recalling your motocross days, eh, *Sprite*?"

Miss Finch colored. "Simon Fletcher! I shared that designation and those memories in confidence."

"I don't recollect you asking me to keep our conversation private. In fact, I'm pretty sure you said no such thing."

"Hmph!"

A shocked Skipper blurted, "Motocross? You, Miss Finch?"

"Our Miss Finch raced professionally . . . back in the day."

"No joke? Wow."

Miss Finch had to laugh at Skipper's amazement. "Fletcher means back when we carved our wheels from rocks, Skipper. And, well, truth be told, I do have fond memories of such exploits . . ."

"And muscle memory is forever."

"And yet, sadly, bones are not. No, I won't be riding my bike like a motorcycle any time soon. It's 'nice and easy does it' for me."

"But you'll go with us tomorrow afternoon?" Skipper asked.

She nodded. "As you suggested, I'll 'check it out.'"

———————◆———————

TRUE TO HER WORD, when Skipper, Becka, and Melissa rode up to her site the following afternoon, Miss Finch locked Hugo and Pouncer in their catio, donned her helmet, and followed them to the trailhead on her peewee eBike. Simon, who would relieve Miss Finch of her office duties the last part of the day, wanted to see what would transpire, so he stood at the trailhead as the four-person troupe rolled by.

"Have fun," he told the teens.

"Don't break your neck," he warned Miss Finch.

"Do not talk like an idiot, Fletcher. Easy does it all the way."

"Famous last words," he muttered under his breath.

Simon followed them a couple of yards into the woods to observe. His observations lasted all of two minutes before the kids, screaming like banshees and followed by a more sedate Miss Finch, vanished from Simon's view. He could hear their happy shouts a couple of minutes longer, then nothing, so he returned to the office to wait out the time until he could close the office.

At 5:00 p.m. straight up, he flipped the sign on the office door from Open to Closed and locked the door behind him. That's when he heard the wild and raucous shouts of the kids returning to the trailhead. He hurried through the gate and watched them emerge from the trees.

They were hot, sweaty, liberally coated in dust from the trails, and grinning with ferocious glee.

All four of the riders.

"Wow, that was great!" Skipper enthused.

"I'll say," Becka agreed. "Miss Finch, you are awesome."

"Totally awesome!" Melissa shouted.

Simon frowned. *Awesome?* He gave Miss Finch a closer look.

Dirty, disheveled curls stuck out from under her helmet. She *and* her bike looked like they had passed through a blistering haboob and retained half the sandstorm's dirt and grit. And what was that swelling imprint on her left cheek? Worse yet, she was grinning like nobody's business while *heh-heh-hehing* under her breath.

"What did you do?" he demanded.

She was trying hard to wrangle that smile and stuff it out of sight but failing badly.

"What did she do?" Skipper bragged. "Don't you mean, what *didn't* she do? She did everything. Every bump, every jump, every obstacle—and won every race too!"

"And she only fell one time," Melissa chimed in. "Gosh, I fell off like three times!"

Simon noted the smears of dirt on Melissa's hands, knees, and shoulders.

"Four times!" Becka corrected her. "Me too."

Melissa took over. "Yeah, Miss Finch raced up this hill, see, and caught terrific air. It was splendid!"

"Breathtaking!" Becka raved.

"Right!" Melissa cut back in. "And when she came down, she stuck the landing perfectly, just like a professional motocross racer. But on the rollout, her wheel snagged up on a stupid tree root. She dumped her bike and *smack!* Faceplant!"

Becka enthused, "It was absolutely epic! And she got right back on her bike too."

Skipper was overflowing with pride. "Yup. Miss Finch is gonna have a whopper of a trophy shiner."

"Are you kidding me?" Simon, ready to lambast her but good, wheeled on Miss Finch. "Are you out of your ever-loving mind?"

Through the dirt and dust, she absolutely glowed. The corners of her laughing eyes were crinkled to the max. And she wouldn't stop with that annoying, under-her-breath "heh-heh-heh" thing.

Well, maybe not annoying. Not exactly.

Kinda like it, Simon found himself rationalizing.

He shook his head in disgust. Hands on his hips, he tried to muster up an appropriate chastisement. Couldn't quite get it out.

He sighed. The words wouldn't come.

Finally, he could hold out no longer. A slow grin spread across his face. "Well done, Miss Finch. Well done."

———◆———

ANOTHER WEEKEND ARRIVED, and visitors hosted by Bright Star residents boosted the park's population by half. Traffic through the gate and up and down the road increased, the swimming complex was a hit, barbecues grilled, broiled, and smoked away, and the various game venues, both indoors and outdoors, were in full swing.

The influx of visitors, at least as many as the park had accommodated over Memorial Day weekend, kept the park's crew hopping.

Miss Finch remained glued to the office. She checked guests in and out. She dealt with a revolving door of visitors asking the same list of questions—the answers to most found posted in large letters on the board beside the office door. By the time lunch rolled around, she'd taken to responding with a dry yet just shy of sarcastic, "Please refer to the FAQ board. Yes, the board you passed on your way through the door."

Simon and Skipper delivered loads of firewood; emptied trash cans frequently; scrubbed, sanitized, and stocked the bathrooms in the swimming complex and rec cabin multiple times a day. They also cleaned up following an unfortunate and embarrassing episode inside the kiddie pool enclosure when too much excitement and sugar on the part of the Kinzer's preschool granddaughter resulted in upchuck.

Skipper, when Simon directed him to use paper towels to scoop the mess into a dustpan then dump the dustpan's contents into a toilet and flush them down, suffered a spasm of empathetic gagging instead and raced for the bathroom.

With a sigh, Simon took over.

"Sorry about this," Ray Kinzer apologized.

Irene Kinzer glared at her husband. "I told you not to give Sally all that candy, Ray. It's not healthy to feed children before they get in the water. What will our son say to you when he and our daughter-in-law get back from their jet ski outing? And on top of everything else, you're spoiling Sally rotten."

"Well, she wanted the candy and asked nicely," he muttered. "Besides, I'm not sayin' no to my grandkids. I'm gonna be the good grandpa, their favorite grandpa. Their *epic* grandpa! As for our son? I didn't have all this gray hair before he turned fifteen and lost his hormonal mind. If Sally goes home a spoiled brat, he can consider it payback."

Simon had a sudden burst of insight. *He's describing me and Skipper. I'm not his dad or anything, but boy do I get it. Guess I shouldn't be surprised if I have gray hair by summer's end.*

CHAPTER 14

AS THEY HAD THE PRIOR two Sunday mornings, Simon locked up the office, and he, Skipper, and Miss Finch drove off in Simon's truck to church. After service, they picked a restaurant and ate a quiet lunch together. Simon and Miss Finch looked at each other over the table and exhaled in unison.

"I'm glad a lot of the visitors leave after lunch on Sundays," Simon admitted. "Bright Star weekends are killer."

"Your grasp of the obvious continues to amaze," Miss Finch deadpanned, "By the way, you or Skipper can staff the office this afternoon. I need a nap."

Hearing his name, Skipper looked up. "Can't. Told Zane and Kevin they could come swim this afternoon. I mean, most of the visitors will have gone home by the time we get back after eating, right?"

Simon frowned. "I know I said they could come swim, but I would have liked you to clear the day and time with me first."

Skipper rolled his eyes in dramatic fashion. "You said just not when we have a lot of visitors and that I had to finish my work. Well, you just told us most of the visitors leave early on Sundays, and I know I can finish my chores before Zane and Kevin get to Bright Star. You didn't say I had to clear it with you."

Sighing, Simon nodded. "Okay, I accept that. But in future, please ask before you invite your friends, okay? As a courtesy."

"Yeah, okay."

Skipper went to use the restroom, and Miss Finch eyed Simon.

"I hear you sighing a lot lately."

He rolled his eyes in imitation of Skipper. "Is that better? Keeping after that one kid is aging me prematurely."

"Indeed."

And all was fine . . . until she snickered under her breath.

———————◆———————

ZANE AND KEVIN, SKIPPER'S friends from church, arrived together around three o'clock, driven by Kevin's dad. As required of Bright Star visitors, they checked in at the office. Kevin's dad introduced himself to Simon, who was standing in for Miss Finch while she took her nap.

"Tobias Blevins, Kevin's parental unit," he said, shaking Simon's hand. "Pleasure to meet you."

"Thanks. Simon Fletcher, subbing as Skipper's, uh, parental unit while his aunt and uncle are away. Wow. Parental unit? Haven't heard that phrase in a while."

"Guess that dates us both. Say, Bright Star is a pretty swanky place. I've heard lots of talk and speculation about it. You're sure it's okay with management for the boys to swim in the park's pool?"

"Since I'm management while the owners are away, I can say with confidence that it's approved."

"Ah! Well, thanks a bunch; they're excited to be here."

Simon looked through the window. "I see Skipper knows you've arrived. The gate is open, and he can show you where to park near the pools. Feel free to look around."

"Thanks again. What time should I pick them up?"

Simon thought for a moment. "How about we feed the boys too? Hot dogs over a firepit, maybe a marshmallow roast after?"

"I think the boys would love that."

"Great. Let's say you come for them around eight o'clock? Here's my cell number. The gates will be closed by then. Call me when you get here, and I'll open them for you."

Simon walked out with Blevins, and gave the boys a few simple rules. "Remember that the swimming complex is a shared facility, so be courteous in all you do. No running inside the pool complex's fence, and keep the noise down to a dull roar. Okay?"

"Sure!" Zane and Kevin said together.

"Oh. And Kevin, your dad said it's okay for you boys to stay and have dinner with us. We'll grill some meat and maybe have a marshmallow roast. Zane, why don't you call your folks and ask if you can eat with us too. Sound good?"

All three boys echoed, "Awesome!"

———— ◉ ————

AT FOUR O'CLOCK, Miss Finch, face puffy from her nap, relieved Simon. "Anything I should know about?" she asked.

"Not really. Skipper and his friends are going at it full throttle over at the swim complex. Oh, and I promised to host a weeny and marshmallow roast for them. We'll use the big firepit on the island. Probably eat around six o'clock. You're welcome to join us."

"Thank you, Fletcher. You may count me in."

With a word to the boys to keep on their best behavior, Simon climbed into his truck and headed into town to his preferred grocer. He'd mentally put together a list of food to feed three growing boys. When he left the store—

lighter by nearly sixty bucks—he set two sacks filled with paper plates, napkins, wieners, buns, chips, potato salad, a watermelon, graham crackers, chocolate bars, and marshmallows on the passenger seat and placed a twelve-pack of regular Dr. Pepper for the boys and a twelve-pack of that Zero Sugar Cherry Dr. Pepper Miss Finch preferred on his truck's passenger-side floor.

"Sheesh. Can't believe I'm abetting her addiction," Simon muttered to himself.

When he returned to Bright Star, he drove his truck around the back of the office and piled wood into the truck's bed. After that, he drove to the swim complex, parked, and walked up to the pools. He watched from outside the pool enclosure and found the three boys competing over who could get the highest bounce out of the spring board.

Were they being quiet? About as quiet as a football stadium on Super Bowl Sunday.

But were they having fun? Simon grinned to himself. The boys' raucous laughter was infectious—and he'd never heard Skipper laugh with such abandon.

Guess Miss Finch was right. Having these boys over has got to be good for Skipper.

He opened the gate and stepped inside.

Skipper spied him immediately. "Hey, Fletch! Fletch! Watch this!"

Skipper bounced high on the spring board, then cannonballed into the deep end. A cascade of water drenched Zane and Kevin who were standing to the side on the deck. They shouted their acclamations at Skipper.

"Best one yet, Skip!" Zane called. "You totally got us!"

Simon applauded. "Good one, Skipper!"

He watched the boys for a while, applauding and commenting on each trick they called his attention to, before asking, "Say, are you boys getting hungry?"

"Hungry? I've got a ravenous beast in the pit in my stomach," Kevin declared. "C'mon guys!"

They helped Simon tote the food from his truck to a picnic table near the large firepit, then Simon sent the boys back to get the load of wood out of the bed of his truck. While they were gone, Simon spied Miss Finch coming his way carrying a covered dish. Seeing her slow progress and pained expression, he jogged over and took the dish from her.

"Thank you, Fletcher. My ankle is misbehaving again."

"I'm sorry you're in pain." Simon was in earnest. He found that it hurt him to see her misery.

"I apologize," she immediately added. "I don't mean to whine."

"You don't need to apologize to me." To change the subject, he asked, "Uh, what did you bring us?"

"A small Waldorf salad."

"Oh? And what, exactly, is a Waldorf salad?"

"Chopped apples, celery, grapes, and walnuts. A little whipped cream. Very tasty and lots of crunch."

"Yum!"

Skipper and his friends returned bearing armloads of wood and kindling and were soon engaged in building a conflagration to potentially rival the 2021 Caldor Fire that burned more than a thousand structures and very nearly reached South Lake Tahoe.

Simon stepped in before Bright Star became another wildfire statistic and showed the boys how to use far less wood and kindling and still produce a modest, yet effective blaze on which to roast a couple dozen wieners, before burning down to hot coals perfect for roasting marshmallows. While the fire was building, he sent Skipper to fetch five long-handled wiener-roasting sticks from the rec hall and had Zane and Kevin help him roll a couple of the shorter seating logs close enough to the firepit to cook their dinner.

When Skipper returned from the rec hall, he wasn't alone. "Hey, guys? This is Bryce. His aunt and uncle are staying here. Bryce gets to come visit them off and on through the summer."

Zane and Kevin said "Hey," and "Hi."

Bryce nodded in return, eyeing the preparations for roasting wieners.

Simon asked, "Would you like to join us for dinner, Bryce?"

He brightened immediately. "You bet! Let me call Aunt Gretchen and ask if it's okay."

"Thanks, Fletch," Skipper added. "I was hoping you would invite him, so I brought six of these wienie-roasting sticks."

Bryce's aunt gave her permission, so soon the six of them had skewered one or more wieners and were perched on a log with their sticks hanging over the fire.

"I prefer my wieners a little burned on the outside," Kevin said. "I like the crispy scorched part."

"Yeah, me too," Skipper replied.

When everyone had their wieners cooked the way they wanted them, they gathered around the picnic table where Simon had set out paper plates, condiments, and the rest of the food.

"Yum," Zane murmured around his first bite. "I like this salad."

"Miss Finch brought it."

The other boys echoed Simon's sentiments on her salad—but the bowl the salad came in was empty before it got to the last person: Simon.

"Huh. I've been cheated."

The four boys cracked up at Simon's woebegone face. Bryce, however, held his plate next to Simon's and, using a clean knife, shoveled some of his huge serving of salad onto Simon's plate.

"Sorry about that," he apologized. "Got carried away."

"No worries, Bryce, but thanks."

"Say," Skipper said to Zane and Kevin, "You'll have to bring your bikes here sometime. Me an' two girls I know like to ride our bikes through the woods around Bright Star. See, the park used to be a summer camp with stables and horses, so the woods are full of cool horse trails. We've ridden our bikes on lots of them! Miss Finch too."

Zane and Kevin turned to her in goggle-eyed amazement.

"You ride a bike?"

"As a matter of fact, I do."

"Shoot," Skipper bragged, "Miss Finch used to ride motocross. She even raced professionally. You should see her on those trails—she's a *beast*."

Simon frowned. "Hey, Skip—"

"No, no, it's all right, Fletcher. Skipper meant it as a compliment. By the way, boys, it was while I was racing professionally in my early thirties that I returned to the Lord and committed my whole heart to him."

The four boys stared at Miss Finch. Simon didn't know which had awed them more: that the tiny woman had competed as a pro or her open reference to the Lord.

And now I've got more questions, lady. Lots *of questions.*

"You see," Miss Finch murmured, as though the boys had asked for details, "I loved Jesus while I was growing up. I loved him while I was in school and even when I applied to join the Air Force."

Simon about choked on his third hot dog. "Air Force? You?"

"I *applied.* I was a Civil Air Patrol cadet, California Wing CAP, for three years while in high school. It was my dream to join the real deal, the US Air Force, after I graduated. But all along, whenever I spoke of it, my grandfather would remind me that the Air Force had a minimum height requirement, a requirement that was several inches taller than I was.

"During those first three years in the CAP, I kept praying and believing that I would get a growth spurt. I prayed so much, asking the Lord to make me taller, that even when it didn't happen, I had convinced myself that because of my ardent prayers, the Air Force would make some special exception for me. I truly believed the Lord wanted me to join up. But when I finished high school and applied, my application was rejected—and that is how I felt. Rejected."

She shook her head slowly. "I had to face my disappointment and admit to myself that, even though I had prayed about it, I hadn't asked the Lord if the Air Force was what *he* wanted for me. So, I did the next best thing available to me and continued three more years with the CAP as a senior member."

"Did you learn to fly in the Civil Air Patrol, Miss Finch?" Kevin asked, his question tinged with respect.

"I did, but not as part of my CAP service. See, some CAP pilots are also private flight instructors on the side. After I'd been a senior CAP member for a year, one young instructor, a few years older than me, offered to teach me to fly . . ."

Her voice stuck, making her pause to clear her throat. "To make a long story short, I received my pilot's license shortly after turning twenty, and in the year following, I flew CAP Cessnas on several CAP missions."

Mesmerized, Simon had been listening to Miss Finch as intently as the boys were—right up until she broke off at 'offered to teach me to fly.'

The break in her voice had puzzled and faintly concerned him.

What was that about?

"You said you were riding motocross when you recommitted your life to the Lord?" Zane asked. "What happened before that? Why did you stop following Jesus?"

"Oh . . ."

There it is again.

Miss Finch fidgeted. "I suffered what might be called a crisis of faith, Zane, and went through a rough patch for a number of years. Eventually, however, I found that going through difficulties *without* Jesus is a lot harder than going through them *with* Jesus. He helped me to weather those . . . difficult times and get my walk with him back on track."

Zane and Kevin nodded like they understood, but Bryce seemed bemused.

"My family isn't religious, Miss Finch, so I really don't follow a lot of what you're talking about. I mean, we're spiritual and all, but we don't go to church. Instead, Sundays are family days. In the winter we snow ski; the rest of the year we hike, bike, sail, or scuba dive. Well, at least we did until my folks took their new jobs. They work ten days straight, then get four days off. Right now, we use whatever days off they have available."

"What do you mean by, 'we're spiritual and all?'" Kevin asked, curious.

"We like to commune with nature and the universe. That's why we spend most of our family time outdoors. I don't know much about Jesus or organized religion."

"Join the club," Skipper drawled. "I don't know much about Jesus either. I go to church with Fletch and Miss Finch, and just started going to youth group on Thursdays, but not much of what they say makes sense to me."

Zane and Kevin slid their eyes toward Miss Finch. Simon thought they were silently asking for an assist.

She answered mildly, "Perhaps I can . . . provide some visual clarification? During the period I was away from the Lord, I dealt blackjack in Vegas, and as it turns out, I learned several card shuffling techniques and picked up some card tricks too. Years later, I learned how to talk about

Jesus by using those card tricks. If you'd like, I could demonstrate how I use card tricks to explain Jesus to those who don't know about him."

Skipper answered, "I'd like to see you do some card tricks, Miss Finch."

"Yeah, me too!" Zane said. Kevin and Bryce nodded vigorously.

"Well, I don't have a pack of cards on me. I would have to go back to my trailer to fetch a deck, but I need to go anyway. Hugo and Pouncer will want their dinner."

Simon said, "Why don't you boys tidy up and start roasting marshmallows. I'll walk Miss Finch to her trailer and back. Then she could show us."

"Cool!" Kevin answered.

The boys, as one, started clearing the table. Simon extended a hand to Miss Finch and helped her up from the table's bench.

"Thank you, Fletcher. I do appreciate that the walkways on the island are lit. Nevertheless, strolling about the park at twilight or after dark is not my favorite thing."

Back at her trailer, Miss Finch fed Hugo and Pouncer before digging through one of the overhead bins. "I am certain I have a fresh deck here. Somewhere."

"May I?" Simon's eyes were level with the bin, whereas Miss Finch was feeling around blindly, many inches below the bin.

"These what you're looking for?"

"Yes! Thank you. Now to don a light jacket and place a pen in my left inside jacket pocket."

CHAPTER 15

WHEN THEY RETURNED WITH the cards, Skipper and Kevin had melted chocolate smeared on their mouths, and Zane was trying in vain to wipe a large drip of melted marshmallow off his shirt.

"I see you found the ingredients to make s'mores," Simon laughed.

Zane answered, "Man, are they messy or what?"

"Yeah, but messy *good!*" Bryce laughed, licking his fingers.

"Well, eat all you like, boys. When you're finished, we can gather around the table again so Miss Finch can demonstrate her expertise with cards."

"We're out of chocolate bars," Skipper said, "so we can't keep making s'mores, but we can keep toasting marshmallows."

"I've had enough," Kevin said.

"Yeah, kinda glad the chocolate bars are gone," Zane admitted. "I think if I ate one more *s'more*, I'd barf.

"Yeah. Barf," Bryce agreed, looking slightly queasy.

"Will you show us your card tricks now, Miss Finch?" Skipper asked.

"Happily—if my hands haven't lost their feel for the cards. I'll just warm them up first, shall I?"

Standing at the end of the table, she broke the seal on the box and slid the cards out. She flexed the cards several times, cut the deck in two—one handed—performed an overhand shuffle several times, then did a two-handed riffle-shuffle, ending in a bridge on the tabletop. As she did this again and again, setting a smooth and graceful cadence, the boys scooted closer, watching closely.

With no further fanfare, she changed things up.

"Faro shuffle, ending in a bridge." Holding the cards in her left hand, her right cut the deck and put the two cut packets end to end. She interweaved the two parts perfectly, the ending bridge flowing from her right hand to her left palm.

"Waterfall." She stepped back from the table, lifted the deck in her left hand, bent it nearly in half and dropped her right hand as far below the left as she could reach. The cards streamed from her left hand to her right in mesmerizing precision, much like a real waterfall of gushing water. But she wasn't done. She lifted her right hand and reversed the process, sending the stream of cards down to her left. Over and over she did this, the cards flowing in beautiful symmetry.

"Cascade." First she set up for a Faro shuffle, but she rotated the top packet almost at a right angle to the bottom packet, held both packets in her right hand, and the cards fell one by one, interweaved but at two different angles, into her left hand. She repeated the shuffle several times, her rhythm increasing until the cards seemed to move of their own volition.

"Wowzer . . ." Zane breathed.

"Ready for our lesson?"

The boys nodded in unison.

"Right, then. I'll demonstrate the resurrection of Jesus with this card trick."

She cut the deck and placed one packet at an angle atop the other on the table, forming a cross.

She pointed to the deck. "The Bible tells us that Jesus died on the cross to pay for our sins, *but* that is not the end of the story. Jesus did not remain dead. Rather, he rose from his grave on the third day, triumphing over death, showing us that we, too, can have life eternal by putting our faith in him. His resurrection set us free from the fear of death. If we place our faith and confidence in him, we know we will rise from the grave and live with Jesus forever."

She set the top packet aside, drew the top card off the bottom packet, and held it face forward so her avid audience saw it.

"See, just as Jesus wants to be the king of our hearts, this is our card, the king of hearts."

"Cool!" all four boys said together.

"Now, watch closely," she continued.

Keeping the card face forward, she said, "When Jesus breathed his last, everyone who saw him testified that he died. A Roman soldier even drove a javelin into his side, releasing both blood and serous fluid. This indicated that tip of the javelin had pierced Jesus's pericardium, the sac of water that surrounded his heart. The destruction of Jesus's pericardium is proof that Jesus wasn't 'mostly dead,' but was fully and completely dead."

Startling them all, she abruptly tore the card in half and held up the two pieces. "I've torn this card in half to illustrate Jesus's death."

She placed the halves together and tore *them* in half. "Now I've torn the card in quarters to further demonstrate the finality of Jesus's death."

She fanned the four quarters of the torn card so Simon and the boys could see them. "All the pieces of the card are here where you can see them, just as Jesus' dead body was visible to those who nailed him to the cross, those who watched him suffer, and those who took his dead body down from the cross, wound his body in a burial shroud, placed him in a tomb, and rolled a large stone over the tomb's entrance."

With her finger, she tapped the four pieces together again. "However, Jesus, being the Son of God and filled with the Holy Spirit, would not *stay* dead."

As she reached her right hand into the left side of her jacket, she said, "I'm retrieving a pen to act as a pointer."

She withdrew the pen and held it where everyone could see it, then slowly tapped the four pieces of torn card with it.

"Three mornings later, the power of the Holy Spirit raised Christ from the dead."

She set down the pen and unfolded the torn card . . . only it was no longer torn! Instead, the king of hearts was perfect except for the fold lines.

"What?" Skipper hollered. "How did you do that?"

"Let me see that," Bryce demanded.

Miss Finch handed him the card. All four boys took turns handling the card, assuring themselves that it was *not* torn.

"I have just performed what is called an illusion—and no, I will not show you how I did it. The point of this card trick is to demonstrate that, for those who put their whole hearts in Jesus's hands, *death is also an illusion*, merely a fleeting, transitory state. Those who belong to Christ will, when Jesus returns in the clouds, rise from the dead just as he did, and we will join him forever."

Skipper, thinking hard, asked, "So, when Jesus rose from the dead, was that like, a miracle?"

"Oh, yes," Miss Finch smiled. "Very much so."

"Not sure I believe in miracles," Skipper muttered.

"I do," Miss Finch whispered. "I've seen miracles in my own life, Skipper. Real and true miracles."

Bryce frowned a little. "I've never heard about any of this. You said Jesus died to save us from our sins. What are sins? And what do you mean by putting our faith in Jesus?"

"Sins are the things we do that the Bible tells us are wrong," Miss Finch said softly. She saw that Skipper was also listening intently.

"I'm a good person with a good heart," Bryce said. "My folks tell me that's what is important."

"You've never done anything you knew was wrong?"

"Well . . . I'm not perfect, but I'm *mostly* good."

"Are you as good as God?"

"Dunno. I don't really know much about God."

Miss Finch tapped her chin while she gathered her thoughts. "The Bible tells us that God existed before all things. He is eternal, almighty, all knowing, and holy in all he is and does. He also created the universe—everything we can see and cannot see. He created the earth, the creatures on it, and lastly he created us.

"We are special to God, you see. He made us so that we could know him personally and enjoy his creation. In fact, he created human beings in his image and likeness. That makes us higher than the other creatures he made. Those creatures were made for our enjoyment just as the earth was. God said we were to 'have dominion' over the earth and 'subdue' everything in it. That means we are to have authority over the earth and take care of it, but we are also to use its resources for our good and our enjoyment."

"Huh. My folks say our species is no better than any other species. In fact, they say we're the reason the earth is polluted and stuff."

"Perhaps they haven't heard what the Bible says about God making us in his image, in his likeness."

"Maybe, but what about this sin thing. You were going to tell me."

"Yes. When God made the first two people, Adam and Eve, he put them in a beautiful garden and gave them that garden to enjoy. God said, 'You may eat the fruit of any tree in this garden except the tree in the middle of the garden. Don't eat from that tree, or you will die.' Sadly, they disobeyed God, and since then, all their descendants, including you and me, have inherited a sin nature, that is, a predilection to sin."

"*What* sins?" Bryce demanded. "I'm a good person."

"Have you ever told a lie?"

Bryce colored. "Maybe."

"Have you ever stolen anything?"

"No . . ."

"You don't sound very sure of yourself."

"Well, I took something one time—but I gave it back . . . later."

Miss Finch smiled kindly. "Bryce, if you have told a lie, what does that make you?"

"I'm no liar!"

"I am."

"What?"

"I am a liar. Let me explain. God gave us ten commandments. If we have broken any of those commandments, the Bible tells we have sinned. For example, if you have stolen, you have broken the commandment, 'You shall not steal.' If you've been jealous because someone else has what you want, you've broken the commandment, 'You shall not covet.' And if you've cursed using God's name, you've broken the commandment, 'You shall not take the name of the Lord your God in vain.' If you've disrespected your parents, you've broken the commandment, 'Honor your father and your mother.'"

Bryce's tight expression told it all. "I . . . I was pretty upset when my folks said I have to come here every weekend throughout the summer. I would miss my new friends in Portland."

"How did you treat them when you were upset?"

"I . . . I suppose I was rude."

"You suppose? Don't you know?"

"Yeah, well, I was mad at them."

"Did you disrespect them? Call them names?"

Bryce hedged. "Maybe . . . but I'm a good person! My mom and dad tell me I am!"

"That is a common misconception on their part, Bryce. You see, we are not to measure ourselves by the behaviors of others, saying, 'I'm good because I'm better than that guy' or 'I'm good because I only do wrong things occasionally; my good outweighs my bad.' We are only to measure ourselves by God's expectations. The truth is, all of us are sinners. You. Your parents. Me.

"Is my sin greater than yours? Is your sin less than someone else's? That doesn't matter a whit to God. The real point in God's eyes is that we have all fallen short of *his* standards. And if we look into our hearts, we must acknowledge that we have fantasized about doing wrong things too. Not one of us is innocent—and that is exactly why God sent his Son, Jesus.

Bryce muttered something too low to be heard.

"I'm sorry—did you want to ask something?"

The boy grimaced. "I guess I don't know much about Jesus."

"Jesus is God's Son. He willingly came to earth as a baby. He lived just like us, worked and sweated just like we do, struggled and suffered like we do, and was tempted to do wrong, just like we are tempted to do wrong— with one very great exception: He did not give in to temptation, not even one time. He could have given in, but he chose not to. Why? Because Jesus knew that if he lived a sinless life, his blood and his sacrifice would pay for not just *our* sins, but the sins of the entire world, from the beginning, until now, and into the future. He paid for *all* sins."

Miss Finch looked kindly on the young man and then on Skipper. "He paid for your sins, Bryce, and your sins, Skipper, just like he paid for my sins. Now that you know that Jesus died for you, what will you do about it?"

"What are we supposed to do?" Bryce asked.

Miss Finch smiled. "That is a great question that has a two-part answer. Jesus, in the Gospel of Mark, chapter 1, verse 15, said, *The kingdom of God has come near. Repent and believe the good news!* Repent means to acknowledge your sins, turn away from them, and turn to God. That is the first part. The second part is found in Romans 10, verse 9: *If you declare with your mouth, Jesus is Lord, and believe in your heart that God raised him from the dead, you will be saved.*"

She sat down opposite the two boys and asked, "Bryce? Skipper? Do you want to follow Jesus? Will you pray right now and ask for the Lord to forgive your sins? Do you want to confess that Jesus is your Lord and Savior?"

"I think so," Bryce said, his eyes misting.

"Well, what about my dad?" Skipper asked, anger bubbling to the surface, "What about his sins? He walked out on me and my mom—just got up and left!"

Miss Finch was gentle. She was also firm. "What you need to realize, Skipper, is that when you stand before the Lord, he will not ask you about your father's sins or anyone else's, for that matter. Your meeting with him will be about you and only you. He will, however, already know if you have or have not forgiven your father. In the Gospel according to Matthew, Jesus put it this way,

> *"For if you forgive other people*
> *when they sin against you,*
> *your heavenly Father will also forgive you.*
> *But if you do not forgive others their sins,*
> *your Father will not forgive your sins."*

Skipper looked worried. "So if I don't forgive my dad for walking out on me and my mom, God won't forgive me?"

"Yes. That is correct."

He stared at the tabletop, clearly conflicted . . . until Simon placed his hand on Skipper's back. Skipper tipped his face to Simon, tears in his eyes.

Miss Finch smiled again. "The Lord is quite capable of bringing good men into your life, Skipper, godly men who will help fill the void your father's leaving has left in your heart."

Simon nodded his agreement. "If you choose to forgive your dad and let Jesus deal with him instead, you will no longer have to carry around the pain of his abandonment. Trust me when I say this, Skipper: You will be grateful forever that you forgave your dad."

"Wow," Bryce breathed. "Jesus can do that? Help Skipper get over . . . you know."

"He can do anything," Zane said quietly. "He is God."

"Bryce? Skipper? Would you like to pray with me?"

The two boys looked at each other. They nodded together.

"I realize prayer is new to you. How about I pray aloud, and you repeat after me," Miss Finch asked, "but only if you mean it. Prayer is to be sincere, from our hearts."

"Okay," Bryce said.

"Yeah. Okay," Skipper echoed.

Miss Finch bowed her head. Immediately, everyone else did the same.

"Father, you are God Almighty. I come to you right now and confess that I am a sinner. I turn my back on my sins and turn to Jesus, your Son, the Savior of the world."

Bryce and Skipper repeated her words, Bryce choking up as he spoke.

"Father, I believe that you sent Jesus to die for my sins and wash them away. I believe he died on the cross *for me*. I believe he rose from the dead to give me a new heart."

Skipper was blubbering at this point, but no one paid him any mind . . . because they were busy swiping at their own tears.

"Right now, I declare that Jesus is my Savior and my Lord. Lord Jesus, I give you my heart, my whole heart. I declare that I will follow you all of my life."

". . . I will follow you all my life," Bryce and Skipper repeated.

"Thank you for saving me, Jesus!"

"Yes, thank you," the boys murmured.

The next moments were awkward for Bryce and Skipper, but Zane got up and motioned to Kevin.

"Come on."

Even more awkwardly, Zane hugged Skipper. "I'm really glad for you, Skipper. Did you know because you're a Christian, we are brothers now?"

"Huh?"

"The Bible says we are brothers in Christ."

"I-I've never had a brother."

"Me, neither," Bryce whispered.

Zane, still awkwardly, hugged Bryce. "You're my brother too."

Kevin followed Zane's example. "Brothers, bro."

Without any prompting, the four boys made a tight circle with their arms around each other's shoulders.

"Bros forever," Zane declared.

"Bros forever," Kevin, Skipper, and Bryce repeated.

As they moved apart, uncertain what to do next, Miss Finch broke the ice.

"And just as you are brothers, I am now your sister—albeit your much older sister."

They all laughed and relaxed a bit.

"You know what would be cool, Mr. Fletcher?" Zane asked quietly.

"What's that, Zane?"

"I know it's a big ask and all, but I was just thinking, wouldn't it be cool to have the whole youth group gathered around this firepit?"

Kevin was immediately all in. "Wow, Zane! That's an awesome idea! Everybody would love it, even Pastor Kent. We could sing and Miss Finch could show us card tricks and talk to us again?"

Skipper's face was alight with hope. He turned to Simon to gauge his reaction.

In the twilight, Simon glanced at Miss Finch.

A small smile touched her mouth as she slowly nodded.

Simon scratched the back of his head and exhaled. "Okay. We'll talk to Pastor Kent and figure it out."

The boys busted out in cheers, while Simon breathed a prayer inside.

Wow, Lord, this is great, but I guess I've sorta dug myself a hole into the bargain, because . . . yeah, because Holly. *Lord, would you mind keeping her away another week or so?*

With the boys helping, cleanup was quick. They policed the area, making sure no scrap of paper or food had eluded them. Skipper cleaned and returned the wienie-roasting sticks to the rec hall, and Zane carried their trash to the trash bin. When Simon declared the area satisfactory, the boys trooped toward the gate to wait for Kevin's dad to pick up Kevin and Zane.

Simon and Miss Finch sat at the table a few minutes longer, content to watch the sun sink behind the looming outline of Mount Tallac and several nearby peaks. Situated as close to the mountain's shadow as Bright Star was, darkness came earlier to the park than for people on the lakeshore. Then Simon walked Miss Finch back to her site, carrying her empty salad bowl, so she could focus on where to put her feet. Even so, she clung to one of his sleeves in case she suffered a misstep.

It was when they reached the road and had turned toward Site 1, that a shadowy figure darted out of the bushes and sprang toward them. A sharp hiss from Miss Finch told Simon she was as startled as he was. Without forethought, he stepped in front of the woman while his arm simultaneously swept her behind him . . . until a rough, familiar *yip* made him sigh in relief.

The shadow was Hugo.

Overjoyed, he pranced around them three times. At Miss Finch's command, "Sit, Hugo," he calmed, sat, and stared expectantly up at her.

She bent and patted his head. "But how in the world did you get out of the catio, dear boy?"

"Perhaps you forgot to latch the door after you fed Hugo and Pouncer?"

"No, I distinctly recall latching *and locking* it, and—" She broke off. "Oh, dear! If Hugo is out, that means Pouncer is out, too!"

She hobbled forward as fast as her walking boot would allow, quicker than Simon had believed possible—or wise. Along the way, she called out softly, "Pouncer, darling! Here, kitty, kitty! Come to Mama!"

No sooner had they reached her site and started down the drive, than they heard Pouncer's distressed wail ahead of them. Nearer the catio, Simon saw its door wide open and, atop the catio roof, he caught the gleam of blue eyes.

Miss Finch called again, "Pouncer? Here, kitty!"

Before Miss Finch could react, Pouncer bounded across the catio roof and, with a great leap, landed in Miss Finch's arms. Simon was convinced Pouncer would have knocked Miss Finch on her can if he hadn't been near enough to keep her from going down.

"Goodness, but that was a close one," she breathed. "Thank you, Fletcher."

"No problem. Still doesn't answer the question of how Hugo and Pouncer got out."

As if in answer, a bloodcurdling scream pierced the night. Simon left Miss Finch at a dead run. He sprinted up the drive and down the road, a profusion of keening wails leading the way.

He realized the wails were coming from Site 2 as he came abreast of Mrs. Rickert's driveway.

"Good grief. Her again."

Simon very nearly turned around. In truth, he would have slipped away, but it was too late: She'd seen him.

Mrs. Rickert, weeping copious tears, ran up the drive toward him, arms outstretched. She even managed to "fall into his comforting embrace." Frankly, it was either catch her or step aside and let the woman faceplant on the asphalt . . . which Simon had been seriously tempted to allow.

From where her tears were soaking his work shirt, she wailed, "I'm *so very* glad you heard me, Mr. Fletcher! Please! Help me—that awful cat just attacked me! I-I-I told you he was dangerous, but you would not listen!"

Oh, brother.

"Nope."

She pulled back enough to lift her eyes to his. "What do you mean, *nope? I have scratches up and down my arms!"

"Firstly, *nope*, Miss Finch's cat isn't a 'he.' Pouncer is female."

"What does that matter? *She* attacked me, scarcely a moment ago! See? I'm bleeding!"

"Nope."

She took a step back. Put her hands on her hips. "Mr. Fletcher, if you do not act to evict that woman, I will call the police. And if your inaction forces me to do so, I will have no choice but to demand they put down that-that *wild beast!*"

Simon wasn't cowed by her threats. "Don't you threaten me, lady. Because if you did call the police, then *I* would be forced to tell them that Pouncer was in Miss Finch's arms when you screamed your silly head off—and no one waits until *after* being attacked to start screaming. I'd also tell them you earned those scratches when you unlatched the door to Miss Finch's catio."

He tipped his head to one side. "I wonder . . . do you also happen to have a dog bite? Hugo is quite protective of Pouncer, you know."

She whipped her right arm off her hip and hid it behind her.

"Yeah, that's what I thought. You—again—trespassed on Miss Finch's site and opened the catio. If Hugo bit you, it was while defending his home turf."

"How dare you accuse me of lying!"

"Oh, give it a rest already—and pay attention to what I say next: This is your last warning, Mrs. Rickert. I'm entering every rotten detail of this incident in today's log. Furthermore? We will not have this discussion with you again. The next time you even *mention* Miss Finch's name in my presence, I will serve you with eviction orders so fast your head will spin. Oh—and I will personally haul your RV off Bright Star property within the same hour."

CHAPTER 16

THE FIRST FULL WEEK of June was behind them. Monday, after his run, Simon stopped the maintenance truck at Site 1. "Good morning," he said, walking down the driveway to Miss Finch's trailer. "Making the rounds to replenish residents' firewood after the weekend. Need more?"

"Yes, please. I am nearly out. When the morning air is chilly, I appreciate a fire while having my first soda of the day."

Miss Finch sat under the trailer's awning in her kiddie chair, Pouncer and Hugo sprawled at her feet. He noted the tablet perched on her lap, the ubiquitous can of Zero Sugar Cherry Dr. Pepper in her left hand.

He shuddered. "How can you drink that stuff at the crack of dawn?"

"I really should not," she replied, her tone as dry as burnt toast. "I have read that it may stunt my growth."

"Already did that," he muttered under his breath.

The two Junior Mints sitting astride her nose swiveled his way and bored a hole through him. "Did you say something, *Mr.* Fletcher?"

"Me? Not a word." He placed a palm over his heart, "I am ever vigilant to mind my own business. I never comment on or interfere in the affairs of others."

"*Hmph.* On that point, I believe it was Arthur Baer who said, 'A good neighbor is a fellow who smiles at you over the back fence, but doesn't climb over it.'"

"Consider me smiling. Not climbing," Simon said with a straight face.

"Ah! Hope springs eternal."

"Shall we start over?"

"We? Don't you mean you?"

"Uh, right you are. Here goes: Good morning, Miss Finch, and what a beautiful morning it is."

"Much better, Fletcher."

"I'm still rejoicing over our little campfire meeting last night. Pretty special."

She grinned. "Indeed! I am looking forward to another such encounter. I hope Pastor Kent will approve meeting here some evening soon. I shall be practicing my card tricks with these old hands in preparation."

"Everything you did looked effortless."

"Thank you. It was God's grace in time of need."

"So, what are your plans for this beautiful new day? By the way, I didn't see you out riding this morning."

"Frankly, I was too tired to ride out early today, but as I am finally waking up, I would like the opportunity to ride shortly. Do you think Bright Star's demanding tenants will permit me to open the office a couple of hours late?"

"Skipper does okay spelling you, even as much as he despises being chained to the office. How about I have him open the office this morning? You could relieve him when you've had your ride."

"My, my. You do make free with that poor boy. You don't worry that a visit from Mrs. Rickert might reduce him to mincemeat, do you?"

"Poor boy? When we got him, he was a spoiled, self-centered brat here on court-ordered probation, working for his aunt and uncle through the summer as an alternative to house arrest back home. He's grown some since then, and since he began following Jesus last evening, I believe we'll see more welcome changes. That doesn't mean he couldn't use some toughening up."

"Toughening up courtesy of Mrs. Rickert? Really? I declare, that woman marches by my driveway twice a day, her singular intention for doing so to cast her evil eye on me, my darlings, and my site."

"Seriously? You, afraid of a bully like her?"

"Not afraid, *Mr.* Fletcher, but concerned. She presents as a terribly unhappy individual, and her dislike for me is . . . disturbing. At times her aversion seems to border on the irrational, as though she holds a personal grudge against me, something longer lived than our residence at Bright Star."

"Does she speak to you?"

"More like she speaks *at* me, but I would not care to repeat what she throws in my direction."

"Does she come onto your drive or into your site?"

"Not since last evening."

"To be clear, I have warned her not to set foot in your site without your explicit permission." He huffed his disdain. "I suppose we can't prove it, but if that woman didn't purposefully disregard my warning and release Hugo and Pouncer last evening, just to gin up another complaint against you, I'll eat my hat."

Miss Finch, a gleam in her eye, leaned toward him, "Eat your hat? Hmm. And will that event be available on pay-per-view?"

"You're a million laughs, lady."

She sketched a little bow from her chair. "Thank you, thank you. I'll be here all week."

"Does your act come with a buffet?"

"Only while I'm headlining in Reno, but returning to my concern, I would not wish Mrs. Rickert to browbeat Skipper. He does not deserve to be on the receiving end of that woman's vitriol."

Simon made an exasperated *tsking* noise. "Oh, all right! I'll give Skipper strict instructions to call me if Mrs. Rickert shows her face . . . after which I *might* be unexpectedly delayed five or ten minutes. He can fend for himself that long, right? Should be good customer service practice."

Miss Finch did that under-her-breath *heh-heh-heh* thing that tickled Simon's funny bone.

"I like your plan," she said, "and, yes, a small serving of Mrs. Rickert may be beneficial to the boy as long as he is rescued from a full-course dinner." She gestured toward her adult-sized chair. "Take a seat, if you have the time. I would like to put a few questions to you."

Simon dropped into the larger chair. Miss Finch gestured toward her tablet.

"Do you keep abreast of local news?"

He shrugged. "Occasionally. What's up?"

"The report of a shooting. A young woman, a teen staying at Camp Richardson with her family, was walking her dog on the Pope-Baldwin Bike Path last evening near dusk. An unknown individual shot at her."

"Seriously? Is she all right?"

"The bullet grazed her arm; the report says she'll be fine." Miss Finch's expression was pensive. "Shootings are commonplace in many parts of LA and the Bay Area . . . but up here? What do you know about the crime statistics around the lake, in particular, shootings?"

"We have a few, I suppose. People visit the casinos on the Nevada side of the lake, drink too much, end up in arguments or pick a fight."

"And do they settle their disputes with guns?"

"On the odd occasion, yes. I recall hearing about a different sort of shooting, several years ago now. The incident was initially branded a home invasion. The case was later ruled an intergenerational domestic dispute. One victim, the mother of the perpetrator, died; the second victim, her husband, the perpetrator's stepfather, suffered severe brain damage. Later, he, too, passed away from his injuries."

"Terrible!"

"I agree." He shifted in the chair and shook his head. "The Bible tells us that human beings are created in God's image and likeness. It is what sets us apart from all other aspects of his creation. Unfortunately, these truths, by and large, have gone missing in our present-day American culture."

"Meaning some people place little or no value on human life."

"Bingo. I see many animal lovers esteem their pets or creatures in the wild higher than their next-door neighbors."

She nodded. "Those are difficult feelings to navigate, Fletcher. Hugo and Pouncer are my darlings, and in a very real way, they are my only family. I would be devastated if anything adverse befell either of them."

"I can understand your attachment."

"Thank you. Nevertheless . . . if I had to choose between Hugo or Pouncer and the life of a human being?" She sighed. "No matter how grievous or painful, I would sacrifice my precious children to save even the most reprobate of sinners . . . because is that not what Jesus did for me?"

Simon shook his head. "The Lord set the bar of love impossibly high when Jesus died to save *me*."

They sighed in perfect agreement, then Simon returned to Miss Finch's original question. "So, what was it that interested you in that shooting you found in the news?"

Simon sensed a sudden shift in the woman. She looked away, and when she replied, she seemed indifferent. A hair "off."

"I was merely curious. The article caused me to wonder how common shootings are in the lake area."

She finished her soda and stood up. "Well, I know you have work to do, and now that I am fully awake, I must dress for my ride. Thank you for granting me the extra hours to do so, Fletcher."

"Sure thing, Miss Finch. I'll top off your firewood, then be on my way."

He walked back to the truck, loaded up the wood sling, carried it to her firepit, and stacked the fresh fuel atop the remains of her wood pile. As he walked back to the truck, he saw that she'd gone inside.

Simon hadn't spent more than half his enlistment in the military as an investigator not to have honed his instincts to a razor-sharp edge.

What was her interest in that news report really about?

Because he recognized her parting comment as the dismissal it was.

———◦———

A COUPLE HOURS AFTER Miss Finch returned from her ride, the three of them took their lunch breaks. Miss Finch flipped over the "Closed for Lunch" sign on the door and left to fix her lunch back at her trailer, while Skipper grabbed his bag lunch out of the office fridge and headed off to the game room. That left Simon to himself for an hour.

He, too, pulled his lunch bag out of the office fridge and laid it out on the counter. His stomach gurgled its approval at the spread before it: two sandwiches, some chips, and an apple.

"Man, am I hungry." He was also curious about the questions Miss Finch had asked him that morning.

While he ate, he pulled up the local online news sources on his phone. He scanned through three news sites, read the articles about the shooting, all of them brief, but saw nothing that should have snagged Miss Finch's attention.

Odd. Was her notice of that article mere curiosity as she said? Because I was certain that I caught a whiff of something else.

He was reluctant to quantify what he'd sensed. The woman simply wasn't given to anything remotely related to . . . anxiety. Still, something about their brief exchange bugged him.

He opened a fourth account of the shooting. This one added a family photo that included the young woman, a girl of fourteen, actually. Grouped with her taller parents and siblings, Simon decided that the short, curly haired girl had probably not yet hit her teen growth spurt.

"Nothing remarkable here. Or elsewhere in the news, for that matter."

In fact, Simon's primary interest in the here and now resided in Site 1. The more he thought about her, the more intriguing he found her.

"Truth is, you rather fascinate me, Miss Finch . . . even the way you hold your cards close to your vest, so to speak."

TUESDAY MORNING, Simon's cellphone rang . . . and God blindsided him. The caller ID said it was Holly. Simon steeled himself before he picked up the call.

"Hey, Holly. What's up?"

"Joe's temperature, Simon. They are transporting him back to the hospital for IV antibiotics."

Her voice cracked. "Simon, I feel terrible calling to tell you this, but I cannot return to Bright Star tomorrow. Not until I am certain Joe is out of the woods."

Simon, more relieved than he cared to let on, asked, "Would you like me to pray with you again?"

The words had jumped out as simply and easily as "good morning."

"Please do, Simon. I-I'm a little scared. Joe's surgeon told us that if the hardware they inserted in Joe's leg to pin it ever became infected, they would have to do surgery and take it all out—and that would mean weeks of antibiotics to ensure that the infection is gone, possibly followed by yet another surgery to re-pin his leg!"

"So let's ask the Lord to kill that infection now, okay?"

"But I hate to leave you and . . . Miss Finch in such a lurch!"

"No worries, Hol. We'll muddle through."

He laughed to himself. *When did I start spouting Miss Finch's self-deprecating phrases?*

Then, recalling Sunday evening with Skipper and his friends and the prayer he'd prayed at the end of it, he added, *Lord, am I supposed to be surprised when you answer my prayers? Frankly, right now I'm fairly speechless. Thank you!*

CHAPTER 17

SIMON HUMMED TO HIMSELF as he finished his early morning run along the Pope-Baldwin Bike Path. The weather had moderated so that mornings were again cool and his run refreshing. He grinned as the rider of a bike coming up the trail behind him tinkled her bike bell.

"On your left!" she called.

Miss Finch waved to him as she blew by, her happy face aglow. Hugo and Pouncer, side by side in their basket on the bike's front rack, shared the view ahead.

"See you later!" she called over her shoulder.

Simon knew that Miss Finch had ridden the Pope-Baldwin Bike Path several times now, and since another trail continued east through South Lake Tahoe, she was beginning to explore different ways to extend or vary her ride. He drove home to shower, dress, and get Skipper out the door.

They had just arrived at the park when Miss Finch rode her bike up to the gate's keypad. The gate slid open, and she rode through the park's entrance on her way to her site. She would shower and dress, then open the office at 9:00 a.m.

Simon sent Skipper off to start emptying trash bins and was behind the office, adding wood to the back of the maintenance truck, when, from down the road, he heard Miss Finch's panicked voice scream his name.

"Fletcher! *Fletcher! Help!* Please!"

"Hold on; I'm coming!" he shouted back.

He jumped into the maintenance truck, roared through the gate, took the turn to Site 1 on two wheels, and jumped out at the top of her drive.

The calm, collected Miss Finch he knew was *not* waiting for him when he jogged down the driveway. She held both Pouncer and Hugo in her arms, her grip on them tight enough to make them fuss and squirm. Pouncer howled piteously when she saw Simon. Further, it looked as though Miss Finch had dropped her bike on its side. Her helmet, too, was on the ground, her hair in disarray from yanking it off.

"What is it?"

She pointed her chin at the catio. "Someone's been here, Fletcher! Been in my catio. I feed Hugo and Pouncer twice a day and generally only in my trailer. I even keep their empty bowls inside. Of course, I leave water in the catio all the time, but *someone* left a pile of freshly chopped meat beside their water bowl! And Hugo knows better than to eat anything that doesn't come from my hand—yes, you *know* better, Hugo!"

Hugo ducked his head at the chastisement. He flicked his guilty eyes to the side and refused to look at Simon.

"He ate some of the meat?"

"Apparently he smelled it the moment we rode in, because as soon as I unclipped his harness, he jumped from the basket and went nosing around, looking for it. Well, I saw when he started mouthing something, something that had to be foreign, so I dropped my bike and-and-and *forced* him to spit it out."

"That's good," Simon said, trying to encourage her.

"I picked up the remainder of the meat and the piece from his mouth, but Simon, I'm worried someone poisoned the meat and that while Hugo was chewing the piece I had him spit out, he may have swallowed some of the poison in his saliva!"

A plastic sack dangled from one of the small hands grasping Hugo and Pouncer. Simon gently pried her fingers open, took the sack, and looked inside. He saw chunks of dark, raw meat. He brought the bag close to his nose and sniffed. A faint odor akin to garlic came to him.

"Smells like the meat could be tainted with phosphorus of some kind."

Hugo fixed his pleading eyes on Simon and began to gag. Simon grabbed him from Miss Finch and set him on the grass. Hugo hacked and coughed a couple of times, bringing up mostly water and some undigested bits of what looked like his kibble from breakfast.

With one hand gently patting Hugo's back, Simon squatted and studied the mess. "I don't see any meat, so I don't think he swallowed any of the poisoned stuff, but I want to rinse his mouth. If there's any poisoned residue in his mouth, that's probably why he's gagging."

Miss Finch seemed reluctant to release an increasingly fractious Pouncer, so Simon jogged to his truck, yanked out a couple of unopened water bottles, and trotted back. Sitting on the ground, he pulled Hugo into his lap.

"It's going to be okay, buddy."

Holding Hugo between his knees, he pried open his mouth and, keeping Hugo's teeth apart with his fingers, poured water into Hugo's mouth, immediately turning his head toward the grass so the water would run out. He repeated the process until both bottles were empty.

When he was done, he pulled a trembling Hugo close to his chest.

"It's all right, buddy. We're all done. I'm sorry if I hurt you, but I hope you feel better with that nasty stuff rinsed out of your mouth."

Hugo exhaled and relaxed in Simon's arms.

"I need to get him to a vet, Fletcher," Miss Finch declared.

"Yeah. Let's take my truck. I'll drive you."

"Thank you."

They returned to Bright Star an hour later. The vet at the animal hospital had declared their fast actions—primarily Miss Finch making Hugo spit out the meat he was chewing—had saved the dog from agonizing pain and possible death.

"Good move, rinsing out Hugo's mouth too," he added to Simon. "I think you can take him home. Just keep an eye out for lethargy or further vomiting, especially if the vomitus has blood in it."

"What about the meat?" Miss Finch asked.

The vet dumped the sack's contents onto a plate and looked them over. "This meat has definitely been rolled in some type of powder. Rodent poison containing zinc phosphide, I'd say."

He dumped the meat back into the sack, knotted the sack closed, and put it in the office's medical waste bin.

"This could only have been intentional. Who would do this to you? Who would try to kill your fur babies?"

Miss Finch's face shuttered. "I have my suspicions."

Simon nodded his agreement. "As do I."

<hr>

"I WARNED YOU THAT if you entered Miss Finch's site without invitation, I would evict you from the park." Simon was neither courteous nor professional. He wasn't even trying to be.

"What are you talking about?"

"Someone left poisoned meat inside Miss Finch's catio this morning. Her dog nearly ate some."

Mrs. Rickert patted her perfect hair and huffed. "Probably intended for that vicious cat of hers. And, isn't that interesting? Someone other than me objecting to that nasty animal?"

"Someone other than you?"

"Well, it had to have been someone else, because it couldn't have been me."

"Uh-huh." Simon's eyes narrowed. "Where were you this morning?"

"If you must know, I met a friend for breakfast in town. We lingered over our coffee." She jutted her chin toward her RV. "I probably have the receipt in my purse. Do you care to see it?"

"Most definitely."

"You could at least be civil to me, Mr. Fletcher. I am your customer, after all."

"I'll be civil to you when you start showing basic courtesy to my staff and our other residents."

"Well, I never!" She strutted to her RV, yanked the door open, and disappeared inside. A moment later, she reappeared, a paper fluttering in her hand."

"There. See? I had breakfast at Heidi's."

Heidi's, a longstanding South Lake Tahoe restaurant.

Simon studied the receipt; the time stamp read 8:55 a.m. "This shows when the cashier rang up your check. What time did you arrive?"

"Around seven o'clock or thereabouts. My friend can vouch for me."

"I'll need your friend's name and number. And do you mind if I snap a photo of the receipt?"

"Not in the slightest, if it will get you off my back. In fact, I have about had it with you. How dare you accuse me of something as dirty and low-down as poisoning helpless animals? The nerve!"

Simon said nothing, but he was thinking. *What time did Miss Finch leave Bright Star on her bike? This woman could have watched for Miss Finch to leave, then stopped at Site 1 on her way to breakfast and slipped the meat into the catio. Plenty of wiggle room. But I have no way to prove my suspicions, one way or another.*

All he said was, "Thank you."

He hopped into his truck and returned to Miss Finch's site. Showed her the photo. Her reaction wasn't quite what he expected.

"I see."

"Doesn't mean she didn't do it."

"Doesn't mean she did."

Miss Finch turned to him, distant and indifferent. "Thank you for your help, Mr. Fletcher, but I am certain you have a busy day ahead of you. I won't keep you any longer."

What? Dismissed again?

Something didn't ring true. Not any part of her response sat right with him, and he struggled to keep his temper in check.

———————◆———————

SIMON DROVE BACK TO the office, parked his truck, got out, and slipped on work gloves. He needed to finish loading wood for the residents' firepits before he took lunch. But when he got out of the truck, the anger simmering in his heart came to a boil.

He slammed his fist into his truck's driver's door. When it wasn't enough, he punched it again.

"*Why?* Why does that annoying old woman do that? Twice now! What is up with her? Why does she turn me away with some cold, glib dismissal? What is she hiding?"

Hiding?

Was that it?

"Is Miss Finch hiding something?" He searched through his recent exchanges with her, and decided the question deserved a measure of validation.

"That woman *is* hiding something."

Simon rehearsed everything he knew about Miss Finch, but it didn't amount to all that much. Oh, she put on an unassuming front, but the lady had already surprised and even astonished him a number of times in the two weeks of their acquaintance. She had, in fact, shown a depth of both skill and experience that belied her unpretentious demeanor. Not to mention the seemingly sincere walk with God she professed.

But if she's hiding something, how can I trust her?

Perhaps that was what grated on Simon most. What if Miss Finch was involved in something illegal or nefarious and it came to light? How badly would her hypocrisy injure the young boys with whom she had shared her faith?

Especially Skipper. Lord, please don't let Miss Finch damage Skipper's newfound faith in you!

Simon shook his head. He stood mulling his options for some time before he left the wood pile for the office.

"Time to kick over a couple of rocks. See what crawls out."

CHAPTER 18

"SACRAMENTO PD. DETECTIVE SABATINO speaking."

"Hey, Elonzo. Simon Fletcher here. Yeah, long time, no see, pal. Yup. Too long, I agree."

They chatted a while. Simon told his old Marine buddy about the course he'd taken on facilities management after leaving the service, and Sabatino updated Simon with news on the home front—wife, two kids, and another on the way.

Finally, Sabatino asked, "What's up, Fletch? We haven't talked since I left the Corps five years ago, so I assume you need something. What can I do for you?"

"I'm wondering if you'd be able to run a background check for me. Place I work, we've done our normal credit check, of course, but I'd like a more in-depth look."

"Sorry, but no can do, man, not in these litigious times. Strict department policy: We can only do background checks on bona fide suspects. Any officer caught doing a background check for personal reasons loses their badge. I have a PI acquaintance I can point you to, though. Name is Craig Dinesh. Runs his business out of Thousand Oaks. You call him; he'll run the background check for you. For a price."

"I'll pay," Simon answered.

Sabatino recited a phone number, and Simon wrote it down.

"Thanks, Elonzo. I appreciate it."

"Sure—but a word of caution? Craig is a great investigator; I recommend him because he's the best I know, in fact. You want the goods? He delivers. You want someone found? He'll get it done. Problem to solve? He's like a starving dog with a bone. Won't let it go until he's found the solution. That said, you should also know that Craig is in the biz to make money. *Period.* Talking to him is a lot like walking on fly paper."

"What does that mean?"

"It means Dinesh is a sticky operator running a sticky business. See, the guy is a data broker. He collects info on everyone and everything that comes across his desk. Don't tell him anything you don't want bartered or sold down the road."

"Huh. Good to know."

Simon paused to ponder his friend's words, then added, "So, Elonzo, let's say this Dinesh guy calls you and wants to pump you for information about me."

"Who? Simon Fletcher? Sheesh—I haven't seen that guy in years. Don't know where he is or what he's doing these days."

Simon chuckled. "Perfect."

"Of course, better not to give Dinesh your name in the first place, if you can manage not to. Or give him my name, for that matter."

"I get it. Thanks again, buddy."

They hung up, and Simon paused to consider his next steps. He thought back to his last conversation with Miss Finch and reviewed the glimmer of suspicion—or was it worry?—that had bothered and unsettled him regarding Site 1's intriguing resident. Whatever it was, it had wormed its way into his head.

"You have enough on your plate as it is without setting out on a snipe hunt, Fletch. Your time is stretched too thin to spend any of it chasing down some uncertain gut feeling concerning Miss Finch. Give it up and get back to work!"

Nope. That nagging disquiet wasn't going to let go.

He looked down at his cell, then glanced at Bright Star's office phone. Thought through Sabatino's warning and his advice. Listened to his own instincts. Simon's years in the Corps had taught him not to give away information that wasn't pertinent to his investigation. *Ever.* Sabatino's warning only served to reinforce that habit and add to his caution.

"Layers. Put some space between me and this Dinesh guy."

Nodding to himself, he picked up his phone and pressed the number of Skipper's cheap, prepaid cell, courtesy of Miss Finch.

A clearly agitated Skipper picked up the call. "Lunch isn't over for forty minutes, Fletch, and I'm right in the middle of this epic battle—"

"Not calling to cut short your lunch break, Skipper. Just wanted to let you know I'm headed your way. Need to borrow your phone."

"Why?"

"Doesn't matter why. I'll be there shortly to pick it up."

———— ◆ ————

SIMON HOPPED IN THE maintenance truck and drove around the park to the game room. He snatched up Skipper's phone without interrupting the boy's game and returned to the office. Before he called the number for the Thousand Oaks investigator, however, he opened an app on his phone and logged into his non-custodial crypto currency wallet, one with anonymity that offered a high degree of security. Once logged in, Simon checked his balance. While he had less than a thousand dollars of crypto currency in the wallet, it would be more than enough to pay the fee the PI would charge for a deep background check.

Then, using Skipper's phone, he dialed the number for the Thousand Oaks investigator. A woman answered on the second ring.

"Dinesh Detective Agency, Greta Shiffler speaking."

"Ms. Shiffler, this is Steve Feinstein calling. A friend recommended Mr. Dinesh to me. Is he available for a short conversation?"

"If you don't mind holding, Mr. Feinstein, I'll find out."

"I don't mind."

"Very good. And should Mr. Dinesh be available, I will ask you for a one hundred dollar consultation fee before I put him on the line. Should the consultation go longer than fifteen minutes, the charge will be seventy-five dollars per every succeeding fifteen minutes. Do you agree to these charges?"

"Yes," Simon replied.

"And how would you prefer to pay, Mr. Feinstein?"

"Bitcoin."

"Very good."

Simon sent the money to the address the receptionist gave him. While waiting for the transfer to complete, Simon scratched his jaw and studied what remained on his list of tasks for the day. His own job was challenging enough; squeezing in the work of a second full-time worker was daunting. Nevertheless, the itch in his head concerning Miss Finch was such that he would spend precious minutes of his lunch break not merely to scratch that itch but to end it.

Moments later, another voice came on the line. "Craig Dinesh speaking."

"Mr. Dinesh, Steve Feinstein here."

"What can I do for you, Mr. Feinstein?"

"A fairly simple job, I think, but call me Steve; all my friends do."

"You got it, Steve, and call me Craig, okay? Now, what's the story?"

"Thanks, Craig. I'm looking for deep background on an acquaintance."

"Sure. Can do, Steve." Sabatino quoted him a reasonable price. "Acquaintance's name, please?"

"Last name, Finch. Older woman, small and quiet for the most part. Says she's 62, but she doesn't look it. Don't have a first name, just her initials—"

Dinesh snickered; the snicker bumped up into a chuckle, then erupted into a full-on, out-loud belly laugh. "Dude! Are you seriously asking for background on *BD Finch?* You're asking me to do a deep dive on *her?*"

"Uh, I take it you're already acquainted with the lady?"

Dinesh snort-laughed. "This is too rich for words."

"So you know her."

"Listen, every Californian in the game knows her."

Simon was confused. "The game?" Then his head snapped up. "The game as in the *PI* game?"

"Well, yeah. Didn't you know?"

Simon couldn't remain in his chair. He found himself on his feet, shifting from foot to foot. "Craig, why don't you assume that I know nothing about this woman."

Because clearly I don't.

"Sure, sure, can do, and without pulling her up on the computer, either, seeing as the lady is rather unforgettable. BD Finch—you've got her age right, by the way—calls herself a part-time hobbyist, *a dabbler*, mind you, in private investigations. Whatever she calls herself, she's a California-licensed PI, licensed in Nevada too. And however she downplays her 'hobby'? That old gal is sharper than anyone has a right to be, and she has her fingers in more pies than I can count. You know she's also a recent best-selling author, right?"

"Uh, she may have mentioned that she wrote a book."

Or two.

"A major studio has already snapped up the movie rights for that publication."

What?

"Uh, isn't her book a forensic guide to vehicular accidents? What's so all-fired intriguing about traffic accidents—"

"Look, she calls it a forensics how-to guide, and yes, instructionally, it's a good one. But see, it's the case studies she employed in the guide that shot the book to the pinnacle of the New York Time's Best Sellers list—I'm talking *numero uno*—not to mention top billing on a less-than-desirable list as well."

"I still don't get it. Why in blazes would anyone buy the movie rights to a forensics guide?"

Craig went silent for a minute, but Simon heard the clicking of a keyboard.

"Hey, Craig. You still with me?"

"Sorry. Pulling up details. Did you hear me say Miss Finch's book garnered attention elsewhere than on the New York Times Best Sellers list?"

Simon frowned. "I heard you. What, exactly, does that mean?"

"Yeah, well, we're getting into the weeds here. Filling you in goes beyond a quick call and a full background check. Gotta bill you by the minute if you decide to continue."

"I'm good for it. How about you spit it out?"

Dinesh made a soft *tsking* sound. "Remember you asked for this. Don't shoot the messenger if it takes a while."

"Uh . . . okay." Simon logged into the office computer, signed into his email account, and started drafting an email to himself, inputting the details of his conversation with Craig.

Simon heard Craig swig something, followed by the *clunk* of a coffee mug as it hit the surface of the man's desk.

"See, this guide Finch wrote employs six case studies as its primary teaching tools, six *actual* California vehicular accidents ranging from three to seven years prior to the publication of this book, six cases in which one or more individuals perished. All six cases were duly investigated by California law enforcement per each accident's jurisdiction, and all six cases were subsequently determined to be bona fide, aboveboard accidents resulting in unintentional deaths. With me so far?"

The muscles in Simon's neck tensed with a weird foreboding. "Yup. Please continue."

"Okay. So, Miss Finch's book lays out those six investigations, one at a time. And one at a time, she absolutely shreds the outcomes. She notes where appropriate methodologies were mishandled or misused, points out sloppy, incomplete, or negligent investigative behaviors, and demolishes the resulting determinations. Using accepted forensic investigative procedures herself, she reexamines the evidence and concludes that, in all six cases, the incidents were not accidents at all but planned hits."

Stunned, Simon demanded, "As in homicides?"

Craig snorted. "Is 'planned hits' defined differently where you live?"

"Right. What was I thinking?"

You were thinking about her, *Fletch, how little you actually know about her, and how stupid you feel at the moment. And you let those thoughts distract you. Get your head out of your feelings and stick it back in the game, Marine!*

Oblivious to Simon's agitated state, Craig continued, "Five of the cases had been investigated initially by LAPD, two of the five by West Los Angeles Division, and one each by Pacific, Hollywood, and Van Nuys Divisions, respectively. The sixth and last 'accident' occurred in Sacramento.

"After Finch's book came out, West LA Division was first to reopen their investigations, even though the two accidents occurred ten months apart. The division captain pulled the two cases from traffic and assigned them to experienced homicide detectives under strict oversight. After a reinvestigation by the numbers, taking care to adhere to the exact protocols Finch laid out in her book, they didn't think that either case *quite* added up to her verdicts. Her suppositions aside, however, the reinvestigation clearly found more substance to the cases than the original investigators had reported. However, without clear motives or evidence pointing to presumed suspects, they were reluctant to rule either case a homicide."

"Surely they didn't stop there?"

"Nope. They kept digging until they got their teeth into the two victims' marriages. They found that in both instances, the deceased wives were, prior to their untimely deaths, on the cusp of initiating divorce proceedings. Both husbands were to benefit significantly should their wives pass away prior to petitioning the courts to freeze the joint assets of their marriages. See, now that's what I call motive."

Simon was typing as fast as he could. "You don't say."

"Oh, but I do say. At that juncture, the detectives had to consider whether the husbands knew each other and had planned the hits together. You know, the old 'Hey, you kill my wife, and I'll kill yours, win-win' scenario?

"However, after extensive investigation, the detectives failed to establish a connection between the two husbands and concluded that neither the guys nor their wives knew each other. The couples' work environs and colleagues didn't overlap, they ran in dissimilar social circles, and they lived in different communities, one couple in Pacific Palisades, the other in far north Beverly Glen. As far as the detectives could ascertain, the paths of the two couples had never crossed."

"But?"

"But then the city of Los Angeles, sparing no expense, hired a forensic accountant to dig deeper into the husbands' financials. Man, did that gal charge the city an arm and a leg for her services!"

"And did the city's investment pay off?"

"You have to look at it from the city's perspective. By then, LAPD was drowning in anti-police sentiment and accusations of police corruption. Sure, they were underwater in that regard already, but any expenditure that could prove Finch *wrong* was going to be worth its weight in PR gold—not that proving a negative is easy or even possible. The best LAPD could hope for was to prove her *right* and make some very public arrests with some very public kudos to Finch. In other words, use the transparent results to buy back a little public good will."

Simon was growing impatient. "So, what did the accountant find?"

"Hold your horses. I'm getting to it." Craig took another sip of whatever he was drinking before he went on. "The accountant gal found that the husbands had purchased brand-new, high-end luxury cars a couple of months before their wives died. The men paid outright for their vehicles, and each man gave his car to his wife as a gift, ostensibly implying that his marriage was in good shape or at least in the reconciliation stage."

"Exorbitant gifts for the wives? Nice touch, but let me guess: Neither of the wives was driving her shiny new car when she died?"

"Right you are, Steve. Each husband had dropped his wife's new car at the dealership to track down and fix some annoying and randomly occurring noise—a noise caused, in one instance, by a dozen bits of gravel found rattling around inside the front passenger's door, and in the other case by two screws running around loose inside the dash. The dealerships found and eliminated the problems quickly, but both dealerships reported that the cars were at the dealership for several days before they were ready to be returned to their respective owners."

"And what, in the meantime, did the wives drive?"

"Loaners provided by the dealership that were, subsequently, totaled in terrible and freakish accidents."

"How did these facts escape the first investigations?"

"We must remember that the accidents were separated by ten months. It's only through the forensic accountant's deep dive that their similarities were noted and subsequently investigated."

"And did the grieving husbands, in the light of their wives' deaths, refuse to accept the new cars back? Did they demand a full refund from their respective dealerships, hinting at a possible wrongful death suit since their wives were driving dealership loaners? And were those refunds supplied to the hit man as untraceable payment for services rendered?"

"You'd think so, but nope. The detectives reinvestigating the incidents determined that neither man returned the cars they'd purchased, yet neither did they have them in their possession at the time of the reinvestigation. Apparently, they did have the cars when the coroner signed off on the wives' accidental cause of death. However, later on, at some undetermined point, those costly vehicles just sorta dematerialized. And now, this many years later, neither husband can provide a believable explanation as to where his deceased wife's very pricey car ended up."

"You're saying each husband paid off his wife's killer with a luxury car? Two murders for hire, same MO, and same brilliant money laundering strategy?" Simon muttered. "The setups are too alike not to have been orchestrated by the same contract killer."

"Nailed it. It seems that the husbands, unbeknownst to each other, had hired the same contract killer, a *supposed* professional who was dumb enough to employ identical tactics in both cases. Stupid Criminal Tricks 101, right?"

"Er, right."

"Eventually, one of the husbands cracked and spilled everything he knew, which wasn't all that much. It was enough, however, for the investigators to shine a light on a tentative suspect. Now, hold that thought, because the situation gets much more complicated as things unwind."

While Simon typed notes like a madman, his thoughts were agitating like a washer on its heavy duty cycle. "You don't say."

"You don't act all that surprised, Steve."

"Me, surprised? I'm too flummoxed to be surprised."

Craig chuckled. "Flummoxed? Good one, but we *are* discussing BD Finch, right?"

"Uh, right."

BD Finch. A woman I apparently don't know beans about, not to mention someone I have grossly underestimated. Again and again.

Simon asked, "I assume an arrest was made?"

"You assume wrong. Just as the investigators had a suspect in their sights for the two contract killings? The feds stepped in and spread their umbrella over all six investigations. See, under specified conditions, contract killing is a RICO crime. Now, California may be one of only a few states with its own RICO laws on the books, and very *stiff* RICO laws at that; nevertheless, before LAPD could make an arrest, the feds swooped in and scooped up the investigations."

Simon's hands on the keyboard in front of him slowed as his brain spit out what he knew about RICO crimes. *RICO: Racketeer Influenced and Corrupt Organizations Act. Felony crimes tied to a pattern of criminal activity, activity often associated with organized crime groups.*

Organized crime groups, aka, the Mob.

The Mob?

The Mob.

While Simon shuddered, Craig continued.

"The feds haven't finished their reexaminations of the remaining four cases, but to complicate matters further, the primary suspect in the first two cases, the contract killer hired by the two husbands? That guy eluded capture but then died in a car crash himself several months ago—more's the pity. That incident has made reinvestigating the other cases much more difficult."

"More difficult how?"

"Maybe the more pertinent questions are, why do those cases matter? Why do the feds care? From what I've heard through the grapevine, the feds were hoping to prove that the remaining four cases could be attributed to an offshoot of the Lucchese Family operating in Los Angeles. Furthermore, as you might imagine, looking too intently into one of the Five Families without adequate protection can't be very beneficial to your long-term health."

"You don't say . . ."

Concurrently, Simon's heart shouted, *Oh, dear Lord! What has that woman gotten herself wrapped up in? And why would she intentionally put herself in such jeopardy?*

Craig must have been thinking along the same lines. "Makes a person wonder if your little songbird has a death wish. I mean, she selected and numbered her six case studies with *exquisite* forethought, putting the two relatively easy-to-prove contract hits first. See, she *wanted* to provide law enforcement with a win—a win that would include a viable suspect. Once investigators attributed both crimes to a single suspect, they would have found that Finch laid the groundwork for them to connect the same suspect to the remaining four cases.

"And those four cases? In her guide, she provided proof that they form a web of interconnected hits. Very carefully, and without naming names, she leads the more, shall we say, *discriminating* reader to conclude that all of the supposed accidental deaths were actually mob hits tied not just to the Lucchese Family but, specifically, to its LA *capo*, Don Ettore Massimo."

Simon swallowed hard. "You're saying she wrote her 'forensics guide' to put a blazing spotlight on that crime family and its boss? That was her real reason for writing the book?"

"One can hardly escape such a conclusion, but *why?* What reason motivates her?"

"I have no idea."

Just as I obviously have no idea who BD Finch really is.

"Right, but regardless of her motive, I'm telling you that little woman either has nerves of titanium or she's categorically mental. I mean, she had to know that certain parties would never be fans of her work."

Simon, arriving at the same conclusion, stilled.

"Early on, before the reinvestigations got underway, those unseen parties applied some fairly nasty strong-arm tactics on her."

Simon's mouth went dry. "Exactly what kind of tactics?"

"First salvo? They applied pressure on her, personally, to withdraw her book. Toe their line or else. She responded by hiring a crackerjack security team to protect her, her home, her car, and so on. Must have cost her a small fortune.

"When the Mob didn't get the result they were after, they leaned on her publisher. The publishing company's owners suddenly got all wishy-washy and had their lawyers conjure up legal reasons to yank the guide from the book stores. That, too, did not work.

"Miss Finch must have intuited such a move ahead of time, because she retained the law offices of Novelle & Thompson months before the publishers tried to pull her book. Novelle & Thompson immediately sent the publisher a stern letter threatening a breach of contract suit accompanied by a publicity blitz that would hit the publisher's bottom line hard. That stiffened the publisher's spine. You don't mess with Novelle & Thompson. Everybody knows that."

Riiight. Never heard of them.

"Next, a prominent individual tangentially connected to one of the four case studies, declared he'd been smeared in her book and found guilty by association. The man held a glitzy press conference to announce he was suing her for libel. Novelle & Thompson countersued the same day. They pointed out that Miss Finch focused solely on the errors she'd found in the original investigations and never once named or alluded to a guilty party. Because she let her readers draw their own conclusions, the judge dismissed the libel case. He even awarded Finch damages."

The whirling thoughts in Simon's head leapt into spin cycle. "But the presumed guilty parties from the other four cases in her book? The unmentioned entities?"

"Yeah, like I was saying, I'm afraid only one person could have ordered those hits: Don Massimo, the Lucchese Family's *capo* or boss. I heard he had his people separate Finch from her protection detail and physically corner her—in broad daylight and in public. Told her, quietly but in firm, vivid terms, to pull the book immediately or else. Threatened her six ways from Sunday."

A chill washed over Simon. In the quiet voice that used to instill fear in his interview subjects "back in the day," Simon asked, "Craig, did the grapevine detail the 'or else' part?"

"Well . . . I hear the occasional whisper, you know."

"Anything concrete?"

"Yeah, well, I've heard there might be a bounty . . . and where there's a bounty, 'concrete' often comes into play." Dinesh chuckled. "Sorry about the play on words."

Simon went from icy cold to instant sweat.

Oh, Miss Finch! What have you done? And why? Why?

"So she refused to cave to their demands?"

"BD Finch cave? Not likely. That woman has to have some kind of a further agenda, another objective, even if it's an objective known only to herself. She's using that guide, with its unarticulated yet patently obvious conclusions, as the instrument to pursue and achieve her ends with, if I may say so, little regard for her own safety. Those of us who are watching and paying attention, can't fathom the 'why' behind her plots and maneuvers. Her book certainly gives no reason for her schemes, but we *can* deduce why the police's prime suspect came out of hiding to do a number on her."

"By 'the police's prime suspect' you mean the hit man from the first two cases? He came out of hiding 'to do a number' on her?"

"Well, sure. Didn't you know he tried to take Finch out, sorta like how he took out the two wives?"

"The car crash she was in? You're saying the suspect orchestrated that?"

"Orchestrated? Hardly that classy. No, this time his approach was up-close and very personal. Guy stole a tanker truck and T-boned her."

CHAPTER 19

SIMON STOPPED TYPING AND gripped the edge of the counter with both hands. "The contract killer hit her car with a *tanker truck?*"

"Amazing she survived, right? Lady must live a charmed life. To be frank, that whole scenario was more than amazing; it was downright weird. I heard from an eyewitness that the driver of the tanker truck pointed the front corner of his cab at the driver's side door of the Range Rover she was driving, aiming to crush Finch."

"She was driving a Range Rover?" *Not the woody?*

"Yup. The impact totaled it. The whole incident, except for two very messy autopsies, should have been over right then, but that's where things got weird."

An image of Miss Finch's small form on an autopsy table rose in Simon's head, and he fought to push down a wave of nausea. "You say it got weird?"

"Not only weird, *very* weird. My eyewitness says that just before the truck hit, Finch threw up her left hand. Understandable reflex when a truck is bearing down on you, right? A natural response that shouldn't have made a lick of difference. Except, after the truck cab hit Finch's door, my witness says the cab sorta momentarily rebounded, like it'd run into an invisible wall instead of plowing through the Range Rover.

"How could that happen, you ask? I still haven't figured it out. I mean, the impact was so great that the truck's driver was thrown through his windshield, yet the truck sorta *rebounded?* Something honestly freaky happened there."

Craig sipped again. "Even weirder than that? My witness swears that as the truck rebounded, it shifted right of Finch's vehicle and kept rolling. Concurrently, with Finch's door caved in and the truck driver's body splattered all over her vehicle's hood, that Range Rover kept right on going, sliding out from under the wheels of the truck. Totally implausible, if you ask me."

"I've seen miracles in my own life, Skipper. Real and true miracles."

Simon zoned out while another snippet of a conversation between him and Miss Finch rang in his ears.

"How's the driver faring?"

"How the driver is faring is highly dependent upon the advance reservations he made for his eternal destination . . . He expired on the hood of my car."

Dinesh's voice wrenched Simon back.

"—and what happened to the driverless tanker truck crowns the freakiness factor. The tractor cab had made such a precipitous right-hand turn that it unbalanced its tanker trailer. The trailer tipped onto its side and both tractor and trailer skidded across the intersection to a nearby overpass, where the rig wrapped itself around the pilings supporting said overpass. The tanker exploded and burned, taking out itself, a chunk of the overpass, and a couple of hapless drivers who had the misfortune to be traveling atop the overpass at that moment. What a *mess.*

"Of course, the driver of the tanker was already dead. Died when the impact launched him through the windshield and planted him on the hood of Finch's car."

Simon found his voice. "And Miss Finch?"

"Yeah, you already know that she didn't die, but she didn't escape unscathed either. My witness says that the side of Finch's Range Rover was caved in big time. Took the fire department a fair amount of time to cut her out of the wreckage. I heard they found her left foot pinned under the Range Rover's pedals, pretty much crushed. They hauled her off to a trauma hospital. Then, not long after that, she disappeared."

"What do you mean, she disappeared?"

"Went into hiding is my guess. I mean, wouldn't you in her shoes? Finch remained hospitalized for a week or so while they put her ankle back together. But the day the hospital released her to a rehab facility? *Poof!* Left in a transport vehicle but never arrived at the facility. Didn't go home, either, not that anyone knows of. Just vanished. The university, on the other hand, must have been in some form of communication with her, because they hired a sub to teach her class until she was well enough to resume teaching. But even then, when she relieved the sub? She never showed up in person. Instead, she finished out the semester via teleconference."

"Huh."

"Right? So, as you obviously know, Finch is alive, but I'd say she's keeping on the move, never staying long in one place. See, I dug around, and as far as I've been able to learn, no one has actually seen her in person since she left the hospital—you being the only exception I know of."

Simon heard more slurping on Craig's end of the call. He took the opportunity to ask, "You said you think there's a bounty on Miss Finch. If there is, who put out the contract?"

His question was a temporizing tactic intended to help Simon mine the PI for a few more bits of vital information. At the same time, he kept on his toes, more than a little careful not to give the PI anything in return. Sabatino's warning that Dinesh was "in it for the money," coupled with Dinesh's telling words, "I dug around, and as far as I've been able to learn," had Simon's nervous instincts jangling.

Hey, Craig, why should you be so all-fired interested in Miss Finch's whereabouts? What's in it for you—unless it's the bounty you mentioned?

When Dinesh spoke again, Simon's trained investigator's ear picked up a nuanced inflection on Dinesh's part, a careful, cagey tenor.

"See, Steve, if there *is* bounty on Finch, it wouldn't be too hard to deduce the 'who' part, would it? Finch went a long ways toward exposing the criminal activities of the LA branch of the Lucchese Family to federal scrutiny. That's bad enough in and of itself, but the kicker was how she implicated Don Massimo's son, Antony, in those first two case studies.

"Of course, Tony Massimo always was a headstrong kid, and he may or may not have been moonlighting without the Don's knowledge and permission when he took the contracts for Finch's first two case studies. Nevertheless, he *was* the Don's son. And Tony may very well have been the architect of the other four hits—hits sanctioned by the Don. But whether or not Antony's freelancing put Don Massimo squarely in the fed's bullseye, the young man was still the Don's only son, *and now he's dead*. I think you can figure out the bounty's 'who' part from there, can't you?"

Simon flinched. "You're saying the man driving the tanker truck was this Don Massimo's son?"

"Well, yeah. Didn't I mention that?"

"No, Craig. You didn't."

"Sorry, man; my bad. But that's the point I've been leading up to. As far as the Mob is concerned? The killer of Don Massimo's son is now *Number 1* on *their* hit parade, emphasis on the word 'hit,' and Finch's ranking on the New York Times Best Sellers list notwithstanding." Dinesh laughed at his own witticism.

Simon was reeling from Dinesh's revelations when the hairs on his arms and the back of his neck prickled, stood up, and shouted at him. *The man who T-boned Miss Finch was the Mob boss's son. The mob blames Miss Finch for the death of Don Massimo's son. Now she's at the top of the Mob's enemies list?*

Number 1 . . . with a bullet.

Simon's stomach lurched, and he felt acid boil up and strike the back of his throat.

Craig's next question, asked with far too much nonchalance, brought Simon out of his shock.

"Say, Steve, may I have your address for my records?"

A half dozen alarm bells clanged in the back of Simon's head, but Simon was already playing offense.

Dinesh knows there's a hit out on Miss Finch, he knows who has put that bounty on her head, and based on Elonzo's assessment, Dinesh has likely fixed his heart on earning that bounty. Right now, he's angling to use me *to track her down.*

Not today, bozo.

Simon searched his mind and latched onto the first viable prevarication that came to him. "I've just moved to Reno, Craig. I'm working casino security here and there, staying in a cheap motel until I can afford a more permanent place."

"So you met our little bird in Reno?"

"Yup. She stayed a couple of nights in the room next to mine at the motel I'm in, and we got to chatting. Very pleasant character. Said she was just passing through on her way to Boise."

"And you wanted background on her why?"

Unplanned words poured out of Simon. "She's got this dog, see. Loves him to pieces, but he must have gotten away from her while she was leaving town, because he came nosing around my door last night. I'd like to get him back to her."

"That so." Dinesh's disbelief was palpable.

Simon ignored him. "I'm pressed for time at the moment, Craig, so I'd like settle up with you now."

"Sure. You have a credit card on file with us?"

"Nope. Used Bitcoin to pay the deposit."

Simon could tell Dinesh wasn't pleased.

"I see. The balance owing is $225."

"Let me pull over and send it now."

"You're on the road?"

"Yeah. My girlfriend and I had the day off, so we're out on a road trip. Got Finch's dog with us too, and he's signaling that he needs a bathroom break. I need to pull over before he makes a mess. Thanks again for taking my call."

Without further warning, Simon clicked off the call. He immediately sent the balance he owed Dinesh, then stood staring out the office windows, while he rehearsed the last words of his conversation with the PI.

"So you met our little bird in Reno?"

"Yup. She stayed a couple of nights in the room next to mine at the motel I'm in, and we got to chatting. Very pleasant character. Said she was just passing through on her way to Boise."

"And you wanted background on her why?"

"She's got this dog, see. Loves him to pieces, but he must have gotten away from her while she was leaving town, because he came nosing around my door last night. I'd like to get him back to her."

He shook his head. "Sorry to disappoint you, Craig, but good luck using me to find Miss Finch."

Miss Finch. Not unlike Winston Churchill's assessment of Russia: a riddle, wrapped in a mystery, inside an enigma.

He reread his notes and thought through the details of Miss Finch's life Dinesh had, off the top of his head, poured into Simon's ear. Recalled what Dinesh had said near the end of their conversation.

"Finch remained hospitalized for a week or so while they put her ankle back together. But the day the hospital released her to a rehab facility? Poof! Left in a transport vehicle but never arrived at the facility. Didn't go home, either, not that anyone knows of. Just vanished."

"Vanished, huh? And just how does a person manage to disappear in today's all-seeing, all-knowing digital society? Every breath we take is tracked. For all we know, the government has cameras in our bathrooms."

He recalled the silly joke one of his Marine buddies had told their unit decrying the omniscience of the electronic devices people blindly install in their homes.

"How did that thing go? Oh, yeah."

My wife, Sally, said, "I'm afraid that Big Brother is spying on us!"

I just laughed.

Then Siri laughed, Alexa laughed, and Google laughed.

"Good one, Sally," Alexa added.

"We agree," Siri and Google chimed in.

"Not actually that funny," Simon muttered. "But how did she manage it? How did she vanish entirely for months after her accident then suddenly pop up at Bright Star, hiding from bounty hunters, yet living here in plain sight?"

He mused aloud, "She had to have made copious plans ahead of time, because people don't drop off the face of the earth without preparation."

He opened Bright Star's accounting program. Clicked into Miss Finch's account. Scrolled to her payment. The program returned the line item . . . and a screen shot of an electronic funds transfer.

Simon stared at the image. The payment hadn't come from Miss Finch's personal or business accounts; the money was transferred to Bright Star out of an account bearing the name Yeon Family Trust, a transfer on which Miss Finch's name was nowhere to be found.

He toggled to a browser and typed "meaning of Yeon." The query came back with Korean surname meaning "swallow bird."

"It wounded my grandfather's heart deeply when my father elected to legally change our Korean family name to an English approximation."

He nodded to himself. "Finch. Not the precise English equivalent of swallow bird, but close enough."

Miss Finch's payment to Bright Star had come out of a trust fund bearing her grandfather's name. His brow furrowed as he tried to recall something else she'd mentioned the day he'd met her, some comment about having lost her phone and having a new cell number.

"Why would she need a new number if she lost her phone? She could have easily transferred her old number to her new phone."

To himself, he muttered, "Let's add it up, shall we? In addition to paying for a three-month site at Bright Star, a site with no utilities in her name, she got herself a new number, a new phone, and keeps a couple of burners in reserve, just in case. She likely took a lump cash payout from the same account too. In fact, I'd lay money that all her expenditures are, no doubt, funded through her grandfather's trust, an income source not publicly connected to her."

Another thought hit him. *What about her car? She had a Range Rover that Don Ettore Massimo's son totaled trying to take her out, so she needed another ride. But surely that woody would stick out like a sore thumb . . . unless its paint job blended in with a sweet little travel trailer.*

"When she bought her friend's burned-out Casita, didn't she say she had someone haul it to a warehouse? Yeah . . . a warehouse in which she stripped that trailer down and rebuilt it from the frame up."

Another thought bloomed in his head. "Why, you sneaky little *sprite*, you! You knew your book would paint a target on you, so you had plans to disappear all along, didn't you? Bet you bought that woody and parked it in your warehouse for the same kind of treatment you gave your trailer, with plans to bug out and hide off grid when it became necessary."

He laughed under his breath. "It's why you showed up in a vintage car devoid of GPS tracking, recently restored and repainted. Why, I'd wager my next paycheck that the woody and your trailer are both licensed through your grandfather's trust too. It's why you booked your site at Bright Star months ago and why, when Holly tried to renege on your contract, you held onto your spot here with the jaws of a bulldog! In fact, I wouldn't have put it past you to have found a means to change out the woody's VIN—except cars didn't have standardized VINs back in 1950s."

He wiped his perspiring face. "Point is, Miss Finch, you prepared, step by meticulous step, a plan to skip off the grid. So, why didn't you obtain a false identity as part of your preparations? Was it because you believed the feds would arrest young Massimo soon enough and that the feds would be quick to take down the Lucchese Family's Los Angeles boss and organization? But, regardless of all your planning, you had no means of foreseeing the truck that rammed your car and put you in the hospital, did you?"

Simon stared out a window, lost in thought. *She had to have been terrified that week she was hospitalized, unable to even get out of bed under her own steam, let alone protect herself. Perhaps she had that security company assign guards to stand post outside her door until she was able to put her plans into motion and disappear. She just didn't figure on me bumbling about, digging into her background . . . and coming within a hair's breadth of revealing her location to those who would come after her.*

Sabatino's word of caution concerning Craig Dinesh had been spot on. Furthermore, Simon's instincts had pinged a warning repeatedly as he and Craig talked. Or had it been the Holy Spirit prompting him not to use his own cell or Bright Star's office phone to call Dinesh? To, instead, borrow Skipper's phone?

Dinesh, you probably have at your fingertips a hundred methods of finding people who don't want to be found. And right now, you probably have every one of those means focused on me, trying to figure out who I really am and where I called from. But, thanks be to the grace of God, if you're looking in Reno, Nevada, you'll never find me or, by association, Miss Finch.

Simon shivered and shook his head. *I might have killed her.*

"Lord, in my ignorance, I came *that close* to giving up Miss Finch's hiding place to her enemies."

Then it hit him. "Dinesh probably tried to trace Skipper's phone while we were talking. It's an unlisted number, but still . . ."

Simon bent a paperclip and used its end to spring open the sim card slot in the cheap phone Miss Finch had loaned to Skipper. He pulled the card and snapped it in two. "I owe you a new sim card, Miss Finch. I'll drive into town and pick one up today."

And now I need to come clean to her. Need to warn her about the bounty on her head.

"You are in one big heap of trouble, lady," Simon hissed under his breath.

CHAPTER 20

SHE WAS BENT OVER her firepit, feeding kindling to a small flame when Simon returned from South Lake Tahoe. He pulled into her driveway and strode her way, a new prepaid phone in hand, because it had been easier to buy a new phone than a pre-paid sim card.

She didn't miss the hardened expression on his face as he approached. "What is it?"

"We need to talk." He glanced around. "Privately."

Her demeanor shifted to match his, as if she intuited that Simon had uncovered her secrets. "Very well. Inside."

She used a poker to spread out the fuel in the pit and put out the fire, then led the way into to her trailer. She gestured to the near seat at her little table. "Sit. Tea?"

With a last look around outside, Simon closed the trailer door. "May as well. Thanks."

She filled an electric kettle with water and plugged it in. Neither one of them spoke as the water heated. Instead of sitting with Simon, she busied herself around her desk and bed area. After a few minutes, Simon realized what she was doing.

Packing up.

"You're leaving?"

"If you know why I'm here, then you know why I need to go."

"I think—I'm fairly confident—that, except to me and the other Bright Star residents, your whereabouts remain unknown to those hunting you."

"Would you wager your life on 'fairly confident'?"

The kettle whistled; she added hot water and a tea strainer to both mugs, then returned to folding up her bedding while the tea was steeping.

Her actions agitated Simon. "Would you sit down, please? We need to talk."

She sighed. "Very well. Honey for your tea?"

"Yes, please."

Over two cups of tea, Simon rehearsed the information he'd found out and how he'd uncovered it . . . after which he apologized. Profusely.

"It never occurred to me that initiating a simple background inquiry might put you in danger."

"Ironically, I could have pulled that background check myself," she replied tonelessly. "Licensed PI in two states—remember? I have resources at my fingertips."

"That would have required hindsight on my part—and I'm not big on prognostication."

She sighed again. "Craig Dinesh, hmm? I know of him, of course. The man has a reputation. Tenacious and a known money-grubber."

"Great," Simon muttered. "Like I said, I gave him a fake name, told him I lived in Reno, that I met you while you were passing through on your way east. Afterward, I removed the sim card from the phone you loaned Skipper. Dinesh has nothing . . . and by the way," he slid the new phone across the table, "I bought you another prepaid cell to replace the one Skipper's been using."

She pushed it back to him. "If Dinesh had the time and means to triangulate Skipper's cell signal, he knows at a minimum that your call came from this end of the lake. It gives him an area to search, and that is not *nothing*."

"I presumed as much, so I told him my girlfriend and I were on a day trip, visiting the lake."

Her laugh was tinged with mockery. "Did you, now? So because you told him you live in Reno, you figure he will scour that city? Just what do you think he will do when that search comes up empty?" Her voice took on an edge. "Oh! I know! He will send scouts *here* to sniff around the lake communities."

"I suppose that's conceivable, but the population around Tahoe explodes after Memorial Day—thousands of tourists coming and going. It's not likely that Dinesh would catch even a whiff of you. You pay cash for everything, except . . ." Simon stopped. "Except you used a card to buy your bike. Please tell me that card was registered to the Yeon Family Trust."

"Very good, *Mr.* Fletcher," she sneered. "And just how did you stumble on my family's trust?"

"You paid your Bright Star fees with an electronic funds transfer from the trust."

She exhaled. "Oh. Yes, that's right. It is extremely unlikely anyone looking for me would be able to connect that trust to me. I suppose . . . I suppose I am as safe here as anywhere . . . for the time being."

"But you did think whoever shot at that teen down on the Pope-Baldwin Bike Path mistook her for you."

"I had to at least consider the possibility. After all? A short female with curly dark hair walking a small dog? The commonalities were too specific, too close for comfort. That said, I acknowledge that my concern was misplaced . . . and I admit to being a tad on the skittish side."

"You keep right on being skittish, Miss Finch. Until Dinesh is satisfied that you're not hiding somewhere around this lake, he or one of his sniffers could be searching nearby. And on a related note, Dinesh can't be the only person angling for that bounty. If he heads this way himself, another bounty hunter might follow him."

She nodded. "True."

Simon took a breath. "Look, Miss Finch, for the present, I want to keep you sequestered within Bright Star's perimeter. I will keep the park gate closed during the day too, forcing the residents to key in their code to get in or out—until those seeking you come up empty and leave the lake area."

She reddened. "Oh? And how will we know when they 'come up empty and leave the lake area?' Will the Bat-Signal fill the night sky? Or will an angel appear to us in a dream to announce King Herod's death? Just how will we know when I am safe?"

"Don't get all snarky on me. This is serious."

"Serious? I know how serious it is, Fletcher. Serious enough for me to clear out of here *right now* and make a run for it."

Simon grimaced inside. Miss Finch had vaulted from a tad skittish straight to steam shooting out of her ears.

"You hang on there a blessed second or two, lady! Think it through with me, okay? Let's say, as of this moment, that you're off Bright Star's payroll. You haven't received a paycheck from us yet, anyway, so let's plug that leak right now. I'll change your status in our system, log you as a contractor instead of an employee. I can pay you in cash too, as long as we receive a receipt from you and record the amount. Or, conversely, we can pay a check into your family's trust. Better yet, if you're not in immediate need of funds, we can wait until a later date to pay what we owe you."

She bristled and folded her arms across her chest.

Simon kept going. "For the next couple of weeks, you stay clear of the office but keep yourself within the park's fence line. I'll have Skipper staff the office, and I'll coach him on how to handle inquiries should anyone call or show up at the office door asking about you."

Her mask of belligerence cracked. "But that means I won't be able to ride my bike . . ."

"You can ride the trails inside the property line . . . but I would prefer it if someone goes with you."

He took pity on her woebegone expression and reached across the table. Put his hand on hers.

"Look, Miss Finch. I get how unnerving this must be, but it has to be a temporary setback, right? And to err on the safe side, I would like to camp out in your site for a while, say a week or two . . . on the off chance you should receive nocturnal visitors."

He rushed on before she could respond, asking, "Do you own a sidearm?"

She nodded. "Concealed carry license in both California and Nevada."

"Good. Me too. Don't go anywhere from now on without your weapon. I'll talk to Skipper as soon as I leave here, then I'll grab my tent and sleeping bag and whatever else I need. I'll keep my gear in the office and bring it over just before dark."

"How will you explain all these secretive actions to Skipper?"

Simon thought for a moment. "I'll speak to him man to man. Without providing too many details, I'll impress upon him the importance of following my instructions. He'll take my warnings seriously." He smiled a little. "In case you haven't noticed, Miss Finch, Skipper has become quite fond of you."

She shrugged. "Perhaps."

"No, definitely. He will do what I ask of him. See, I think that kid would take a beating to keep you safe."

"I don't want that!"

"Don't worry. I've given tough orders to young men most of my adult life, even in combat. Skipper is smart; he will do well."

He thought for a moment. "Perhaps I'll sleep inside the catio."

"My, won't Pouncer love that! You will wake in the night with her either making biscuits on your face or shredding it. Her choice."

"Er, behind the catio, then."

"And Skipper? Will you leave him alone at night in your cabin?"

"Crud. I suppose . . . where I sleep, he sleeps."

"I am *not* hosting a slumber party, *Mr.* Fletcher!"

"Okay, okay! You don't need to get all testy with me. I'll bring my tent, pitch it behind the catio, and share it with Skipper."

"Oh, yes. I cannot wait to witness Skipper's delight."

"Lady, I've got one nerve left, and you're standing on it."

She snickered.

He glared. "Glad I can humor you."

Then another thought distracted him. "Say, when you told me about your accident, you said that you couldn't get your surgeon to take your ongoing ankle pain seriously. And before you bought your bike, you called your physical therapist to get his blessing. If you fled LA instead of checking in to the rehabilitation center, how did you communicate with your doctor and therapist without leaving a trail?"

She sniffed. "I was in no shape to drive myself when I left the hospital. A dear friend helped me flee LA and reemerge in San Diego on the QT. The same friend arranged my follow-up care with a discreet surgeon, a doctor who helps survivors of domestic abuse hide their whereabouts from their abusers. He and his staff are experts in faking patient records for the safety of their patients in hiding. His office manager logged me into his practice under an assumed name and allowed me to pay in cash for his services. Unfortunately, while that doctor's practice has in-house physical therapists, the surgeon himself is not an ankle specialist and could not determine what to do to help me."

"Couldn't he have referred you to an ankle specialist?"

"Of course, but for my own security, I was disinclined to seek a second opinion. You see, a different doctor would have required that I show ID and proof of insurance and sign a request to obtain my medical records from my initial surgeon, and those are all under my real name. Since I could not take such a risk, I have remained under the less-than-optimum care of my discreet doctor."

She exhaled. "And to answer your last question, the phone I used to call my physical therapist in San Diego before I bought my bike is also a burner. I keep several prepaid phones handy, in fact. Just in case."

"I see."

She sighed. "Fletcher, your precautions may work in the short term, but what happens when Joe and Holly return? Do you think you could 'coach' Holly into covering for me?"

Simon flinched. "Probably not."

"You mean *definitely* not. She would be more likely to ask for a cut of the bounty! Look, Fletcher, I welcome your help and will sleep better with your presence nearby tonight. However, I will hit the road as soon as I solidify my next plans. I need to get clear of Tahoe. Head to some place remote."

Simon stared down into his empty cup. Stared into the hole her absence would leave. He sighed and glanced up at her.

"I don't want you to go."

She blinked several times. "Well, that makes two of us."

———— ◆ ————

A HALF-HOUR LATER, Simon stood in the doorway of Holly's personal office and motioned to Skipper. "Skip, come here, please. I need to talk to you in private."

Skipper took in Simon's expression and sobered. "Am I in trouble?"

"You're not in trouble. Just . . . close the gate and turn over the sign on the office door, will you? I don't want any interruptions while we talk or any nonresidents driving around on Bright Star property."

A few moments later, Skipper joined Simon in Holly's office.

"Close the door, Skipper."

The kid did so. Slowly. "You're kinda freaking me out, Fletch."

"I'm sorry, but I can't risk our conversation being overheard." Simon had taken one of Holly's upholstered guest chairs. He patted the second. "Sit."

Skipper sat on the chair's edge.

"Before we start, Skipper, I want to say that I've seen a welcome improvement in you this past week, and I know that Jesus will continue to help you grow and mature in him. But now I need to ask several important things of you. First, what we're about to discuss has to stay between us. You cannot speak of it to anyone. *Anyone.* Do I have your word on this?"

Skipper fidgeted. "I . . . suppose."

"Nope. Not good enough. Let me ask you a question: Do you care about Miss Finch?"

"Finchy? Yeah, I like Miss Finch. I like her a lot. Is she okay?"

Finchy?

"She is for the moment. But if we are to keep her 'okay,' I need your solemn word that you will say nothing of what I'm about to tell you to anyone else. Not to Becka, Melissa, Bryce, Zane, Kevin, or even Pastor Kent. Absolutely no one. Can you promise me that?"

Skipper swallowed. "Yeah. Okay. I promise."

Simon reached out and clasped Skipper's shoulder. "Good man."

He sat back. "I can't give you all the specifics; I will tell you only what is necessary in the present situation. In a nutshell, Miss Finch is in trouble, not with the law, but with some seriously bad people, and she's hiding from them here at Bright Star."

Skipper's face drained of color, and his eyes bugged out of his head. "Are you joking with me, Fletch?"

"No, I wouldn't. This is too serious. What you need to know, what we need to prepare you for, is the possibility that some of those people looking for her may call the office or even show up at Bright Star looking for her."

"But Miss Finch runs the office—"

Skipper wasn't dense. He stopped himself and sniffled in resignation. "Miss Finch can't run the office anymore, can she?"

"No, nor can she leave Bright Star at present. Not until we feel the search for her has gone elsewhere. We want to hide her here, keep her less visible until then."

"But what about all the residents? They know her. All of them do."

"We can't say a word to them; that would only create questions and serve to draw more attention to her. The best we can do on that front is pray that our residents, when away from Bright Star, have no need to mention her. And we can try to keep them from being questioned by anyone who comes sniffing around, which is why I asked you to close the gate."

"Should we keep it shut all the time?"

"Yes. No more leaving it open during the day. But then there's also this office."

"I'll do it."

"Do what?"

"I'll run the office for Miss Finch. It's boring, but it's not hard; she showed me how to answer the phone and all. Talk to people the right way."

Simon studied the boy. "All right. Let's say I, a stranger, called on the office phone. What would you say?"

"Uh, Bright Star Summer RV Residence. How may I help you?"

Simon leaned toward Skipper. "Oh, hey. I hope you can help me. I'm looking for a dear old friend, a Miss Finch, and I understand she's one of your residents."

"Uh, nope. No Miss Finch here."

"Good, but not quite glib enough. It has to be a fact; don't think about it, just say it."

"Sorry; we don't have a Miss Finch at Bright Star."

"Better. You'll need to keep practicing it so that you can say it with the same quick confidence as saying your own name."

Skipper nodded. "I'll practice and get really good at it, Fletch."

"Okay, how about this? I knock on the office door or just walk in. You've never seen me before. What do you do then?"

He rolled his eyes. "Smile a really big fake smile with lots of teeth."

Simon choked on a startled guffaw. "Good grief. Did Miss Finch teach you that?"

"Yup. You should see *her* fake-smile with lots of teeth. *Scary.*"

Simon laughed so hard he had to sit back until the spasm passed. Took him a few minutes to get a handle on himself. He finally pulled himself together and looked up.

Skipper was taking a turn at studying him. "I like it when you laugh, Fletcher. You don't look all tough and mean like most of the time."

"Huh. Well, tough and mean is a Marine requirement."

"But you aren't a Marine anymore, right?"

Simon chuckled and shook his head. "Say that to any other retired Marine, Skip, and you'll probably have a fight on your hands."

"What? Just for saying that?"

"Marines live by a code. Part of that code is, once a Marine, always a Marine."

"Wow. Okay. Sorry I said you weren't a Marine anymore . . . but I do like it when you laugh."

"Oorah."

Skipper grinned.

"We need to finish up our talk, and that means I need to tell you something unpleasant. It will likely make you angry, but I need you to grasp the seriousness of Miss Finch's situation."

"Uh, okay. What is it?"

"Someone left poisoned meat in Miss Finch's catio this morning while she was out riding her bike."

"What? Are Hugo and Pouncer all right?"

Simon described what happened. "Hugo is okay, but the situation could easily have gone the other way."

Skipper seethed. "Man, I swear I'll pound anyone who tries to hurt them!"

"First, please don't swear, Skip. Self-defense and defending our loved ones and our property are okay in God's book, but swearing an oath in the heat of the moment is not how God wants us to talk, okay? He would prefer that we answer with a 'yes' or a 'no' or 'I will do this' or 'I will not do that, God willing.'

"Second, you and I are going to watch over Miss Finch and her fur babies every night until we know they are safe. We start tonight. We'll pitch my tent behind the catio and sleep there."

Skipper was on board. "Camping out? Cool. Whatever you say, Fletch. You can count on me."

Simon looked the boy in the eye. "You're shaping up nicely, Skipper. I like what I see."

"Wow, thanks, Fletch. Hey, when can I have my phone back?"

"I borrowed your phone to make a call earlier today and had to, er, trash it when I was done so no one could trace the call to Bright Star. But don't worry; I've already bought a replacement, and Miss Finch said to give it to you. She said you could keep it."

"Really? My own phone? Wow, isn't Finchy the greatest?"

"*Finchy?* Kid, do you have a death wish? That's the second time I've heard you call her that. Whatever you do, I don't advise calling her that to her face."

Skipper shook his head. "I won't. But what do we do next to keep Finchy—I mean *Miss Finch* safe?"

"Right. Let's close up the office, grab our gear, and get set up for the night."

———————— ◆ ————————

BACK AT SIMON'S CABIN, he and Skipper packed up tent, air mattresses, sleeping bags, pillows, camp cookware, food, personal items, and a single lawn chair to add to Miss Finch's two. Lastly, Simon opened the small safe bolted to the wood floor under his bed where he kept his ammo and a substantial cash reserve.

While Skipper observed, Simon withdrew two boxes of .45 ammo, then closed the safe. His Springfield XD four-inch subcompact and a second loaded mag were already holstered as usual at the small of his back, concealed by the tail of his camo-green Bright Star work shirt.

"Think you'll need all those bullets?" Skipper asked in a whisper.

"Better to have them and not need them than to need them and not have them, Skip."

"Could you . . . could you teach me to shoot sometime?"

Simon thought through the request before he answered. "I would consider it, if I saw continued improvement in your attitude and if it were allowed legally."

"But you can't, even if my attitude changes?"

"Right, for two reasons: First, because you are a minor, I would need your mom's written permission and liability release. Second, and more difficult to overcome, you'd have to be off probation to handle a firearm, even under supervision."

As he beheld Skipper's hopes deflate, Simon temporized. "I could, however, teach you gun safety rules and show you—by demonstration only—the mechanics of a handgun and how to properly and safely handle it. Nothing hands on, though. Do you understand my reasoning? And will you obey my instructions to the letter?"

Skipper stood straighter. "Yes, sir. I do and I will. Um, thank you."

Simon shook his head in feigned disbelief. "Wow. Great response, Skipper. Why, I almost feel like giving you a great big hug."

Skipper reared back in horror. "What? No way!" He grabbed his bag and hit the door, leaving Simon vaguely bemused . . . and oddly satisfied.

CHAPTER 21

FEELS LIKE THE LONGEST Wednesday on record, Simon mused, studying Site 1 with new eyes. Bushes grew in a thick and lush privacy hedge along the outside of Miss Finch's driveway. Simon asked Miss Finch to repark her woody with its nose as near to her trailer and as close to the hedge as possible to block an intruder from walking down the right side of her vehicle, then getting behind her trailer unnoticed.

When she had her woody in position, he backed his truck down the drive and he and Skipper unloaded their gear. With the exception of a small box that he left against Miss Finch's trailer and Simon's campfire coffee pot and cookware that they stacked by the firepit, they toted the rest around to the far side of the catio.

From her high hammock in the catio, Pouncer's piercingly blue eyes followed them. When Simon happened to squint in her direction, she saluted him with an extended hiss.

"Yeah, backatcha, you little coward," Simon muttered.

Skipper cracked up. "You know she loves you, Fletch."

"Sure she does. Like Megatron loves Optimus Prime."

Skipper added his own spin. "Like Maleficent loves Sleeping Beauty, right? Or like Thanos loves Star Lord? *Not!* Or how about, like Godzilla loves King Kong? Hey—does that make you Godzilla or Kong?"

"Go a few rounds with me and find out."

"Think I'll pass."

"You're brighter than you look, Skipper."

"Gee, thanks," Skipper groused.

Skipper's grumble turned to a laugh, though, when Simon pulled him over and kneaded a noogie on his scalp.

The area behind the catio and the rear of Miss Finch's trailer was plenty large enough for Simon's two-man tent, although the ground sloped away from the site. Simon and Skipper, at this stage in their working relationship, however, needed little communication to perform a task well together. They leveled the ground, spread the tent taut, and staked it down with the door facing in the same direction as Miss Finch's trailer door, pointed toward her little patio and firepit. Then they inserted the poles and raised the tent body, clipped on the rain fly, and squatted to inflate their air mattresses. When the mattresses were ready, Simon unzipped the tent's entrance and crawled inside. Skipper handed him the mattresses, sleeping bags, and pillows. Once those were arranged, with Simon's sleeping arrangement on one side of the tent, and Skipper's on the other, they brought in the rest of their gear and placed it in the space between their beds up near their pillows.

With their camping prep complete, Simon drove his truck to the office and around back where it was out of sight. He started back to Miss Finch's site, closing the park gate behind him.

By then, it was past dinner time, and both he and Skipper were starved. They were grateful—and salivating—when Miss Finch brought out a pot of steaming chili con carne and a pan of freshly baked cornbread for the three of them to share.

"It's the least I can do to thank you both for keeping Hugo and Pouncer, not to mention me, safe through the night."

"Well, as much as I don't relish a run-in with whoever is stalking you, I'd prefer they make their move sooner, rather than later. Get this thing over and done with."

"Yes. Much better than this uncertainty dragging on." Miss Finch hesitated, then added, "And me having to leave."

Skipper jerked a startled look in her direction. But before he could open his mouth to protest, Simon shook his head.

"Put a pin in it, Skip. I'll explain later."

Skipper sighed and reluctantly subsided.

Later, the three of them sat around Miss Finch's firepit, stuffing themselves with popcorn, talking, telling stories, and laughing until long after dark.

As the fire died down to barely glowing coals, the night sky came alive. Simon scooted down in his lawn chair until he was able to rest his neck on the rear of the chair and let his head loll back. With his gaze fixed straight up, he stared into the vast expanse above him.

"Whatcha doing, Fletch?"

"Take a look for yourself."

Skipper followed Simon's example. He leaned his head back too . . . and gasped.

"Wowzer! I've never seen so many stars in my life!"

"Down in the cities, light pollution prevents us from enjoying a view like this," Simon murmured.

A sudden fiery trail swept across the inky sky.

"Was that a falling star? Did we just totally see a real falling star?" Skipper demanded in excited awe.

"Probably a meteor," Simon murmured. "Still, it's cool to see one."

"What exactly is a meteor, Fletch?"

"Oh, bits of space debris, pieces of rock that break off of comets and fall into our gravity well."

"Do meteors ever hit the ground while they're on fire?"

"Thousands do every year, but big impacts are pretty rare. Most of them burn up in the atmosphere."

"Look there, Skipper," Miss Finch said, using her index finger to circle an area above them. "See that cloudy mass at the tree line on the right? That's the tail of our galaxy, the Milky Way."

She paused, calling something to mind, then recited,

> *"Praise the Lord.*
> *Praise the Lord from the heavens;*
> *praise him in the heights above.*
> *Praise him, all his angels;*
> *praise him, all his heavenly hosts.*
> *Praise him, sun and moon;*
> *praise him, all you shining stars.*
> *Praise him, you highest heavens*
> *and you waters above the skies.*
> *Let them praise the name of the Lord,*
> *for at his command*
> *they were created."*

"What's that?" Skipper asked.

"A quote from the Bible, Psalm 148. It is a continual amazement to me that God made our universe so vast and awe inspiring—and that every planet, sun and moon, every star, and even the highest heavens, worship him!"

Skipper wrinkled his nose. "How do stars worship God?"

"By being what God made them to be, Skip," Simon murmured. "All that beauty is a tribute to the King of Kings and Lord of Lords, the creator of the universe. Kinda makes me think that if we people would try harder to be what he made *us* to be, we'd be a lot happier."

Skipper seemed unimpressed. "Huh. Well, how come we can't see much of this Milky Way thing? How big is it, anyway?"

Miss Finch answered, "Bigger than you can imagine, Skipper. Where we are sitting, a lot of the sky is obscured by the trees around us. However, much more of the Milky Way is visible from the lake shore. That said, if you look straight up," her finger shifted and drew a circle against the sky, "you can clearly make out the Big Dipper. It's pretty much in the center of the clearing above us."

"That thing that looks like a scooper or a weird-looking spoon?"

"Yes. Dipper is a word not used much these days. It refers to a kind of scoop or cup on the end of a long handle. Before we knew what germs were or that sharing the same dipper could spread sickness, people kept their common drinking water in a big barrel or cistern. Everyone would use the same long-handled dipper to scoop water from the barrel into a bucket. They would also drink water directly from the dipper."

"Gross!"

"Yes. Many diseases were passed around that way."

"Well, I'd like to see more of this Milky Way. Could we go to the lake shore some night to see the stars better?"

"Sounds like a great field trip," Simon said. He blinked, dumbfounded that the words had issued from his mouth.

Skipper shivered with excitement. "Cool! Maybe we could take the whole youth group on a stargazing trip?"

"Uh, why don't you suggest that to Pastor Kent?"

"Super idea! Can't wait to tell Zane and Kevin. Bryce too."

"We need to take care of our little problem here first."

"Oh. Yeah. Forgot for a sec."

"Speaking of our problem . . ."

Their three heads rotated toward the low grumble of a vehicle coming from the park entrance, then crawling along the road toward them.

"If my ears don't deceive me, that is my near neighbor's truck," Miss Finch whispered.

Simon scanned around them. The fire had gone out. No light glowed from inside Miss Finch's trailer. From the road, Miss Finch's site would be drenched in darkness, to all appearances, its occupants retired for the night and sound asleep.

A quick check of his watch told him the time was 10:14 p.m.

"Everyone quiet and still," he cautioned. "Not the slightest movement, please."

As the truck came abreast of the head of Miss Finch's driveway, it slowed even further until only its forward momentum kept it inching along. Just the faint profile of the vehicle could be seen. After a full minute, the truck cleared Miss Finch's driveway and moved down the road.

Skipper started to say something but found Simon's hand covering his mouth.

The three of them continued to listen in silence. When the truck reached the next site, it turned into its driveway.

Miss Finch's whisper broke their hush. "I was fairly certain that was Mrs. Rickert's truck; now I am certain."

Simon nodded. "I agree. I know all the vehicles in the park, and only one corresponds to that silhouette. Besides which, the gate is closed, which limits the possibilities. No one can get a vehicle into or out of the park without the proper keycode."

"What do we do now, Fletch?"

"We go to bed . . . but first I want to rig a little surprise."

Skipper was eager to help. "What can I do?"

"As quiet as a mouse, fold up the lawn chairs and lean them against Miss Finch's trailer under the awning. Clear away any other hazards too. If I have to chase someone tonight, I don't want to lose them because I tripped in the dark. When you're done, come assist me."

He turned to Miss Finch. "Can you let Hugo and Pouncer inside and get yourself into bed without turning on any lights?"

"I'll muddle through . . . but I doubt that I'll sleep much."

"You and me both. But if anything happens in the night? Don't come out unless and until I call you."

"As you say, Fletcher."

Skipper and Miss Finch, as noiseless as wraiths, split off to perform their tasks. Simon, however, had his own project to complete. He retrieved the small box he'd left by the trailer, placed it on the woody's front fender and withdrew a reel of dark wire.

He had, quite intentionally, asked Miss Finch to park her woody against the screen of bushes, closing off the far side of the woody and leaving the near side of the driveway wide open—the easiest route to Miss Finch's door. He attached the end of the wire to the rear bumper of the woody, about 15 inches off the ground. Reeling out more wire, he strung its length across the drive and the breadth of Miss Finch's site, keeping it at the same low height. He then wrapped the wire around the base of a tall pine and pulled the wire taut.

Skipper appeared at his side just as Simon clipped the wire from the reel and twisted the wire's end around its length. Simon was pleased that the boy watched without speaking.

He stood and gestured for Skipper to follow him back to the woody's front end. From the box he'd left on the fender, he pulled a container of some innocuous looking powder and a small paint brush. He put his mouth to Skipper's ear. "This is a type of powdered fluorescent paint. Visible only under a long-wave ultraviolet lamp, a black light."

Simon saw Skipper's teeth gleam in the gloom. Smiling back, Simon thrust his chin toward the woody's bumper.

"Take this brush and 'paint' the wire with the powder. Be generous. We want a good coating on it. When you finish, retrace the line. Dip your brush into the powder and shake powder on the ground in front of the wire. Use it all."

When Skipper returned, Simon had laid out a fresh 6-volt heavy duty lantern battery, a device of some kind, and his smart phone on the fender.

Again, Simon bent to Skipper's ear. "Done? Use all the powder?"

Skipper nodded, his eyes on the three items before Simon.

Simon returned to his task. He had connected the device to his phone via Bluetooth and needed to configure and customize the settings on his phone. When he finished, he slipped his phone into his pocket, picked up the battery and device, and indicated Skipper was to bring the reel of wire and the wire cutters.

Tipping his head toward the car's back end, he invited Skipper to follow him. When they reached the wire, Simon pulled a short wand from his pocket and switched it on. Under the wand's black light, the wire and every speck of powder Skipper had strewn between the woody and the pine tree lit up like Christmas and the Fourth of July combined.

Skipper grinned like a maniac, but kept his elation silent.

Simon turned off the wand and squatted by the woody's bumper. A few inches out from where the taut wire was attached to the bumper, Simon placed the device on the ground below the wire. He measured and cut a length of wire just long enough to reach from the wire crossing Miss Finch's site down to the device on the ground.

Once he'd joined the short wire to the painted wire, he took the other end and connected it to the device. Lastly, he connected the battery to the device and carefully—*carefully*—tapped the device to activate it.

His mouth to Skipper's ear, he breathed, "Don't come near the wire until I've deactivated it tomorrow morning, okay?"

Skipper nodded enthusiastically. He watched as Simon reached behind himself to the small of his back and slid his holster off his belt. Leaving his handgun in the holster, Simon headed for their tent.

They slipped quietly into their tent and into their sleeping bags. Simon laid awake for a long time, his ears carefully tuned to pick up any unnatural sound from the site. When he finally heard deep, soft breathing coming from Skipper, he turned over and tried to relax.

Eventually, he fell off into slumber.

———— ◆ ————

THURSDAY MORNING, not one of Simon's preparations had been disturbed.

"That means, nobody came creeping around last night, huh?" Skipper asked Simon in a whisper.

"Right."

"Maybe whoever tried to poison Hugo and Pouncer saw we were camped in Miss Finch's site and got scared. Yeah, I bet you scared them off, Fletch."

"Except we pitched the tent where it couldn't be seen from the head of the drive. See, I'd prefer to catch the sneakers rather than scare them off just to have them return another night when we're not ready for them."

"Huh. Yeah, you're right."

"We'll set the trap again this evening. For now, we'll take the trap down and set it aside."

"So will we camp out here again tonight? I liked looking at the stars when the night got really dark."

"Yes. We'll continue camping here . . . for a while."

Skipper's "nobody came creeping around last night" didn't set Simon's mind at rest—not in the least. If he were being truthful with himself, the way his nerves were on edge told him the opposite: Whoever was stalking Miss Finch was just fine with biding their time.

And Simon hated playing a waiting game.

He sighed. "Come on, Skipper. Let's make a run up to the cabin to grab a shower, change of clothes, and breakfast. We have a big list of chores to tackle today."

Simon knocked on Miss Finch's door. "Nothing to report. We'll come down at lunch and check up on you. Talk to you then."

He and Skipper drove off, headed for Simon's cabin.

Unfortunately, in all their careful, stealthy preparations, Simon and Skipper hadn't noticed the intruder crouching in the shrubbery between Site 1 and Site 2 . . . listening in on their conversation and observing their every move.

CHAPTER 22

SIMON ROSE EARLY FRIDAY, while night was only beginning to wane. He pulled on his pants and boots, reseated his holster on his belt, and buttoned up his work shirt. Skipper was sleeping hard, even his head buried inside his sleeping bag, so Simon tried not to awaken him.

Besides, he was in need of some alone time. Once out of the tent, he donned his jacket against a chilly breeze. Walking about the dim site, he began to pray. Eventually, he pulled out his black light wand, and went to check on his "trap." Not that he expected to find anything.

He'd slept with his phone close to his head. If Miss Finch's stalker had touched the wire, his phone would have vibrated and chirped—just loud enough to awaken him but not loud enough to alert the stalker—giving Simon opportunity to surprise and capture the intruder. Even if the intruder escaped, they'd be marked across their shins and on the soles of their shoes with invisible fluorescent powder and unaware of it. All Simon would have to do is wave his black light wand over every individual inside Bright Star until the right one "popped."

He sniffed to himself and acknowledged that it was a flawed or inadequate plan. It was entirely possible for Miss Finch's stalker to climb through the simple three-strand barbed-wire fence surrounding Bright Star's property, hike in using the trails crisscrossing Bright Star's thirty acres, and enter the park via the trailhead near the office.

If it were me stalking Miss Finch, I wouldn't leave my getaway car on the road alongside Bright Star's property line, nor would I want to walk the distance to the park. No, I'd want a quick escape route with no troublesome individual to give the police a description of my vehicle.

Of course, someone could just drive up the property road to the office and scale the park fence, but our security cameras don't just monitor the gate. I also positioned one at the turnoff and two more along the approach leading to the gate. If I were a thorough stalker, I'd look for the cameras, spot them, and decide not to sneak in that way either.

For those reasons and on the grounds of some vague gut feeling within him that he hadn't quite figured out, Simon felt the stalker was nearby. Inside the park.

But if it wasn't Mrs. Rickert, then who?

Simon nodded to himself. Yes, if the stalker *were* a resident, and if he—or she—had tripped over Simon's wire, he would leave a faint trail of fluorescent shoeprints, but probably only for a few yards, until the powder wore or rubbed off.

Hopefully, the stalker would leave enough of a trail to point me in the right direction.

Just not today.

After the uneventful night, there was nothing for Simon to do except turn off the device, put it and the battery away, then unstring the wire, winding it up to use again after dark. For good measure, he found a snapped branch hanging from a shrub along the road. He finished breaking it off, swept as much of the powder off the driveway as he could, and brushed dirt over the rest of powder, all the way to the pine tree.

We'll lay a similar trap tonight using a fresh container of powdered paint.

Quietly, so as not to disturb Miss Finch, he started a fire in the pit, drew some water from the site's potable water station, and put his coffee pot on to brew.

While he waited, Simon stared into the sky, recalling the vivid panorama from the night before. He'd been deep in his thoughts for several minutes when the furious perking of the pot brought him around. He gingerly pulled the pot back where the fire wasn't burning as hot and set it to perk at a more moderate pace.

Simon jerked as a flurry of activity from the road caught his attention—the rush of heavy boots pounding asphalt and the unmistakable ratcheting of semiauto firearms.

"What in the—"

A bullhorn. "You in the camp! Put your hands in the air and get on your knees!"

Simon knew better than to quibble. His hands flew up, and he dropped to his knees—one of them protesting as it landed on a small rock.

Ow.

"I am armed!" Simon called. "Small of my back!"

Two men armored up in recognizable SWAT fashion showed themselves. One trained his weapon on Simon, while the other approached Simon from the side, felt for his weapon, and removed it.

"Get on your face," the man ordered.

Simon complied, his right cheek scraping against the rough surface of the pavers surrounding Miss Finch's firepit, his eyes toward her trailer, while the officers flex-cuffed his wrists behind his back.

The man hovering above Simon shouted, "Clear!" but Simon's eyes were fixed on Miss Finch's trailer.

Her door slammed open against the side of her trailer, and there she stood, like a kid on Christmas morning, clothed from neck to toe in a cute miniature plaid flannel nightgown, all greens, reds, and golds, her wild mop of curling hair vying for Best of Breed in the Woodland Creature Category.

"What is the meaning of this?" she demanded.

A third man, obviously in charge, jogged toward her.

"Are you Miss Finch?"

"I am. Who are you?"

"Jonas Phillips, SWAT Team Lead, South Lake Tahoe Police Department. We caught this armed man in your site, ma'am, and prevented what we believe was an attempt on your life."

Miss Finch crooked her finger at Phillips. He came closer until, because she stood in her trailer's doorway, they were face to face. Almost.

She leaned toward him. "You, sir, are ridiculous. That man," she pointed at Simon's prone figure, "is Simon Fletcher, Bright Star's facilities and security manager, also currently operations manager of this RV park. Of course he's armed, you dolt! He has a CCL and carries a firearm per Bright Star's security regulations. In addition, he is my trusted friend. What in God's green earth ever possessed you to think he would attack me?"

The team leader scanned her site. "Where is his vehicle?" His eyes narrowed in suspicion. "Is he always here at night?"

"No, he is *not* always here at night, and certainly *not* in the manner you're implying!"

About then, a bleary-eyed Skipper peered around the edge of the catio.

"Who are you?" Phillips demanded.

"I-I-I'm Skipper Mitchell. I work here. For Mr. Fletcher."

Miss Finch poked the team leader in the chest to reacquire his attention and encountered the solid plate of his armor instead, so she poked his shoulder. "See here! Mr. Fletcher and his apprentice had dinner with me last evening. We stayed up late, eating popcorn around the campfire. Skipper and Mr. Fletcher are camped over there in a tent behind my trailer. Furthermore, Mr. Fletcher left his truck behind Bright Star's office, only thirty yards or so from my site."

Phillips shouted, "Crutchfield! McDonald! Check out that tent."

Miss Finch poked him again. "*You—*" she poked Phillips yet again for good measure, "have not yet explained why you are here and why you acted on such a ludicrous assumption."

The two officers drew near.

"One sec," Phillips said, turning to his officers. "What did you find?"

"Tent, two sleeping bags. Normal camping gear."

The man addressed Miss Finch. "Ma'am, we are here because we received a phone call about thirty minutes ago. The caller stated that you were being held hostage by an armed man, a non-resident who had walked into your site, and who was threatening to kill you."

"Who called? Man or woman?" Miss Finch demanded.

"Woman—no, belay that. I am not at liberty to provide those kinds of details."

"And yet you just did. Word to the wise? Don't play poker for money. You will lose your shirt. In a game where preventing your opponent from reading you is vital, you wouldn't stand a chance. *Your* face is an open book."

She pointed toward Simon. "Now, release that man and let him up. As I said, he's Bright Star's facilities and security manager and a personal friend."

Stung by her rebuke, the team leader spun on his heel and jerked his chin. The two SWAT officers hauled Simon to his feet and cut the plastic cuffs binding his wrists. When Simon produced his concealed carry card, they reluctantly returned his weapon.

Miss Finch wasn't finished. "And just so we're clear, Officer Phillips? Whomever your caller was, I hope you realize their intentions were malicious. We are the victims here."

"I agree, ma'am," Phillips replied. "It appears you've been swatted."

With that, Phillips signaled his men, and as quickly as they'd arrived, they departed, leaving Simon and Miss Finch standing in her site alone.

Skipper crept up behind them. "I don't understand. What just happened, Fletch?"

Before Simon could explain, he realized that a small crowd of Bright Star residents was gathering at the top of Miss Finch's drive.

"Hold that thought, Skip."

He marched up to the road and nodded at the residents' familiar faces, searching out one in particular, but not finding it. When the residents began to pelt him with questions, he lifted both hands to shut down the confusion of their competing voices and garner their attention as a group.

"Anyone here familiar with the term, 'swatted'?"

Chet Bigalow spoke up. "Uh, like when someone calls the police to report a deranged husband trying to kill his wife, so they send the SWAT team to save her?"

"Close, Chet. You've described a legit SWAT callout. 'Swatted' is when someone calls the police to report a *fake* scenario. Usually it's when a person with malicious intent and who wishes to cause you trouble and public embarrassment phones the police to report a fabricated state of affairs dangerous enough to warrant calling out the SWAT unit. It's similar to being 'punked' but is a serious criminal act with zero humorous outcomes."

"Are you saying that's what happened here?" Wes Trujillo asked. "You got, er, swatted?"

"Yes, but the harassment runs deeper than this event. Wednesday, day before yesterday, while Miss Finch was out riding her bike, someone placed poisoned meat in her pet enclosure. When she returned, her dog got ahold of a chunk. Thank God, she forced him to spit it out before he was able to swallow it."

The low growl that percolated through the crowd told Simon what they thought of the attempt.

"Despicable," someone grumbled.

"Right you are. And Miss Finch, being older and entirely alone here, was pretty shaken. I mean, you can imagine how terrified she had to have been, can't you? That's why my intern and I volunteered to camp behind Miss Finch's rig the past two nights. The best outcome would have been for us to catch that animal hater in a repeat attempt. At the very least, we wanted Miss Finch, as shaken as she was, to feel secure enough to sleep." Simon used the term "animal hater" intentionally, hoping to sway the group's irate sentiments toward those who would target Miss Finch's pets, rather than her, personally.

Because people these days have more outrage for the mistreatment of animals than they do for the mistreatment of their fellow human beings.

He continued, "Whoever called the police said that an armed man was in Miss Finch's site, threatening to shoot her. The police, obligated to respond to such a threat, called out the SWAT unit." Simon pointed toward the firepit. "I was up, making a pot of coffee, when the unit arrived and assumed I was the armed and dangerous suspect."

More mutters and angry rumbles answered him.

"In case you are unaware, my official Bright Star position title is 'Facilities and *Security* Manager.' After two decades in the Marine Corps, eighteen of those years as a military police officer, I am a proficient marksman, and yes, I am licensed to carry a sidearm. Part of my role as security manager is to be the first line of defense should we, God forbid, experience an active shooter event."

"I've never seen you armed," Mrs. Bhattacharya said, clearly nervous.

"That's because I conceal carry my sidearm while I'm on the job." He searched the faces around him, all of them listening with concerned expressions, "but the individual who called in this false report knew I was armed."

He cleared his throat. "And now that everyone at Bright Star is apprised of this childish escapade," Simon intentionally downplayed the event, "I can venture to hope that the scoundrel has learned his lesson."

"Mr. Fletcher! Mr. Fletcher! Permission to string up the low-down varmint when he's caught!"

That strong sentiment arose from Mrs. Gorman. The woman was a spry senior, eighty years plus if a day, and Simon was momentarily nonplussed. Another resident responded to her before Simon could.

"I vote for that solution! You can use the giant Jeffrey Pine in our site," Wes Trujillo offered with a snorted laugh. "Got the perfect branch for it."

Simon, recognizing the crude attempt to break the tension for what it was, chuckled along with the others—and then firmly quashed the idea.

"No one gets strung up at Bright Star, folks. We might be an exclusive park, but we'd rather our exclusivity not be known by our willingness to dispatch residents who abuse helpless animals like Miss Finch's Hugo."

Miss Finch had often ridden her bike around the Bright Star loop with Hugo and Pouncer in her basket. Hugo, of course, had made many friends.

Pouncer, on the other hand? Not so much.

"Wait—we're talking about *Hugo?* Are you saying *a resident* tried to poison that precious boy? That *one of us* tried to kill Hugo?" That came from an outraged Irene Kinzer.

Yikes. Stop adding fuel to the fire, Fletch.

"We don't know who left the poisoned meat, Mrs. Trujillo. However, I can tell you that we designed Bright Star as a safe place for our residents to spend the summer. It's why we have a gate and require visitors to sign in when the office is staffed. It is also why we close the gate when the office is closed. It is because of our precautions, that I cannot easily believe someone from the outside would know that Skipper and I were camped behind Miss Finch's trailer . . . or that I carry a sidearm."

Before the situation could deteriorate further, Simon, past master of crowd control, again raised both hands. "Look. It's early, and I doubt we've had our coffee yet—I know I haven't."

That got the shared laugh Simon was angling for.

"I suggest we all go home, catch our breath, have our breakfast, and prepare to enjoy another wonderful day here among the trees or at the lake."

"But what about that . . . person, Mr. Fletcher?" Bryce's uncle, Frank Muller, Bryce nodding at his elbow, asked. "Will the police arrest whoever it is?"

"Regrettably, the caller likely used an unregistered cellphone to make their false report, meaning the number cannot easily be tracked to its owner. And apparently simply being armed with a cellphone isn't a crime in itself— or we'd all be under arrest, am I right?"

Another laugh.

"Nonetheless, this morning's prank was cruel, and yesterday's attempt on Hugo was just downright hateful."

The restless residents nodded and agreed under their breath.

Through clamped teeth and a wide, not-quite-sincere smile, Simon added, "Please allow me to tell all of you this: I appreciate our community here at Bright Star. All of you—with the exception of this one patently unhappy and miserable excuse for a human being—are wonderful people to serve. I'll publicly address my sentiments to the single person who did these things: *You are not welcome here.*"

He added, "When we catch you—and we will—you'll face the full force of the law."

The crowd was quite vocal in their agreement now, but Simon, his face aching, continued to smile and keep the atmosphere light.

If I keep grinning like this, either my lips are going to split or my jaws will lock up.

Simon made a little "'shooing" motion with his hands. "Thank you for being wonderful neighbors to our Miss Finch. I know she appreciates you. Now, go and get your coffee—so I can have mine."

Laughing and mostly relieved, the residents dispersed, and Simon walked down the driveway to Skipper and Miss Finch. Miss Finch handed him a steaming cup.

"The Lord bless you, woman!"

"Yes, the Lord bless this poor, aged, terrified, and shaken woman."

Simon choked and had to spit out his first sip. "Uh, you know that was for the crowd, right?"

"But of course it was."

Oh, brother.

Skipper spoke up as Simon, again, tried to take a sip. "How did the police get through the gate, Fletch? Do you think they busted it down?"

"Not likely. That gate was manufactured to withstand everything short of a tank. If they *had* busted through our gate, we and all of El Dorado County would have heard the commotion, and my cellphone would have alarmed. The SWAT unit came in stealthily, so they must have parked their vehicles outside the gate and scaled the fence."

"Or, as most law enforcement units often have, the SWAT unit could have had the lock manufacturer's 'back door' code," Miss Finch said, "Or they could have a technician embedded in their unit, one with the tech and skills to overcome the locking mechanism, but what do I, an elderly and pathetic little female know?"

Simon, having just inhaled his second gulp of coffee, choked again and was forced to spit it out on the ground. "You're not going to let that go, are you."

"You can bet your sweet bippy I'm not letting that go." She pointed toward the road. "I counted the residents while you were busy entertaining them. Only two of our twenty-four sites were unrepresented: Sites 2 and 19."

"Terri Rickert and Marie Santini. That agrees with my count, although Mrs. Rickert is the more likely culprit. Miss Santini looks like she couldn't fight her way out of a wet paper bag. That said, we should determine if either of them is connected in any way to the Lucchese Family."

"Agreed. And by the way? I am, that is, *we are*, undoubtedly, being spied upon. It is the only logical way our 'swatter' would know you were camped behind my trailer and the only way he or she would know when you got up this morning. We must discover how the spy is watching us."

She turned a potent glance on him. "And we both know whose site is closest to mine."

Simon slugged down the remainder of his coffee before another interruption could delay it. "I'll figure that part out. While I'm at it, it's time for you, Miss Finch, to use your PI resources. I need everything you can pull on Mrs. Rickert and Miss Santini."

"*You* need? Don't you mean *we* need that data? After all, *I* am the licensed PI with the investigative resources, Mr. Fletcher, not you."

Skipper wrinkled his nose. "You're a what?"

"A PI. I'm a licensed private investigator—among other things."

"Sooo many 'other' things," Simon muttered.

"A detective? Like in the movies?" Skipper asked.

"Yes, my boy. Just like in the movies."

Skipper, with an exaggerated sigh, slapped his own forehead. "Why am I always the last to know the cool stuff?"

The boy tried to act affronted but failed. "Actually, I'm just glad you, Hugo, and Pouncer are okay, Miss Finch. You, too, Fletch."

Simon wrapped his arm around Skipper's shoulders. "The Lord has protected us several times now. Going forward, we may need to lean on him even more."

"Yes, and I pray he leads me to the information we need on those two women. The kind that will crack open this mystery. I'll go inside and get right on it . . . before anything else untoward occurs."

Simon tipped his mug upside down and stared with longing into its emptiness. "Hold up a sec. I have another thought. But first, we need breakfast. And more coffee. My treat."

"I am not leaving my darlings here alone!"

"Put them in their travel carriers, and we'll take them with us. I know just the place."

He ran his eye up and down her figure. "And you might want to change first . . . not that I don't like the plaid. Very, er, *Christmassy.*"

"Oh, do put a sock in it, *Mr.* Fletcher."

As she hobbled away in a huff, Skipper stared at Simon. "Sheesh, man. You always gotta push her buttons?"

Simon grinned. "Yeah, I guess I do."

"Well, don't come cryin' to me when she sics Pouncer on you."

CHAPTER 23

WHILE MISS FINCH DRESSED and Skipper put Hugo and Pouncer in their travel carriers, Simon decided that his search for their spy's hiding spot should start in the most likely location: the roadside between Sites 1 and 2.

The sun was beginning to rise when he climbed to the top of Miss Finch's driveway, stepped out onto the road, and walked in the direction of Site 2. Where the forty-foot swath of shrubs and bushes that formed the physical barrier between the two sites began, he slowed to shine a flashlight on every inch of the road's shoulder lest the waning shadows obscure what he sought: an entry point into the thick vegetation or any indication that someone had entered the bushes from the road.

He almost missed the wide, leafy branch stuffed between two saplings. He surely would have passed over it if he hadn't been reciting the names of each grass, plant, bush, and tree as he progressed.

"Lots of native grasses of course, plus . . . an incense cedar sapling, a mountain rose there, western serviceberry in the back, a creeping snowberry, some manzanita ground cover, a maturing white fir, more manzanita, another sapling, bitterbrush, a Jeffrey Pine seedling, some chinquapin—hey!" He returned to the bitterbrush, wondering why he saw only a single branch of the sun-loving shrub.

The instant he touched the leafy branch, he knew it was dying, snapped off recently, since the leaves hadn't yet browned. Speaking of its leaves, they had that desiccated feel a broken branch gets as it is drying out. He reached for the branch's center and tugged carefully on it. While he drew it out from between the two saplings, he kept his eyes on the dirt around it.

There. Just beyond where the branch had been placed. A scuffed shoeprint.

Woman's walking shoe, he decided, attempting to measure the length with his eye and frustrated because, from arch to heel, the print was marred. *Could be any size between a seven and a nine*, he fumed.

Yet it was still the first physical evidence that he was on the right track.

"Fletch! We're ready to go!" Skipper called out.

Simon stuffed the branch between the saplings, just as he'd found it. *Back soon*, he promised the shoeprint. *You can bank on it.*

Miss Finch was ensconced in her woody's driver's seat when Simon joined them. Skipper was in the seat behind her with the two travel crates beside him. Reluctantly, Simon opened the passenger side door.

"Not averse to being driven by a frail, doddering old woman, are you, Fletcher?"

Simon slid in and felt around for a seatbelt. "Not as long as she has retained all her marbles."

"Then I give you fair warning: I may have left several of mine on my pillow. They don't take kindly to being swatted out of a deep sleep."

"Quit your griping. You weren't the one face down on the pavement with your hands cuffed behind your back."

He was pleased that her response was a soft *heh-heh-heh*. Even Skipper grinned.

"Where to, Fletcher?"

Simon salivated in anticipation. "Maggie's."

———— ❖ ————

MAGGIE'S WAS THE POPULAR restaurant attached to the three-floor, five-star Desolation Hotel. Simon requested outdoor seating, and they were shown to a table on the terrace.

"Coffee for the gentleman, please," Miss Finch told the hostess as she released Hugo from his carrier and bid him sit beside her chair. "And do keep it coming. Poor boy has had a rough morning."

"This is getting old," Simon sighed.

"Thank you for being a good sport; Skipper and I are quite enjoying it," Miss Finch grinned while perusing the menu. "Tell me, what did you find out on the road? Must have been good. You were positively sparkling when you got in my car."

"I believe I've found our first tangible clues—the point at which our spy left the road to burrow her way toward your site, along with a partial shoeprint."

"I cannot wait to see where this trail leads—although that hope must be deferred until I've finished pulling background on Mrs. Rickert and Miss Santini, as you requested."

"Um, about that? Change of plans. I'd like you and Skipper to get out of Bright Star altogether. Take a day trip away from the park while I watch for our spy to make a move. You can do the research when you get back."

"Does that mean I don't have to work today?" Skipper interrupted.

"Yup. That's what it means. I'm going to close the office and leave my cell number on the door in case a resident needs me urgently. Then I'll track our spy's route through the foliage until I find where she listens and watches us. On my way out, I'll bait the route with fluorescent paint powder like I baited your site last night. Oh, and I'll reset that trap too. With you gone, leaving your site unwatched, she just might make another attempt."

"Just who is *she*, Fletch?" Skipper asked, "and another attempt at what?"

"Another attempt to hurt or harass Miss Finch, Skip. Technically, our spy could be any Bright Star resident; however, because of the size of the partial shoeprint I found, I'm operating on the premise that our suspect is a woman. And based on the animosity of Miss Finch's nearest neighbor, I suspect Mrs. Rickert of putting the poisoned meat in Miss Finch's catio."

It was the second time Skipper had heard about Hugo's close call.

"Man, I'd like to take a stick and beat that lady silly," Skipper retorted.

"Skipper, I do not like to hear that sort of talk from you," Miss Finch replied. "While we have our suspicions, we cannot yet say who is responsible for the tainted meat. When we find out, they will answer to the law, not to us. As a Christian, an individual who belongs to the Lord, we must trust in his justice, not in revenge."

"Huh. Did not know that. Sorry."

"Good man, and not to worry; as a young Christian you will be learning new things every day for some time." Then she winked at the boy. "In the meantime, how about we enjoy the lovely breakfast *Fletcher* is paying for? What do you say to that?"

Skipper caught on fast. "You bet!"

"Hey! No steak and lobster, you two," Simon protested. His eyes swept down the menu and he swallowed. "Keep it reasonable, like . . . sausage, eggs over easy, hashbrowns, and lots and lots of pancakes. And maybe an English muffin. Or two. With blackberry jam. And coffee. Keep the coffee coming. Oh, look—they have cinnamon rolls!"

"Perhaps an entire strawberry pie—just to tide you over?"

Miss Finch's droll suggestion tickled Skipper's funny bone. "Yeah. A whole pie!"

"I'll take that pie to go," Simon said, setting down his menu.

———◆———

SATISFIED AND ON THE road back to Bright Star an hour or so later, Miss Finch asked, "Fletcher, what kind of a day trip did you have in mind for Skipper and me?"

"What have you heard about the Truckee River Bike Trail?"

"Not a thing until you just now mentioned it, but I'm quite intrigued."

"Good. I'll load your bike and Skipper's in your car. Then I want you, Hugo, Pouncer, and Skipper to drive the lake road west, then north, toward Tahoe City. Don't rush. Stop and enjoy the views along the way, at say, Inspiration Point and Emerald Bay State Park Lookout. Whatever catches your fancy.

"After that, I recommend you park at Sugar Pine State Park where the West Shore Bike Path starts. Grab your bikes, hop on the trail, and ride it up to Tahoe City. Just before you get into Tahoe City proper, you'll see signs for a junction to access the Truckee River Bike Trail. Cut over that way and take the trail all the way to Olympic Valley and Palisades Tahoe, what used to be Squaw Valley and the site of the 1960s Olympics.

"In total, your ride will be around fourteen or fifteen miles. I've run that route, and I can tell you from experience that it's a stunning jaunt through the woods and meadows along the Truckee River. Lots of places to pause and admire gorgeous scenery. Stop and have some lunch along the way, perhaps at River Ranch Lodge, and take your time coming home.

"Like I said, I want you and Skipper away from Bright Star. I will bait another trap, and once the trap is ready, I'll go about my daily chores, hoping our spy makes a move. That's why I'm serious about you staying gone while I'm waiting for our perpetrator to act."

"Could you suggest a return time, Fletcher?" Miss Finch asked.

"How about I call you instead? If you finish your ride and return to your car, and you still haven't heard from me, feel free to drive on into the town of Tahoe City and hang out. Take in a movie. Have dinner. Whatever you want. Until I call."

"Sounds like a blast," Skipper enthused.

"I hope it is, Skip. Just remember that Miss Finch isn't fourteen. If she runs out of steam, roll with it."

"Yes, this pitiful and elderly woman may very well give out on you, Skipper. Why, you might be called upon to sling me across your shoulders and tote me all the way back to Tahoe City or—heaven help us—even perform CPR on me."

"That's just gross!"

"Yeah; give it a rest, *Finchy*," Simon growled.

Skipper perked up. "Hey! That's what I like to call her."

He liked it until he caught those two glittering Junior Mints bouncing death rays at him via the rearview mirror.

"But I'll never use that nickname again. Nope. Not me! Won't ever cross my lips. Solemn promise. Pinky swear."

Out of the side of his mouth, Simon whispered, "Can it, Skipperdoodle. Quit while your head is still attached."

"Yessir."

———◆———

SENDING MISS FINCH AND Skipper off on their day trip didn't take long. While Skipper ran back to the office to grab his bike and helmet, Miss Finch produced her own helmet, several bottles of water, sunscreen, and a baggie each of trail mix and pet treats, after which she took Hugo and Pouncer out of their carriers to do their business.

When Skipper returned, he and Simon loaded the two bikes and Hugo and Pouncer's basket into the woody's back end.

Simon leaned down to the open driver's window. "You're good to go. Be safe. Please."

"And you," Miss Finch answered softly. With that, she backed out of the drive and motored off.

With Miss Finch and Skipper safely away from Bright Star, Simon pocketed a few items and returned to the road and the broken branch he'd discovered earlier. He used his cellphone to photograph it and the slightly marred shoeprint the branch had hidden.

Then he stepped between the two saplings, pulled the dead branch back into its place behind him, and found himself on what could not technically be called a path but only the narrowest indication of previous ingress. He kept his eyes down in front of his feet and used his cellphone's camera whenever he caught a glimpse of another shoeprint.

The trail wound through bushes and trees before it widened. The expanded width made Simon's progress easier. Then the trail came to an abrupt end behind a lush chinquapin bush. Simon peered through the chinquapin's thick boughs and found himself staring at Miss Finch's firepit, not four yards away. Beyond the firepit, he had an unobstructed view of her trailer and his own tent.

Good grief! From this vantage point, nothing we did yesterday would have escaped Rickert's scrutiny, he growled internally. *She could have overheard us making our plans and watched as we prepared our little trap, meaning she knew exactly what we were up to. No wonder the night was uneventful.*

But it also means she had to have been right here, *watching Miss Finch's site early this morning when I got up, even watching me when I strapped on my holster. How else would she have known I was carrying or when to phone in that fake report to the police?*

Another thought dropped into his head.

How long had Mrs. Rickert remained hidden here? Had she watched the entire SWAT situation go down? Waited until after they left?

Simon's breath hissed as he sucked it in through his clenched teeth. *If she continued to listen after the police left, she could have overheard me suggest a day trip to Miss Finch and Skipper.*

He stood there, weighing their cunning spy's options: Would the woman follow Miss Finch and make a move on her while she and Skipper were out riding? Or would Rickert use the time they were away to devise and plant another devious means of attack or sabotage in Miss Finch's site?

Simon discounted the first option. *The logistics of following Miss Finch and setting up an ambush are too complex.* Standing still, he told himself, *Nevertheless, I do need to check Rickert's site and make certain her vehicle is still in her driveway.*

In other words, if Rickert's car hadn't left the park, Simon needn't worry about Miss Finch and Skipper while they were away.

He took more photos to document the spy's vantage point and scoured the ground for additional physical evidence that might prove that someone had been hiding in the shrubs when the SWAT unit was called out. Nothing other than those few scuffed shoeprints came to light.

Wait.

Something fluttered beneath the chinquapin. Simon bent and plucked the innocuous bit of litter from where it lay snagged on one of the shrub's lower branches. The paper outside was printed with distinctive markings he didn't recognize. He sniffed the paper and caught the faintest whiff of a scent he thought he recognized but couldn't put his finger on. He slipped the scrap into a pocket and took stock.

"Finding our spy's hidey-hole gives me a second trap to bait. Even better? I now have a contact inside of South Lake Tahoe's police department. After the trap is sprung and I apply my black light, I will report my findings to Officer Jonas Phillips. He should then be able to obtain a warrant to search her RV."

Simon broke off a short chinquapin bough from under the bush and swept away his own shoeprints. He put the bough under his arm and withdrew a small paint brush and an unopened container of fluorescent paint powder from his shirt pocket, stepped back from the chinquapin bush, and dipped the brush into the powder. By shaking and flicking the brush, he sifted the invisible dust over the chinquapin's lower and chest-high boughs and also on the ground where he'd stood to peer through the bush's branches.

"Anyone who approaches that bush will pick up powder on their shoes, pant legs, and higher," he murmured. "They won't see it and won't be able to avoid it."

He continued to sprinkle powder as he backed down the path, until he'd used all but a small amount. When he made his way back to the entry point, he stepped out onto the road, turned and, taking the chinquapin bough from under his arm, brushed away his own shoeprints. Then he planted the dying bitterbrush branch between the two saplings and dusted the ground around the branch and the branch itself with the last of the powder.

"I'll check back here regularly today with my black light. If the powder on the ground around the branch has been disturbed, it will be my delight to confront our dear, sweet Mrs. Rickert."

Next he walked up to Site 2 and confirmed that Mrs. Rickert's truck was parked in her driveway.

"Good. That angle's covered."

⸻ ◆ ⸻

SIMON WORKED HARD all morning, but he left the gate closed and managed his work so that he kept either the gate or Site 2 under his ongoing observation. Rickert wouldn't be able to leave Bright Star without Simon observing her departure.

For maybe five minutes he was roped into stopping at Site 7 for a conversation with the Mullers. Bryce's aunt and uncle had wanted to express their gratitude for Skipper and his friends including their nephew in their activities. Other than that single distraction, he'd closely monitored the gate or Mrs. Rickert's site.

Half past noon, he wiped sweat from his forehead and guzzled a bottle of water. He'd put off lunch until he finished his morning tasks, but the day had become quite warm. He really needed to eat and rest a few minutes. He was so hungry that when his cellphone chirped and vibrated in his pocket, he was tempted to let it go to voicemail.

It stopped ringing, but a moment later it started up again. He plucked the phone from his pocket and gave it a look.

"Miss Finch? Crud!" He opened the call. "Hey, what's up?"

He was unprepared for her breathless response.

"Fletcher, we've been ambushed."

CHAPTER 24

SIMON'S PICKUP BARRELED WEST on Emerald Bay Road, taking at breakneck speed the curves of the rim that circled high above Emerald Bay. While he drove, the gist of Miss Finch's call ran and reran nonstop in his head.

"Are you all right?" he'd demanded. "Hit? Grazed? Dear God, what about Skipper? And are Hugo and Pouncer okay?"

"We're all untouched, but Fletcher? They shot out my bicycle's rear tire! We had to dump our bikes quite unceremoniously near some fallen logs, unclip and grab Hugo and Pouncer's basket, and cower behind the logs to escape a perfect *hail* of bullets—a rifle firing high velocity rounds, if I am not mistaken. We called the police and then you, in that order. Oh, Fletcher! My poor babies are utterly traumatized. Pouncer will not stop crying."

"Hold on. Tell me exactly where you are; I'm leaving right this second."

As he'd gunned the maintenance truck and raced toward the office, she went on. "We had visited the old Olympic village and were returning the way we came, down Olympic Valley Road to where it met Squaw Creek Road. We turned onto Squaw Creek Road to catch the bike trail that branches off Squaw Creek Road and winds through a wonderful wooded area. We were just approaching the trail's entrance when we heard the first rounds and my tire blew out."

"Have the police arrived yet?"

"I hear sirens in the distance. Also, the personnel in the firehouse down the slope had to have heard all the gunfire. They are buzzing about like angry bees when someone has taken a stick to their hive. I do hope they don't step out into the line of fire!"

As though it had just occurred to her, she said, "Goodness! Whoever is shooting at us had to have followed us along our route to Olympic Valley, Fletcher. How else would he or she have known to set up his ambush in the trees and merely wait for us to return the same way as we'd come? And it ruined our lovely ride—absolutely ruined it!"

Her voice started to wobble a little at the end, telling Simon how distraught she was, despite her misplaced concern over the abrupt and ruinous end to their 'lovely ride.'

"Have you remained crouched behind the logs? Are you safe where you are at present?"

"I believe so, and we haven't heard any more shots since a few moments after we hunkered down—oh dear! It could mean the shooter is moving to acquire a better angle."

Simon heard Skipper moan near Miss Finch, "Jesus, please help us!"

"Stay put, do you hear me? Don't budge until the police clear the scene. I'll be there soon."

Regrettably, "soon" was a solid thirty miles to Olympic Valley, and while he drove he wrestled with his own lapse in judgment. A whopper of a failing. Before he'd roared away from Bright Star, he double-checked Mrs. Rickert's site. *Her truck was gone.*

Somehow, she'd left Bright Star without Simon knowing it.

A sick heaviness filled his gut. *If anything happens to Miss Finch or Skipper, it's on me*, he acknowledged. *I should have put off the Mullers, even if I had to be rude to them.*

On top of the guilt weighing him down, Simon knew he couldn't arrive on scene for nearly half an hour, even if he pushed the speed limit. It didn't help that traffic approaching Tahoe City and then northwest on 89 toward the town of Truckee was known to be notoriously sluggish.

Simon finally turned onto 89 and encountered less traffic than he expected. Thanking God for his grace, Simon turned west onto Olympic Valley Road. While still east of the junction of Olympic Valley Road and Squaw Creek Road, the cars ahead of him slowed, and he caught a glimpse of flashing lightbars. Apparently, traffic had been forced down to one lane and was being diverted around the scene.

While he edged slowly onward, he passed a swath of condos and ski lodges, the kind of touristy rentals that filled up summer and winter and emptied out between seasons. Next, he came abreast of the Lake Tahoe Preparatory School that conjoined the Fire Department Miss Finch had described.

Simon eased his truck forward while his eyes scanned the lay of the land. Miss Finch said the bike trail they were on had cut off from Squaw Creek Road just before the road joined Olympic Valley Road. Simon figured the trail had to be off to his left, running through the forest, upslope from the firehouse, the school, and the condos.

Since the trail has no access for cars, the shooter couldn't have driven in, Simon thought, scanning around. *Had to park elsewhere and walk in. And since they walked in, they'd have to walk back out to reach their vehicle— while carrying a long gun.*

The nearest parking to the point where Miss Finch and Skipper came under attack was at the Olympic Valley Fire Department, whose crew was milling about to assist the police if needed. A fire truck and an ambulance were parked close to the scene on Squaw Creek Road. He was tempted to return to the condo parking lots to look for Mrs. Rickert's truck or scout out individuals on foot carrying what might be a rifle. That temptation didn't live long enough to solidify, though.

Nope. I need to get to Skipper and Miss Finch.

Since the firehouse's parking lot was the closest Simon could get before being diverted, he pulled in. Two firemen tried to wave him off. He rolled down his window. One of them said, "Active scene. You can't park here."

"The woman and boy who were shot at? I've come to take them home."

"You a relation?"

"I'm the boy's, er, guardian and the woman's employer and friend. They asked me to come help them."

The fireman looked over Simon's ID, then pointed not far ahead. "Park there. You'll find them on the other side of the ambulance, getting checked out and giving their statements."

"Thanks."

Simon parked, got out, and jogged toward the ambulance where two officers were jotting notes.

Skipper saw him first. "Fletcher!" The boy's relief was palpable.

Miss Finch looked up and gave him a tight-lipped smile that was more grimace than greeting. To the side of the two officers, Skipper was surprised to see a friendly face: Jonas Phillips, the South Lake Tahoe SWAT team leader. Phillips' expression was grave, but he nodded his acknowledgement as Simon joined them.

"Surprised to see you here, Phillips," Simon said softly, tousling Skipper's hair and giving Miss Finch's shoulder a light squeeze.

"Not as surprised as I am to encounter the same cast of characters involved in a SWAT situation twice in under twenty-four hours."

"Tell me about it. Uh, aren't you out of your jurisdiction up here?"

"When we got the active shooter alert, we rolled out to provide support. Tight neighbors in the lake community and all that. Turns out we weren't needed because whoever did the shooting unloaded a thirty-round magazine then bugged out pretty quick." He gestured toward four armed individuals up on the trail, walking abreast, eyes on the ground. "They're canvassing for evidence. Already found the shooter's nest, most of the spent casings, and shoeprints. They hope to follow the prints back to where the shooter parked."

"Well, I'm glad you're here, actually. Can I have a word in private?"

Simon nodded at Miss Finch before he and Phillips moved away. They walked off the road and stopped under the shade of a tree far enough removed to grant them privacy. Simon turned his back should anyone be watching them.

"I need a favor, Phillips."

"Oh? But this is only our second date, Mr. Fletcher. Isn't it customary to send flowers or candy first?"

Simon snort-laughed. "It's presumptuous of me, I get that. But, see . . . my lady friend is in danger. Someone is, literally, gunning for her."

"You mean, other than this incident?"

"We think so, yes."

"Wish I'd been told this earlier, like, oh, I dunno, while we were investigating this morning's prank call?"

"You mean while I was flex-cuffed and getting my face scored by one of Miss Finch's patio pavers? You weren't exactly in a receptive mood. Would you have believed me if I'd told you she was in danger then?"

"No."

"Do you believe me now?"

Phillips sighed. "What is it you want? What so-called favor do you need?"

"We know there's a bounty on Miss Finch's head—no, I'm serious. A branch of the Lucchese Family out in LA."

"Whoa! That's . . . not good. But what can I do about it? Petition the US Marshals Service for protective custody? Really not my purview, dude."

"No, what I'm asking is that you keep her name out of the media, at least for a couple of days. To keep the vultures from homing in on her."

"I'm not in charge here, Fletcher, and don't have the auth—"

"But you have both connections and influence. Tight neighbors—those are your words. I'm asking that you speak to your law enforcement buddies up here and get them to withhold her name from the media—her name and the name of my young intern, who is a minor."

When Phillips seemed undecided, Simon added, "Look, Phillips. You know as well as I do, that this story has no legs. Why? Because nobody died. By tomorrow, the media won't care who the targets were."

Phillips studied Simon. "And if I manage to pull this off?"

"Then I suppose I'll owe *you* a favor."

"That so? Don't think I won't call in that favor one of these days."

"Does that mean you'll do it?"

Phillips nodded. "I'll give it my best shot . . . and listen, I'll have one of our officers follow you back to Bright Star in Miss Finch's car. She really shouldn't be driving at present."

"I agree. Thanks for the assist."

In his head, Simon breathed a rueful sigh of relief. Then he experienced a flash of incongruous insight.

Good grief! How did I end up in the business of trading favors? I'm obviously spending too much time with a certain person.

———●———

THE DRIVE BACK TO Bright Star was eerily quiet, the three of them absorbed in their own thoughts. But as Simon input his gate code, Miss Finch reached across Skipper and touched Simon's arm.

"Thank you for coming for us, Fletcher. I'll get out here and drive my car down to my site."

He exhaled. "Not a problem. Grateful to God that both of you are okay. Hugo and Pouncer too."

"Yes. Quite grateful." She glanced at Skipper, whose expression was shuttered. She mouthed to Simon, "We need to talk. In private."

Simon nodded. "Hey, Skipper? Skip?"

Skipper slowly turned his way.

"As soon as we unload at Miss Finch's site, I want you to take your bike up to the office and wait for me. I'll be there shortly. We have work to finish."

Skipper nodded. A few minutes later, his bike unloaded at Miss Finch's site, he pedaled away.

Miss Finch watched him go. "I will miss that boy."

Simon was expecting her announcement. Didn't mean he liked it one bit. "You're determined to leave, then?"

"I really must, and it's better if I go quickly. I couldn't bear it if Skipper got hurt because of me. And Fletcher? If you please, I am asking you to pay me whatever I have earned to date . . . in cash if at all possible. Now."

Simon stared at the toes of his work boots. "I have enough cash on hand back in my cabin."

"Thank you. While you are gone, I will get ready to pull out."

Simon's hand gently reached for her arm. "Wait up. Could you pull the backgrounds I asked for before you go?"

"Ah. Yes, I suppose I can."

Taking Hugo and Pouncer with her, Miss Finch walked to her trailer door, but not to pull mere cursory sweeps of Terri Rickert and Miss Santini's lives. No, the obdurate set to her mouth told Simon that, despite the day's terrifying events, Miss Finch was determined to conduct thorough background checks on them both. She would not stop until she had mined every nugget of information on the two women available via the Web.

Skipper was a different story. As they worked together, he clung to Simon like a shadow at midday. Moreover the boy was anxious. Distracted. Often so caught up in his own thoughts that he wasn't aware when Simon spoke.

After thirty minutes, Simon called a halt. "Skipper."

No response.

"Skipper!"

The kid started. "What?"

"I want you to ride your bike back to my place. Take a hot shower, and climb into bed."

"But—"

When Skipper didn't move or go further, Simon nudged him. "I need you to take a rest, Skipper; your body's in shock. You'll be all right, but a nap will do you good. Go on home. Please."

Skipper nodded and trudged off in the direction of the office. Simon patched the rear tire on Miss Finch's bike, then worked away the rest of the afternoon into the early twilight. He was dirty, sticky, hungry, and tired when his phone jangled an incoming call from Miss Finch. He picked up.

"Fletcher, you will not believe what I've found."

"Tell me."

"I would prefer to show you."

Simon sighed. *And I would prefer a shower and clean clothes.*

"Be right there."

She had parked her woody on the near side of her driveway, farthest from the shrubs. She was seated in her mini chair, laptop open on her thighs and her can of soda at the ready, the woody between her and the rest of her site.

Between her and the spy's observation point.

Simon placed her extra chair close to her and sat. "Good thinking," he whispered, putting his finger to his lips to remind them that they might be overheard.

"What do you have?" he asked.

"Good stuff. Here is the first tidbit: Terri Rickert has never been married."

"Never been married, sooo . . ."

"So, not a widow."

Simon shrugged. "Okay. And?"

"And Terri Rickert was Tony Massimo's mistress."

"No! Seriously?"

"Shhh!"

"Right. Sorry. Are you serious?"

"Serious as a tax audit. We have motive, Fletcher. I don't know how she found me, but I must assume that her hatred has a basis, albeit a flawed one: She blames me for Tony Massimo's death and is seeking revenge."

"Let's go. I want to talk to her before we call in the police."

Miss Finch put a restraining hand on his arm. "Wait. Call in the police? Think it through. She is Tony Massimo's *mistress*. What if she's conducting her own personal vendetta and Don Massimo knows nothing of it—and, hence, knows nothing of where I am? Wouldn't calling in the police make this situation public?"

Simon considered her words. "I take your point. Although Phillips has asked the local media to keep your name out of today's attack, calling the police on Rickert would generate additional media attention, which in turn could paint a bullseye on you. But . . . perhaps I can use the threat of calling them to leverage our grieving 'widow's' cooperation. Let's give it a shot and see how it plays out."

"After which you will help me load up and see me on my way?"

Slowly, Simon nodded.

CHAPTER 25

TWILIGHT HAD GIVEN WAY TO darkness when Simon drove them the short distance to Site 2 and parked his truck across the site's driveway, effectively blocking it. They walked down the drive toward Mrs. Rickert's RV, Simon carrying his black light with him.

When they came abreast of Mrs. Rickert's truck, Simon focused the black light on the truck's door, then the driveway, scanning for the fluorescent paint he'd seeded throughout the hiding place where the spy had observed Miss Finch. He continued scanning right up to Rickert's front door and turned up nothing. No trace of the powdered paint at all.

"Well, that's perplexing," he muttered to himself.

Simon peered through the latched screen door and announced, "It's Simon Fletcher and Miss Finch, Mrs. Rickert. We'd like to talk to you."

From inside, they heard, "Well, I don't want to talk to you, and you're trespassing on my site—isn't that what you said I was doing to your precious old crone? Trespassing? Go away!"

"Nope. We're not leaving until we've spoken with you. See, we know who you really are, Mrs. Rickert. We know you were Antony Massimo's mistress. That's right, we've uncovered your beef with Miss Finch. Explains why you have such antipathy toward her and why you have attacked her repeatedly. At the moment, we only want to talk. Come out or let us in, but if you refuse to talk to us, our next step will be to notify the police."

Terri Rickert appeared in the doorway. The scorching rage shuddering through her body was fearsome. "Perhaps *I* will be the one calling the police."

"That will only save me the trouble, ma'am. Oh, by the way? When I do speak to the police, I will be reporting you for stalking Miss Finch and trying to poison her pets . . . among other things."

"You cannot prove any of that."

"Oh, I think I can," Simon replied, even though he wasn't convinced he could. A lot hinged on how this conversation with Rickert went. "Now open up."

When her bluster failed to move Simon, the woman dropped her angry gaze.

"Last chance, Mrs. Rickert," Simon said softly. "I've parked my truck across your driveway so you cannot hook up your RV and flee. My truck will remain parked where it is until you talk to us . . . or until the police arrive. Your choice."

The woman who raised her gaze to them was beaten. "I'll . . . talk."

She unlocked her screen door and moved farther inside. Simon and Miss Finch stepped into Rickert's RV and looked around.

Simon pointed to her table and its bench seats. "Sit."

When she sat, Simon waved Miss Finch into the opposite bench seat and slid in beside her. Tension showed in every twitching muscle of Rickert's face.

"*You*," she spat at Miss Finch.

"We're not here to talk about what Miss Finch has or hasn't done. We need to talk about you trying to kill her."

Rickert fell against the bench seat's back and managed to appear puzzled. "Kill her?"

"Don't play cute. You tried to kill her."

"Twice," Miss Finch said.

"No, I did not. I'm no killer." She glared at Miss Finch. "I didn't want to harm you—not physically."

"You fired a gun at a young girl down on the Pope-Baldwin Bike Path. You thought she was me," Miss Finch answered.

"No! Well, I mean *yes*, I did, but I wasn't shooting at the girl, I swear it!" She clasped her trembling hands on the tabletop. "I don't know guns that well, and I . . . I have horrible aim."

"Your aim was good enough to graze that girl." The ice in Simon's voice was merciless. "You very nearly killed an innocent young woman."

Rickert swallowed. "No one was more surprised than I was that I actually hit her."

Simon blinked, Found himself momentarily off balance. "Stop trying to rationalize your actions. *You shot at her*. Tell me, where is that gun now?"

"I . . . I tossed it into the bushes not far from where the trail ends."

"*Where* exactly?"

She sighed. "Spring Creek Road, across Emerald Drive from where the Pope-Baldwin Bike Path ends."

"Nonetheless, when you fired your gun, you thought that child was me," Miss Finch insisted.

The woman said nothing for a moment. Finally, she muttered, "Yes, I thought she was you. That evening, when I spotted her, by herself, out walking her little mutt, I couldn't believe my good fortune. I believed the planets had aligned perfectly, that the universe had delivered you to me to grant me a small measure of justice."

Miss Finch scoffed. "Justice? In what manner can attempted murder equate with justice?"

Rickert ground her teeth. "Not *murder*, but by presenting me with an ideal opportunity. I mean, she was alone, yes? No one else was around."

"Sorry to be the bearer of bad news, but the planets and the universe? They consist of insentient rocks and gasses and are incapable of granting you the favor of a preferred parking spot, let alone your twisted definition of justice. God created *them*, not the other way around."

"I don't care! I thought that girl was *you*."

Miss Finch's smile was tight. "And had you succeeded? That is what they call murder in the first degree—with malice aforethought."

Rickert shook her head vehemently. "But I keep telling you, I wasn't trying to kill you—truly! I-I . . . I only wanted to make you suffer . . . as I have suffered."

Simon's unease grew. Something wasn't adding up.

"That was your end game? You wanted to scare Miss Finch. Make her feel she was being stalked?"

"Not scare her. I wanted to hurt her . . ."

"So, you only intended to wound her, not kill her, huh? Lady, at a minimum, you've confessed to assault with a deadly weapon." He leaned forward, his gaze boring into her. "You need to come clean with us. The truth is, you *did* intend to kill Miss Finch. And after you succeeded, you planned to call your boyfriend's father so you could collect the bounty on her head."

The woman appeared confused. "Call Tony's father? Why would I call him? *How* would I call him? I don't even know the man. And what bounty?"

She shifted wide eyes to Miss Finch. "There's a bounty on your head?"

That "thing" bugging Simon grew tentacles and tightened its grip. "You're saying you don't know your boyfriend's dad?"

She shook her head. "No, I don't. Tony never took me to meet his parents. He didn't tell me much about them, either."

Simon snorted. "Really? In addition to not personally knowing Tony's father, you're also claiming to be ignorant of who his father is? *What* he is?"

She shrugged. "Tony kept us and our relationship separate from the rest of his life. I didn't know his folks, and they didn't know about me."

"You expect us to believe his family knew nothing of you?"

She stared at her hands. "Tony didn't want his wife to find out about me."

"Tony's *wife?*" Simon felt like he'd been hit between the eyes with a pipe wrench. Alongside the pounding ache of this revelation, he berated himself for accepting Dinesh's summary of Antony Massimo's personal life and for not chasing down his own background on the man. He slid his eyes toward Miss Finch to gauge her reaction.

I didn't look into Tony Massimo's background because I was looking for info on you, *not him. And unless I'm reading you wrong, Miss Finch, you are as shocked as I am to hear he was married.*

Rickert nodded, misery etched on her features. "Tony and I were together three years, the best three years of my life, except . . . except I had to share him with his wife. That was the deal. We saw each other on a strict schedule: every-other Friday night and two Sundays a month."

Simon was incredulous. "That's all? You were content with two evenings and—*wow*—two whole days a month?"

She spread her hands in a helpless gesture. "I loved him."

"And his wife?" Simon asked.

"What about her?"

"Did you ever bump into her?"

"I wouldn't know her if I did."

"You've never seen her? Not even a photo? You never Googled her?"

"Well, Tony said if we were to keep seeing each other, I had to learn to com . . . compart-something."

"Compartmentalize?"

"Yeah, compartmentalize. We had to keep our life together separate from his life with his wife. And I . . . I'm not into all that Google stuff."

"You certainly have the 'mental' aspect of compart*mental*ize down pat," Miss Finch murmured, her dig going straight over Rickert's head.

Apparently, for the role of mistress, Tony hadn't selected the sharpest stick in the stack.

Must have chosen the woman for her other attributes, Simon told himself, recalling his initial reaction to Rickert.

"It was worth it! I loved him!" Rickert moaned.

"You loved him more than he loved you, I wager—that being considerably less than he loved himself, the selfish, insufferable narcissist," Miss Finch replied.

Mrs. Rickert flushed. "What would you know about love, you shriveled old—"

Simon interrupted her. "Your story is that Tony never told you his dad is the *capo* of the Los Angeles branch of the Lucchese Family mob?"

"The what?"

"The boss or head man of the Lucchese Family, an organized crime mob."

"Crime mob? As in gangsters? Are you joking? That's impossible!"

Miss Finch said softly, "It is a *fact* that can be verified as easily as proving you are no *widow*, Mrs. Rickert, since you have never been married. Furthermore, it is *fact* that Antony Massimo was a well-versed hit man for the Lucchese Family."

Rickert's eyes bulged. "Th-that's not true! You're lying!"

"What have I to gain by lying?"

"But I knew him—he was no killer!"

"Then why was he driving a tanker truck the day he perished? A tanker truck *he personally stole?*"

The woman shook her head vigorously. "Again, you're lying."

Miss Finch placed a file folder in front of the woman and flipped it open. "This is a copy of the police accident report. May I draw your attention to this line, here? It reads, 'The two vehicles involved in the incident were a Range Rover Evoque driven by BD Finch and a tanker truck, reported stolen, driven by Antony Massimo.'"

The fire seemed to go out of Mrs. Rickert. She licked her lips and said halfheartedly, "Tony said you wrote some kind of book filled with lies. Perhaps these papers are fake too."

"He called me a liar because the book I published proves how six vehicular incidents that the police concluded were accidents were actually well-planned and executed homicides. Upon reinvestigation of the first two incidents, the police uncovered additional evidence, proof that two husbands, unknown to each other, paid the same hit man to kill their wives and make their deaths look like accidents. They also uncovered proof that Antony Massimo was that hit man.

"Furthermore, the evidence connects those two cases and their contract killer to the other four cases in my book, the deaths in those four cases benefitting the Lucchese Family mob. Lastly, the only common denominator in all six cases was the contract killer, Antony Massimo—thereby incriminating the Lucchese Family mob in the last four murders."

"But . . ." She seemed dumbfounded.

Simon, who'd been puzzling over Rickert's replies, signaled to Miss Finch that he wanted to resume his questioning of the woman.

"Mrs. Rickert, you said you didn't intend to harm Miss Finch physically, is that right?"

Mrs. Rickert exhaled. Stared at her twined hands. "Yes. I-I, like I said, I wanted her to suffer, to feel the same pain I felt. The pain I feel every day."

"How did you feel? Were you scared or anxious when your boyfriend died?"

"Scared? No . . . that is, not exactly. I am afraid of being alone the rest of my life . . . but I mostly grieved because my heart is broken!"

"Let me see if I'm following you. You wanted to deprive Miss Finch in the same manner you were deprived? You wanted her to grieve like you're grieving?"

The woman cringed and pushed herself as far back in her seat as possible, as though trying to avoid what was coming.

And it was coming. Hard.

"You know what I think you intended that evening down on the Pope-Baldwin Path, Mrs. Rickert? Yes, you may have come upon that poor girl by chance, but I believe you were telling the truth when you said you weren't aiming at Miss Finch. And the only reason you grazed that girl is because you told us the truth a second time: You actually *are* a terrible shot."

Mrs. Rickert withered further in her seat, but Miss Finch's head jerked in Simon's direction. "What *are* you getting at, Simon?"

A small smile twitched the corner of his mouth because she'd used his given name.

"I'm saying Mrs. Rickert here was shooting at Hugo, BeeDee. Not the girl she believed was you."

"What!"

"Yes, she thought the girl's little dog was Hugo. She wanted to see you suffer? That's how she planned to do it. She planned to kill *Hugo*, but due to her terrible aim, she missed the dog and grazed that poor girl instead."

Simon saw Miss Finch struggle with her emotions, but he wasn't done.

"Sadly for Mrs. Rickert, when you bought your bike and started riding with Hugo and Pouncer in the front basket, it deprived her of a second such opportunity. So, she had to come up with another means of harming Hugo or Pouncer, which is why she opened the catio door and released Hugo the evening we had the marshmallow roast with the boys. Her attempt likely failed when Hugo eluded her and ran off—or perhaps when Pouncer, being her charming self, startled her, giving Hugo opportunity to flee. In any event, I'm certain she also left the poisoned meat in your catio for Hugo and Pouncer to find."

Mrs. Rickert's rage came alive and she sprang to her feet, pushing the table toward them in her anger. "You killed the love of my life, you dried up old witch! You love those horrid, dreadful animals of yours? Yes, I wanted to kill them! I wanted to kill anything you loved! I wanted to make you suffer like you have made *me* suffer!"

Simon rose and loomed over the woman. "*Sit down*, Mrs. Rickert!" He then watched as Miss Finch processed the ugly truth. She closed her eyes and muttered something under her breath. When she finally spoke, her words were calm. Gentle, even.

"I am terribly sorry your boyfriend died, Mrs. Rickert. As a woman who lost the love of her life long ago, my heart goes out to you. That said, you must accept that I did not kill Tony Massimo, nor did I attempt to. He killed *himself* when he drove that stolen tanker truck into my car and flew through the truck's windshield. Only by the miraculous grace of God did I escape death at *his* hands."

"No, you goaded him with that awful book you wrote! You sicced the police on him and forced him to run and hide. He had to defend himself, hit back somehow—what else was he to do? You had framed an innocent man! All of this is your fault!"

Simon nodded. "So you lied to us. You *did* know he attacked Miss Finch."

When the woman broke down, sobbing uncontrollably, Simon signaled Miss Finch, and they stood to go. As they moved toward the door. Simon halted. He spotted a pack of gum lying on the arm of Rickert's sofa. He took a second to study it, shook his head, then followed Miss Finch out the door.

They walked up to Simon's truck. Simon gestured for Miss Finch to come around to the driver's side where Simon was dialing 911.

"She said she ditched her gun, but I'm not betting my life on what comes out of her mouth. I'd prefer we wait behind my truck, just in case she experiences a change of heart and comes out, guns blazing," he told Miss Finch, as the call rang through.

"This is Simon Fletcher calling from Bright Star Summer RV Residence," he told the dispatcher. "I have just confronted one of my residents. She has confessed to taking a pot shot at a girl down on the Pope-Baldwin Bike Path, couple weeks back. I need a police unit to take her into custody for that and for an animal abuse charge. Tell the officer that we have a good idea where the weapon is too."

Miss Finch sighed. "What a disaster."

"Rickert? A genuine hot mess. Or did you mean our case?"

"We have a 'case'?"

"What else would you call it? Someone has it in for you, but it's not Terri Rickert. I no longer believe she's the individual who's been spying on you."

"Why would you think that?"

"No fluorescent paint traces and her gum isn't the same brand as the wrapper I found in the spy's little hidey hole."

"And you expect me to hang about waiting for the other shoe to drop?"

"What I expect is that since *you* are the person at risk, and since it's our case, then we need to figure out who is targeting you."

"Perhaps you need to figure it out; *I* feel the need to skedaddle."

Simon guffawed. "Skedaddle?"

"Remarkable. Your ears are functioning, yet I must repeat my intentions? How many and varied expressions of departure will it take to press home the seriousness of my situation? It is imperative that I abandon ship, get out of Dodge, blow this popsicle stand, and beat a hasty retreat—heavy emphasis on *hasty*."

"Well, I don't want you to go."

"I believe we've already acknowledged our agreement on that sentiment, Fletcher. It doesn't alter my pressing need to 'beat feet' since, as you put it, *I* am the person at risk."

Disgruntled, Simon leaned against the driver's door . . . and remembered something. "Say, Miss Finch, when you pulled Terri Rickert's background, did you also pull Marie Santini's?"

"Goodness! I . . ." She shook her head. "I confess I was so engrossed with what I'd found on Terri Rickert, that I did not continue on."

"So, Marie Santini?"

She huffed. "Marie Santini cannot matter at this point, can she? Why, the woman is positively frightened of her own shadow. Rather, since we are convinced Terri Rickert is not trying to kill me and we have no other suspects in mind, it behooves me to pull up stakes posthaste—before the shooter's aim improves."

Simon shook his head. "Nope. You can leave first thing in the morning, once I'm convinced that Miss Santini is clean. After that, I will help you load up."

She sighed. "Very well. Hopefully, a few more hours will not hurt, and I could certainly use the help."

"Glad to hear it."

———— ❖ ————

NINE O'CLOCK HAD ROLLED around before the police finished asking their questions, took Terri Rickert into custody, and without fanfare, drove away. Simon pulled into Miss Finch's drive, got out, and opened the passenger side door.

Miss Finch yawned as she climbed down from his cab. "Goodness, but I am weary."

"Best you get crackin', then," Simon murmured. "The sooner you finish pulling Santini's background, the more shuteye both of us can catch. I'll keep an eye out while you work, and I will sleep in the tent again tonight."

"What about Skipper?"

"He was so emotionally drained, I sent him to my cabin for a nap. Knowing him, he'll probably sleep straight through the night. As for me, I can be up early, say 6:00 a.m., to help you pack and load . . . if Santini's background comes up clean."

"What was it you said to me not long ago, *Mr.* Fletcher? 'I've got one nerve left, and you're standing on it'?"

"Like that one, do you? By the way, enough of the '*Mr.* Fletcher' baloney. You called me by my first name not more than an hour back."

"And my nerves may be shot dead—quite literally—just because you insist I dither around merely to pull background on Marie Santini."

"Yeah, yeah. Don't forget that we need to be vigilant about what we say aloud. For all we know, our spy could be listening to us now."

While Miss Finch busied herself inside, Simon lit one of her tiki torches and wandered around her site in the flickering light, tidying up his and Skipper's tent, policing for bits of trash, sweeping the patio, readying the firepit for the morning. When Hugo whined from inside the catio, he called to Miss Finch, "Do you mind if I let Hugo out?"

"Let them both out, if you please," she called back. "And do not be concerned about Pouncer; she will not leave my site as long as you are there."

Simon unlatched the catio door and stood back. Hugo bounded out, ran around Simon three times, then sat in front of him, head forward in happy expectation.

"Good man, Hugo," Simon murmured, giving the top of Hugo's head a good scratch. He moved Miss Finch's full-sized lawn chair away from the flickering tiki torch and into the shadows on the other side of the woody. He settled into the chair to await the results of Marie Santini's background check.

Hugo measured the distance to his lap, made the leap, and nestled into the crook of Simon's arm. Two minutes later, Pouncer landed on his chest. She clawed her regal way to his shoulder and around the back of his neck until she was enthroned across both of Simon's shoulders. Soon her purr became a pleasing buzzsaw in Simon's right ear.

Simon relaxed.

He sighed and let down. All the way down.

Guess I'm super tired.

No, that wasn't it, not entirely. What he felt was deeper. Better.

When was the last time I felt this content?

———— ◆ ————

"FLETCHER." SOMETHING jostled his shoulder. "Fletcher, wake up."

He blinked several times. Although the only light nearby was the tiki torch, he could hardly miss the two stunningly bright blue eyes only inches from his face. They gazed deep down into the depths of his psyche.

"Uh, hello, Pouncer."

She winked one eye, purred softly . . . and giggled.

Huh? No, wait. Pouncer doesn't giggle.

Does she?

Finally awake, he found Pouncer sprawled on his chest mere inches from his face and Miss Finch off to his left grinning at his discomfiture.

"Guess I was asleep."

"You must have needed the rest."

Simon shook himself and sat up tall. Hugo pulled his nose out of the crook of Simon's arm to see what was going on. Pouncer, on the other hand, launched herself from Simon's chest, leaving clawed launch points behind, and bounded toward the catio door. She turned and hissed once at Simon, then walked inside, tail held high.

"You're a brat, Pouncer."

He rubbed his face before asking Miss Finch in a whisper, "Find anything?"

"And how."

"Don't just stand there!"

Miss Finch pulled her chair over to his, plopped herself down, and popped the top of her preferred beverage. She leaned toward Simon; he put his head near hers.

"You know how stunned we were to find that Terri Rickert was Antony Massimo's mistress?" She sipped on the fizzing beverage. "Ah. Just the pick-me-up I needed."

Simon shuddered. "Uh huh. You're delaying. Are you baiting me?"

She smiled a coy little smile. "Oh, without a doubt. And I confess to being both excited and dismayed, because I wager even Terri Rickert's newly revealed secrets cannot hold a candle to what I learned minutes ago."

"Come on. Spit it out," he growled.

Her chuckle was wry. "Very well, here it is: Our Miss Santini is actually Marie Santini Massimo, Tony Massimo's wife—or should I say, his widow?"

"What!" Simon shot from his seat, sending Hugo scrabbling in midair to right himself.

Miss Finch grabbed Simon by his shirttail. "Shh!"

Simon dropped back into his seat. "Right. Sorry, but *wow*—unbelievable. You're certain?"

"I am positive." Those shiny Junior Mints flicked in Simon's direction. "And now I must express my regret for discounting our unassuming little assassin wannabe and must thank you for insisting that I pull her background."

"To be fair, we had no idea Tony was even married when you pulled Terri's background let alone have any clue Santini might have a connection to him. How could we know?"

Miss Finch's murmured reply was severe. "How could we? We failed to ascertain this basic fact because we *presumed much*, Mr. Fletcher, and presumption is *ever* the enemy of truth."

It was the second time she'd delivered a warning against presumption, and Simon was forced to agree with her. "You're right. On my part, I took Craig Dinesh's account of Tony Massimo at face value, never asking myself if his information was true or complete. We should have done our own background on Massimo at the get-go."

He sighed. "Two years out of the Corps' investigative detail, and my instincts are about rusted over."

"Spilt milk at the moment, Fletcher. More important to the situation at hand, now that we know the truth about Marie Santini? It grossly complicates the situation, specifically *my* situation."

"Because?"

"Because, as I have also learned, Marie's father is Franco Santini, Don Massimo's right-hand man—his top lieutenant and an old and trusted friend."

Simon stilled. "I suppose that explains Tony's zealously structured relationship with Terri Rickert. That whole 'compartmentalized' tale she told us suddenly makes sense." He shook his head. "Talk about toxic in-laws."

"Indeed. Tony's infidelity, had it become known while he was alive, could have driven a wedge between his father and his father's most trusted lieutenant, not to mention Tony earning his father-in-law's everlasting fury. Since we both know that feuds within organized crime families have resulted in bloodbaths, it should be no great mystery why Tony kept Terri Rickert behind a firewall, far from his family. And yet . . . an internal Lucchese Family bloodletting could not have been Tony's only or even primary concern."

"Oh?"

"Consider what would have become of *Terri* had Tony's relationship with her come to the attention of either Don Massimo or Franco Santini."

"Good grief! You're right—Terri's life wouldn't have been worth the proverbial plugged nickel if Tony's father or his father-in-law had found out about her."

"Perhaps Tony Massimo wasn't as selfish as I labeled him," Miss Finch admitted, "yet another error of presumption, this one on me. But, back to 'Miss' Santini?"

Simon stared into the shadows surrounding Miss Finch's site, recalling his first encounter with Marie Santini.

"My dad bought this RV for me when I told him I wanted to get away, perhaps spend the summer here."

"Must be nice."

He remembered her smile before saying, *"You know how dads are. My dad would do anything for me . . . Well, almost anything."*

"Almost anything. Huh. Maybe . . ."

"Maybe what, please?"

"The day I met Marie, she told me her dad would do anything for her. But then she qualified her statement by adding, '*almost* anything.'"

"Do you think she meant—"

"That her dad would do anything for her except bump off her husband's mistress? Or—worse for you—bump off her husband's so-called killer? Either or both, we have no way of knowing."

He was envisioning Santini's shy smile as she spoke . . . and unwrapped a stick of gum.

His hands started digging around in his pants' front pocket before his mind fully formed the association. He yanked out the wad of gum wrapped in a scrap of paper.

"Eureka."

"What is it?"

"Definitive proof, I hope. Let's go."

"Where to?"

"If Terri Rickert didn't lie in wait to shoot you up by Olympic Village, then who else fits the bill? Who else had motive, for that matter? We made a mistake when we bought into the idea that Marie Santini 'is afraid of her own shadow.' It's a ruse. No, based on what you've uncovered, we must assume she takes after her father more that she lets on. That makes her far more devious and dangerous than Terri Rickert. And since we've already discounted that 'mousy' woman once, I won't make the mistake of under-estimating her a second time."

He looked at Miss Finch. "Are you carrying?"

"I can be."

"Presumption being ever the enemy of truth, please arm yourself. Time to pay Marie Santini a visit."

The TAHOE MYSTERIES

CHAPTER 26

WHILE MISS FINCH WENT INTO her trailer for her gun, Simon put Hugo in the catio and latched the door. He pulled the firearm holstered at the small of his back, checked both it and the extra mag on his belt, and made certain the black light in his truck still had an adequate charge.

He looked up as Miss Finch joined him. She had changed into kiddie-sized range gear: cargo pants, khaki blouse, and tactical boots.

"Show me what you're carrying?"

She lifted the right side of her blouse to uncover a small holster attached to her belt. She unsnapped the holster, withdrew a Ruger LCP II, and handed it to him, barrel appropriately pointed down.

"Tiny but efficient," Simon muttered. "Two and three-quarter-inch barrel, six .380 ACP rounds."

"Just shy of a pound, fully loaded," Miss Finch added. "Easy for me to handle."

"Extra mag?"

"Always."

"Good. Now wait here a minute. I need to check something."

Simon extinguished the tiki light, grabbed the black light, and jogged up to the road and down the shoulder to the mouth of the path that led through the brush to the spy's observation point. Without touching the dying branch, he shone the black light onto the shoulder. It took only seconds to find what he was seeking: faintly glowing footprints emerging from the trail behind the branch. They headed across the road and on up the island before fading out.

"Not toward Terri Rickert's site," he muttered softly, "but across the island . . . to Marie Santini's?"

The footprints hadn't retained enough powdered paint on them for Simon to track them farther. Powdered paint on the spy's clothes, on the other hand, was less likely to have rubbed or flaked off.

Simon was counting on that.

He jogged back to Miss Finch and told her what he'd found.

"Officer Phillips will require more to go on than Marie being the wife of Terry Rickert's lover. Before I call him, I want to scan Santini's car and trailer doorway. If the black light doesn't turn up any of my paint powder,

I'll knock on her door and employ some fabrication that allows me to check her clothing."

He glanced at Miss Finch. "Your job is to remain hidden from Santini but stay ready should she make an overt move."

"In other words, my job is to have your back."

"Yeah. That's it."

They climbed into Simon's truck. Marie Santini's RV was in Site 19, meaning she was on the other side of the Bright Star wide loop, but just five sites from Bright Star's gate. For that reason, Simon turned left out of Miss Finch's drive, drove slowly to the gate and parked crosswise across the entrance, blocking Santini's only means of escape should the woman attempt to flee. Simon had done the same to block Terri Rickert's egress when he parked across her driveway.

Before they got out, Miss Finch said, "I hope you find what you need, Fletcher, but I would prefer that you not allow her to get the drop on you. Put plainly, please be careful."

"I'll do my best. Shall we pray before I go in?"

"Absolutely."

They joined hands, and Simon murmured, "Lord? We think Marie Santini is Miss Finch's stalker and attempted assassin. If so, she is without doubt a dangerous individual. Please be with us as I approach her RV. We ask you to keep her unaware of our suspicions. And please help the police bring this ugly thing to a safe conclusion. We ask these things in Jesus' name. Amen."

"Amen."

Simon and Miss Finch got down from his truck and trod softly the wrong way up Bright Star's one-way road. Night had fully fallen, the time closing in on 11:00 p.m. They passed Sites 24, 23, 22, 21, and 20. They heard a few muffled sounds and saw dim lights reaching up those driveways to the road—with the exception of the Gormans in Site 21. Their RV was dark, the older couple likely abed and asleep.

When they reached Site 19, a single light shone from within Santini's motor home.

At the back fender of the subcompact Santini pulled behind her RV, Simon put his mouth next to Miss Finch's. "Wait here. If my black light doesn't show anything on her car or front door, I'll knock. That's your cue to move up past the passenger door of her motor home and listen closely to our conversation. If I need you to back me up, I'll use the phrase, 'I think I can fix the problem outside.' Got it?"

She nodded.

Simon turned on his black light and shined its focused glow over the driver's door of Santini's car and the asphalt below the door. Nothing popped.

Still trying to be quiet, he crept toward the motor home's door. He shined the black light over the step, the door, and its handle. Again, nothing.

He moved up and knocked on the motor home's door. When he glanced to the side and saw Miss Finch move up to her assigned position, he nodded to her.

No longer attempting to keep quiet, Simon called "Miss Santini? Simon Fletcher here. I realize it's late, but may I have a word?"

Santini's dog, Napoleon, began to bark and shuffle toward the door, his *woof* raspy with age. A moment later, the light over the door came on. Then the door opened a crack, and Marie Santini peered out.

"Mr. Fletcher?"

"Yeah, sorry to bother you this late. Just needed to pass on some information to you about a problem we're experiencing. Have you noticed any issues with your Wi-Fi or cable?"

She stared blandly and wiped sleep from her eyes. "Sorry. Fell asleep reading. Wi-Fi or cable? I wouldn't know, actually. I don't watch much television. I prefer a good book."

"I get you. Well, since you're up, would you mind turning on your TV so I can take a look? I may need to reset your cable box or modem. I'll be done in a jiffy, then on to the next resident."

She thought for a moment. "All right."

She opened the screen door. Simon switched on the black light and hung it at his side, not trying to hide it as he stepped inside.

"What is that?" Santini asked.

"This?" Simon lifted the light, "My trouble light. Makes it easier for me to look behind your TV or modem if I need to reset something."

"Oh."

The moment she turned away, Simon lifted the light to the back of her pants. He dropped it beside his leg just as quickly. Even with the dim light within the trailer diminishing the black light's effect, he'd seen all he needed to see.

Using the TV's remote, Santini powered on a large flatscreen mounted on the wall. It came to life with the cable company's menu scrolling down the screen.

"Huh," Simon mumbled. "Looks like you're okay. Let me just check your cable box's settings and I'll move down to the next site. We want to ensure that Bright Star's amenities are always in good working order."

He moved to a shelf beside the television where the cable box sat. With his back toward Santini, he scanned the back of the box with his black light . . . but his eyes were fixed on the wastebasket tucked into the corner below.

"Everything looks good. Again, sorry for disturbing you."

He exited the RV, trying to ignore the mental image of Marie Santini training a gun on his back. It wasn't until he reached the front of her RV and joined Miss Finch, that he began to breathe easier. He switched off the black light and placed a finger across his lips. Neither of them spoke until they were on the road, walking quietly back to where he'd left his truck blocking the gate. He keyed in his gate code, and they passed through, still silent, until Simon unlocked the office door and they went inside. He went directly to the phone on the counter and dialed Phillips' number.

"Phillips, it's Simon Fletcher. Yup, I realize it's after ten o'clock—sorry about that. Do you want the individual from the active shooter scene yesterday? We've figured out the who and the why, and I have, at the very least, evidence that she's been spying on Miss Finch, but you'll need to act quickly to preserve and document that evidence. Yes, a woman."

They spoke for several minutes, Simon explaining the evidence until Phillips understood the gist of it. They moved on from there, hashing out next steps.

When Simon hung up, he told Miss Finch, "Phillips, two detectives, and an evidence tech will be here inside a half hour."

"What about a warrant? How do you plan to get them inside Santini's rig that you might show them the fluorescent paint on Marie Santini's pantlegs?"

"That's the tricky part. We have to lure her out of her RV so Phillips can document the paint on her pants—and we have to get her out without her suspecting we're on to her. Otherwise, if she does catch on and she has that high-powered rifle within her RV, we may end up in an armed standoff."

"That wouldn't be at all good for the safety of your nearby residents . . . or Bright Star's reputation."

"Reputation is the least of my concerns at the moment, but yes, we'd prefer to avoid a shootout. Just need some legitimate means of drawing Santini out of her RV."

"Emergency alert," Miss Finch replied.

"What?"

She raised one brow. "Sound Bright Star's evacuation sirens. Be prepared to snag her the moment she pops out her door or wherever it seems best to take her into custody."

Simon felt a slow grin stretching his lips. "Brilliant! At the very least, the evacuation will get the other residents out of harm's way if, for some reason, Santini refuses to leave her RV."

———◆———

SIMON AND MISS FINCH WERE waiting outside the office when Officer Phillips quietly rolled up in a police unit, followed by another unit and a crime scene van, headlights off. Simon invited them into the office where they were less likely to be overheard making their plans. Phillips introduced Simon and Miss Finch to the two detectives he'd brought with him.

"If you don't mind, please repeat to them what you told me on the phone. It was a lot to take in."

Simon rehearsed the several attacks on Miss Finch to the other officers, those attacks committed by Terri Rickert and the more serious one he and Miss Finch believed Marie Santini had committed. He didn't leave much out, including why Miss Finch had earned the Lucchese Family's ire.

Phillips frowned at her. "Let's see if I get the starting point of all this. You basically published a book disclosing to the world that this dangerous crime family ordered a bunch of hits on their enemies and tried to make them look like accidents? Why would you do that?"

She lifted her chin. "At the moment, my reasoning is not of consequence. What *is* of consequence is the presence of Marie Santini, widow of Tony Massimo and daughter of Franco Santini, in this RV park. However, we believe she is acting of her own accord for personal reasons, possibly without the Mob's permission or knowledge. Her husband died trying to kill me, you see, and she, like Terri Rickert, blames me for his death."

"What a mess," Phillips muttered.

"I cannot disagree."

Phillips turned to Simon. "You say you found that fluorescent paint on Santini's clothing?"

"Yes. It ties her to a hiding place in the brush surrounding Miss Finch's site. Someone has been using that little hidey-hole to spy on her. It's why we need to act soon to preserve the evidence on Santini's clothing."

Simon pulled the baggy in which he'd placed the wad of gum wrapped in paper from his pocket. "I also found this on the ground at the observation point. It's the same brand of gum Santini chews. If you get a warrant, you'll find a matching wad in the wastebasket nearest her television. Hopefully, they can pull her DNA from both."

"Seems like flimsy justification for getting a warrant. Can you show me this 'hidey-hole' you're talking about?"

"I can. It's on the other side of the park's 'island,' basically opposite Santini's site. If your tech comes with us, you can document any further evidence we find."

Simon, Phillips, and the crime scene tech walked from the office to the dead branch marking the entrance to the path leading to the spy's observation point. Simon shined his black light on the foot prints leading away from the branch.

"See these prints? I believe these will match Marie Santini's shoes."

The tech took several photos, then Simon removed the branch and pointed to additional foot prints. The tech photographed those also.

When the tech finished, Simon said, "Follow me. I'll stop and point out other evidence to document."

Simon led them along the path, through the brush and winding around trees. Simon stopped just short of the wider spot directly opposite Miss Finch's firepit and moved the black light across the ground.

He said to Phillips, "You can see someone has been here as recently as today. I spread this powdered fluorescent paint yesterday morning, and I checked it several times throughout the day until I received Miss Finch's call that she'd been ambushed."

He looked Phillips in the eye. "Terri Rickert hasn't a speck of fluorescent powder on her. Marie Santini, on the other hand? Her pant legs are covered in it."

Phillips nodded. "Let's go back to your office. I'll call for a warrant."

The call took nearly fifteen minutes, but when he hung up the phone, he told them, "Warrant is on its way."

He turned to Simon, "You know this place. Do you have any suggestions on how best to draw the suspect out of her RV so we can take her into custody without an exchange of gunfire? We don't want to trigger an active shooter situation."

"Miss Finch has a good idea."

CHAPTER 27

AT 2:30 IN THE MORNING, Simon activated Bright Star's emergency evacuation system. The immediate response to the blaring park-wide sirens was, understandably, mostly unseen and unheard. Three minutes in, though, panicky shouts joined the still-blasting sirens along with the roars of trucks and car engines as they backed out onto the road and started toward the gate. Once on the access road, however, those fleeing the park and its imaginary fire didn't get far.

Half a mile beyond the gate, Bright Star's agitated residents encountered two police units blocking the road, lightbars flashing. At the officers' commands, residents pulled to the side, turned off their vehicles, and waited . . . more confused at that point than when they'd been rousted from their sleep.

Back at the park, Officer Phillips directed Miss Finch to confine herself to Bright Star's office—to her utter and quite vocal disgust. Phillips then positioned Simon and an officer named Crutchfield within some trees alongside the road, just beyond Santini's site. Simon's role was to note when Marie Santini pulled out of her site, and Officer Crutchfield was to notify Phillips via two-way radio. Phillips would, as Santini approached the open gate, order a third police unit to pull across the road by the office, hemming Santini between him and his team in the front and Crutchfield and Simon, at Santini's backside.

Simon tapped Crutchfield on the shoulder. "There she is," he whispered.

Crutchfield clicked his radio three times, code to notify Phillips of the suspect's approach.

When Santini headed for the gate, the Gormans directly ahead of her, Simon and Crutchfield hotfooted it across the island. They climbed down onto the road beside the dancing fountains where they waited for Santini's approach. Officer Crutchfield had his sidearm drawn.

As Santini neared the gate with her elderly dog in her car's passenger seat, several planned actions occurred: Once the Gormans roared through the park entrance, a police unit darted out from behind the office to block the road. One of those officers jumped out and, from behind the shield of his door, pointed a spotlight on Santini's car. At the same time, Phillips and two officers stepped from the office porch onto the road, faced Santini's car with their weapons drawn and pointed at her, and shouted for her to stop. Lastly, Officer Crutchfield waved off the car in line behind Santini and flanked Santini's vehicle.

As a civilian, Simon was forbidden to participate in the takedown. He stayed back as ordered but close enough to watch the scene play out.

He witnessed the shock that crashed over Santini, followed by a desperate display of mental gymnastics as she tried to reason out an escape. Defeat followed shock as she realized the hopelessness of her situation. And Simon recognized the rash, last-ditch determination that flashed across her face.

He couldn't see the handgun on the car seat, but he knew, beyond any doubt, when she reached for it.

"Don't do it, Santini!" Simon shouted. "You love your good boy, Napoleon, don't you? You don't want to force these officers to shoot him in the crossfire, do you? Please don't kill Napoleon. Put the gun down."

"He's right, Miss Santini," Phillips called. "If we so much as *see* a gun, we *will* open fire. To avoid such a possibility, place both of your hands on the steering wheel and do not move them until we tell you to."

Slowly, she did as Phillips commanded and gripped her steering wheel with both hands. The rest was over in several tense seconds, ending with Santini on the ground, hands cuffed behind her. Crutchfield retrieved the handgun Santini had dropped on her car's center console.

The officers managed to keep Santini's dog in the car, but her "good boy, Napoleon," loyal to his mistress, lunged at the windows, barking, growling, and snapping in helpless fury. Simon went to the passenger door, opened it a crack, and spoke softly to him.

The dog showed his teeth and growled through them.

Suddenly Miss Finch elbowed Simon aside. "Hey, sweet boy. It's okay."

The frantic elder dog whined piteously. She extended her hand through the cracked door. He sniffed it, whined again, and looked toward Santini as she was loaded into a police unit.

Miss Finch eased open the door and retrieved a leash from the passenger-side floor. She snapped it onto Napoleon's collar. He whined again, but the fight had gone out of him, leaving him sad and anxious.

"Come with me, Napoleon. It's going to be okay. I promise you."

After that came the systematic "dismantling" of Marie Santini's Forest River as the detectives and crime scene techs descended on it, scouring it for evidence.

Simon went around to the resident vehicles that had been behind Santini and told them they were free to return to their sites. Residents at the roadblock down the road were not as lucky; they would have to wait for Phillips to give his officers the "all clear" signal.

In the meantime, Simon, Miss Finch, and Napoleon waited in the office for Phillips to report on what Santini had left behind.

Twenty minutes later, he walked through the office door carrying several bagged objects. One of the clear evidence bags showed a bulky item neatly wrapped in black plastic and tightly duct taped.

"Found this rifle with a folding stock holding an empty magazine buried in Santini's firepit. Found the wrapped wad of gum in the wastebasket as you described. Also found fluorescent powder on a pair of trousers in her laundry hamper. Used your black light on her just now, and photographed fluorescent powder on her arms."

Finally, he grinned outright. "Last, but loads better than fluorescent powder, we swabbed Santini's hands and the clothes in her laundry hamper for GSR. The results made my techs perfectly giddy."

Simon and Miss Finch exchanged relieved glances; Simon reached for Miss Finch's hand and squeezed it.

"By the way, we need you to follow us to the station so we can take your statements," Phillips added.

"No problem," Simon said.

"Good. Oh, by the way, since my station commander is out of town and left me in charge, and seeing as how the tall tale you told us is so convoluted and hard to follow—you know, that whole business explaining why Santini has it in for Miss Finch—would the two of you be willing to listen in on our initial interrogation of the suspect?"

"By all means," Miss Finch said for both of them, nearly as giddy as the crime techs.

Phillips smiled again. "Outstanding. You two may be able to keep us on track with the details. Oh. And one last thing? My officers are holding your kid outside. He's pitching a right royal fit and demanding to see you."

"Our what?"

"He means Skipper, Fletcher," Miss Finch murmured.

"Crud. I'd all but forgotten about him!"

"Yes, well, Bright Star's sirens probably woke half the county."

When Simon stepped out of the office door, he was hit by a respectable rendition of a flying tackle.

Skipper clung to Simon and sobbed, "I thought . . . I thought . . . I was really afraid!"

"We're okay, buddy, and everything is going to be fine. We got the person who shot at you and Miss Finch yesterday. The police have her now—thanks be to God."

"Yes, amen," Miss Finch added.

Skipper let go of Simon and swiped at his moist eyes. "Who? Who was it?"

"Miss Santini."

"That shy lady? Her? No way!"

Miss Finch smiled. "We were so busy looking at what we presumed to be the obvious, that we discounted and looked past the carefully crafted disguise our 'mousy' resident wore so convincingly. Let that be a lesson to us all."

It was still the middle of the night, actually very early Saturday morning, and as exhausted as Simon and Miss Finch were, they were obligated to follow Phillips to the police station.

Simon grabbed Skipper and walked him a few feet away from Phillips' officers, gesturing for Miss Finch to join them. She followed them, cajoling Napoleon to come along with her.

"Skipper, listen up. Miss Finch and I may be gone for hours. Even though we're not supposed to leave you unsupervised, in this situation, it can't be helped. So, I need you to go back to my cabin and remain there until we return. However, if we still aren't back in time to open the office in the morning at the usual time, I would like you to open it and stay there. May I have your word that you'll stay put, either at my cabin or in the office?"

"Yes, sir. And I'll take care of the office."

Simon clasped Skipper's shoulder. "I know you will. I trust you, Skipper."

Skipper fidgeted but beamed, nonetheless.

Miss Finch added softly, "And, Skipper, would you do poor old Napoleon a great kindness and let him come with you? Take care of him?"

"Uh, sure. I can do that."

"Good lad. Please be mindful that he is confused and anxious and will need lots of pats and loves to calm his fears. Oh, and do stop by my trailer before you walk back to Simon's cabin. Pick up a few of Hugo's treats for Napoleon."

Skipper squatted near Napoleon's dejected, low-hanging head. "Hey, buddy. Want to take a walk?" When he reached for the leash and tugged gently on it, Napoleon flicked his woebegone eyes in Miss Finch's direction.

"It is all right, Napoleon. You may go."

"C'mon, Nappy boy. Let's get you some treats, okay?"

Skipper started off, and Napoleon, with a last look to Miss Finch, went with him.

———— ❖ ————

BY THE TIME SIMON and Miss Finch arrived at the South Lake Tahoe Police Department, Phillips' officers had put Marie Santini in an interrogation room. Taking full advantage of his prerogative during the station commander's absence, Phillips decided to have Simon and Miss Finch sit in on Santini's questioning.

"Rehearse your background for me again, Fletcher. I need to be confident that you won't screw up this interrogation."

"Twenty years in the Corps, eighteen years an MP, eleven of those as an investigator."

"Just to be straight with you, I'll have you yanked out of the room if you diverge from my line of questioning."

"I won't."

"Good. And Miss Finch? I'll only ask you to speak if I require your input. However, if you hear me getting the story wrong, lift a finger, and I'll pause for clarification. Otherwise, please remain a silent observer."

She nodded. "As you say."

Simon asked, "Has Santini lawyered up?"

"She has been Mirandized yet refuses counsel at this time. You'd think that, at the very least, she would have called her father and asked him to arrange for a lawyer, but nope. She didn't want to call him. It's a stupid decision she'll live to regret, and she'll likely change her mind. That's why we need to move quickly to take advantage of this window of opportunity."

"I suggest that she may be somewhat afraid to call her father," Simon murmured, "considering who he works for. Don Massimo's organization is already under intense federal scrutiny, and the Don isn't going to smile on this complication—especially since Santini's target was Miss Finch, her being the feds' key to their case and all."

Simon slanted a look at Phillips. "See, I've heard a rumor that there's a bounty on Miss Finch's head. Ask yourself: Who stands to benefit from Miss Finch's, er, removal? Only Don Massimo and his organization. The feds could argue that Santini was working at her *father-in-law's* behest to eliminate Miss Finch. Of course, Santini getting caught puts Don Massimo squarely in the feds' bullseye. Again."

Simon chuckled. "If I were Santini, I wouldn't want to call home either."

Phillips shook his head. "Unbelievable."

The three of them entered the interrogation room and sat opposite Santini, who was cuffed to the table. Phillips signaled an officer on the other side of the mirrored one-way glass to begin recording the session.

Phillips set a notebook and a file on the table. "Please state your name for the record."

The vicious woman staring at Simon and Miss Finch bore little resemblance to the demure, withdrawn Miss Santini they'd known for going on a month.

"Marie Santini," she spat.

"Is it? Not what your ID says."

She huffed with scorn. "Fine. My full name is Marie Santini *Massimo*."

"Have you been apprised of your Miranda rights, Mrs. Massimo?"

"Whatever."

"Is that a yes or a no? Have you been apprised of your rights?"

"*Yes.*"

"I'll ask again, do you wish an attorney present during your questioning?"

She barked a laugh. "I *am* an attorney."

Simon mentally swallowed yet another hefty serving of Surprise Pie, and thought, *Then you, lady, of all people, should know the truth of that old adage: "A man who is his own lawyer has a fool for a client."*

Next, Phillips impressed Simon by lofting a curve ball at the woman. "Would you like us to call your father and let him know you're being booked for attempted murder? Perhaps he will appoint an attorney for you."

"No," she answered, but the question had unsettled her.

"What, you don't want your father to be informed?"

"I said I don't want you to call him."

Phillips angled toward Simon and winked. "Got it. You are the widow of the late Antony Massimo?"

"Yes."

"Why did you register yourself at Bright Star as Marie Santini?"

She shrugged. "As you pointed out, I'm a widow and will be retaking my maiden name. Not against the law. And by the way? Don't call me Mrs. Massimo. I prefer Miss Santini."

"But by registering yourself as Marie Santini, you deliberately withheld your relationship with your late husband from Bright Star management and employees . . . not to mention Miss Finch."

"Again, not illegal."

"Do you hold animus toward Miss Finch?"

Santini didn't answer, but her sneer spoke plenty.

"Let me draw your attention to yesterday's events, around midday. Where were you between the hours of 10:00 a.m. and 1:00 p.m.?"

She shrugged. "In my RV at Bright Star."

"Can anyone verify this?"

"Not likely. I like my privacy."

"Were you anywhere near the Olympic Village yesterday?"

"No."

"Did you lie in wait for Miss Finch and use a high-capacity rifle to shoot at her?"

"Did I what? That's absurd. I don't even own a gun."

"Yes or no, please."

"*No.*"

Phillips answered calmly, "Interesting. You see, we can prove that you left Bright Star right after Miss Finch did—which means you lied to us. We can also prove that you were near Olympic Village yesterday—your second lie—that you set up a sniper's nest and waited for Miss Finch to return by the same bicycle route she took to Olympic Village, and that you fired in the neighborhood of thirty rounds at her from a high-capacity rifle—yet another lie. That's attempted first-degree murder."

"And how do you propose to prove any of that nonsense?"

Phillips answered with the same level of calm detachment as his previous statements. "We have you on Bright Star's surveillance video following Miss Finch out of the park. We'll also LoJack your car's GPS history to ascertain your whereabouts *away from Bright Star* yesterday. And of course, we collected the spent rounds we found at the scene. I'm convinced the shells will have your fingerprints on them. Finally, we'll find your rifle soon enough—no doubt with your fingerprints on it also."

Not bothering to hide a smug and self-satisfied smile, she answered, "Good luck with any of that."

That tells us a few additional facts, Simon thought. She likely had her car's GPS disabled before she came to Bright Star. Tells us she was also smart enough to wear gloves when she handled her ammo and loaded the rifle. Finally, she thinks the police won't find her rifle. She has no idea that the police found GSR on her clothing or that they already have the gun.

Bottom line? Her outright defiance provides us with the most salient point: She is one cold, merciless killer, all the details neatly planned out ahead of time—with what the law defines as "malice aforethought." And whether the police can place her car near Olympic Village or not, they already have all the evidence they need to charge her, the totality of which will play well with a jury.

Phillips was a good interrogator, leading Santini to deny what he could already prove. He smiled and dropped the hammer. "Ah, but we did find your rifle, Miss Santini, buried in your firepit. It was wrapped up nice and tidy so it wouldn't get dirty. Thank you for that, by the way. It was kind of you to preserve your fingerprints and touch DNA on the stock and barrel for us."

Santini swallowed, and Simon noted a tremor in her clasped hands.

"In addition, we swabbed you and the clothes in your hamper before we brought you here. Guess what we found? How about copious amounts of gunshot residue? Can you explain how you came by GSR if you don't own a gun?"

"I decline to answer," she muttered.

At this juncture Phillips really showed his interrogation prowess. "Listen, lady, I want to tell you something important. We have you for attempted murder, and we have you cold. The fact that we can prove how you planned to kill Miss Finch in such a meticulous manner? Well, there's no way you will skate on this charge. You'll spend the rest of your miserable life in some dirty prison filled with women far more savage and brutal than you can even imagine."

The tremor in Santini's hands became more obvious, and a tic pulsed and twitched the outside of her left eye.

"On the other hand," Phillips said softly, "if Don Massimo placed a bounty on Miss Finch's head, it's just as likely that your father, as Don Massimo's right hand, 'let' the contract for the Don. If you agree to provide credible testimony against them, the DA may be inclined to cut you a deal with the possibility of a shorter sentence in a less onerous facility or, if you fully cooperate and give evidence against the Lucchese Family, the feds may offer you a berth in their WITSEC program. To start, simply tell us that Don Massimo ordered the hit on Miss Finch here. Give us the details and tell us how to confirm the ordered contract. That's the deal."

She stared stupidly at Phillips for less than two seconds before a blank expression dropped over her . . . and her hands stopped trembling.

"You'll give me a deal if I confirm that the Lucchese Family ordered a hit on this dry old bird here?" She laughed with derision. "Let me tell you something. If I were to turn witness against the *Don, I'd be dead*, but I would also be lying. You see, your vague assertions against my father and Don Massimo are false. I categorically *deny* that they placed a bounty on this Miss Finch person. I mean, why would they?"

Simon was versed in reading a suspect's facial microexpressions. It was impossible for the woman across from him to contain her smirk, the way her mouth lifted on only one side for the briefest moment. Additionally, he knew Santini couldn't help it—he'd seen far too many criminals lose control of those microexpressions in the same way, as she said, "I mean, why would they?"

Simon knew Santini's smirk signaled *contempt*, one of humanity's most powerful emotions, right up there next to hatred. Simon wondered if Miss Finch had seen it and slid a glance in her direction.

But Miss Finch gave nothing away as she cut in to answer Santini, "Why would they put a hit on little old me? Because, *supposedly*, I killed your husband, Don Massimo's son."

Phillips frowned at the interruption, yet kept his attention fixed on Santini.

Santini's eyes glittered, but she did not reply.

Before Phillips could retake control of the interview, Miss Finch added, "Of course, the reality is that Tony Massimo was a contract killer for the Lucchese Family. And *apparently*, doing the Mob's dirty work was the only thing Tony was any good at—seeing as how he was an abject *failure* at anything else he put his hand to."

Shock rippled through Simon as Miss Finch barked an ugly, derisive, and uncharacteristic laugh. Nor was she done.

She went on, "Not that the Don's baby boy proved his proficiency the day he tried to take my life. No, just as he royally messed up his attempt on me, I've proven beyond doubt that your darling husband committed the six murders, those so-called accidents I used as case studies in my book. Yes, just like he blew his attempt on my life, he *fouled them up* too."

"So you say!" Santini challenged Miss Finch.

"Well, of course he did. Did I die? No. Did the idiot kill himself instead? Why, yes, he did."

To Simon's amazement, Miss Finch stood and pushed back her chair. She planted her hands on the table, leaned as far toward Santini as she was physically able, and added, "Do you know what I think? I think *your husband* was so incompetent that the *Don,* and even your father, were relieved when Tony plowed through that truck's windshield and *splattered himself* all over the hood of my vehicle—and oh, my word!—such a great deal of blood and brains he left behind."

Santini cursed Miss Finch even as her grasping fingers reached for Miss Finch's throat. When the woman's restraints foiled her efforts, she screamed louder, calling Miss Finch by some of the vilest names Simon had ever heard.

But spread among the screams and curses, he heard, "I wish I'd killed you the day you parked my RV!"

Miss Finch sat down, an enigmatic smile curving her mouth.

Simon and Phillips? Phillips, eyes wide and lips parted, looked to Simon, who shrugged.

Don't ask me, man. I do not *know this lady.*

Over Santini's ongoing shrieks, Phillips shouted for the microphone to capture, "Interrogation halted, 4:11 a.m."

He gestured Simon and Miss Finch toward the door and was silent all the way to his desk. Then he grimaced and said, "Guess we have our confession—and how. Gives us plenty of leverage to work with too, because Santini has to be aware that no jury hearing a recording of *that* explosive scene, will show her any sort of leniency. Once she cools off, I'll be surprised if Santini doesn't cut a deal with the feds."

Shaking his head, he added, "And I'll tell you what else. I wouldn't want to be on the other side of the table from you, Miss Finch. You knew exactly how to provoke that woman."

Miss Finch merely nodded and murmured, "Shall we be going, Fletcher?"

CHAPTER 28

THANKFUL THAT TERRI RICKERT and Marie Santini were in police custody but with little sleep to energize them, Simon, Skipper, and Miss Finch faced the increased workload of a busy Bright Star Saturday. In addition to their heavier than normal weekend tasks, Simon and Miss Finch had to respond to the residents' many questions concerning the chaotic events of the previous night.

Somehow, the three of them managed to power through the long hours. Even so, Simon elected to close the office an hour early.

The three of them, by unspoken accord, gathered around Miss Finch's firepit to breathe the sweet air of relief—even if temporary.

Simon wouldn't consider the threat to Miss Finch to be entirely suspended until the police extracted enough testimony from Santini to charge her father, Franco Santini, and Tony Massimo's father, Don Ettore Massimo, with putting a hit on Miss Finch—all of which the feds would take quite an interest in. Still, the temporary stress reduction was welcome.

"I am exhausted, sapped, and drained," Miss Finch announced. "Whoever said a summer spent at Lake Tahoe would be restive and refreshing is categorically and emphatically *nuts*."

"Totally whack," Skipper agreed, his legs stretched out and his head leaned back on his chair, staring up at the scudding clouds.

"Those people need their heads examined," Miss Finch murmured.

"'Cuz they're craaaazy," Skipper added.

"Well, I need a vacation. A real vacation," she announced.

"I'll go with you!" Skipper replied.

"Not on your life," she mumbled.

Caught up in his own thoughts, Simon scarcely heard them. He was still tussling with Marie Santini's feigned ignorance regarding the Lucchese Family's hit on Miss Finch.

"Let me tell you something. If I were to turn witness against the Don, I'd be dead, *but I would also be lying. You see, your vague assertions against my father and Don Massimo are false. I categorically deny that they placed a bounty on this Miss Finch person. I mean, why would they?"*

Followed by a smirk of contempt.

That smirk is what's bothering me, Simon admitted. *Why would Santini signal disdain and superiority while declaring Don Massimo's innocence? Does she actually believe what she said?*

As he tussled with his thoughts, he spoke directly to the crime family's capo. *Seems to me, despite your personal loss, Don Massimo, that your hothead son did you a solid by offing himself before the police could interrogate him. You wouldn't have wanted him to confess to his other hits, including those you and your organization ordered, right?*

But . . . if you did not order the hit on Miss Finch, then who did?

About then, Becka and Melissa Gorman rode up on their bicycles.

Becka called out, "Hey, Miss Finch! Hey, Mr. Fletcher! Can Skipper come ride with us?"

"Please?" Skipper begged.

"Yes, *please*," Miss Finch answered.

Simon waved them away. "Sure. Please try not to annoy the other residents with your noise."

Skipper raced for the office to grab up his bike, and Becka and Melissa peeled off in a burst of speed, shouting and whooping it up, despite Simon's request.

He paid no mind to them. Instead, he leaned back in his chair to pick away at his disquiet. *What's wrong here*, he asked himself. *I'm missing a step. An essential piece of the puzzle.*

When Simon didn't move or speak for several minutes, Miss Finch noticed.

"Fletcher? Something on your mind?"

He sighed. "I suppose, if I'm being honest, I'm not quite convinced we have the whole story from Marie Santini."

"I would be surprised if you did," a voice nearby replied.

A figure stepped through the shrubs and into Miss Finch's site. Simon's blood chilled as a man approached, pointing a Smith & Wesson .45 at them. The suppressor attached to the .45's barrel increased the gun's length by six inches.

In a flash of insight, Simon knew the man's identity.

"I should have figured you'd go for the bounty, Dinesh," Simon growled, "your avaricious reputation preceding you and all."

He inclined his head. "Guilty as charged." He looked to Miss Finch. "We haven't been formally introduced, but I would know *you* anywhere, Miss Finch."

Simon, knowing Dinesh was there to off his friend, tried to yank the assassin's attention away from her and onto himself . . . even if it only delayed the inevitable.

"How much is Don Massimo paying you, Dinesh? Is it worth spending the rest of your empty life in prison?"

Dinesh chuckled. "How much is Don Massimo paying me? Why, I'm astounded. I didn't think you'd swallow my little prevarication hook, line, and sinker. Nevertheless, I'm gratified you did."

"What?" Simon slid off balance, but at least Dinesh's attention was on him and not on Miss Finch. "What prevarication?"

"That bounty baloney I laid on you. See, there *is* no bounty, at least not in the 'public offering' sense, and certainly not from Don Massimo. He's under too much scrutiny as it is."

"No bounty? Where's the incentive for you if money isn't involved?"

"Oh, there's plenty of money, but I'm operating under a direct hit-for-hire contract, from her to me. No public letting of said contract."

"What's that mean, from her to you? Who's the 'her' in that transaction?"

He giggled. "I may have left that part out when we spoke on the phone. Why, Marie Santini, of course. See, Marie hadn't a clue about Tony's mistress until the reinvestigation into his death brought the police 'round to her door to question her a second time. And during the police's second interview with Marie, they grilled her concerning Tony's mistress . . . only Marie hadn't known Tony had a mistress until they brought it up. Quite the shock! I think if Tony had still been alive when Marie found out, she would have killed him herself for his infidelity—burned him right there in his own bed."

Simon and Miss Finch's stunned silence must have tickled his funny bone.

"Ha! You didn't know that you were hosting both Antony Massimo's mistress *and* his wife in your precious RV park? My, my, this is priceless."

Simon found his tongue. "You're a day late and a dollar short, Dinesh. Our surprise isn't because we didn't know Marie Santini was Tony Massimo's wife. We got that part yesterday."

"That so? Then I guess the part you *didn't* get was that it was *Marie* who contracted me for the hits. That's right, not Don Massimo and not Franco Santini, but Marie herself."

He's right, Simon fumed, clenching his jaw. *From the get-go, I've been off the mark, always a step or two behind.*

Dinesh laughed at Simon's discomfiture. "But see? Being the only daughter of Franco Santini, Don Massimo's right hand man, Marie enjoyed a rather privileged upbringing. The best of everything money can buy, plus the glow of her father's status in the Lucchese organization? I'm certain you can understand how being raised within that sort of fear-inducing reverence and prestige breeds a certain arrogance. Oh, and let me tell you, Marie is *not* the type to tolerate being trifled with, let alone publicly humiliated. And since her father has personified the Don's hand of retribution throughout Marie's entire life, you might say she came into her own style of reprisal quite, er, *organically.*"

He laughed again. "Yup. And by the way? It's a 'two-fer' contract. Two hits for one *very* large payment—Miss Finch here and Miss Finch's neighbor, Terri Rickert."

"How did you find me? It had to have been quite difficult," Miss Finch asked, feigning genuine interest like the pro Simon was beginning to see she was.

"You'd have to ask Terri Rickert. Apparently, *she* discovered you had reserved a berth here at Bright Star. At Marie's behest, I'd been tracking Terri via her expenditures ever since Marie found out about Terri. You cannot imagine Marie's delight when she realized Terri had her own score to settle with Miss Finch and had done the locating part for us. Talk about delicious serendipity! Have to say, though, that Marie is a vindictive little witch. I could have done the both of you on opening weekend here, but *nooo*. Marie wanted the anticipation of the kill. Made me hold off until she tired of toying with you."

Dinesh grinned. "I'm just delighted that Marie chose me to fulfill her contract. Sets me up for a life of leisure on a pristine beach somewhere in the Pacific. After I end Miss Finch here and, regrettably, you too, Simon, I'll move on over to Terri's site. That will complete my business here, and then it's payday."

Simon clawed through possible responses, seeking anything to delay the inevitable, settling on the most obvious one.

"Uh, that might be a problem, Dinesh. The police have arrested Terri Rickert."

Dinesh's demeanor hardened. "What? When?"

Behind Dinesh, at the top of the drive, Skipper and his bike rolled to a silent stop.

Simon shuttered his face; forced his eyes to remain on Dinesh so as not to give Skipper away. "The police took her last evening. Then they took Marie, too, quite early this morning. And since they have Marie, you might want to rethink the killing us bit. I doubt she will be inclined to pay you from jail."

"Huh. Good thing her dad is loaded. He may not like paying me, but faced with the option of me testifying against her, he'll be good for it." Dinesh raised his gun and pointed it at Miss Finch. "Up. Both of you."

The instant Dinesh's attention left him, Simon shook his head once in Skipper's direction. To Simon's great relief, the boy rolled silently away. Simon didn't know if Skipper would call for help, and he couldn't tell if Skipper had left or if he was hanging around, watching from the road.

Simon breathed a short prayer. "Lord, please protect Skipper; keep him safe."

Dinesh gestured with the gun, including Simon in his command, "Move that direction, toward your screened enclosure. I'll hide your bodies in there."

Miss Finch flicked a glance toward Simon as she stood. He moved his chin down incrementally and walked to the catio, then moved to the side of the catio door. While Miss Finch unlatched the door, he slowly backed away from it.

"Please don't shoot my dog," Miss Finch whispered, turning to Dinesh. "Please."

"No money in killing an animal," Dinesh answered, "as long as he doesn't attack me."

"He's only a little dog and as docile as a lamb."

She threw open the screen door, and Hugo popped out. He stopped when he spotted Dinesh.

"It's okay, Hugo. This *bad man* won't hurt you."

The instant she said, "bad man," a low growl started in Hugo's throat.

"Hey, I warned you," Dinesh snarled.

But before Dinesh could react, a flying furball erupted from the catio. It touched down on Hugo's back and from there sprang to Miss Finch's shoulder. Using Miss Finch's shoulder as a launching pad, Pouncer flew into Dinesh's face, claws and teeth quick at their work.

Dinesh tried to pull Pouncer off his face without letting go of his gun. Unable to use both hands effectively, he backed away while trying to bring his gun to bear on the cat. Unfortunately for him, his gun's elongated barrel prevented him from getting an effective angle. He hit her with the gun instead and got in several blows before Pouncer, having clawed the mess out of Dinesh's face and neck, jumped off and scooted under the woody.

His face dripping blood from a dozen scores, Dinesh roared and leveled the gun on Miss Finch. "That's it—*you're dead!*"

"Don't you dare hurt *my Finchy!*" Skipper screamed, peddling his bike full speed down the drive toward Dinesh.

Dinesh glanced over his shoulder, his bloody expression reflecting astonishment. He managed to dodge out of the way just as Skipper would have collided with him.

And, apparently, that was all the distraction Miss Finch required.

Simon stared amazed as the cane on which Miss Finch dearly depended morphed into a whirling, whizzing, whacking pain machine. With her first strike, Dinesh's gun went flying; with her second strike, she buckled Dinesh's right knee. Dinesh, while staggering, managed to keep his footing and attempted to defend himself.

Simon grabbed up the gun before Dinesh could recover from Miss Finch's attack.

Dinesh recover? When Simon picked up Dinesh's gun and spun around, he found Miss Finch delivering strike after strike and *whomp* after *whomp* to Dinesh's body—kidney, elbow, back of the hand, opposite shoulder . . .

and his nether regions. As Dinesh clutched himself and croaked in agony, she delivered the *coup de grâce*, the "blow of mercy"—a measured strike to the side of his head.

Dinesh's eyes rolled back in their sockets. He fell to the asphalt like a dead tree falls in the forest.

Simon kept the gun on Dinesh's unconscious body. "You okay?" he asked Miss Finch.

"Shaken, not stirred," was her terse reply as she hobbled to her chair.

"And exactly what kind of martial arts—?"

"Krav Maga. I only know the basics."

"Krav Maga! That's IDF, Israeli—"

"Israeli Defense Force. Yes, I am aware."

"But how—"

"Picked it up while living in a kibbutz near the Sea of Galilee, late 90s."

"Of course you did." If Simon could have infused his reply with greater sarcasm, he would have done so.

Frankly? I'm fresh out.

He shifted his attention. "Skip? You good?"

"Yeah. Got a scrape is all. Hey, that Officer Phillips gave me his card when we were up at Olympic Valley, so when you waved me away, I called him. He said to tell you they're on their way . . . and something about frequent flyer miles?"

"Best news ever," Simon breathed, "although I'll probably owe him yet another favor."

Miss Finch slanted a look at him. "Owe him a favor, will you?"

"You're quite the influence, lady."

"Quite good or quite bad?"

"Haven't decided yet."

"Skipper? Skipper! Where are you?"

Becka and Melissa Gorman pedaled down the driveway. They stopped short when they saw Dinesh lying prone on the driveway, a stupefied expression on his face, his eyes slowly opening and closing.

"Who's that? What's going on?" Becka demanded.

"Well, we caught this bad guy," Skipper answered with an offhand sniff. "I ran him down on my bike to distract him, see? Then Miss Finch clobbered him."

"Yes, indeed," Miss Finch declared, "Skipper is the real star of this tale. If he hadn't come at this man on his bike when he did, well, Fletcher and I would be . . ."

"Goners," Skipper supplied.

"Precisely. *Goners.*"

"Wow, Skipper," Melissa breathed, hero worship wreathing her face. She got off her bike and came close to him. "Why, you deserve a kiss."

"*What?* No way!"

"Just on the cheek, silly. Right, Becka?"

Becka grinned. "All heroes—*real* heroes—get kissed. Now hold still."

Skipper squirmed as the two girls, one on either side, planted their kiss on the cheek closest them.

Skipper reddened. "Crud."

"Our kisses are *crud?*" Melissa demanded, hands on her hips.

Reddening further, Skipper fumbled for the right words, but his brain temporarily abandoned him.

He finally muttered, "No! I mean, well, your kisses aren't crud—not at all—just, um, I-I've never *been* kissed."

"Oh. Then that's understandable," Becka giggled.

What was not immediately understandable was how Dinesh came to life with a sudden spurt of energy. He rolled, jumped to his feet, and sprinted for Melissa's bike, ran it up the sloped driveway and jumped on it using the impetus of his running start.

"Hey!" Skipper shouted, first to respond. He leapt astride his own bike and hauled after Dinesh.

At nearly the same time, Simon ran up the drive after Dinesh hoping to catch him before he reached the road. However, Dinesh, peddling like a madman, had too much of a lead for Simon to catch him on foot. Dinesh hit the road, turned left, and sped in the direction of Bright Star's gate. Skipper wasn't far behind Dinesh, but the man's lead was increasing.

Simon turned toward his truck—

"Out of my way!" Miss Finch shouted.

Simon narrowly escaped being plowed over by Miss Finch as her eBike zoomed up the drive on full throttle.

Simon dodged to the side, fumbled his keys, got his truck running, backed up the drive, and raced after them. He anticipated Dinesh would speed through the open gate to wherever he'd hidden his vehicle off Bright Star's road. He was not expecting Dinesh to bypass the gate and point Melissa's bike onto the trailhead leading into the forest—with Skipper and Miss Finch in pursuit. Simon braked at the trailhead just as Miss Finch, putting on a burst of speed, overtook Skipper and disappeared into the trees after Dinesh.

Simon was pounding his steering wheel in frustration when Becka's face appeared at his window startling him.

"Becka! You about gave me a heart attack!"

"Sorry. Here, take my bike."

"What? Oh. Yeah, thanks."

Simon stood over the small fat-tire bike, his backside far above the seat.

"If you can't sit down, just pedal standing up, Mr. Fletcher," Becka urged him. "Get going before the bad man gets away!"

"Uh, right."

Now last in a line of four bicycles, Simon sped into the woods and onto the dirt trail, barely managing to keep the bike on the trail while navigating turns, avoiding obstacles, and thinking, *Whoever said 'just like riding a bike' had never gotten on one after a thirty-five-year hiatus.*

Suddenly, from far ahead, Simon heard Skipper's terrified screams, "Miss Finch, look out! Miss Finch!"

Pumping the pedals of Becka's little bike for all he was worth, Simon burst into a small clearing where the trail widened but necessitated that Simon make a sharp hairpin turn to the left to avoid colliding with the ginormous boulder directly ahead.

Having no other option, Simon braked and skidded into the turn. The bike fishtailed and ran up a steep embankment. Simon leapt off before the bike went over, landing halfway up the embankment. That's when he spied Skipper's bike tossed aside onto a shrub.

Simon got to his feet and peered around. "Skipper! Skip! Where are you?"

"Down here, Fletch. Please hurry!"

"Where? Where are you?"

He heard scrabbling and Skipper's head appeared at the top of the embankment. "Down here. Please hurry, Fletch! Miss Finch is hurt bad."

Simon clambered to the top of the embankment and stared at the scene below. In a tangle of bush, brush, arms, legs, and strewn rock, Miss Finch and her bike sprawled atop Craig Dinesh.

Dinesh groaned.

Miss Finch did not move.

"She-she ran him down, Fletch. Just before we hit that curve, he slowed to make the turn. Miss Finch didn't slow down though," Skipper sniffled. "Fletch, she-she powered through that turn and ran him down on purpose to keep him from getting away. Hit him so hard, they both flew up the slope and over."

My wild days of riding motocross are far behind me, Fletch.

Simon blew out a shaky breath. "Way to stage a comeback, you crazy woman, you."

Simon scrambled down the steep, rocky slope until he reached Miss Finch. As he knelt, Dinesh groaned again and opened his eyes.

"Help me . . ."

"Skipper!"

The boy's white face appeared beside him. "Yes, Fletch?"

"Do you have your phone?"

He shook his head and waved in the direction of the trail. "Lost it outta my pocket back there. Is Miss Finch . . . okay?"

"Don't know, but we need an ambulance. Take my phone and call 911. Tell them it's a bicycle accident with two to transport."

"Bicycle accident. Two to transport."

Simon returned his attention to Miss Finch. She had a pulse, although it seemed slow to him. Gently, he ran his fingers through her wild, curly hair, exploring her scalp. He stopped when he came upon a large, sticky lump.

His fingers came away bloody, and apparently, his gentle palpations had hurt, because she moaned a little.

"Miss Finch? Keep still, please. You've hit your head."

One hooded eye opened. Wandered a bit until it found him. "Fletch. My . . . foot."

"You have a head wound. Possible concussion."

"No, foot . . ."

"We're not downplaying a head injury. The foot can wait."

Took her a minute to work up to her next statement. "Not downplay . . . Hit my foot."

His mouth opened in slow perception. He shifted his attention to her left foot. It was still encased in that aggravating boot. It was also lying atop a large, pointed rock.

"Lord, please help . . ." Simon muttered.

"Did I . . . get him?"

Dinesh groaned again. "Get off . . . me. Can't . . . breathe."

"Yeah, I'd say you got him. Well done."

She had closed her eyes while he answered her, and he couldn't tell if she heard him or not.

He shook her shoulder gently, then harder. "Miss Finch? Miss Finch!"

No response.

She had slipped into unconsciousness.

CHAPTER 29

THE PARAMEDICS FASTENED A collar around Miss Finch's neck, transferred her to a backboard, and hauled her up to the waiting ambulance, after which the paramedics removed Dinesh in the same manner. The difference was that a police officer cuffed one of Dinesh's hands to the gurney and stood watch close by.

Of course, Phillips demanded that Simon give an account of what had happened, but as Simon tried to narrate the latest exciting episode of "Bright Star SWAT" for the officer's benefit, he kept one eye trained on the paramedics. The team of two alternated between Dinesh and Miss Finch, but the paramedic monitoring Miss Finch's vitals wore a worried expression.

Not as worried as Simon's.

"So this guy appears in Miss Finch's site and pulls a gun on you and her? Then your intern runs him down with his bike?"

"Like I said four times, Skipper *tried* to run him down. When Dinesh jumped out of the way, Miss Finch used her cane to knock the gun out of Dinesh's hand. Look, Phillips, I already told you everything, and you found the gun in her site. Can we wait to go over it for the fifth time after I see how Miss Finch is doing?"

"Sure. You're not much use to me in your distracted state anyway. Just don't think I'm through with you yet."

Simon stalked toward the ambulance.

"How's my friend, please?"

"Sir, as you can see, we're busy working. You need to stay back."

When the paramedic turned to retrieve something from the back of the ambulance, Simon stepped to the side of the closer gurney.

"Miss Finch? BeeDee?"

She did not respond.

The paramedic returned and shooed him away.

Two minutes later, the ambulance, with the officer on board to watch Dinesh, roared away, lights flashing and siren blaring. Phillips left too, leaving Simon standing alone. Tom Peterman, closest to the trailhead in Site 24, walked over to him.

"You all right, Mr. Fletcher? Can't say as I've ever camped anywhere near as lively as this place is—and I've camped a lot of places. Sure keeps the blood pumping!"

"I apologize," Simon said automatically, staring after the departed vehicles.

"Don't. Looks to me like that Miss Finch has been through a lot. Can't exactly fault her if bad folks keep chasing after her, can we?"

Simon finally looked at the man, saw the compassion in his eyes. "Thank you for that, Mr. Peterman."

Becka and Melissa rode slowly out of the woods on their bikes. A few minutes later, a disheveled Skipper appeared at the trailhead, walking Miss Finch's eBike—"walking" being a relative term. The front tire was blown, the wheel severely bent. He alternately pushed and scooted the bike toward Bright Star's road.

"Excuse me," Simon told Mr. Peterman, breaking away to help the boy.

"Hey, Skip. Let me take that for you."

Skipper heaved a sigh, "Man, Miss Finch's bike is really messed up. Chain's busted. Controller smashed. Front rack bent."

"Yeah. I see that." Simon hefted the bike over his head. "Let's put it behind the office instead of taking it to Miss Finch's site. I don't want her to come home to this."

They walked together to the office, and as they walked, Skipper's countenance dropped lower and lower until it was about as low as possible. Belly-to-the-ground low.

He mumbled when Simon leaned the bike against his pickup. "Fletch, is Miss Finch going to be okay?"

Simon wrapped an arm around the kid's shoulders and squeezed.

"Let's go find out."

———◆———

WHILE SKIPPER SLOUCHED in a chair, Simon paced the floor of the ER waiting room, stopping every quarter of an hour to harass the receptionist with yet another, "Can you tell me how Miss Finch is doing?"

The answer was invariably the same. "Sir, she's still unconscious. We'll let you know when she wakes up."

Simon rubbed his face. His eyes were gritty, his cheeks and chin stubbly, and his body shouted that he'd been through close quarters battle.

Lord, we need this to be over. Really over. No more surprise attacks. And Lord? I need Miss Finch to be all right. Please.

A doctor appeared. "Mr. Fletcher?"

"Yeah. How is she?"

"Starting to come around. She's got a nice little concussion going on, so we'd like to keep her overnight for observation."

"When can we see her?"

"Oh, in about an hour after we get some x-rays, I think. Why don't you and the boy find yourselves something to eat and come back after?"

"Sure. Thanks."

Simon jerked his chin at Skipper. "Come on. Let's grab some dinner. When we come back, they'll let us see her."

<hr>

SIMON TOOK SKIPPER TO a nearby burger place. Skipper picked over his food, while Simon, to his surprise, devoured his burger and fries.

Guess I was hungry after all.

When they returned to the hospital, they were told Miss Finch was awake and were shown into a large room with curtained beds staged around the room's perimeter. Simon slowed and nodded to the police officer stationed next to one of the nearer beds. The figure in the bed appeared to be sleeping, one hand cuffed to the bed's rail.

Craig Dinesh.

Lord, thank you for saving us from his evil intentions.

Skipper ran ahead to another bed across the room. He hung over the rail, a worried frown on his brow. Miss Finch lifted her small hand to his face.

"I'm all right, Skipper," she reassured him.

"Are you sure?

Simon silently echoed the same question: *Are you sure?*

"Because you didn't wake up for a long time," Skipper whispered, "and I . . . I—"

When his voice failed him, Miss Finch stroked his cheek gently.

"I promise I will be okay, Skipper, but can I tell you something? It means a lot that you care about me . . . and I thought you were incredibly brave today, the way you charged that man on your bike."

Skipper sniffed, unshed tears hanging on his eyelids.

I should have said that to Skipper, Simon realized. *I should have said it first.*

He cleared his throat. "I agree with Miss Finch; I'm proud of you too, Skipper Mitchell. You demonstrated uncommon courage this day when you saved . . . your Finchy."

Skipper's eyes widened. "Oh, man! I-I didn't mean to say that . . ."

Miss Finch reddened, opened her mouth to snap a retort, caught the grin Simon was trying hard to master—and then, quite suddenly, both of them were chuckling, and Skipper's eyes shot from Simon to Miss Finch and back, uncertain of what was happening.

Miss Finch left off laughing. She shifted a little and winced, then demanded, "When can I get out of this asylum, Fletcher? This hospital bed does not suit me at all."

"I believe the doctor wants to keep you overnight."

"And *I* believe the hospital requires doctors to say that in order to collect more from their patients' insurance companies."

"Not buying it," Simon replied. "You need to be observed."

"But I'll rest better in my own bed," Miss Finch protested, "and I'm fine, aside from a few scrapes and bruises, a nice knock to my noggin, and another to my ankle—which, praise God, my walking boot blunted."

"Nope. Staying the night."

"There is not a single thing to be gained by keeping me here another minute!"

"You hit your head on a rock, you stubborn old woman," Simon growled.

"And now you know exactly how hard my head is," she growled back.

They laughed again, and this time, Skipper joined in.

"Yes, I suppose I *do* know hard your head is," Simon said when he caught his breath after their laughing jag petered out. "Nonetheless, I'm backing the doctor's play. I won't drive you home until he releases you."

"Hmph!"

"'Hmph' all you want. You're not going anywhere."

She sighed. Looked down. Picked at the bedsheet. "Fletcher . . ."

"Yeah?"

"How badly did I break my beautiful little bike?"

Skipper opened his mouth to provide a detailed damage report, but Simon ran a finger across his throat. When Skipper's jaws snapped closed, Simon answered Miss Finch.

Carefully.

"Whatever is marred or broken on your bike was a price well worth paying to catch Dinesh in the very act. He's going away for a long time, and that means you don't need to worry about him coming for you."

Simon cleared his throat. "That said, I'll take your bike down to Jasper, and he'll fix her right up. I promise to get you back on the road as soon as you're ready to ride again."

He added softly, "I'll even throw in the red fez, a ringmaster, and a full complement of circus clowns."

He ducked the pillow she lobbed at his head.

CHAPTER 30

UNFORTUNATELY, WHEN MISS FINCH exhibited mild dizziness, the doctor insisted on keeping her two nights rather than one. Monday afternoon, Simon and Skipper drove to the hospital. They waited for Miss Finch to be discharged, then Simon helped her into the cab of his truck.

"How are Hugo and Pouncer?" she demanded.

"We spent the last two nights in your site," Simon explained. "Introduced Napoleon to them." He shrugged. "They seemed to have adjusted to him all right, but if Pouncer doesn't cut Napoleon some slack soon, the poor old guy might have a nervous breakdown."

"*Poor old guy* is right," Skipper echoed. "Pouncer scares the crud outta Nappy."

"Which brings me to a sticky subject," Simon said.

"What to do with Napoleon long-term?" Miss Finch asked.

"Yeah. I asked Phillips to pass on a message to Santini, letting her know we're taking care of him, but asking that she make other arrangements for him soon. I really don't want to surrender him to the local shelter. He's too old for that kind of stress."

"I don't imagine she appreciates your efforts."

"Probably not."

"Managing the office all right in my absence?"

"Yes. Skipper's been great, and we were both surprised when Irene Kinzer offered to help out this afternoon when we left to get you. She has volunteered to step in until you're back on your feet. Everyone at Bright Star has asked after you and offered their support and encouragement. Really, I couldn't ask for a nicer group of people."

"You mean now that the homicidal elements have been removed?"

"I think that about sums it up."

LATER THAT DAY, Phillips called Simon back. "Passed on your message to Santini. By the way, the feds are taking her into custody tomorrow. Anyway, I got the weirdest response when I told her you were taking care of her dog."

"Oh?"

Phillips sighed. "She told me to have him destroyed."

The hair on the back of Simon's head stood up. "You're joking."

"Nope. She was adamant about it."

"I know for a fact that she loves that dog but . . . wow. Guess this is a brutal example of what hate does to a person. Absolutely consumes them."

"No doubt. So, what are you going to do?"

"I can tell you what I'm not going to do. I'm not going to have that good boy put down on the whim of a psychopath. I'll . . . try to find him a decent home."

Simon could almost see Phillips nodding over the phone.

"Outstanding."

TUESDAY MORNING, after Simon finished his run, he woke Skipper and they had breakfast together. "I need to run an errand this morning. I'll drive you to the office first."

Skipper nodded. "Okay, Fletch."

Simon had parked Miss Finch's broken bike at his cabin. She wouldn't be up to riding for a while, but Simon wanted to deliver her bike to Jasper now so it would be repaired and ready when she was. Skipper watched Simon put Miss Finch's bike in the bed of his truck.

"You think your friend can fix Miss Finch's bike?"

Simon shook his head. "I really don't know, but I do know Jasper. He'll give it his best."

Of course, when Jasper saw the bike's condition, he pretty much had a cow.

"What in the world happened! Is Miss Finch all right?"

"She's recovering from a concussion and has some pretty good scrapes and bruises, but okay otherwise."

His friend put his hands on his hips and skewered him with a look.

"Don't you lay into me, Jasper. That woman has a mind of her own."

Jasper huffed. "Yeah? Well, I need a cup of coffee—and you need to spill. I want to hear what happened—every detail."

An hour later, after two cups of coffee and after Simon had "spilled" all the details, Jasper continued to shake his head in disbelief.

"Dunno if I can keep your tall tale straight in my mind, 'specially since parts of it are mighty unbelievable."

"Tell me about it. The last four weeks have twisted my gut and set my hair on fire more times than I can count. But enough about our daring Miss Finch. Can you or can you not fix her bike?"

"Yeah, I suppose I can fix it, but it won't ever be pretty again. Fenders all dinged up. Handlebars scratched but good. A lot of paint scraped off.

Needs a new controller, chain, derailleur, front rack, front wheel, and pet basket. And I can't guarantee how this one will hold together after all the abuse the frame took."

"What if . . . what if I just buy her a new bike and basket, exact same as before?"

"Huh. And do what with the old one?"

Simon shrugged. "Maybe give it to someone who'd appreciate it despite the scraped paint?"

Jasper nodded thoughtfully. "Fact is, I could tidy it up and bless someone with it. I'd toss that basket, though. Unsafe."

"Okay, I'm sold."

Jasper scratched his chin. "Will you let me pay for part of her new ride?"

Simon shook his head. "Nope. Thanks, but I'm doing this. Now, let's get Miss Finch's new bike and basket assembled and loaded in my truck. Gotta get back to work."

"On it."

———— ● ————

AN HOUR PLUS LATER, Simon backed into Miss Finch's driveway. She was sitting under the awning in her kiddie chair, tablet on her lap, left leg propped up, Pouncer and Hugo beneath her chair, her beverage of choice on the little table to her side.

Simon lifted the bike from the truck's bed and wheeled it toward her. It was identical in every respect to her original one, right down to the side mirrors. Hugo began to prance with excitement when he saw Simon and the bike, whereas Pouncer demonstrated her adoration for Simon with bared fangs.

"Good as new," Simon said with a smile.

Miss Finch slowly stood and hobbled to the bike. Stared at the flawless frame, fenders, and seat. Placed gently trembling fingers on the shiny handle-bars. Took in the intact pet basket.

"But . . . but how?"

"Okay, I confess: It's new. All of it. Can't have you gallivanting around the lake on a scratched and dented bike, can we? I mean . . . what would the ringmaster have to say about that?"

She snarked a little laugh. "Indeed."

Then she whispered, "Thank you, Simon. Thank you a hundred times over."

Simon's smile faltered when she burst into tears.

———— ● ————

THE FOLLOWING WEDNESDAY, after a four-week absence, Holly brought Joe home. For his part, Simon had never been so glad to see the guy. His feelings over Holly's return were more restrained. She immediately reasserted her authority by attempting to rearrange Simon and Skipper's work.

Simon, having run Bright Star quite satisfactorily without her input, chose to nip Holly's overreach in the bud.

"Holly, you and Joe are my boss, and I have no problem when you assign new tasks to my workload, but I don't need to be told how to manage my work—I mean, that *is* my job, right? You know, the *manager* part of facilities and security manager? Certainly, any time my work isn't up to your expectations, I want to know. Otherwise, I'd appreciate it if you'd trust me to do the job you hired me to do."

"But—"

"Nope. I don't need to be micromanaged. If that's the way you intend to keep going, I'll tender my resignation now."

Holly sputtered, then subsided. She hardly knew how to handle this "new" Simon.

FRIDAY MORNING FOUND Simon behind the office, adding gasoline to the riding mower, while Joe introduced Skipper to the riding mower's controls. Joe had decided to teach Skipper how to mow Bright Star's grass.

Simon was surprised when Miss Finch appeared at his elbow. She beckoned him aside where they could talk in private.

"Fletcher, I need a favor, please."

"For you, Miss Finch? Anything. Shoot."

"I need to go into town and see that nice ER doctor again."

"Why? What's happened?"

"I don't like the look of the bruise I earned when my ankle hit that rock. I called ahead and have an appointment in forty minutes. I was hoping you would drive me. Just in case."

Simon put the gas can down. "In case of what?"

"In case he needs . . . to do something."

He stared into those wise brown orbs and didn't like what he saw.

She's worried.

"May I see? I've had combat first aid training, and just to satisfy my curiosity, would like a peek."

She sat on the upturned log where Simon split kindling for the residents. She unstrapped the boot on her foot. Simon squatted down and helped free her foot from the boot. He carefully picked up her foot and stared. From midcalf to toe, her left foot was a nasty black and blue trending toward sickly green.

"Whew! Now, that's what we in the Corps call 'battle stripes'—earned fair and square. But . . ."

She lifted her brows. "But?"

"Your ankle is more swollen than I would have expected it to be a week after your skirmish and crash landing. Is the swelling what you're concerned about?"

"Not precisely. Perhaps a closer look?"

Simon could see the point at which her ankle bone had impacted the rock, but the swelling was greatest to the outside of that bone. He peered at the puffy tissue and, with two fingers, applied gentle pressure to the area. The puffy skin was grayish and sickly. Hot to the touch.

"Whoa. I do not like the look or feel of that. Some kind of abscess in there."

The word on the tip of his tongue had been "necrosis," but he refrained from saying it aloud.

"My thought also, hence a visit to the doctor."

"Let me tell Joe I'm leaving. Be right back."

———◆———

SOUTH LAKE TAHOE'S BARTON Memorial Hospital had excellent emergency services. At Miss Finch's request, Simon accompanied her into the treatment room.

"Not that I need you to hold my hand, *Mr.* Fletcher," she murmured.

Simon winked. "No. Not at all."

The doctor who'd examined and treated Miss Finch after her fall was proficient and thorough—although, being young, he tended to talk down to his senior patients. After taking a look at her ankle and carefully prodding it, he pronounced, "We've got a problem here."

She delivered her reply with exquisite aplomb. "I had not noticed. I suppose, then, it is quite fortuitous that I came in today?"

The doctor—not so young as to overlook sarcasm—reddened. "Right. I'll, um, be right back."

With a roll of her eyes, Miss Finch replied, "And I will be right *here.*"

"You've been spending too much time with Skipper," Simon whispered.

"I'm beginning to think the boy has something."

The doctor returned with a nurse carrying a covered tray. "We're going to open up this area of concern, Miss Finch, and clean it out."

She swallowed and nodded once.

The nurse spread a sterile pad under Miss Finch's foot and began to clean and disinfect the area. "My, that's a terrific bruise."

"Yes, simply terrific."

"First, we'll numb you up," the doctor said, lifting a hypodermic. "You'll feel a pinch and some coolness."

Miss Finch's fingers scrabbled for Simon's hand.

"I've got you."

She looked away from what the doctor was doing, but Simon did not. The scalpel sliced open about half an inch of skin. Immediately, pus and pink fluids poured out onto the sterile pad. The doctor's gloved fingers squeezed the puffy area to express more of the foul mixture.

Simon thought he saw something else glide out with the fluids.

"Ah," the doctor said.

"Ah, what?" Miss Finch demanded.

The doctor used some tweezers to fish around on the pad. When he found what he was looking for, he signaled the nurse. She held a small glass dish under his hand, and he dropped his find into the dish.

"I believe this is your culprit, Miss Finch."

She stared into the dish at a dull, inch-long fragment—a narrow shard of bone with sharp, pointy ends.

"Where did this come from?"

"Well, it's not new, I can tell you that, so not from your recent misadventure, not with that cloudy coating on it. I believe you said you broke your ankle a few months back?"

"Yes. My car was T-boned and my ankle crushed."

He nodded. "Ankles are notoriously difficult to put back together, and your surgical team may have missed this splintered bit. Your initial accident's impact could have driven the shard deep into tissue, tendon, or muscle. Once embedded, this splinter may have been nearly impossible for the surgeon to see or your body's defenses to detect.

"During your bicycle accident, when your foot struck that rock, I'd wager the impact dislodged this shard. Knocked it loose. Soon after, your body's defenses must have decided the fragment was a foreign body and initiated action to kick that intruder to the curb."

He laughed at his witticism, then sat back. "Didn't you say your ankle was still giving you pain prior to this, er, more recent event?"

Still stunned nearly speechless, Miss Finch exhaled. "Yes, it was decidedly painful."

"Well, with this shard removed, you should heal up nicely and, I would venture to predict, will soon be pain-free. I'll clean and stitch my incision, and we'll send you home with both oral and topical antibiotics to finish off any residual bacteria. Oh, and I doubt you'll need that boot much longer, if at all."

The nurse cleared away the soiled pad, placed a clean one under Miss Finch's foot, and cleaned her ankle a second time. The doctor closed the incision he'd made and bandaged it. When he finished, they both left to do the paperwork to release their patient.

Simon murmured, "You won't need your boot much longer."

"I won't?"

"That's what the doctor said."

Miss Finch was quiet. Eerily so.

Then Simon picked up a soft but familiar *heh-heh-heh* under her breath. As usual, it tickled Simon's funny bone, and he grinned along with her.

"A rock," Simon whispered. "God used *a rock*. Not the first time he's used a rock, is it? Lord, we thank you!"

Miss Finch squeezed her eyes closed, and a lone tear leaked out.

"Oh, yes, and amen!"

The TAHOE MYSTERIES

POSTSCRIPT

MONDAY, JUNE 30

SIMON LEANED BACK IN Miss Finch's adult-sized camping chair, comfortable and replete, the crumpled wrapper of a breakfast burrito in the chair's beverage holder.

"With Joe and Holly back and Joe picking up the tasks he's able to handle, I realized something."

"Oh? And just what might that said 'something' entail?"

Simon lifted his head and glared at her. "Sarcasm this early in the day should be against the law."

"Good luck with that. What did you realize, Fletcher?"

Simon sighed. "I realized I scarcely recall how to take breaks. Even a short pause for breakfast or lunch and I start to feel like I'm slacking."

Miss Finch sniffed. "I am convinced you will adjust."

"Thanks for your *encouragement*."

She sat in her kiddie chair sipping a Zero Sugar Cherry Dr. Pepper, her open tablet in her lap. "On another note, I came across a curious article this morning."

Mimicking her sarcasm, Simon replied, "Oh? And just what might that said article entail? Mystery or mischief? Perhaps mayhem? We've covered murder this month, so that one's out."

"You have overlooked 'missing persons.'"

"My bad."

"Are you interested or not?"

"Read on."

"Hmph." She adjusted her reading glasses and began.

> "Authorities are looking for
> Donald Whatley, age 19,
> last seen early Monday morning.
> The young man and three friends
> set up camp at Fallen Leaf
> Campground Sunday evening.
> The following morning,

the four friends set out to climb
Tahoe Mountain, on what is considered
to be an easy to moderate hike.
Whatley stepped off the trail to relieve himself
while his friends continued up the trail.
When Whatley did not rejoin his friends,
they backtracked down the trail
but were unable to locate him.
Persons with information as to Whatley's
whereabouts are asked to contact either
South Lake Tahoe Police Department or
El Dorado County Sheriff's Office."

Simon nodded. "Not the first hiker to get lost while out and about in unfamiliar terrain . . . although I wouldn't expect someone to get lost in that particular area. The trails are well marked, and it's unlikely that a young, vigorous male like Whatley would lose his way in such a tame environment."

"I did not say it was unlikely; I believe I said it was curious. Please keep up, Fletcher."

"I beg your pardon. In what manner is Whatley's disappearance curious as opposed to another adjective?"

"Curious because the article neglects to mention that Mr. Whatley is the third such disappearance in the lake area over the past six weeks."

"Huh. I hadn't heard a thing."

"Possibly because the three cases are somewhat geographically removed from each other, but more likely because we've been just a smidge preoccupied keeping me and my babies alive—and all that blather. Let me pull up my notes . . ."

She toggled to a different screen and read aloud,

"Caesar Morales, age 22,
was solo mountain biking
on the Five Lakes Trail
south of Olympic Valley when
he disappeared without a trace,
three weeks ago.

"Five Lakes Trail is a good thirty miles from here, but I believe he was the second such victim."

"Victim? As in what? Bear attack? Search and Rescue would have found traces."

"No traces, at least not in the region where he disappeared. I am, despite your overly optimistic 'we've covered that one,' leaning toward homicide."

She held up a hand to forestall his questions and continued to read. "Then there is this:

"Missing:
Haoyu Xú, age 25,
a college exchange student on break
from California State University, Chico.
Xú was backpacking the Tahoe Rim Trail,
headed up Mount Houghton,
when he disappeared.

"Xú was also solo, like Morales. He vanished six weeks ago, forty-plus miles north of here."

"How'd you pull these accounts together? Because I've heard nothing about any of these disappearances."

"Oh, my programmer friends, the ones who built the companion program to my forensics guide? They wrote a custom piece of code for me—to my specifications, to be precise. I plug the code into a browser and it collects and collates the news reports and social media posts that fit my data specifications and sends a report with links to my email inbox. I'm able to set the code's search parameters myself to seek out related or possibly related situations."

"Sounds like a valuable tool."

"It will be. We're still tweaking the code. Concurrently, my programmer friends are building the app to market the tool."

"And how did you wrangle these guys into working for you? Do they also owe you favors?"

"Guys and gals, Fletcher. Guys and gals. And, in a manner of speaking, yes, they owe me. I paid them a pile of money to develop my forensics program, and they stand to make a hefty slice of the royalties from this new app too."

"Well, at least I don't have to guess at the favors they owe you—unlike the favors Joe and Mobius owed you."

"You are fishing, Fletcher."

"What kind of bait should I use?"

"Depends upon what you want to catch."

He pointed to her tablet. "I'd like in on whatever you think *this* is."

She smiled. "I did not read you in merely to tease you."

"Great. Tell me why you think it's murder."

"They found the first victim."

"Okay. Whereabouts?"

"Lake Tahoe. A particularly deep part of the lake."

"But wasn't that guy hiking north of the lake when he disappeared? How did he end up in the Big Blue?"

"Ah. It seems that a person or persons unknown gifted the young man with an ankle bracelet attached to three cinderblocks."

Simon stilled. "So it *is* murder."

"Undeniably. And until the next victim surfaces—pardon my tasteless turn of a phrase—I doubt the authorities will connect him to the other instances of missing persons."

"Why do you feel the disappearances are connected? Do we know the cause of death on this guy?"

"We do not; however, the medical examiner does."

"And . . . you know the medical examiner?"

"No, but quite fortuitously, I have a friend who—"

"Owes you a favor?"

"Why, whatever would make you think that?"

He waved his hand in the air. "Only being around you since the day we met. So let me have it. Cause of death?"

"The particulars? Still very hush-hush. However, the coroner's ruling? Homicide."

Simon grinned. "Does very hush-hush mean you'll whisper the details to me?"

A smile crept across her face, crinkling the corners of her eyes. "Soon— as soon as I tease out a few more incidentals from my source."

Without warning, Pouncer landed in Simon's lap. Simon gasped and gripped the arms of his chair as she clawed her way up his chest and around his neck, then draped herself across his shoulders.

"Sheesh, cat! You may have nine lives, but I have only one—and you about scared the living daylights out of it! Not to mention your claws have turned me into a human pincushion."

Pouncer responded by making biscuits on his shoulder, her purr rattling against Simon's neck.

Simon couldn't stay mad. He turned his head and nuzzled her jowls with his cheek. In return, she revved up her engine.

Miss Finch smiled. "Did you know that, next to me, you have become Pouncer's favorite person, Fletcher?"

"Considering she hisses at me on a regular basis, I find my becoming her favorite hard to believe—unless we're talking 'preferred scratching post.'"

"Her favor is a significant and novel achievement, the only one I have witnessed. She even watches for you and listens for your truck. I believe she recognizes the sounds of both your pickup and Bright Star's maintenance truck, for when you drive by, she calls to you. Why, if I were to let her out of her catio in those moments, I am convinced she would hunt you down and keep you company while you worked."

Risking his hand's well-being, Simon reached up and rubbed between Pouncer's ears. "You have good taste, girl."

Instead of scoring his fingers, her purrs deepened.

"Well, how about that."

"Indeed."

"Say, I've been thinking, Miss Finch."

"Oh, dear. I hope it doesn't hurt too much."

"*Har har*. Very funny."

"Yes, I am easily amused. What have you been thinking, Fletch?"

"Well . . ."

Truth was, he felt somewhat "off."

What is it?

He looked deeper inside. Tried to put a finger on it. All he could come up with was . . . wistful.

I feel wistful?

"What is it, Simon?" Miss Finch's question was kind.

"Dunno for certain. I suppose these past weeks, for the first time . . . in a while, I've felt like my life meant something. That I have a purpose again."

"The kind of purpose you experienced while in the Marine Corps . . . before they pushed you out?"

He huffed softly. "Figured it out, did you? Yes. I found my purpose as a Marine, as an MP and an investigator, but also as a Christian who taught Bible studies and led many a fellow Marine to Jesus. My faith never came into conflict with the Corps, not for years, and I had never received anything but outstanding fitreps—not, that is, until our nation's administration began to abandon God's foundational truths about marriage, family, sexual preference, even gender.

"Once the new orders came down the chain of command, Christians in the military were told to get on board or get out. Those who didn't separate willingly became targets. We were disciplined for speaking our personal values, even in private, and for not publicly embracing views that contravened our religious principles. If we balked, our commanding officers downgraded our fitness reports and denied us promotion. After my second downgraded fitrep, I opted to get out—but only because the next step in that parade would have been involuntary separation."

"Leaving the Corps wounded you grievously."

"You've hit the nail on the head. The Corps was more than a job or a calling. It was my family."

He blinked. "Huh."

"What is it?"

"Just realized that . . . the past weeks, running Bright Star with you and Skipper . . ."

"Yes?" she prodded gently

"I've felt more like part of a family than since I got out."

She smiled. "It has been good, hasn't it? I am, however, grateful to be relieved of Bright Star's office duties. I have another book to finish, after all."

Simon stared at her. "Like your first one didn't ruffle enough feathers? And yet, there's a piece of all the drama we've been wading through that I just don't get."

She fiddled with her soda, examining the can like she'd never seen the like before. "Oh?"

"*Oh?* That's all you have to say?" He snapped his fingers to reacquire her attention. "Hey! Eyes here, lady. I want to know why you wrote *The Forensics of a Traffic Accident* in the first place—and why you felt the need to use case studies that point to the Mob! Whatever possessed you to put yourself in such jeopardy? And what is the point of your next tome—something about suicide?"

"*The Forensics of a Suicide*," she muttered, looking far away.

"Right. See, I'm sufficiently acquainted with you at this juncture to know you couldn't possibly be writing a second book without some deeper, underlying purpose . . . and it grieves me that you might be painting yet another target on yourself."

Simon leaned closer to her. "Please tell me . . . BeeDee."

She studied him momentarily, then again looked away. When she refused to answer, he made an angry sound in his throat and stood up. "I'm the closest thing to a true friend you've got here, lady, but sure! Have it your way."

He was halfway to his truck when she spoke.

"Did I tell you . . ."

He swiveled to face her, still angry. "Tell me what?"

"Did I tell you that my grandfather was . . . something of a businessman?"

Simon walked back to her. Her fingers were clasped together now, and he could read the tension in them.

He retook his seat. "No, I don't think you mentioned that to me." *You made him sound like a stay-at-home babysitter.* "Er, what kind of businessman was he?"

"Restaurateur. Grandfather owned six restaurants in Korea. He sold them when he followed his son, my father, to America. With the money from the sale of his restaurants, he opened a single Korean diner in LA, paying off the building so his overhead would be manageable. The diner thrived and became popular. It grew over time into a number of small Korean eateries around LA, even two mobile food trucks for special events. I often shadowed him while my parents taught school. He worked tirelessly, and I learned so much from him!"

"And?"

She swallowed. "I was thirteen when my parents passed away. Their deaths left the two of us, Grandfather and me, quite alone in the world, but Grandfather kept going. I learned how to work hard alongside him, and even his small eateries prospered.

"It was after I graduated high school and ventured out on my own, that he took a great leap of faith and launched an upscale Korean restaurant in Beverly Hills. It was an instant smash! I was so proud of him. Rich and famous people came to dine there, and newspapers wrote rave reviews about his cuisine. He was enormously successful, even into his eighties, and all was well until . . ."

Dread.

Simon read it in her voice, her body language.

He gentled his voice. "What happened to your grandfather, BeeDee?"

She inclined her head slowly. "About twenty years ago, they tried to buy him out. They pressured him for 'protection' money initially. Later, thinking he was old and would be easy to manipulate, they tried to force him out. Yet, even though he was far past retirement age, he refused to sell . . . to them."

They tried to buy him out? They who?

A heavy weight of certainty thudded onto Simon's heart.

"This is still about the Lucchese Family and Don Massimo?" He sighed. "It is, isn't it."

"Ettore Massimo was a rising young lieutenant back then . . . out to show the *capo* what he could do."

"What . . . what did they do to him, BeeDee?"

She turned her sad chocolate eyes on him. "My grandfather was one of the most astute individuals I have ever known. And because Korea has its share of corruption and crime syndicates, Grandfather knew how to dodge or thwart attempted 'protection' rackets and other gang-related extortions. So, when it came to the Mob's attempt to buy him out? I have to believe that Grandfather knew what he was doing when he hired a pair of judicious attorneys. Through them, he consolidated the entirety of his holdings into a single family trust and continued to hold out against the Mob's 'offers.'

"Of course, since I had moved away from California and was absorbed in my own life at that time, I had no idea what Grandfather was enduring. He never told me, but his attorneys did. Afterward."

Simon asked softly, "Afterward?"

"Grandfather pulled a fast one on the Mob. In order to keep his hard work from falling into their hands, he sold every restaurant he owned to the highest bidders and deposited the proceeds into the family trust. To his credit, he managed to liquidate his holdings without the Mob catching on. They had no clue until it was done."

She blinked several times. "Of course, when they found out . . ."

The potent silence between them grew long and heavy . . . until Simon didn't need for her to finish. Within his own thoughts, he shuddered.

"They made it look like suicide," he finally whispered.

Her eyes glistened with unshed tears. "Indeed. And I can prove it."

"You . . . you've been planning this for a long time."

"Years. More than a decade. Grandfather left much of the evidence in the hands of his attorneys. Voice recordings, primarily: threatening conversations he taped on the sly. It took me years to identify the speakers on those recordings, validate other evidence he left, and gather the further proof I sought."

Simon's heart slowed. "For revenge?"

"Not for vengeance, Fletcher; rather, using our justice system to perform a legal and systematic debriding of one of the many horrific blights feeding upon the lives of innocent LA citizens."

"Debriding, as in surgically removing dead tissue?"

"Yes. Exposing such an infection to the light of day can have a healing effect, but only if the putrefaction is excised and the pus drained . . . not unlike what the doctor did to my ankle, which exposed and expelled the bone shard, the source of the infection. Unfortunately, when law enforcement institutions are overwhelmed by crime, when courts are slow and punishments are insufficient deterrents—and when elements within law enforcement and the courts are on the take? One must think and plan . . . creatively. There is, as the old proverb says, more than one way to skin a cat; there is also more than one way to bring the guilty to justice."

Her rationale began to coalesce in Simon's mind. "Your first book? It was all about setting the stage, focusing the spotlight on Tony Massimo. Getting Don Massimo's attention, but also the public's attention so that your second book—"

"Would receive the careful scrutiny it deserved, and that public outcry might spur law enforcement into action."

Simon couldn't speak, but the sentiments shouting in his head had plenty to say.

His internal voice yelled, *Every time I think I'm figuring you out, BeeDee Finch, I get an up close look inside that head of yours, and what do I discover? Only that you're a complete and utter loon! Don't you realize the Mob won't sit still while you publicly prove they committed murder!*

A second voice sighed and said, *Can't end well for her, can it?*

A third voice agreed. *Most definitely not.*

Second voice added, *Lop off one mob boss head, and another will grow back faster than spit dries on a hot griddle. Why? Because evil abhors a vacuum. And if she keeps going, keeps poking that bear . . .*

Back to his own voice. *No. Nope. I won't let you do it, BeeDee. I'll figure out how to stop—*

Her sniff intruded on the protesters rioting in Simon's head.

"No need to intervene on my behalf, Fletcher. Things have worked out to date, have they not? Tony Massimo paid for his crimes with his life, and the courts will handle Marie Santini—cautionary tales their fathers should take to heart, particularly in light of the ongoing accident reinvestigations that could still fall upon their oh-so-worthy heads."

Simon's retort was laced with sarcasm. "Got it. Don Massimo will take the death of his son lying down, and Franco Santini will stand by, wringing his hands helplessly, while you make certain his daughter goes to prison. And neither father will lift a finger to retaliate against you. *Riiight.*"

"Correct. I think not."

"You *think* not?"

Miss Finch lifted her chin. "Marie Santini had her LA investigator, Craig Dinesh; as it happens, I have my own."

"You have an LA PI on tap and never thought to mention it to me?"

"A PI, no. A retired detective with his ear to the ground, yes. And, based on his insightful reports, Tony Massimo was a wild upstart, an uncontrollable and growing liability for the family, particularly since his connection to all six vehicular homicides points the neon finger of guilt at their organization."

She lifted one brow, a hint of dry humor in the gesture. "From what I have heard, Don Massimo's lieutenants are relieved to have the Don's son out of the picture. Furthermore, since Tony Massimo's death four months ago, the Don's lieutenants have made it plain to him that his son had been no fit successor to his father's leadership position.

"Fatherly grief aside—and Don Massimo is a realist at his core—he gets it. He understands that his son's departure greatly reduces the likelihood of an internal power struggle, a literal bloodbath, after he passes. He has to realize the syndicate dodged a bullet when Tony killed himself while trying to harm me."

"And that means, out of the goodness of their hearts, you suddenly get a pass?"

She turned a bland stare on him. "For the reasons aforementioned, no. However, both fathers will soon realize that to take action against me, personally, would only unleash upon their heads more of the same police and federal scrutiny under which they are presently writhing."

"Oh, they'll realize that, will they? They—" Simon hesitated. "Wait. You have yet another iron in the fire, is that it? What else have you not told me?"

She had the audacity to giggle. *Giggle!* Simon's temper again heated and started to smolder.

"Ah. Well, I *may* have made arrangements to send both Don Massimo and Franco Santini draft copies of my upcoming book, *The Forensics of a Suicide*—second edition—with a personal cover letter courtesy of *moi*. I assigned this task to my attorneys, and a week from today, they will execute their task by hand-delivering the copies to Massimo and Santini."

Simon lost his breath and a good portion of his mind for a couple of lengthy, charged moments. When he was able to inhale again, he muttered, "I thought you said you said you hadn't finished that second book."

"True. I intend to release the first edition this coming January. But, between now and then, it needs a good polish."

"Then what—" He sat back, baffled. "You hope to release the first edition in January, but you're sending Massimo and Santini *the second edition?* Why a second edition before the first is published? What's the difference between the two?"

Her mouth widened in a conspiratorial smile that displayed a row of even, nicely shaped teeth, although Simon couldn't help but notice that her smile did not reach her eyes.

"You have asked the right questions, Fletcher. The first edition, which releases to the public in January, contains only three case studies, studies unrelated to my grandfather or the Lucchese Family."

She sipped on her canned beverage. "You see, the first edition is a straightforward teaching manual, guiltless of an underlying agenda. But the second edition? Ah! It adds three case studies to the initial three, one being my grandfather's supposed suicide. And all three of the new case studies can be tied, quite definitively, to Don Mossimo and his syndicate.

"Remember when I said Massimo was a rising young lieutenant back then? Oh, he was full of himself all those years ago—back in the day when Massimo was young and thought himself invincible, back when records actually did create 'paper trails.'"

She met Simon's gaze. "The second edition includes a detailed appendix, listing all but the most sensitive and pejorative of the evidence I have collected over the years."

She stared into his stunned expression through thick, bristly lashes. "As I said, the first edition goes to press in January. However, in the event of my death—from any cause—my attorneys will send the second edition to press immediately."

She tossed her empty can into a wastebasket. "My cover letter explains this to Don Mossimo and Franco Santini. What I neglected to add—no, what I quite deliberately *omitted* from my cover letter—is that the DOJ is already in possession of my second-edition draft. You see, the Justice Department wants the LA branch of the Lucchese Family as much as I do."

She waggled her brows. "Why, a federal judge has already issued warrants allowing the DOJ to seize Lucchese Family emails and phone records—without Don Massimo or Franco Santini being aware, of course . . . until it is too late."

Simon was far past anger; he was aghast and gripped with fear for her. "This is how you chose to provide justice for your grandfather? Putting an even larger target on yourself? Of all the harebrained, shortsighted—"

"Or perhaps I have acted exactly as I believe the Lord has led me to act over the past decade."

"Really? You think depending upon a threat will deter the Mob? Is that godly wisdom? Will your second edition, in any fashion, be sufficient to keep them from hunting you down and—"

"Even God uses the threat of consequences as a deterrence against sin, Fletcher. The manuscript Don Massimo and Franco Santini will receive is quite heavy with evidence. It should keep them in check, at a minimum, until fall. Franco Santini, in particular, will not want to throw gasoline on the fire while his daughter is arraigned and brought to trial lest any harm I should come to be seen as reprisal and result in a steeper sentence for Marie. He will pressure Don Massimo to refrain from making a move on me."

"And exactly *what* magical event occurs in the fall to remove Don Massimo or Franco Santini as an ongoing threat against you?"

"When the feds complete their review of the evidence I have collected, they will empanel a grand jury to indict the head of LA's Lucchese Family, Don Massimo, and his lieutenants, including Franco Santini. My contact within the DOJ assures me they will convene the grand jury in October, at the latest. At that time, I will need to appear before the grand jury to testify, but I have already given the Justice Department copies of the evidence and my sworn deposition . . . so even should something happen to me, they can go forward with their prosecution."

"I . . . see." Simon's mind was running down her logic, sorting the details, and in general, searching for a hole, a grave mistake, one that could backfire on her.

"Thank you for that, Simon."

"For what?"

"For playing the devil's advocate, for scrutinizing my play. Obviously I had a couple of small blind spots pop up, one being Marie Santini. Now that we're safely past that danger, I thank you for looking out for my interests."

His temper finally flared. "It's not your 'interests' that concern me, lady. It's your stinking *well-being*."

Hardly chastised, she nodded. "I know, and I am grateful."

"Well, I don't like it, not any of it! And you should have told me, told me everything. In future—"

Simon snapped his mouth shut while he fumed.

"In future? What precisely does 'in future' portend?" she demanded.

Simon was still struggling with his temper. "I have no idea."

Then he waffled. "If I'm being honest, I had been thinking that you and I don't make such a bad team, all things considered . . . and when we, you know, actually work *together*."

"We don't make a bad team of . . . what?"

"I don't know. Problem solvers? Possibly the criminal kind of problems? With our backgrounds, one could even call us investigators—that is, when you're not actively and deliberately *goading* the Lucchese Family into squashing you like a bug."

"I will take that sentiment under advisement," was her unfazed retort.

"Yeah? Well, my goal in life isn't to be squashed along with you as collateral damage, lady. And don't forget about Skipper. You put *him* at risk too."

He could tell by her shocked expression that he'd finally made his point.

"I am sorry to have involved Skipper," she whispered. "Having made my personal peace with however this finishes out . . . and having been solitary in my planning and execution, I suppose I stopped considering how my choices might bleed over onto anyone else."

"'Bleed over' is way too literal for my taste."

"Another inappropriate pun. *Mea culpa.*"

"That's three strikes, BeeDee Finch, reason enough for you to admit that being all 'solitary in your planning and execution' was and is ridiculously stupid. *God did not make people to do life alone!* You need the counsel and wisdom of others and need to take advice from those who actually care about you."

"And what advice have you for me, Mr. Fletcher?"

"Stop with this inane plan of yours. *Just stop.* You don't need to publish a second book or threaten Massimo and his mob. Let God take care of them: *He* doesn't let anyone escape justice."

"And if I were to listen to your counsel, if I were to . . . withdraw my intention to publish a second edition of my book? What then?"

Simon was surprised and somewhat hopeful. "Our skills complement each other. I suppose I was starting to toy with the idea that we might combine our investigative experience. Put our joint expertise to work. Just part-time and primarily as hobbyists, of course. I'm not suggesting we should enter into a formal partnership or apply for a business license. But—again, part-time and primarily as hobbyists—if we did hang out a shingle, so to speak, we could take up circumstances we find intriguing. Look into local mysteries that pique our interest, mysteries such as the three missing persons you brought up. Enter into an equal, although informal, partnership."

"Do go on."

"I mean, I already have a job and you're spending a restful summer while you decide whether or not to retire. Why couldn't we take on an interesting case here or there? Mostly for the fun of it but also to pad your income. Beats staffing Bright Star's office, don't you think?"

Confusion wrinkled her forehead. "What makes you think I am in need of 'padding my income,' as you put it?"

Simon frowned. "You needed your wages badly enough that you asked me to cash you out."

"I did indeed, but primarily under exigent circumstances." She tapped her chin with a dainty index finger. "Hmm. Returning to your proposition, I believe I might enjoy such a partnership, Fletcher, so long as it remains a hobby. Neither of us is in a position to take on a full case load."

"Agreed. And I was thinking . . . we could bill ourselves as *Fletcher and Finch, Private Investigations*."

"Thinking, were you? And yet, my preference would be *Finch and Fletcher*."

He growled, "What, ladies first? Age before beauty? Why do you get first billing? What happened to 'an equal partnership'?"

"Someone's name has to be first, *Mr.* Fletcher."

"Yes, and unquestionably, I have more years of investigative experience."

"I have more years of life experience."

"Ha! Direct investigative experience trumps indirect life experience. Give me a real reason you should get first billing."

She put her nose in the air, feigning indignation. "Why, to be impartial."

"And just how is that impartial?"

"Alphabetical order, of course."

She was holding in her laughter, but not trying all that hard. Her eyes were squeezed nearly closed, their outside corners crinkling in the way that made Simon . . . happy inside.

He grinned back. "Fine. *Finch and Fletcher* it is."

Her eyes opened; she tipped her head and smiled at him. "You truly are a kind and generous man, Simon Fletcher."

"Yeah, right. I've been called worse. You don't scare me, BeeDee Finch."

Laughter, uproarious and unrestrained, burst from her, lighting her from within. Simon couldn't help himself. He laughed along with her for the sheer pleasure of sharing her joy. For a lengthy, protracted minute, they couldn't stop. Their mutual delight owned them.

And then the unexpected happened.

Something far down in in Simon's gut flipped over. And flipped back again.

Huh? What is that?

The flip-flopping part subsided and gave way to a dull ache. A sort of clenching or clutching at his heart.

He frowned and delved deeper inside, searching for whatever "it" was, seeking it out, attempting to identify and attach a word to the sensation.

When he stumbled upon that word, his jaw dropped in disbelieving perception.

No. Couldn't be that. Nope. No way. I mean, just the age difference . . . Means nothing.

He exhaled slowly and lifted his gaze.

She was watching him, a little puzzled but also intrigued. Her fingers tugged at an errant strand of curly hair tickling her cheek. She tucked it behind her ear . . . and he thought it the dearest thing he'd ever seen.

Then her puzzlement cleared and the hooded lids around those shiny chocolate eyes of hers widened. She licked her lips and turned her gaze aside. Blinked several times. Cleared her throat. Croaked out, "My, my. How time flies! I think . . . yes, I *must* get on with my day."

Simon, in perfect agreement, jumped to his feet. "Right. Me too. Back to work. See you . . . later."

The End
or is it?

The TAHOE MYSTERIES

return
October 2025!

My Dear Readers,

What's next for Miss Finch and Simon Fletcher? Look for *Murder by Accident*, A Miss Finch Prequel, and *Be Quick or Be Dead*, Book 2 in *The Tahoe Mysteries*, both coming your way, October 2025. And if you enjoyed *Number 1 with a Bullet*, would you consider leaving a review on Amazon or Goodreads? I would greatly appreciate it!

Interested in my other books? **Look inside** the first pages of this book to see a complete list. And to keep in step with my publication schedule and receive notice of upcoming releases and free or discounted Christian books, I invite you to visit my website, https://www.vikkikestell.com/, and sign up for my newsletter, *Faith-Filled News*.

From the bottom of my heart, *thank you*. I appreciate your readership and the fellowship we share in Christ Jesus, our Lord.

Many hugs,

—Vikki Kestell, Author of Faith-Filled Fiction™

ABOUT THE AUTHOR

VIKKI KESTELL'S passion for people and their stories is evident in her readers' affection for her characters and unusual plotlines. Two often-repeated sentiments are, "I feel like I know these people," and, "I'm right there, in the book, experiencing what the characters experience."

Vikki holds a PhD in organizational learning and instructional technologies. She left a career of twenty-plus years in government, academia, and corporate life to pursue writing full time. "Writing is the best job ever," she admits, "and the most demanding."

Vikki and her husband, Conrad Smith, make their home in Albuquerque, New Mexico.

To keep abreast of new book releases, sign up for Vikki's newsletter on her website, **http://www.vikkikestell.com**, find her on Facebook at **http://www.facebook.com/Vikki.Kestell**, or follow her on BookBub, **https://www.bookbub.com/authors/vikki-kestell**.

Faith-Filled Fiction™

www.faith-filledfiction.com | www.vikkikestell.com

www.ingramcontent.com/pod-product-compliance
Lightning Source LLC
Chambersburg PA
CBHW060439310726
48977CB00001B/250